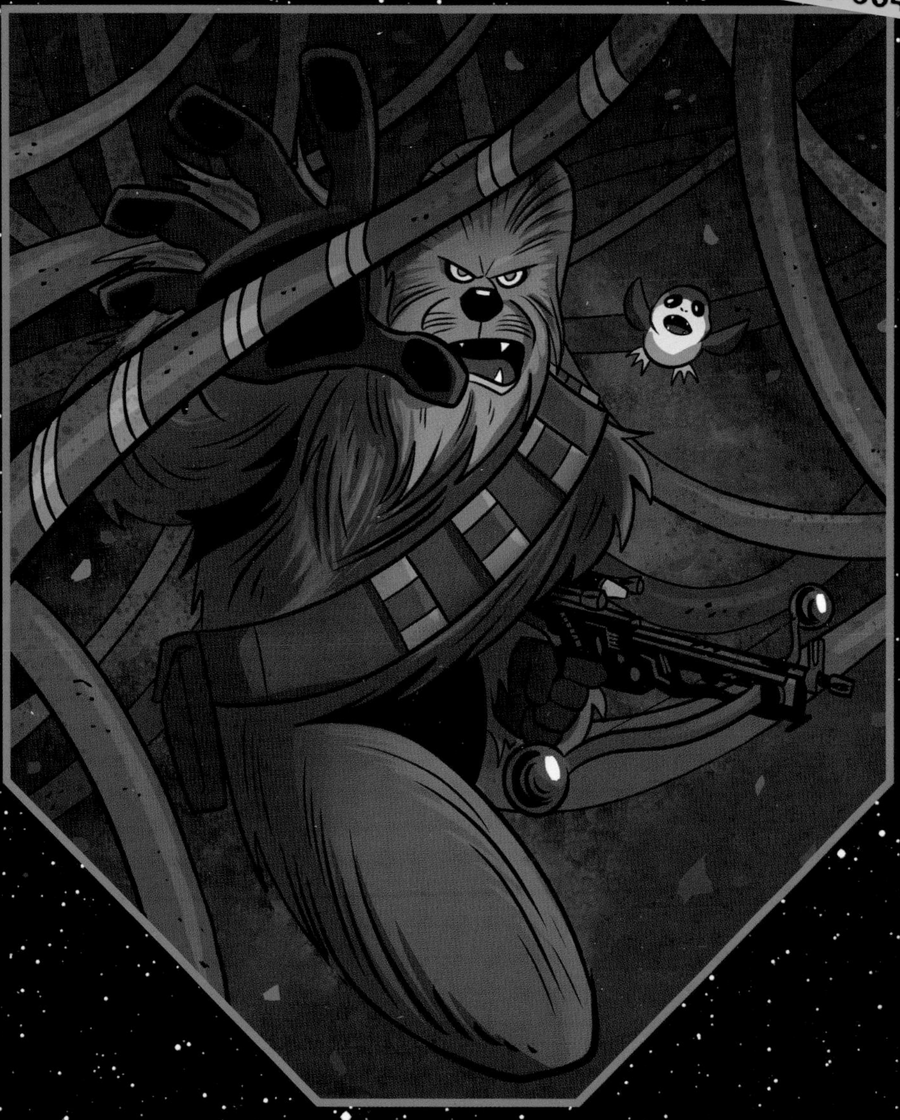

STAR WARS™ ADVENTURES

RISE OF THE WOOKIEES

Facebook: **facebook.com/idwpublishing**
Twitter: **@idwpublishing**
YouTube: **youtube.com/idwpublishing**
Tumblr: **tumblr.idwpublishing.com**
Instagram: **instagram.com/idwpublishing**

COVER ARTIST
DEREK CHARM

LETTERERS
JAKE M. WOOD
& TOM B. LONG

SERIES ASSISTANT EDITOR
ELIZABETH BREI

SERIES EDITOR
DENTON J. TIPTON

COLLECTION EDITORS
ALONZO SIMON
& ZAC BOONE

COLLECTION DESIGNER
CLYDE GRAPA

ISBN: 978-1-68405-736-8   24 23 22 21   1 2 3 4

STAR WARS ADVENTURES, VOLUME 11: RISE OF THE WOOKIEES.
JANUARY 2021. FIRST PRINTING. © 2021 Lucasfilm Ltd. & ® or ™
where indicated. All Rights Reserved. © 2021 Idea and Design Works,
LLC. The IDW logo is registered in the U.S. Patent and Trademark
Office. IDW Publishing, a division of Idea and Design Works, LLC.
Editorial offices: 2765 Truxtun Road, San Diego, CA 92106. Any
similarities to persons living or dead are purely coincidental. With
the exception of artwork used for review purposes, none of the
contents of this publication may be reprinted without the permission
of Idea and Design Works, LLC. IDW Publishing does not read or
accept unsolicited submissions of ideas, stories, or artwork. Printed
in Korea.

Originally published as STAR WARS ADVENTURES issues #27–32.

Jerry Bennington, President
Nachie Marsham, Publisher
Cara Morrison, Chief Financial Officer
Matthew Ruzicka, Chief Accounting Officer
Rebekah Cahalin, EVP of Operations
John Barber, Editor-in-Chief
Justin Eisinger, Editorial Director, Graphic Novels & Collections
Scott Dunbier, Director, Special Projects
Blake Kobashigawa, VP of Sales
Lorelei Bunjes, VP of Technology & Information Services
Anna Morrow, Sr Marketing Director
Tara McCrillis, Director of Design & Production
Mike Ford, Director of Operations
Shauna Monteforte, Manufacturing Operations Director

Ted Adams and Robbie Robbins, IDW Founders

Lucasfilm Credits:
Robert Simpson, Senior Editor
Michael Siglain, Creative Director
Phil Szostak, Lucasfilm Art Department
Matt Martin, Pablo Hidalgo, and
Emily Shkoukani, Story Group

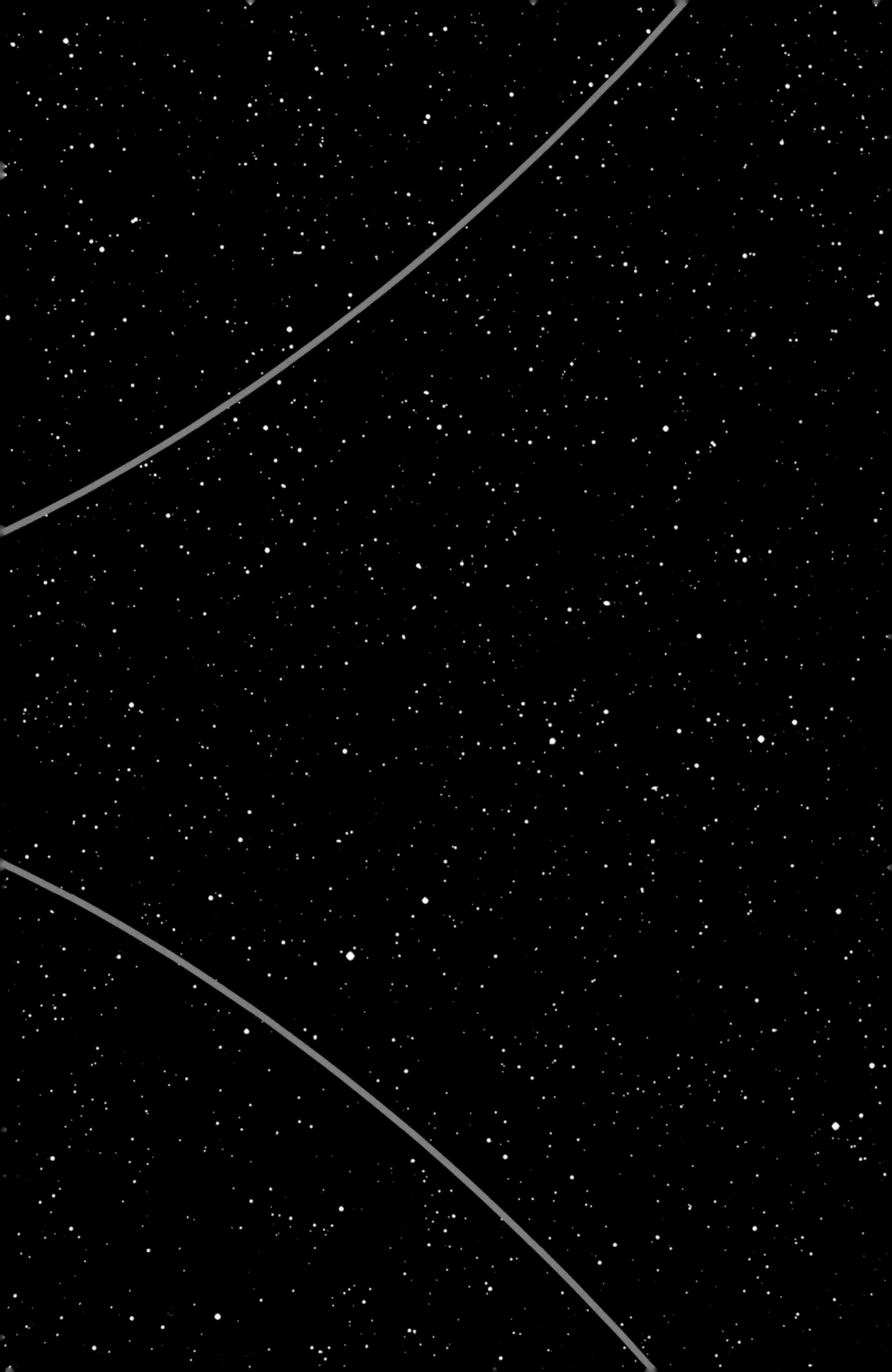

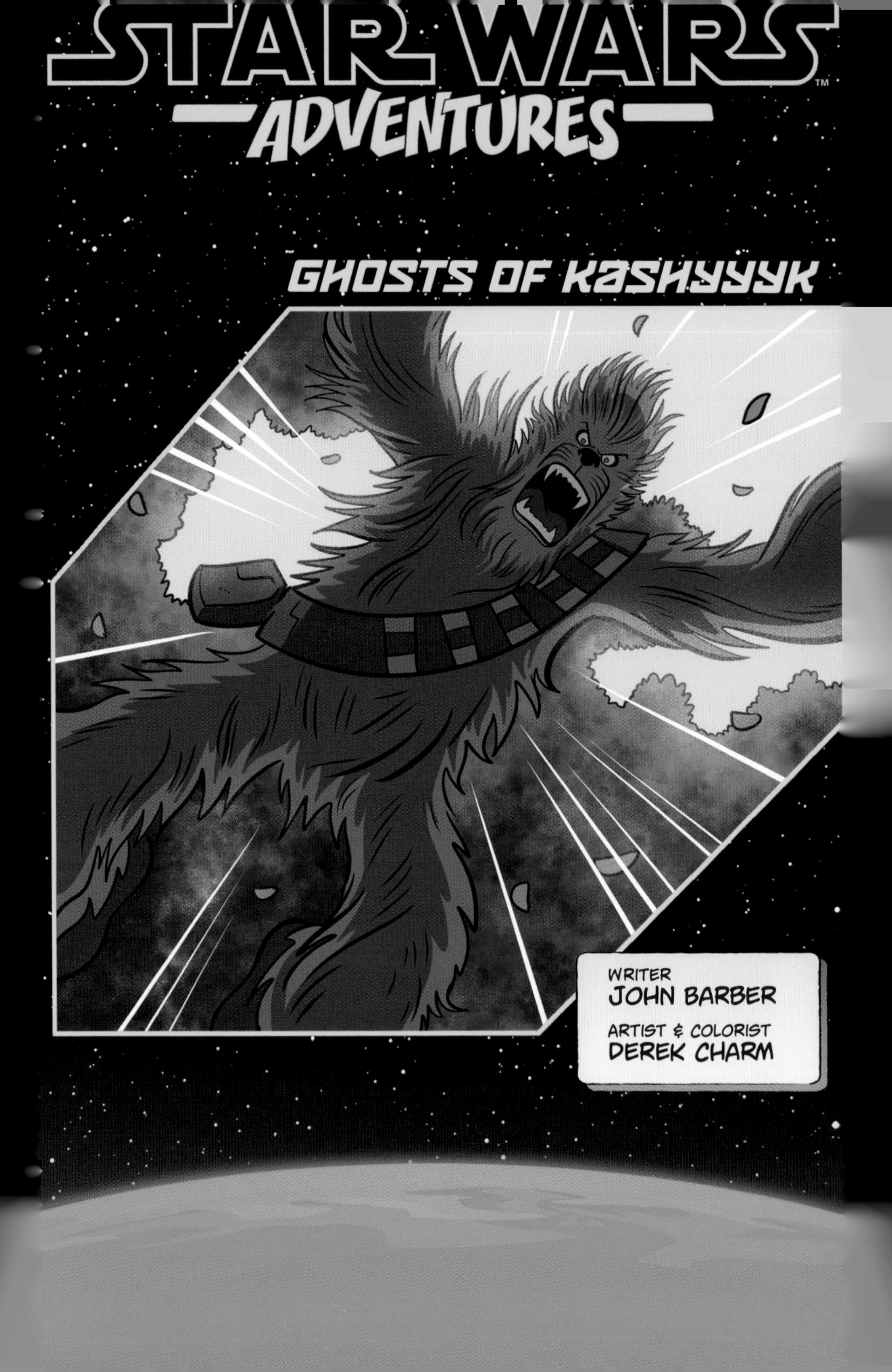
STAR WARS ADVENTURES
GHOSTS OF KASHYYYK
WRITER
JOHN BARBER
ARTIST & COLORIST
DEREK CHARM

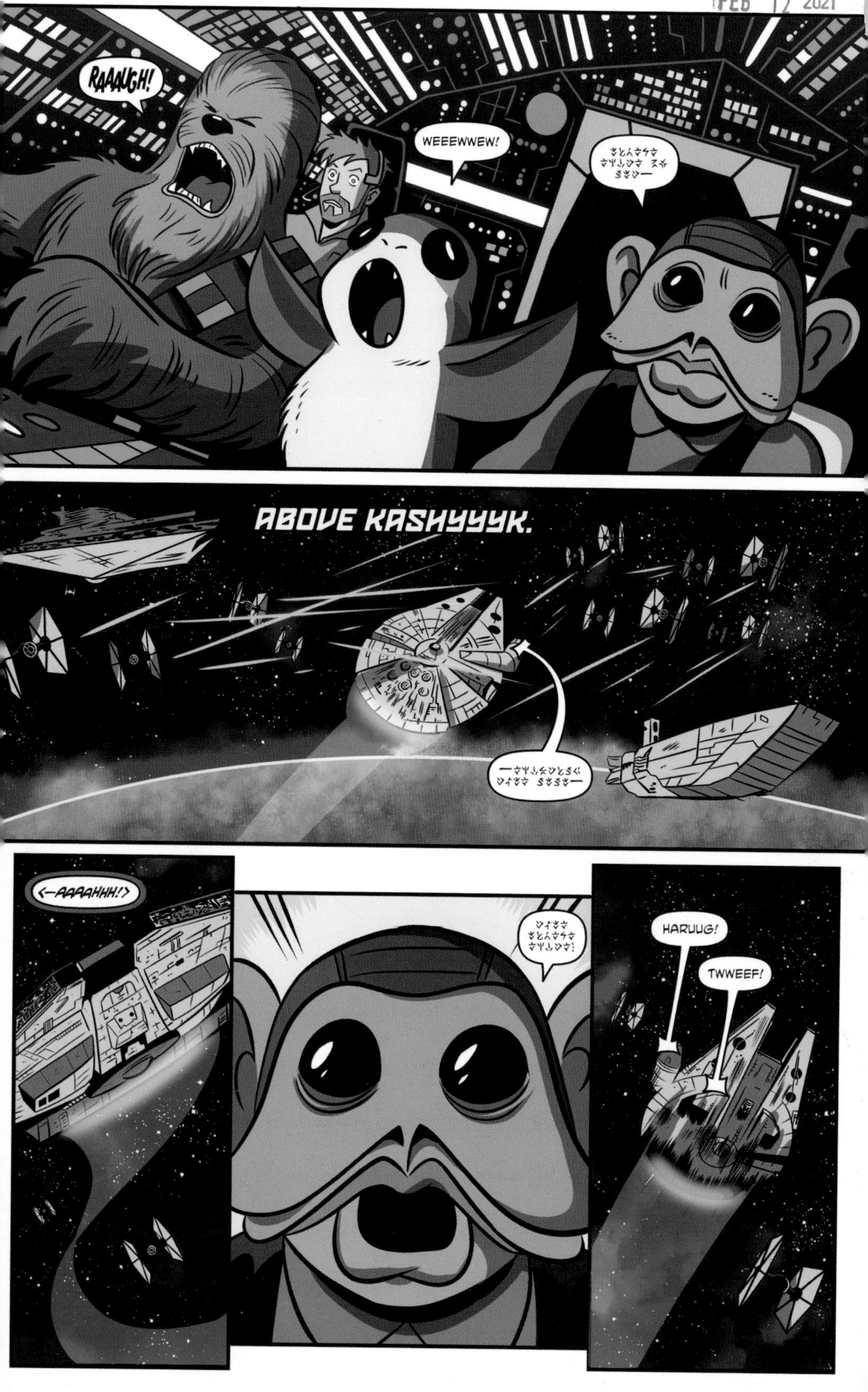
RAAAUGH!
WEEEWWEW!
ABOVE KASHYYYK.
<—AAAAHHH!>
HARUUG!
TWWEEF!

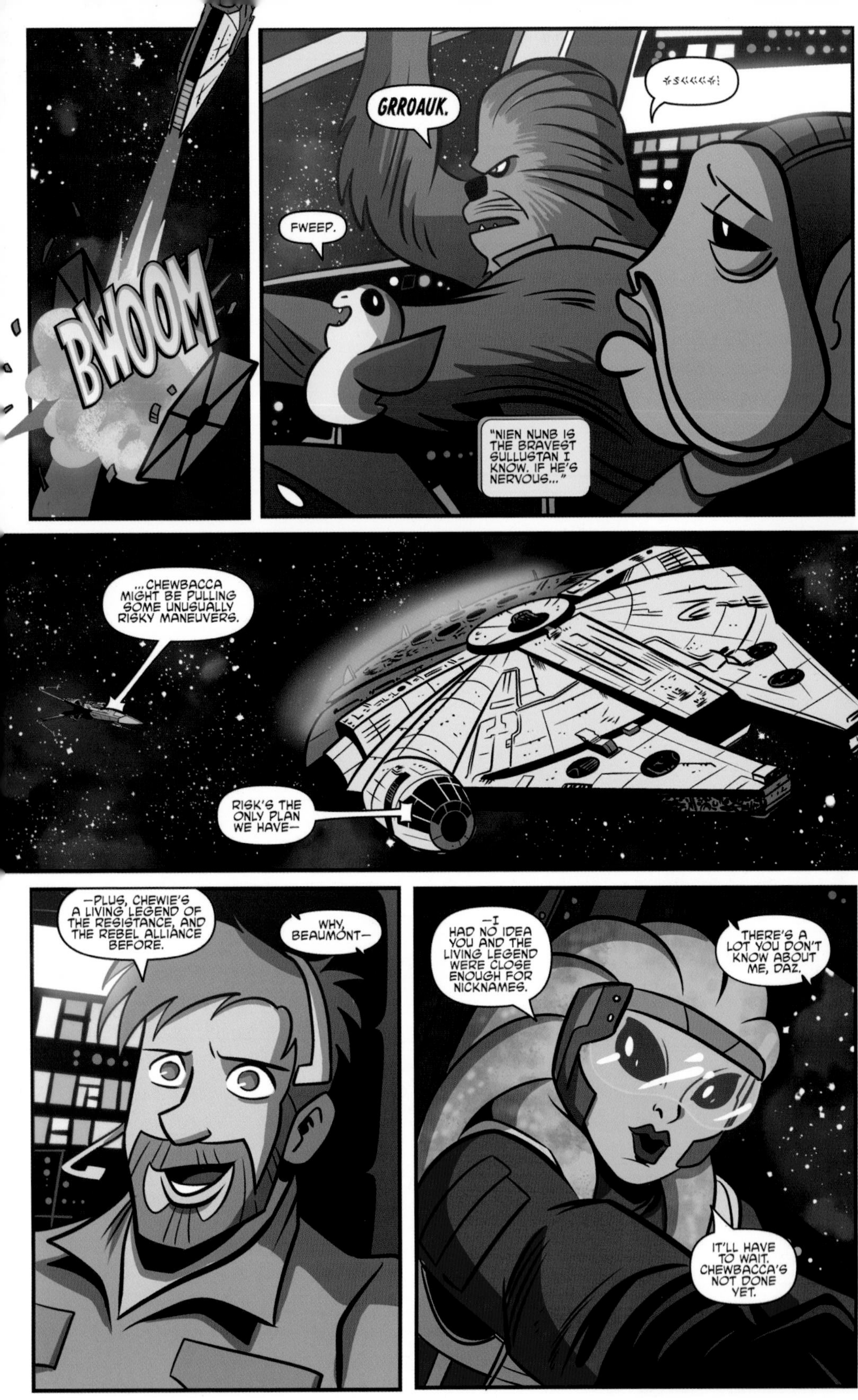
BWOOM
GRROAUK.
FWEEP.
"NIEN NUNB IS THE BRAVEST SULLUSTAN I KNOW. IF HE'S NERVOUS..."
...CHEWBACCA MIGHT BE PULLING SOME UNUSUALLY RISKY MANEUVERS.
RISK'S THE ONLY PLAN WE HAVE—
—PLUS, CHEWIE'S A LIVING LEGEND OF THE RESISTANCE, AND THE REBEL ALLIANCE BEFORE.
WHY, BEAUMONT—
—I HAD NO IDEA YOU AND THE LIVING LEGEND WERE CLOSE ENOUGH FOR NICKNAMES.
THERE'S A LOT YOU DON'T KNOW ABOUT ME, DAZ.
IT'LL HAVE TO WAIT. CHEWBACCA'S NOT DONE YET.

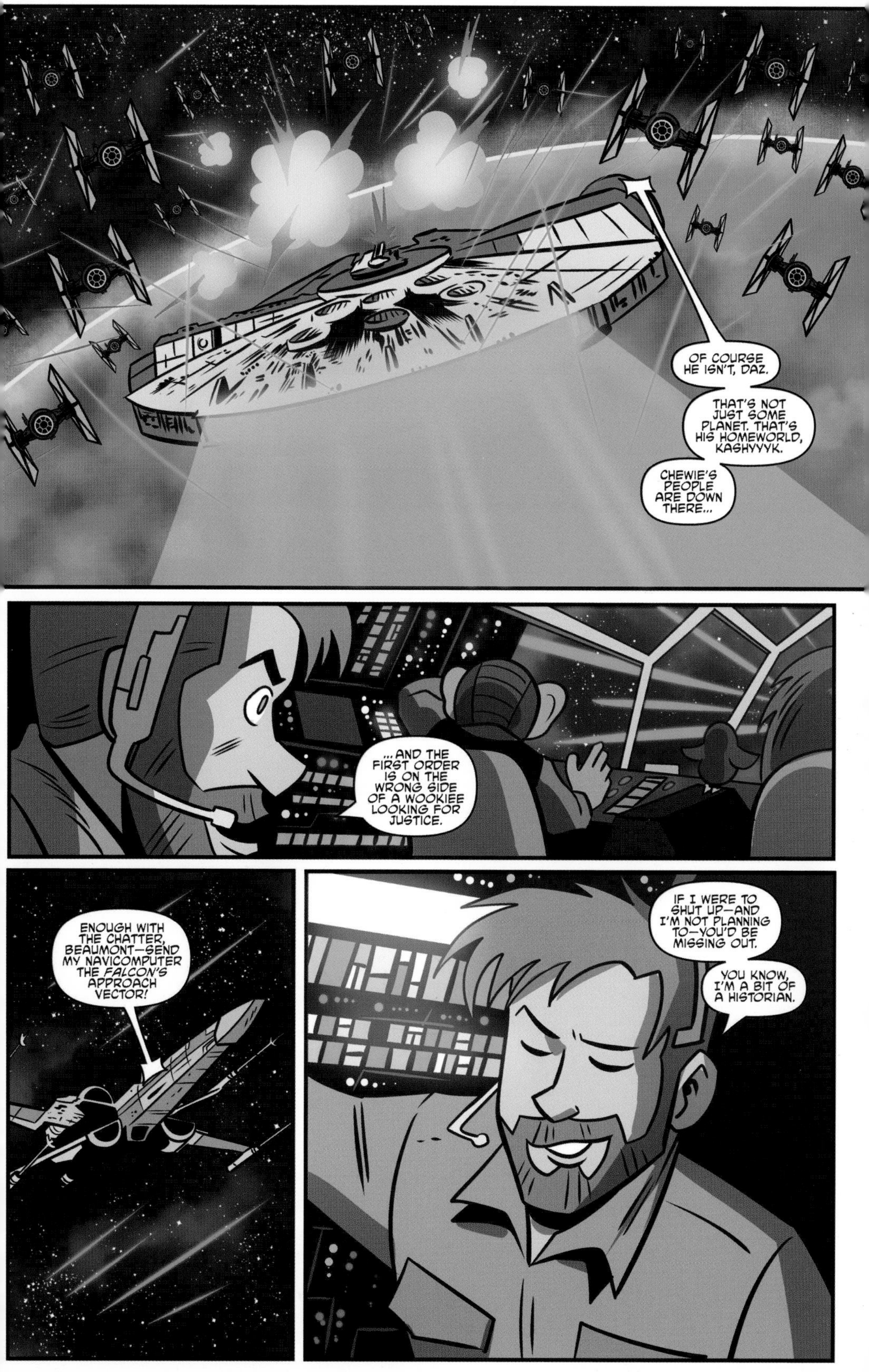
OF COURSE HE ISN'T, DAZ.
THAT'S NOT JUST SOME PLANET. THAT'S HIS HOMEWORLD, KASHYYYK.
CHEWIE'S PEOPLE ARE DOWN THERE...
...AND THE FIRST ORDER IS ON THE WRONG SIDE OF A WOOKIEE LOOKING FOR JUSTICE.
ENOUGH WITH THE CHATTER, BEAUMONT—SEND MY NAVICOMPUTER THE *FALCON'S* APPROACH VECTOR!
IF I WERE TO SHUT UP—AND I'M NOT PLANNING TO—YOU'D BE MISSING OUT.
YOU KNOW, I'M A BIT OF A HISTORIAN.

CONCENTRATE ON NOT GETTING BLASTED, BEAUMONT!

I CAN DO TWO THINGS!

ANYWAY— I LIKE TO KNOW WHO I'M SAVING.

ᛒᛈᛏᚵᛸᚵᛋᛉ ᛉᛃᛃᛃᛃᛃ ᛉᛈᛘᛃᚷ ᛉᛈᛘᛃᚷ

GRUUNK.

FEEEP.

DURING THE CLONE WARS, EVERYBODY WAS AFTER KASHYYYK BECAUSE IT WAS AN IMPORTANT NAVIGATIONAL HUB...

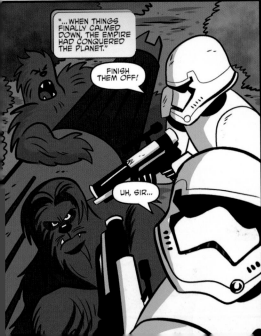

"...WHEN THINGS FINALLY CALMED DOWN, THE EMPIRE HAD CONQUERED THE PLANET."

FINISH THEM OFF!

UH, SIR...

...COMPANY.

"SO, CHEWIE'S GOT A VESTED INTEREST IN NOT LETTING THAT HAPPEN AGAIN."

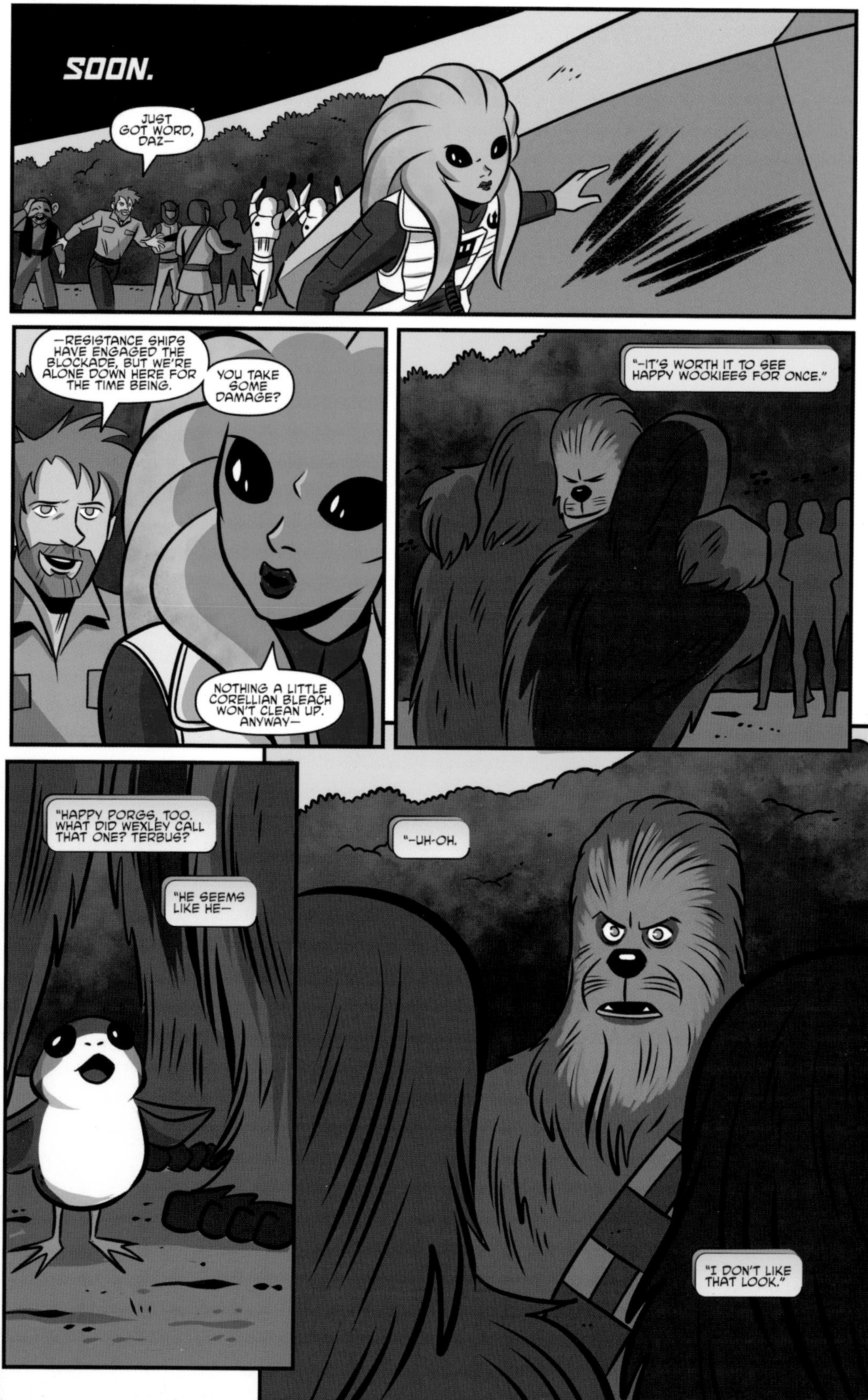
SOON.
JUST GOT WORD, DAZ—
—RESISTANCE SHIPS HAVE ENGAGED THE BLOCKADE, BUT WE'RE ALONE DOWN HERE FOR THE TIME BEING.
YOU TAKE SOME DAMAGE?
NOTHING A LITTLE CORELLIAN BLEACH WON'T CLEAN UP. ANYWAY—
"—IT'S WORTH IT TO SEE HAPPY WOOKIEES FOR ONCE."
"HAPPY PORGS, TOO. WHAT DID WEXLEY CALL THAT ONE? TERBUS?
"HE SEEMS LIKE HE—
"—UH-OH.
"I DON'T LIKE THAT LOOK."

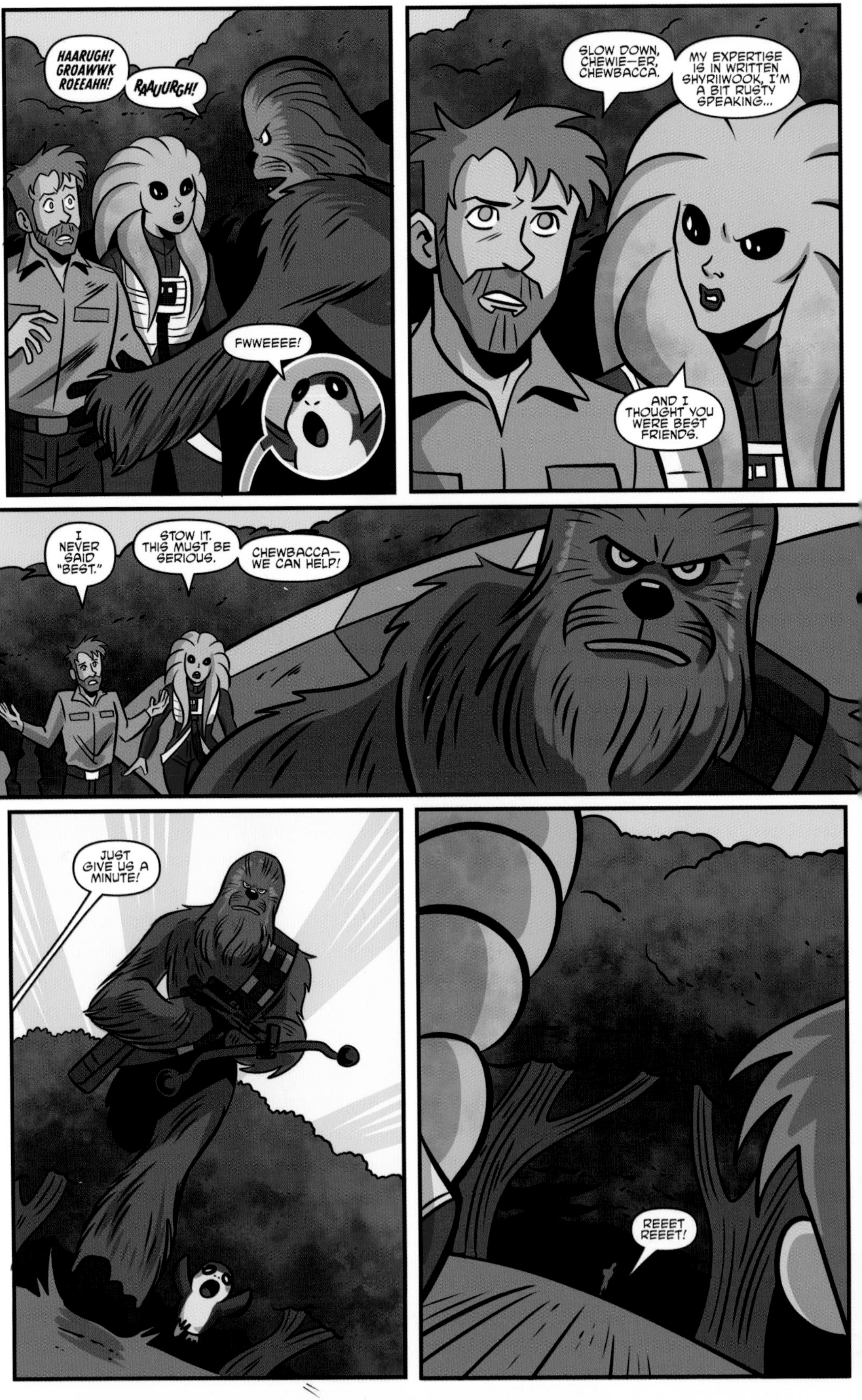
HAARUGH! GROAWWK ROEEAHH!
RAAUURGH!
FWWEEEE!
SLOW DOWN, CHEWIE—ER, CHEWBACCA.
MY EXPERTISE IS IN WRITTEN SHYRIIWOOK, I'M A BIT RUSTY SPEAKING...
AND I THOUGHT YOU WERE BEST FRIENDS.
I NEVER SAID "BEST."
STOW IT. THIS MUST BE SERIOUS.
CHEWBACCA— WE CAN HELP!
JUST GIVE US A MINUTE!
REEET REEET!

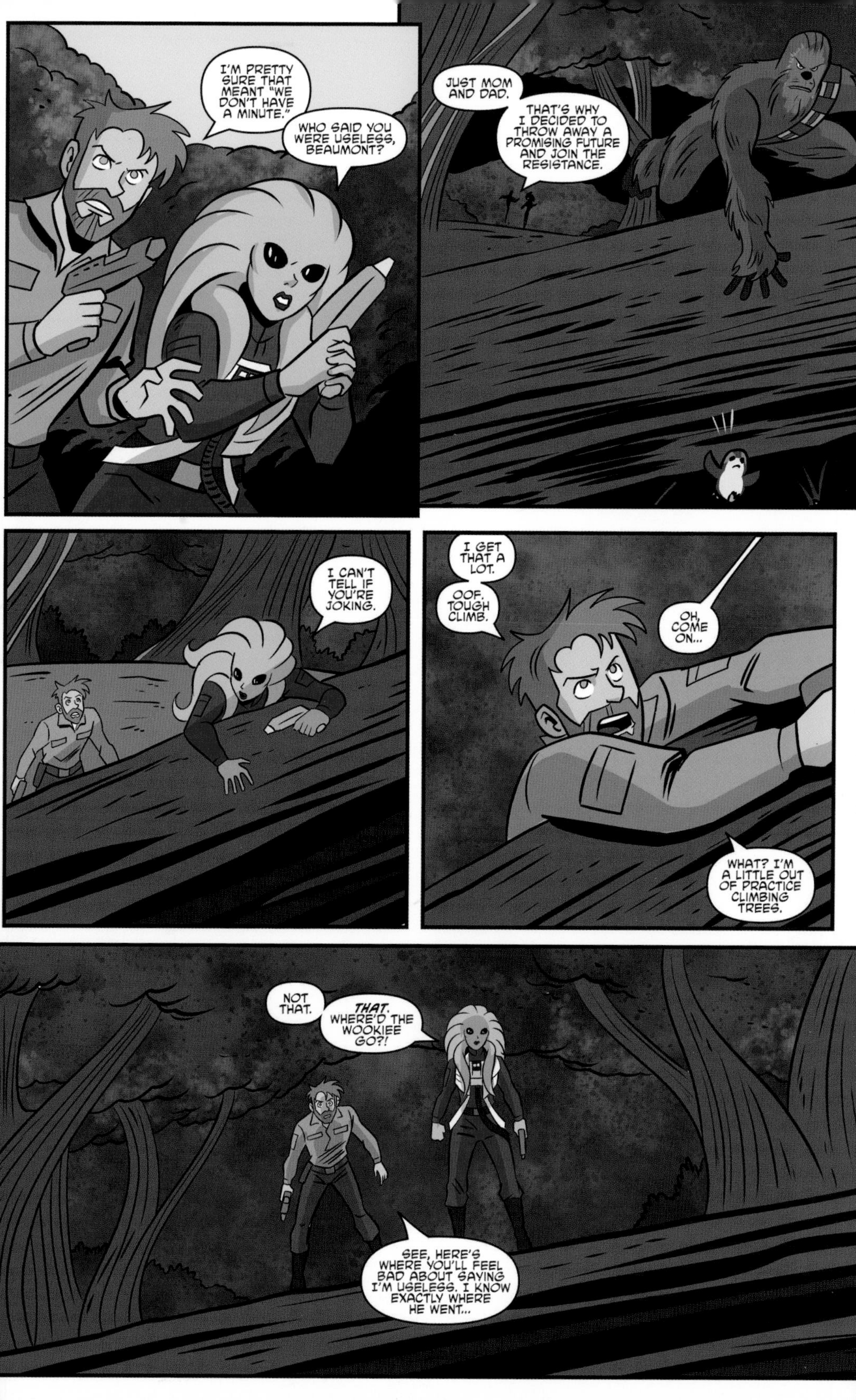
I'M PRETTY SURE THAT MEANT "WE DON'T HAVE A MINUTE."
WHO SAID YOU WERE USELESS, BEAUMONT?
JUST MOM AND DAD.
THAT'S WHY I DECIDED TO THROW AWAY A PROMISING FUTURE AND JOIN THE RESISTANCE.
I CAN'T TELL IF YOU'RE JOKING.
I GET THAT A LOT.
OOF. TOUGH CLIMB.
OH, COME ON...
WHAT? I'M A LITTLE OUT OF PRACTICE CLIMBING TREES.
NOT THAT.
THAT. WHERE'D THE WOOKIEE GO?!
SEE, HERE'S WHERE YOU'LL FEEL BAD ABOUT SAYING I'M USELESS. I KNOW EXACTLY WHERE HE WENT...

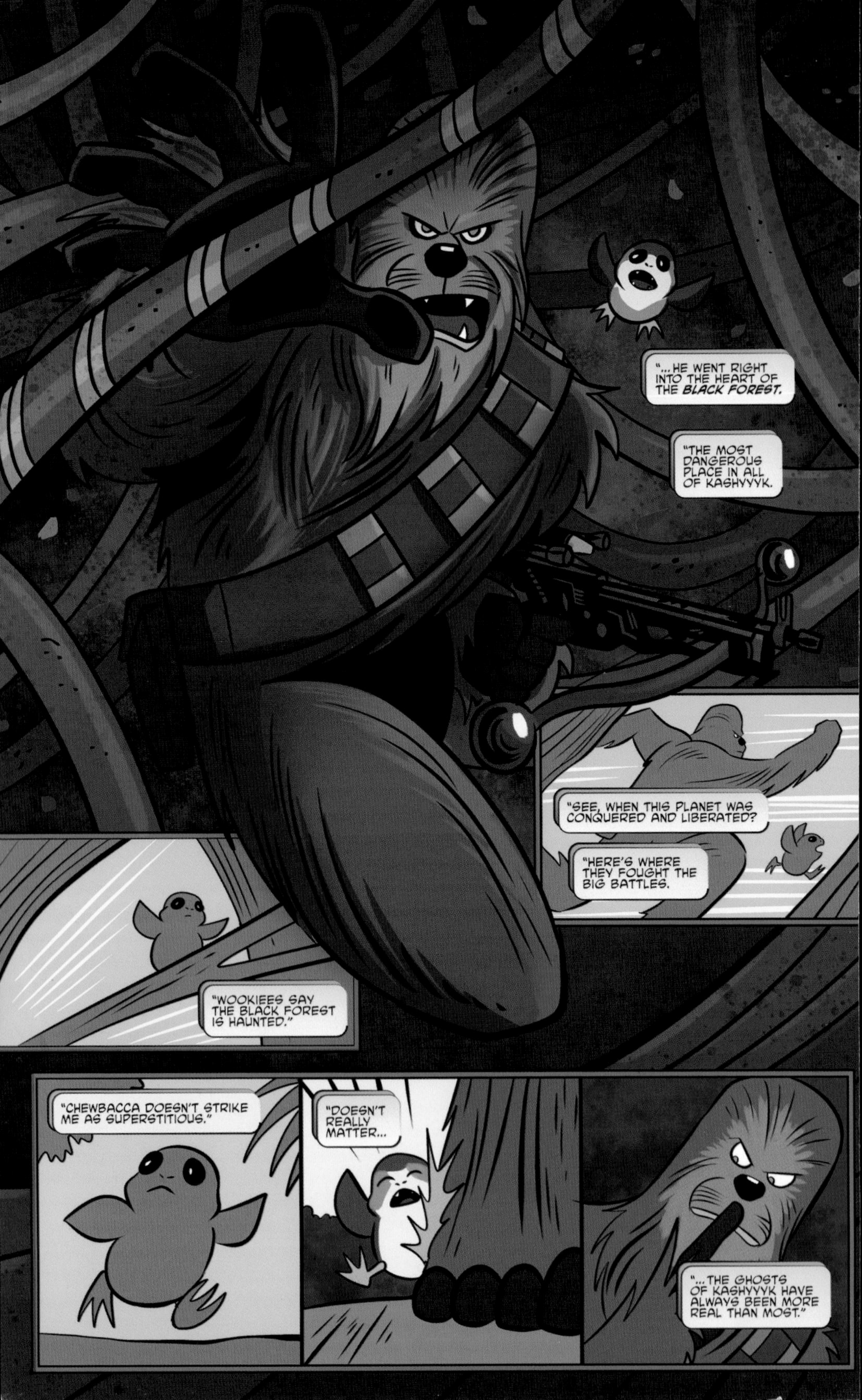
"...HE WENT RIGHT INTO THE HEART OF THE BLACK FOREST.
"THE MOST DANGEROUS PLACE IN ALL OF KASHYYYK.
"SEE, WHEN THIS PLANET WAS CONQUERED AND LIBERATED?
"HERE'S WHERE THEY FOUGHT THE BIG BATTLES.
"WOOKIEES SAY THE BLACK FOREST IS HAUNTED."
"CHEWBACCA DOESN'T STRIKE ME AS SUPERSTITIOUS."
"DOESN'T REALLY MATTER...
"...THE GHOSTS OF KASHYYYK HAVE ALWAYS BEEN MORE REAL THAN MOST."

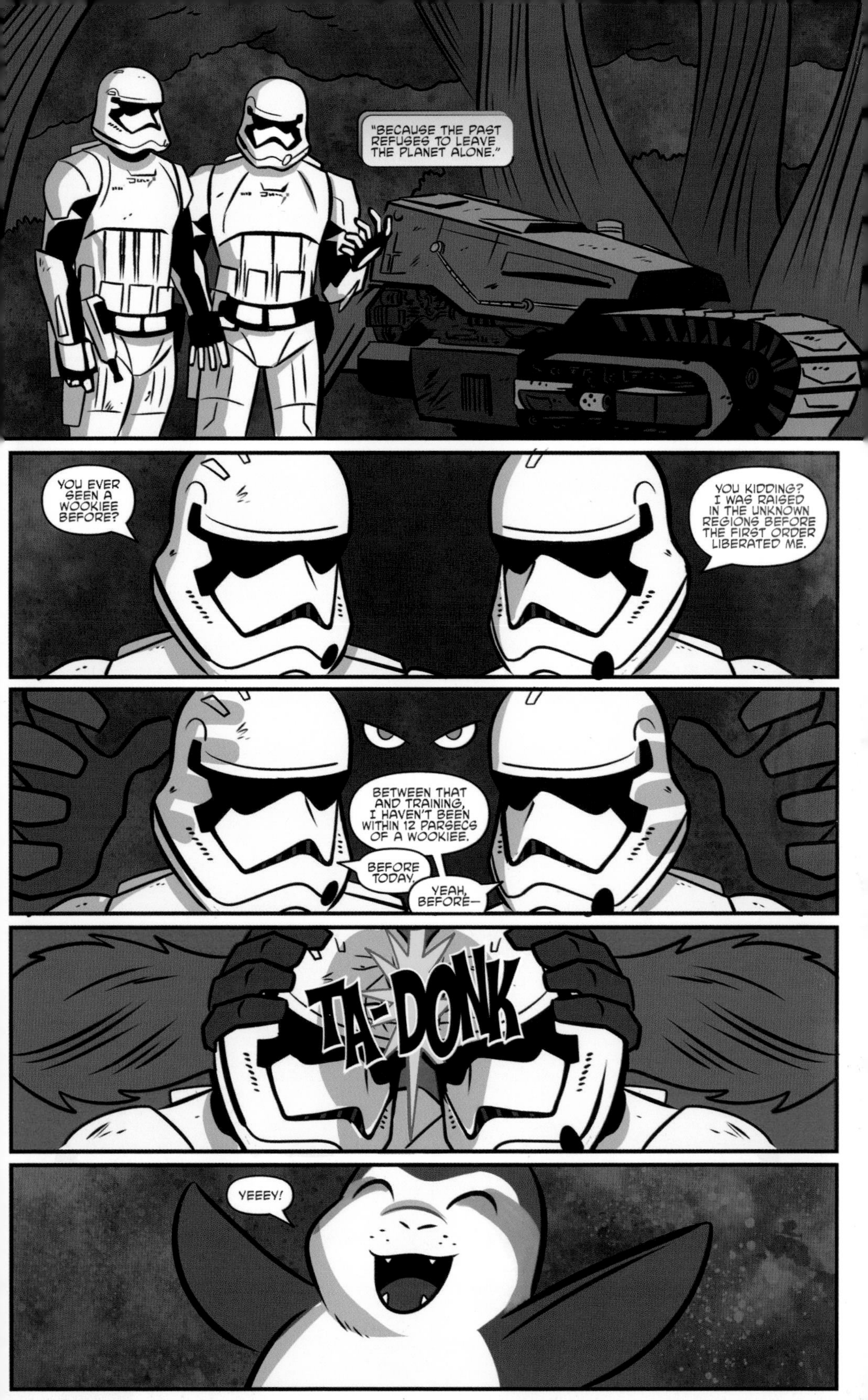
"BECAUSE THE PAST REFUSES TO LEAVE THE PLANET ALONE."
YOU EVER SEEN A WOOKIEE BEFORE?
YOU KIDDING? I WAS RAISED IN THE UNKNOWN REGIONS BEFORE THE FIRST ORDER LIBERATED ME.
BETWEEN THAT AND TRAINING, I HAVEN'T BEEN WITHIN 12 PARSECS OF A WOOKIEE.
BEFORE TODAY.
YEAH, BEFORE—
TA-DONK
YEEEY!

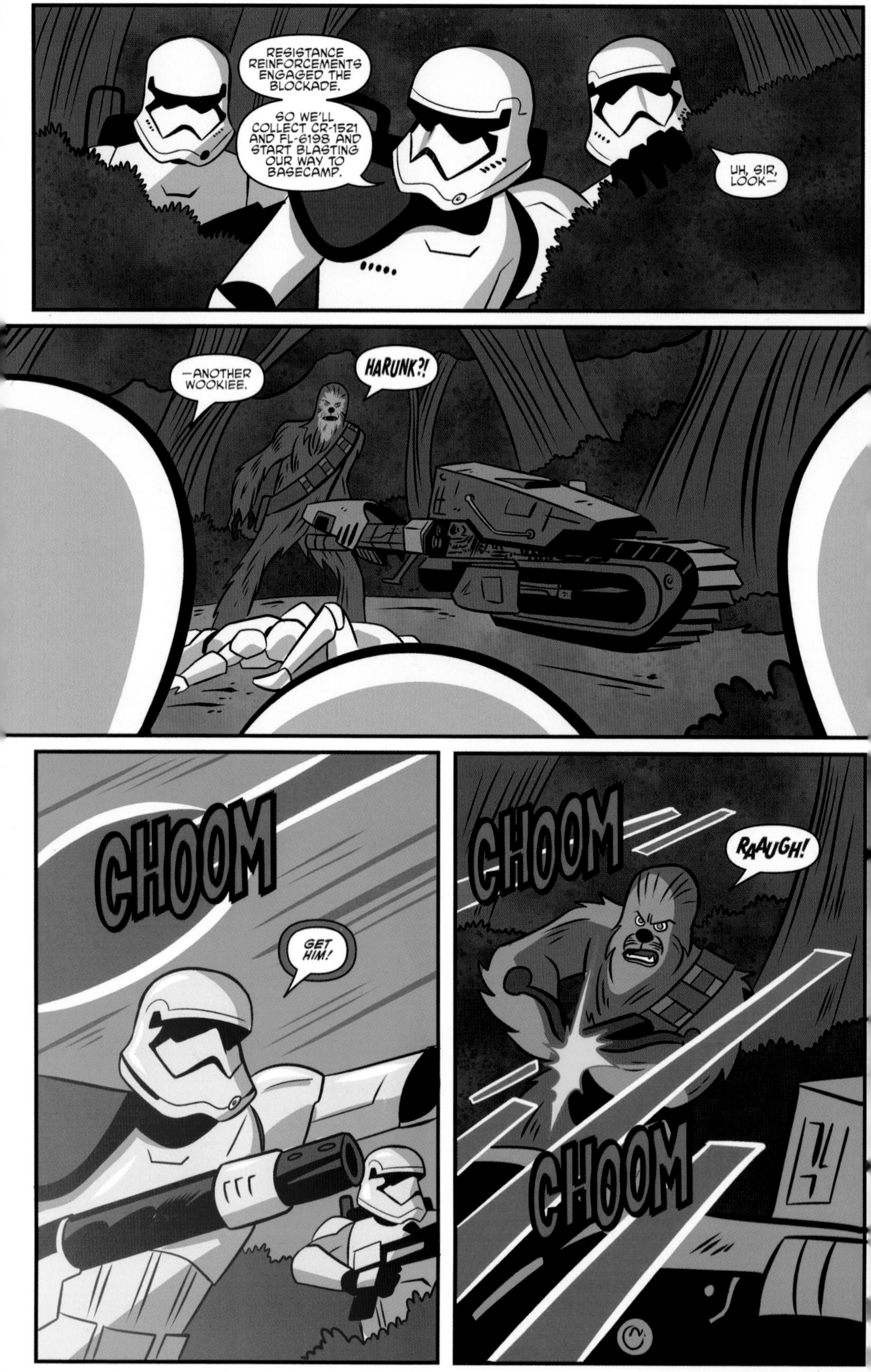
RESISTANCE REINFORCEMENTS ENGAGED THE BLOCKADE.
SO WE'LL COLLECT CR-1521 AND FL-6198 AND START BLASTING OUR WAY TO BASECAMP.
UH, SIR, LOOK—
—ANOTHER WOOKIEE.
HARUNK?!
CHOOM
GET HIM!
CHOOM
RAAUGH!
CHOOM

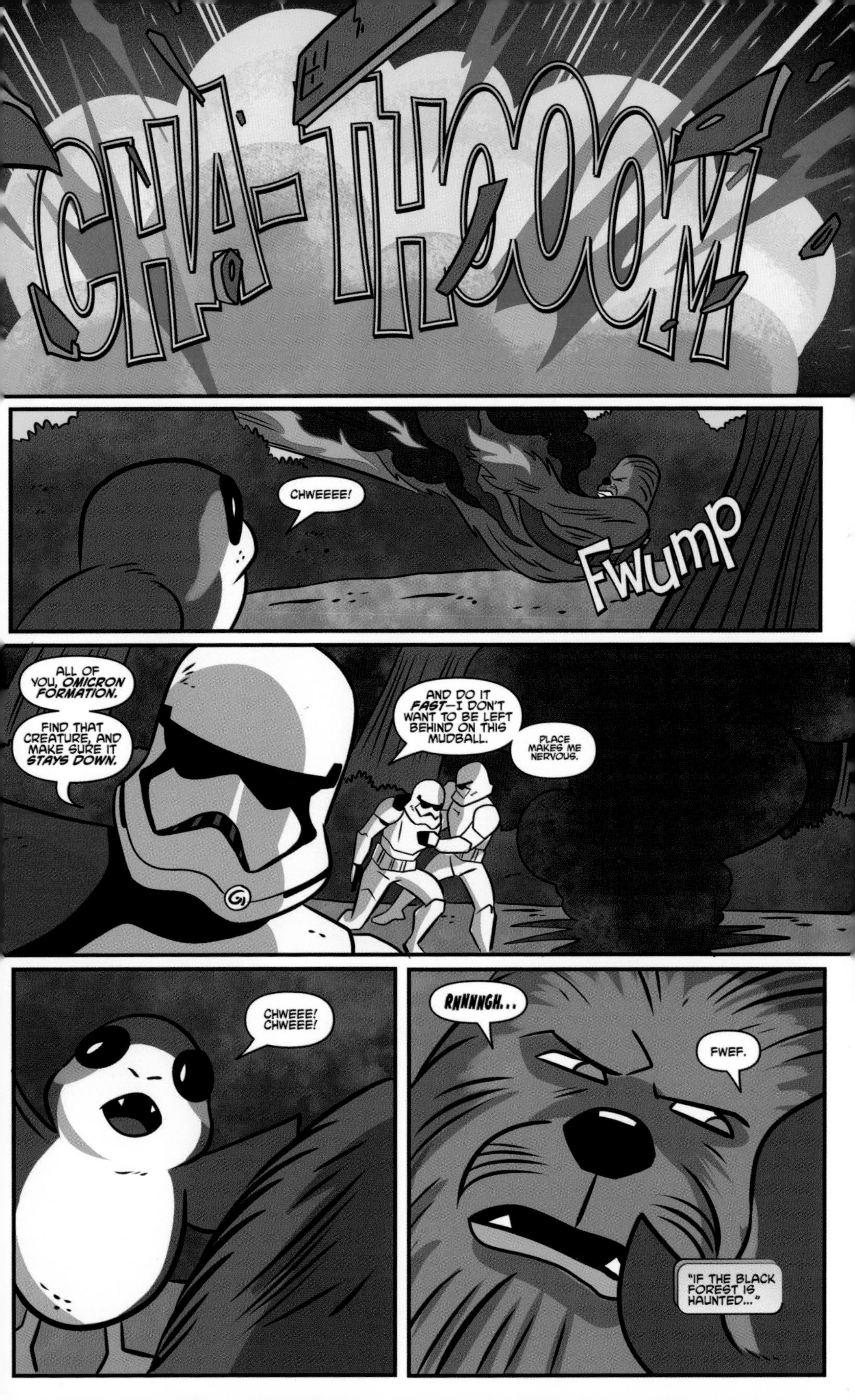
CHA-THOOOM
CHWEEEE!
FWUMP
ALL OF YOU, OMICRON FORMATION.
FIND THAT CREATURE, AND MAKE SURE IT STAYS DOWN.
AND DO IT FAST—I DON'T WANT TO BE LEFT BEHIND ON THIS MUDBALL.
PLACE MAKES ME NERVOUS.
CHWEEE! CHWEEE!
RNNNNGH...
FWEF.
"IF THE BLACK FOREST IS HAUNTED..."

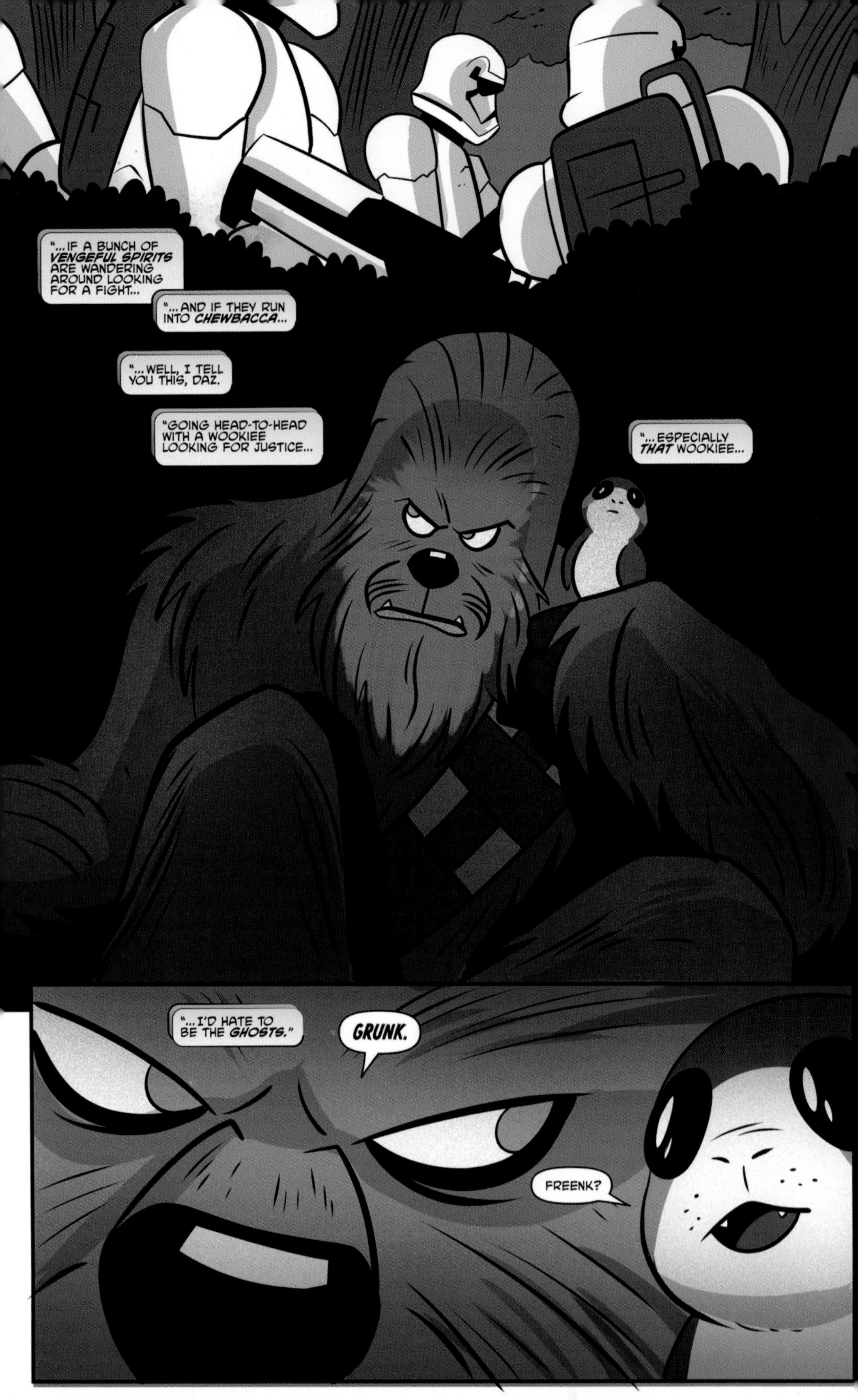

"...IF A BUNCH OF *VENGEFUL SPIRITS* ARE WANDERING AROUND LOOKING FOR A FIGHT...
"...AND IF THEY RUN INTO *CHEWBACCA*...
"...WELL, I TELL YOU THIS, DAZ.
"GOING HEAD-TO-HEAD WITH A WOOKIEE LOOKING FOR JUSTICE...
"...ESPECIALLY *THAT* WOOKIEE...
"...I'D HATE TO BE THE *GHOSTS*."
GRUNK.
FREENK?

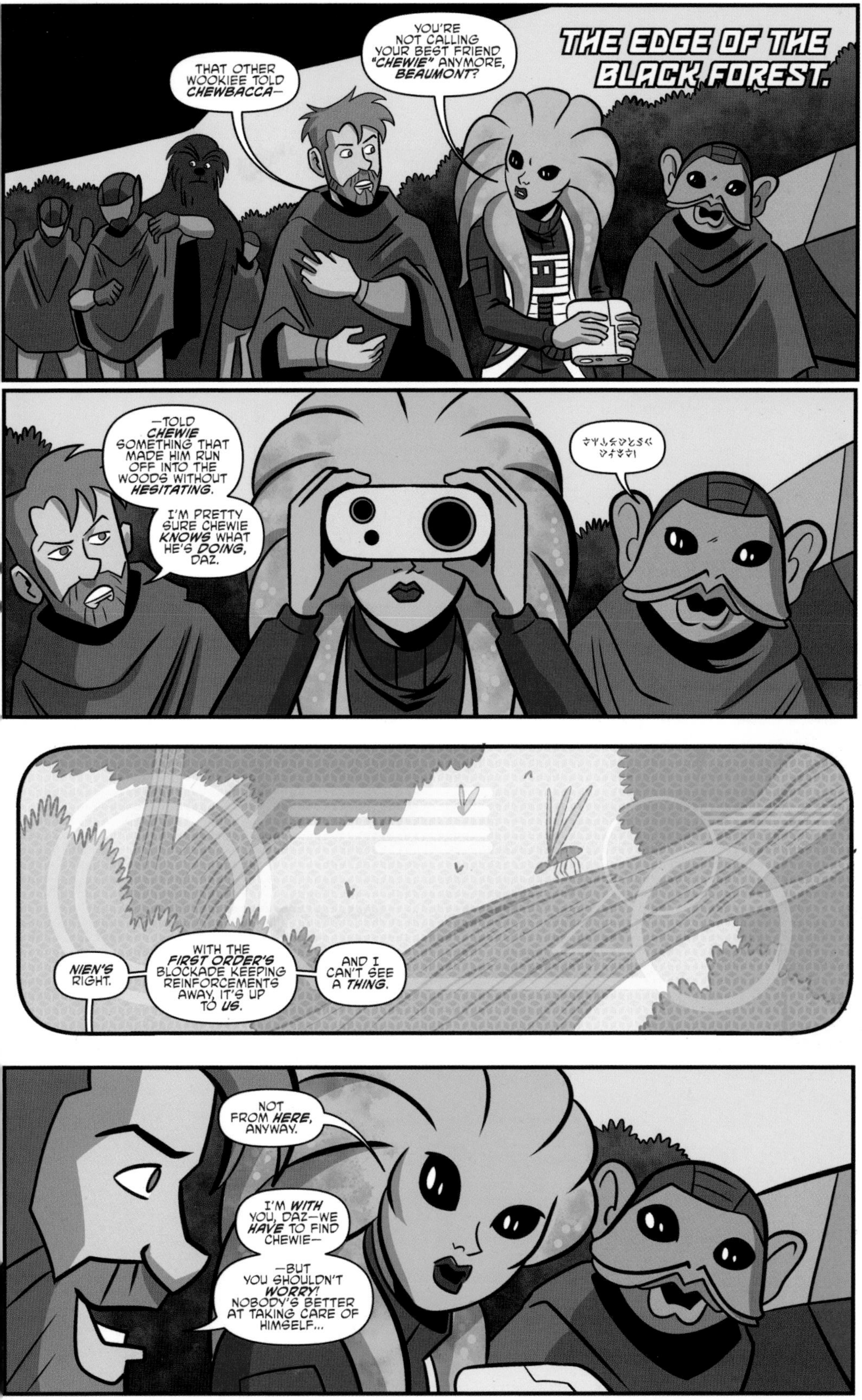
THE EDGE OF THE BLACK FOREST.
THAT OTHER WOOKIEE TOLD CHEWBACCA—
YOU'RE NOT CALLING YOUR BEST FRIEND "CHEWIE" ANYMORE, BEAUMONT?
—TOLD CHEWIE SOMETHING THAT MADE HIM RUN OFF INTO THE WOODS WITHOUT HESITATING.
I'M PRETTY SURE CHEWIE KNOWS WHAT HE'S DOING, DAZ.
NIEN'S RIGHT.
WITH THE FIRST ORDER'S BLOCKADE KEEPING REINFORCEMENTS AWAY, IT'S UP TO US.
AND I CAN'T SEE A THING.
NOT FROM HERE, ANYWAY.
I'M WITH YOU, DAZ—WE HAVE TO FIND CHEWIE—
—BUT YOU SHOULDN'T WORRY! NOBODY'S BETTER AT TAKING CARE OF HIMSELF...

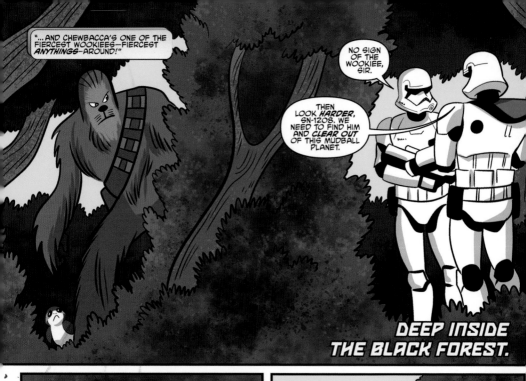

"...AND CHEWBACCA'S ONE OF THE FIERCEST WOOKIEES—FIERCEST *ANYTHINGS*—AROUND!"

NO SIGN OF THE WOOKIEE, SIR.

THEN LOOK *HARDER*, SN-1208. WE NEED TO FIND HIM AND *CLEAR OUT* OF THIS MUDBALL PLANET.

DEEP INSIDE THE BLACK FOREST.

CRAC

THERE—I HEARD SOMETHING.

GO-GO!

GOING, SIR!

BY THE AUTHORITY OF THE FIRST ORDER—

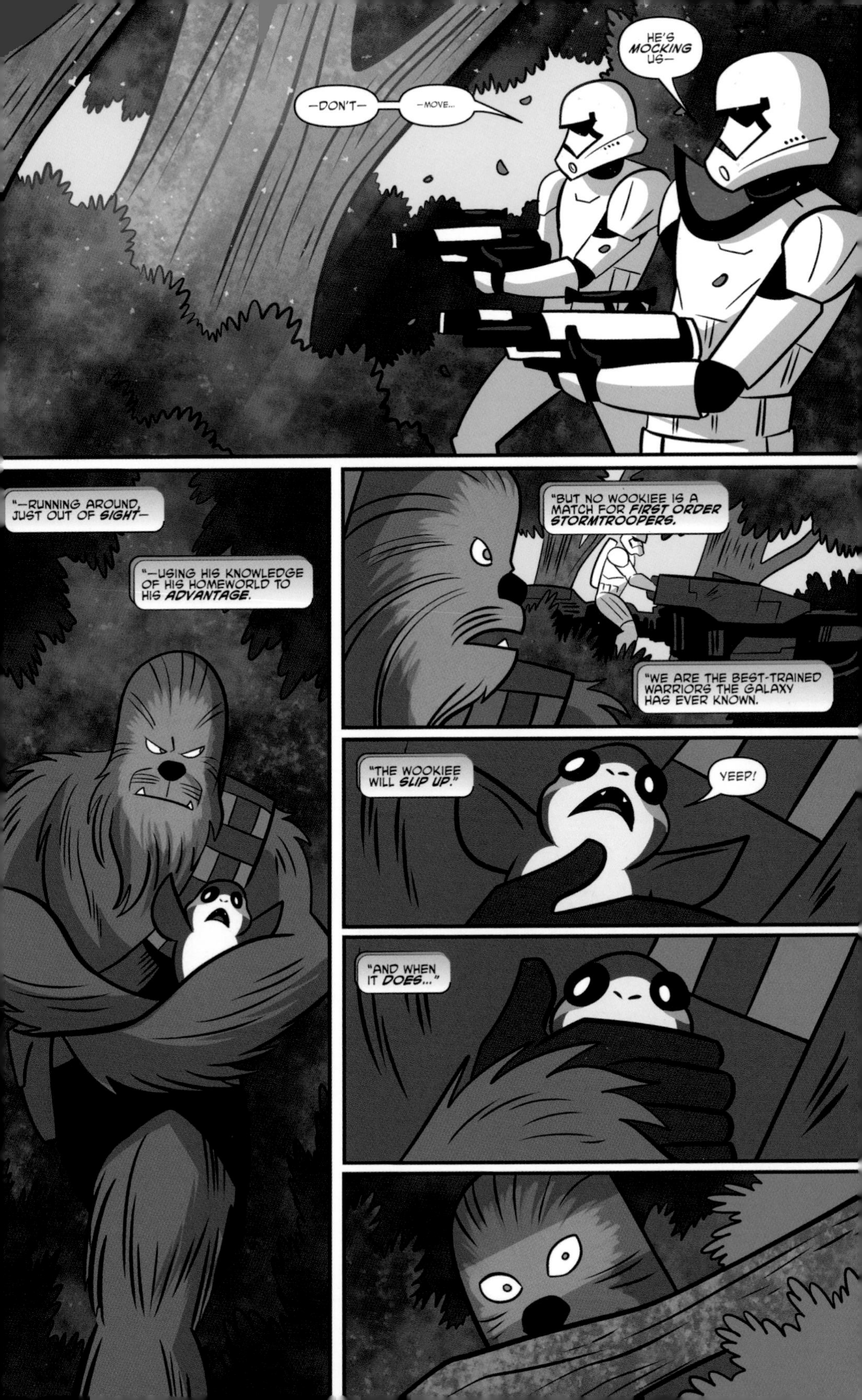

—DON'T—
—MOVE...
HE'S MOCKING US—
"—RUNNING AROUND, JUST OUT OF SIGHT—
"—USING HIS KNOWLEDGE OF HIS HOMEWORLD TO HIS ADVANTAGE.
"BUT NO WOOKIEE IS A MATCH FOR FIRST ORDER STORMTROOPERS.
"WE ARE THE BEST-TRAINED WARRIORS THE GALAXY HAS EVER KNOWN.
"THE WOOKIEE WILL SLIP UP."
YEEP!
"AND WHEN IT DOES..."

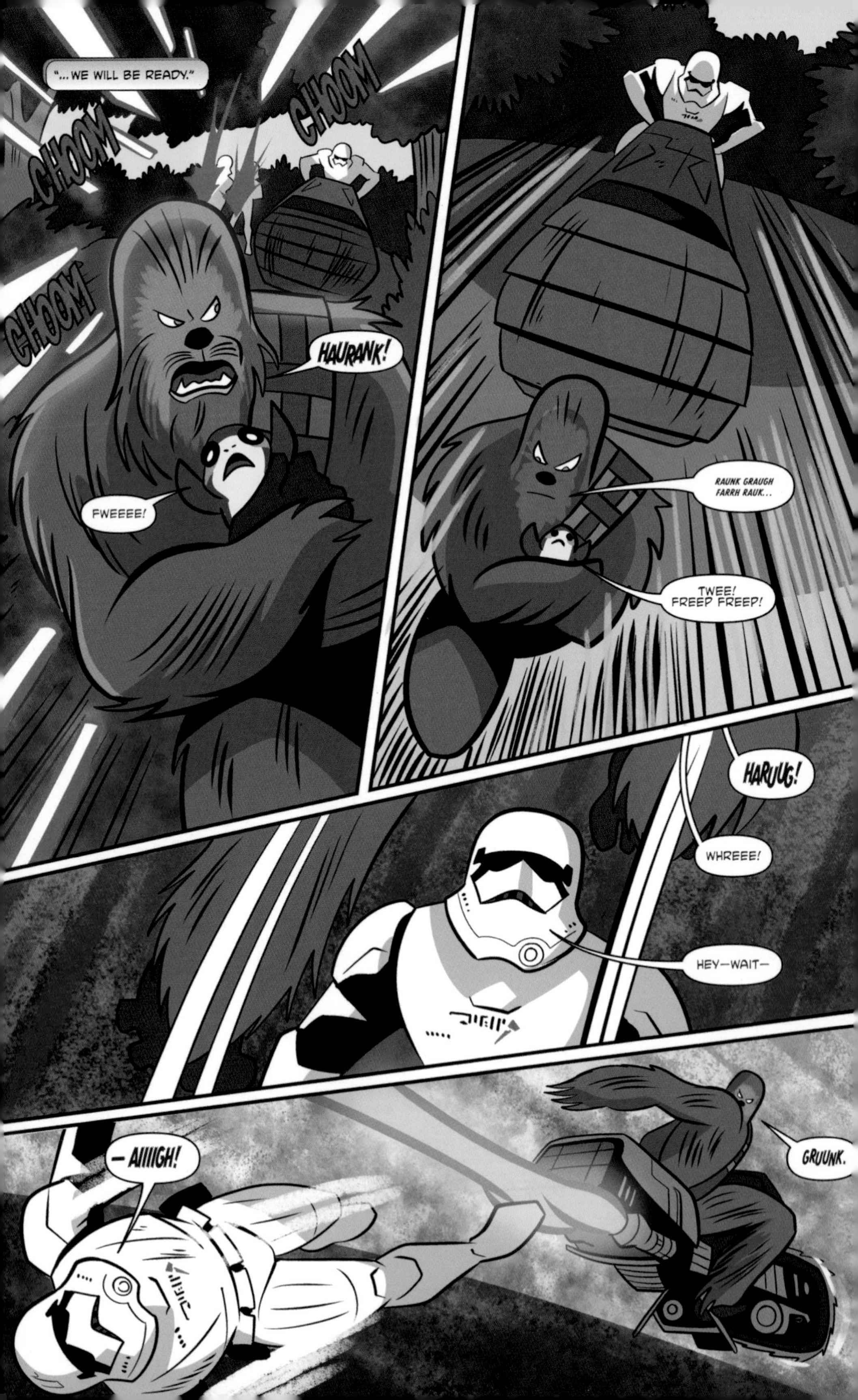
"...WE WILL BE READY."
CHOOM
CHOOM
CHOOM
HAURANK!
FWEEEEE!
RAUNK GRAUGH FARRH RAUK...
TWEE! FREEP FREEP!
HARUUG!
WHREEE!
HEY—WAIT—
—AIIIGH!
GRUUNK.

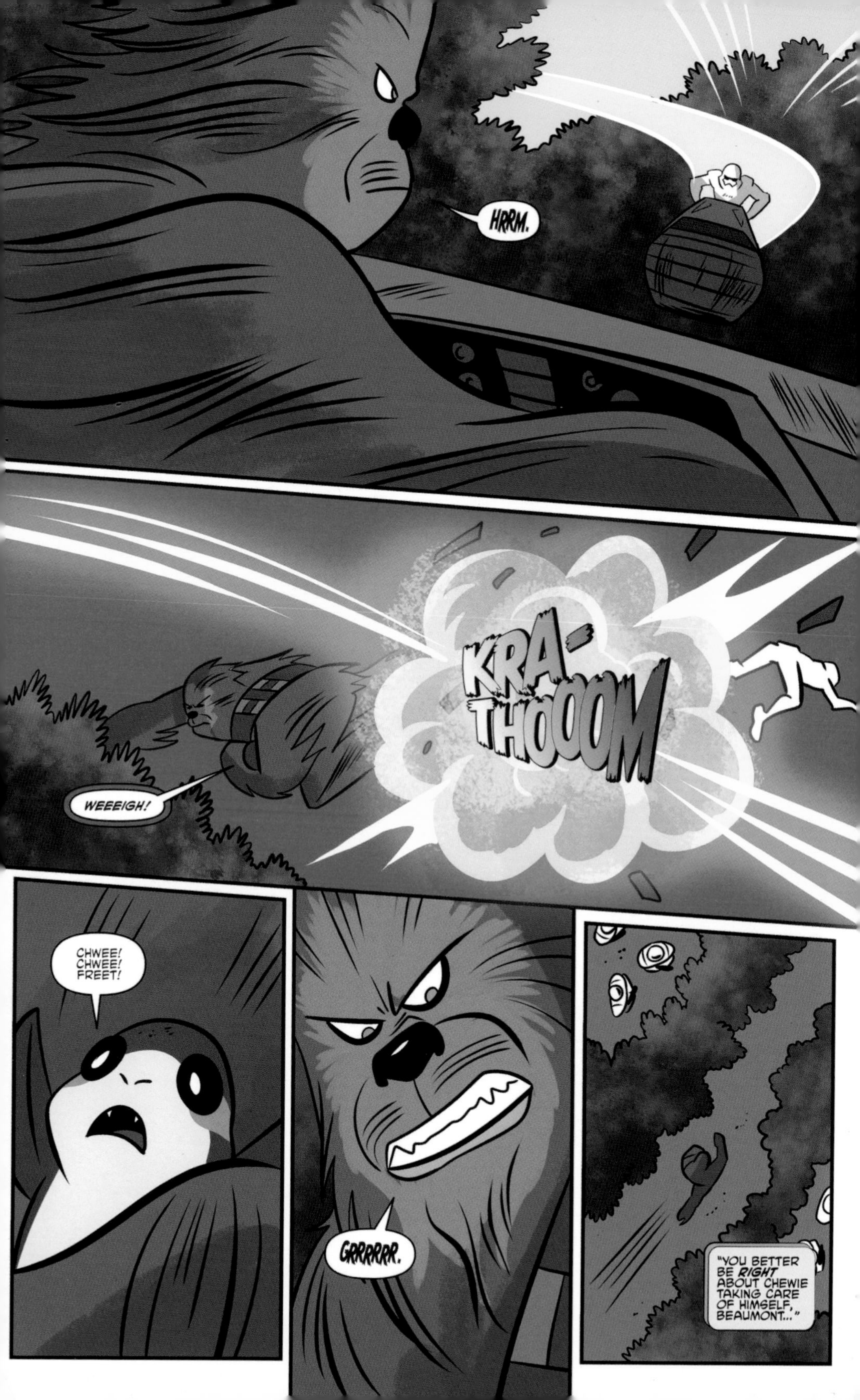
HRRM.
WEEEIGH!
KRA-THOOOM
CHWEE! CHWEE! FREET!
GRRRRR.
"YOU BETTER BE RIGHT ABOUT CHEWIE TAKING CARE OF HIMSELF, BEAUMONT..."

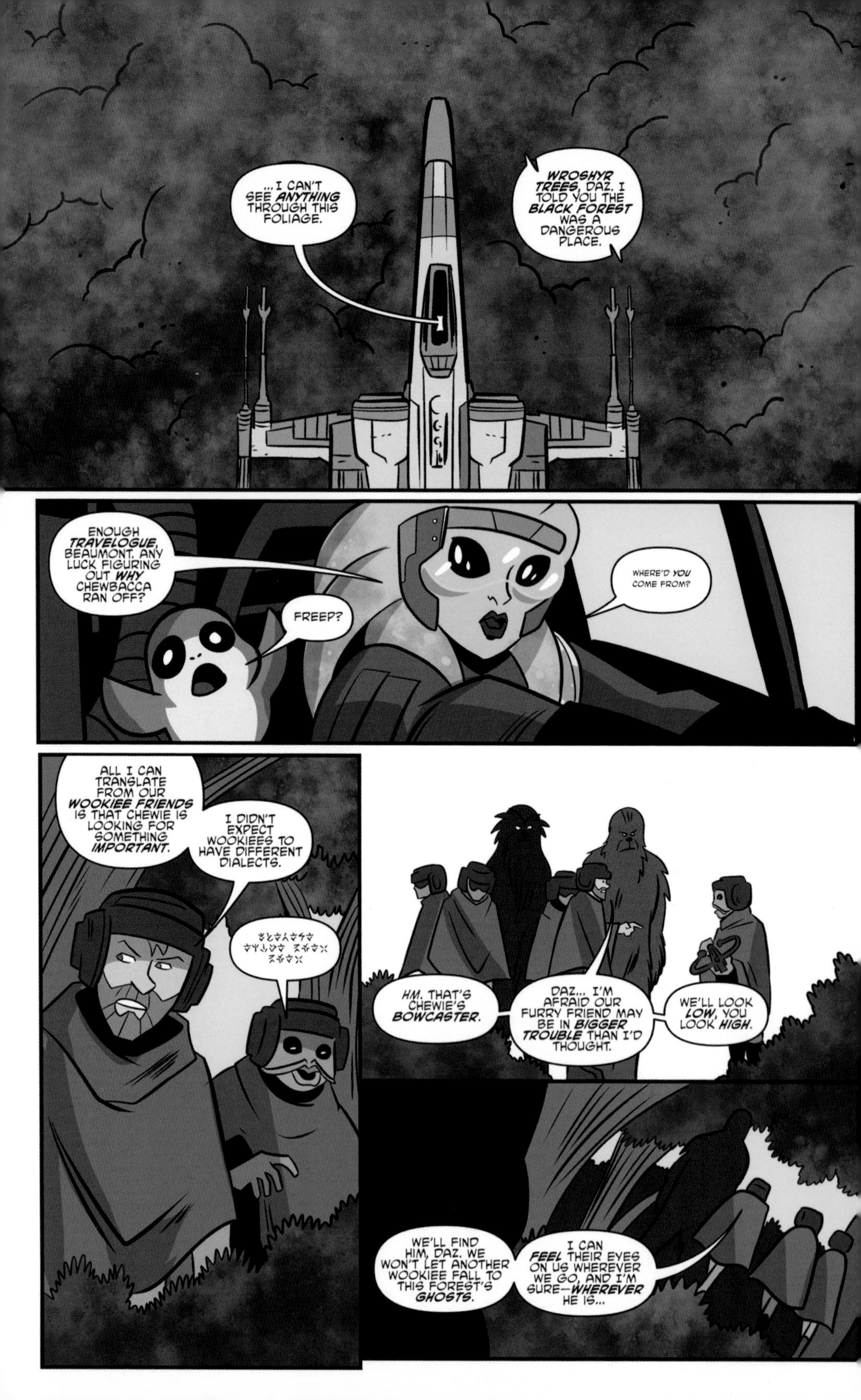
...I CAN'T SEE ANYTHING THROUGH THIS FOLIAGE.
WROSHYR TREES, DAZ. I TOLD YOU THE BLACK FOREST WAS A DANGEROUS PLACE.
ENOUGH TRAVELOGUE, BEAUMONT. ANY LUCK FIGURING OUT WHY CHEWBACCA RAN OFF?
FREEP?
WHERE'D YOU COME FROM?
ALL I CAN TRANSLATE FROM OUR WOOKIEE FRIENDS IS THAT CHEWIE IS LOOKING FOR SOMETHING IMPORTANT.
I DIDN'T EXPECT WOOKIEES TO HAVE DIFFERENT DIALECTS.
HM. THAT'S CHEWIE'S BOWCASTER.
DAZ... I'M AFRAID OUR FURRY FRIEND MAY BE IN BIGGER TROUBLE THAN I'D THOUGHT.
WE'LL LOOK LOW, YOU LOOK HIGH.
WE'LL FIND HIM, DAZ. WE WON'T LET ANOTHER WOOKIEE FALL TO THIS FOREST'S GHOSTS.
I CAN FEEL THEIR EYES ON US WHEREVER WE GO, AND I'M SURE—WHEREVER HE IS...

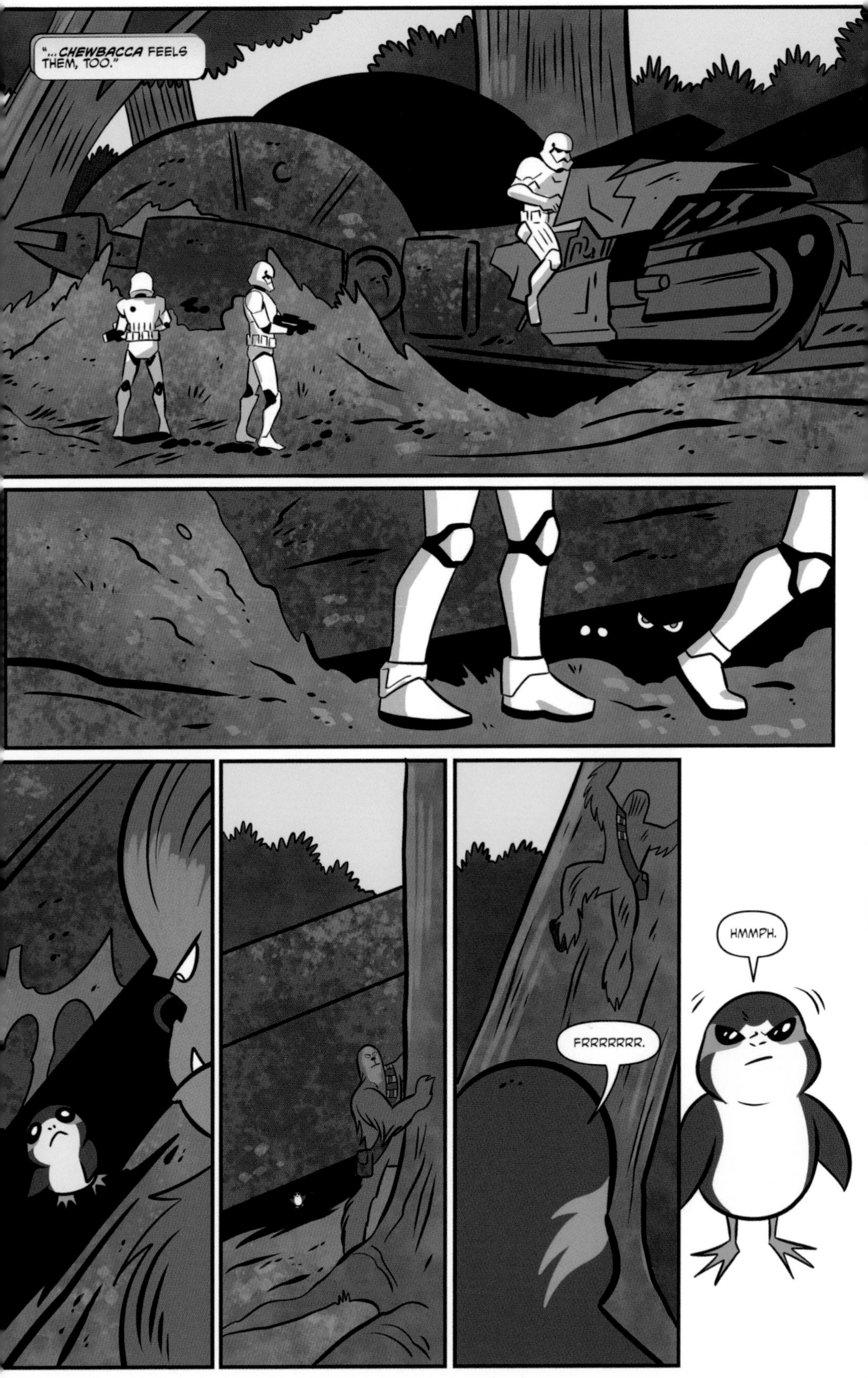
"...CHEWBACCA FEELS THEM, TOO."
FRRRRRRR.
HMMPH.

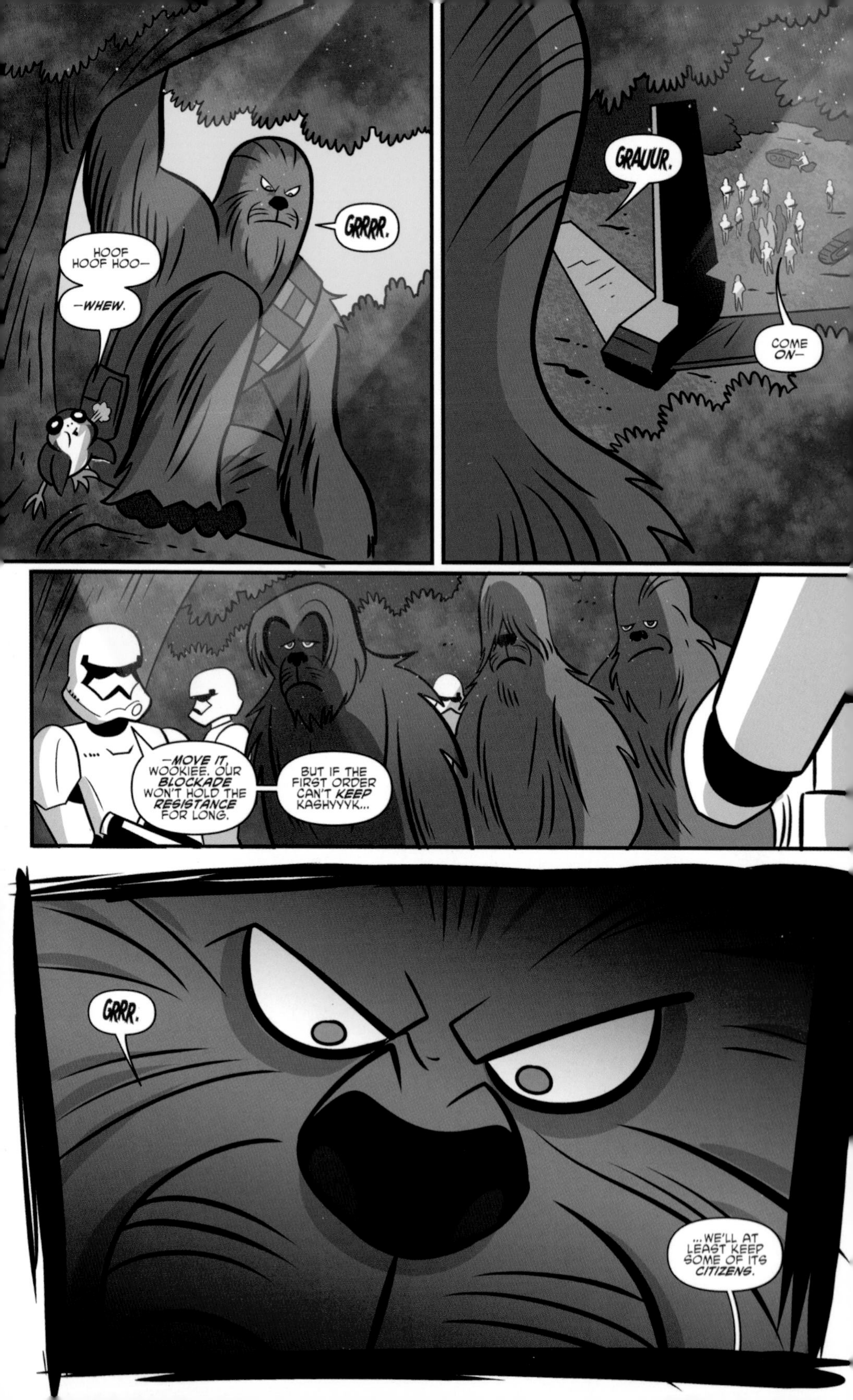
GRRRR.
HOOF HOOF HOO—
—WHEW.
GRAUUR.
COME ON—
—MOVE IT, WOOKIEE. OUR BLOCKADE WON'T HOLD THE RESISTANCE FOR LONG.
BUT IF THE FIRST ORDER CAN'T KEEP KASHYYYK...
GRRR.
...WE'LL AT LEAST KEEP SOME OF ITS CITIZENS.

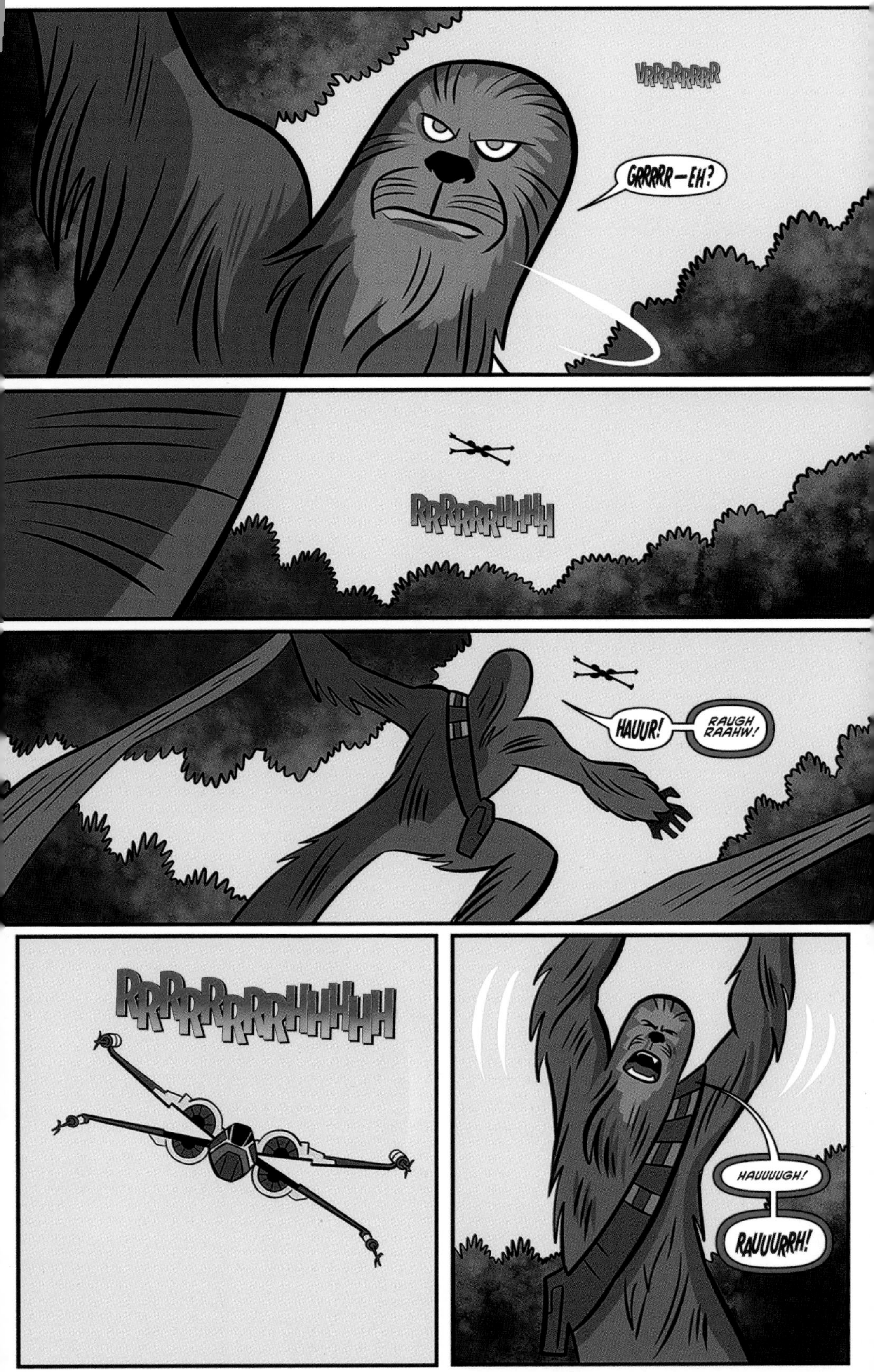
VRRRRRRRR
GRRRRR—EH?
RRRRRRRHHHH
HAUUR!
RAUGH RAAHW!
RRRRRRRRRHHHHH
HAUUUUGH!
RAUUURRH!

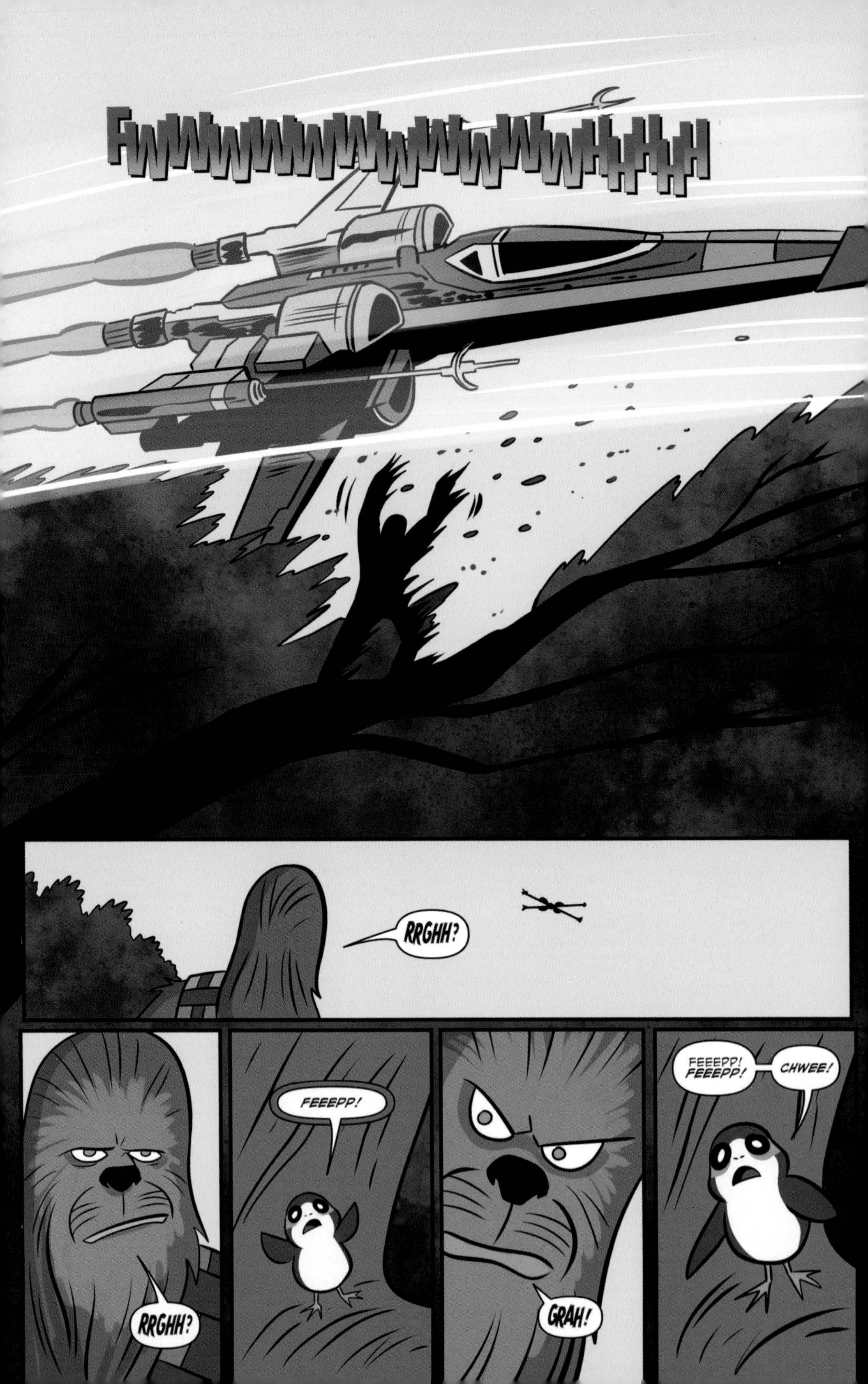
FWWWWWWWWWWWWWWWHHHHH
RRGHH?
RRGHH?
FEEEPP!
GRAH!
FEEEPP! FEEEPP!
CHWEE!

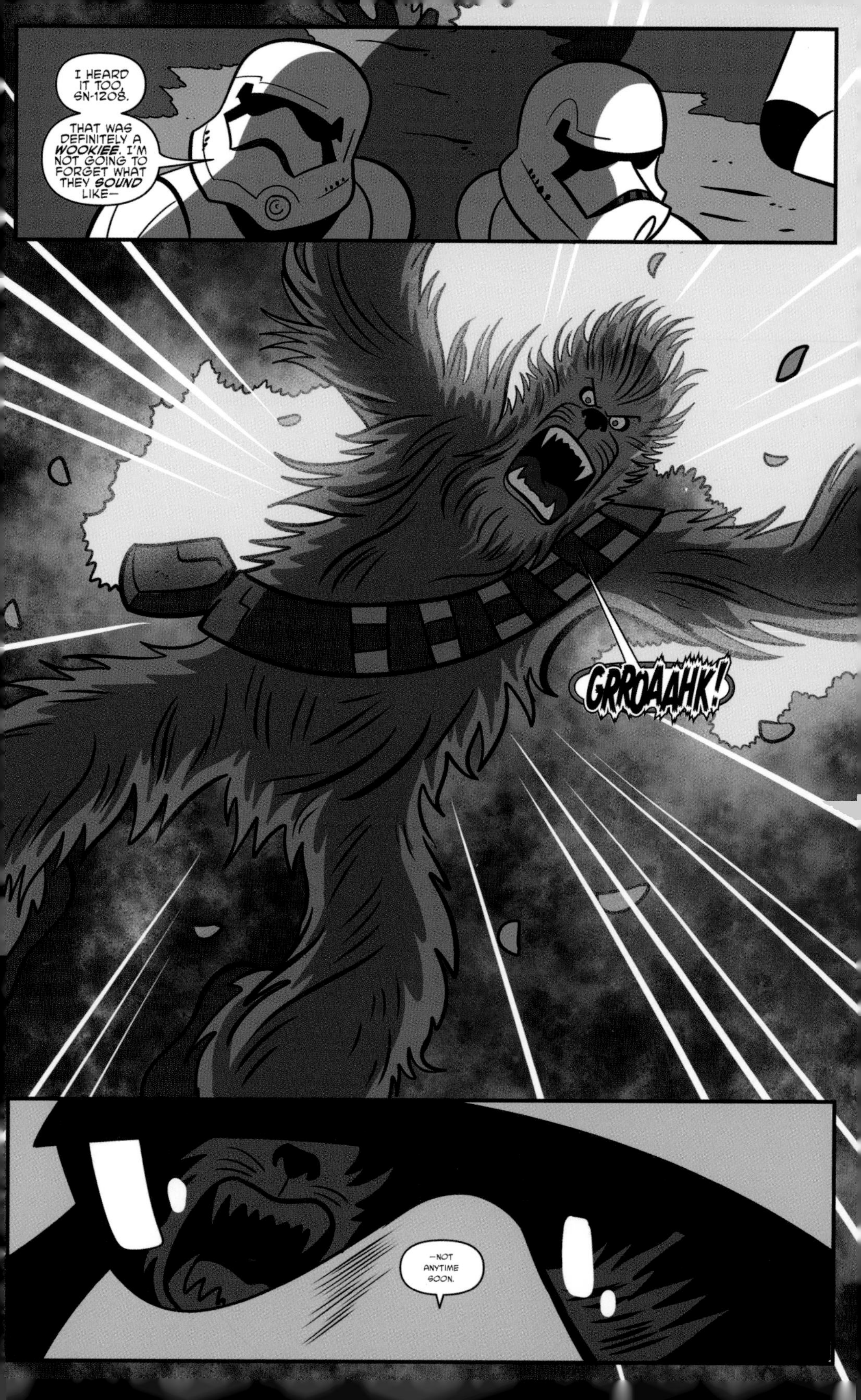
I HEARD IT TOO, SN-1208.
THAT WAS DEFINITELY A WOOKIEE. I'M NOT GOING TO FORGET WHAT THEY SOUND LIKE—
GRROAAHK!
—NOT ANYTIME SOON.

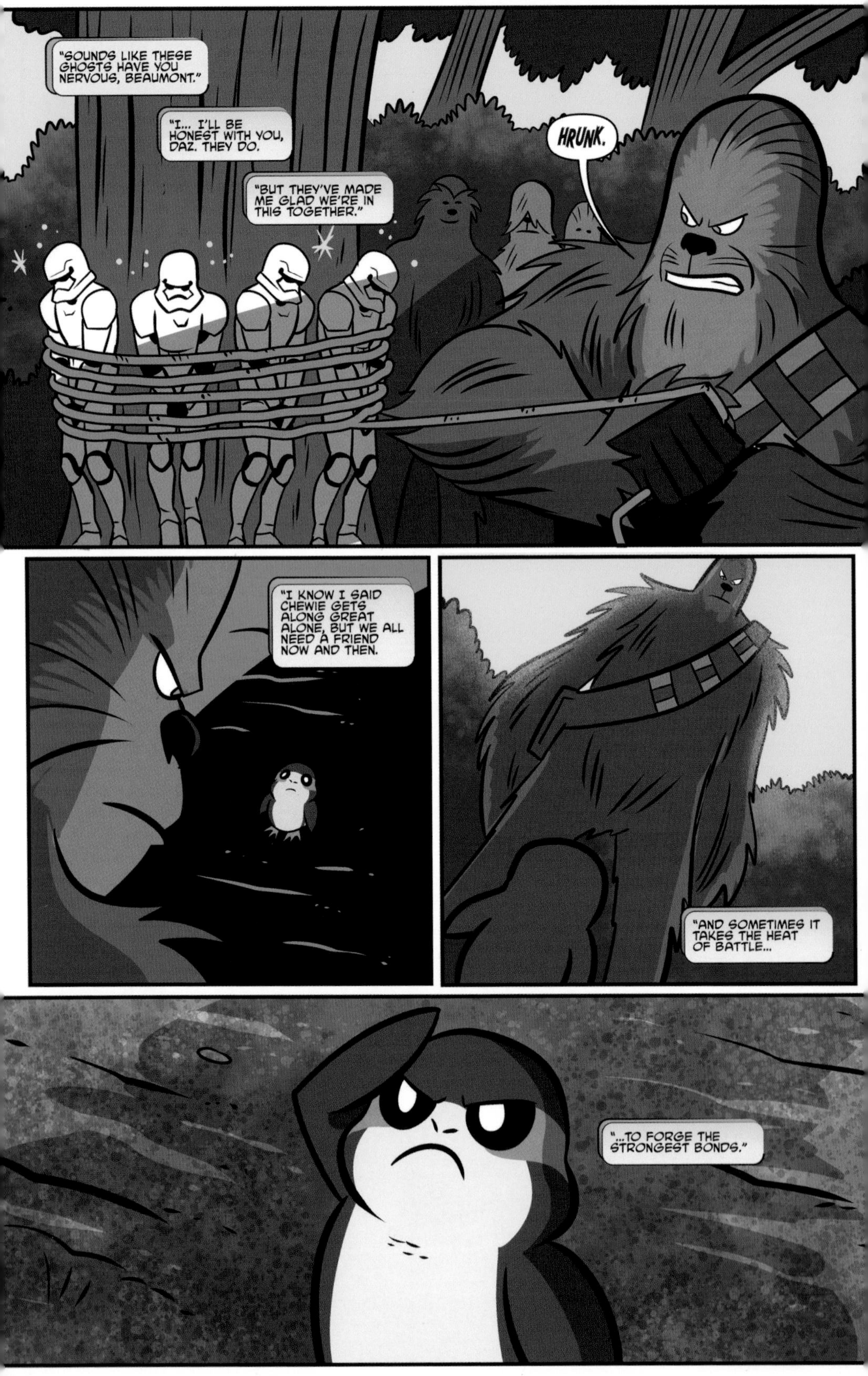
"SOUNDS LIKE THESE GHOSTS HAVE YOU NERVOUS, BEAUMONT."
"I... I'LL BE HONEST WITH YOU, DAZ. THEY DO.
"BUT THEY'VE MADE ME GLAD WE'RE IN THIS TOGETHER."
HRUNK.
"I KNOW I SAID CHEWIE GETS ALONG GREAT ALONE, BUT WE ALL NEED A FRIEND NOW AND THEN.
"AND SOMETIMES IT TAKES THE HEAT OF BATTLE...
"...TO FORGE THE STRONGEST BONDS."

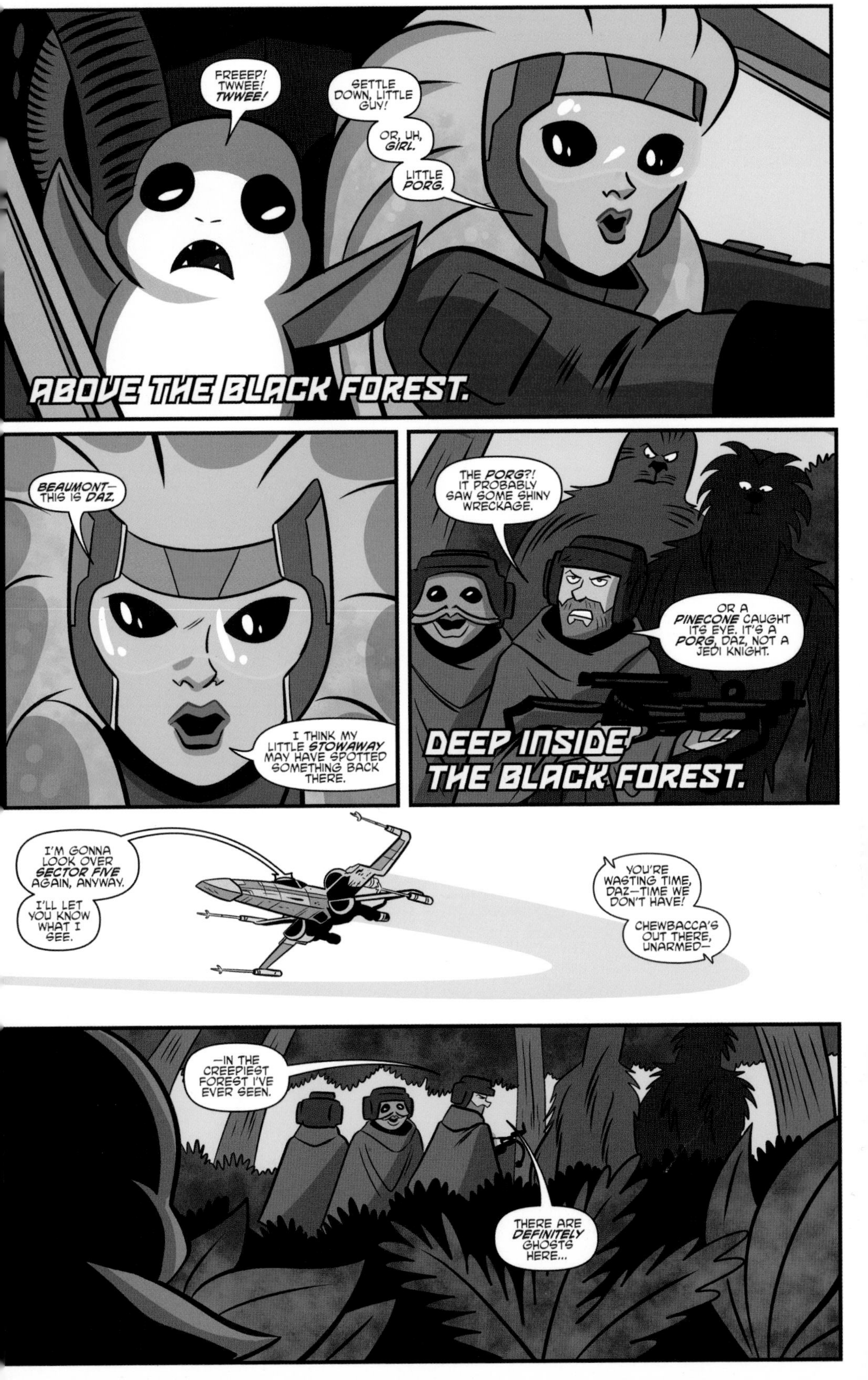
FREEEP! TWWEE! TWWEE!
SETTLE DOWN, LITTLE GUY!
OR, UH, GIRL.
LITTLE PORG.
ABOVE THE BLACK FOREST.
BEAUMONT— THIS IS DAZ.
I THINK MY LITTLE STOWAWAY MAY HAVE SPOTTED SOMETHING BACK THERE.
THE PORG?! IT PROBABLY SAW SOME SHINY WRECKAGE.
OR A PINECONE CAUGHT ITS EYE. IT'S A PORG, DAZ, NOT A JEDI KNIGHT.
DEEP INSIDE THE BLACK FOREST.
I'M GONNA LOOK OVER SECTOR FIVE AGAIN, ANYWAY.
I'LL LET YOU KNOW WHAT I SEE.
YOU'RE WASTING TIME, DAZ—TIME WE DON'T HAVE!
CHEWBACCA'S OUT THERE, UNARMED—
—IN THE CREEPIEST FOREST I'VE EVER SEEN.
THERE ARE DEFINITELY GHOSTS HERE...

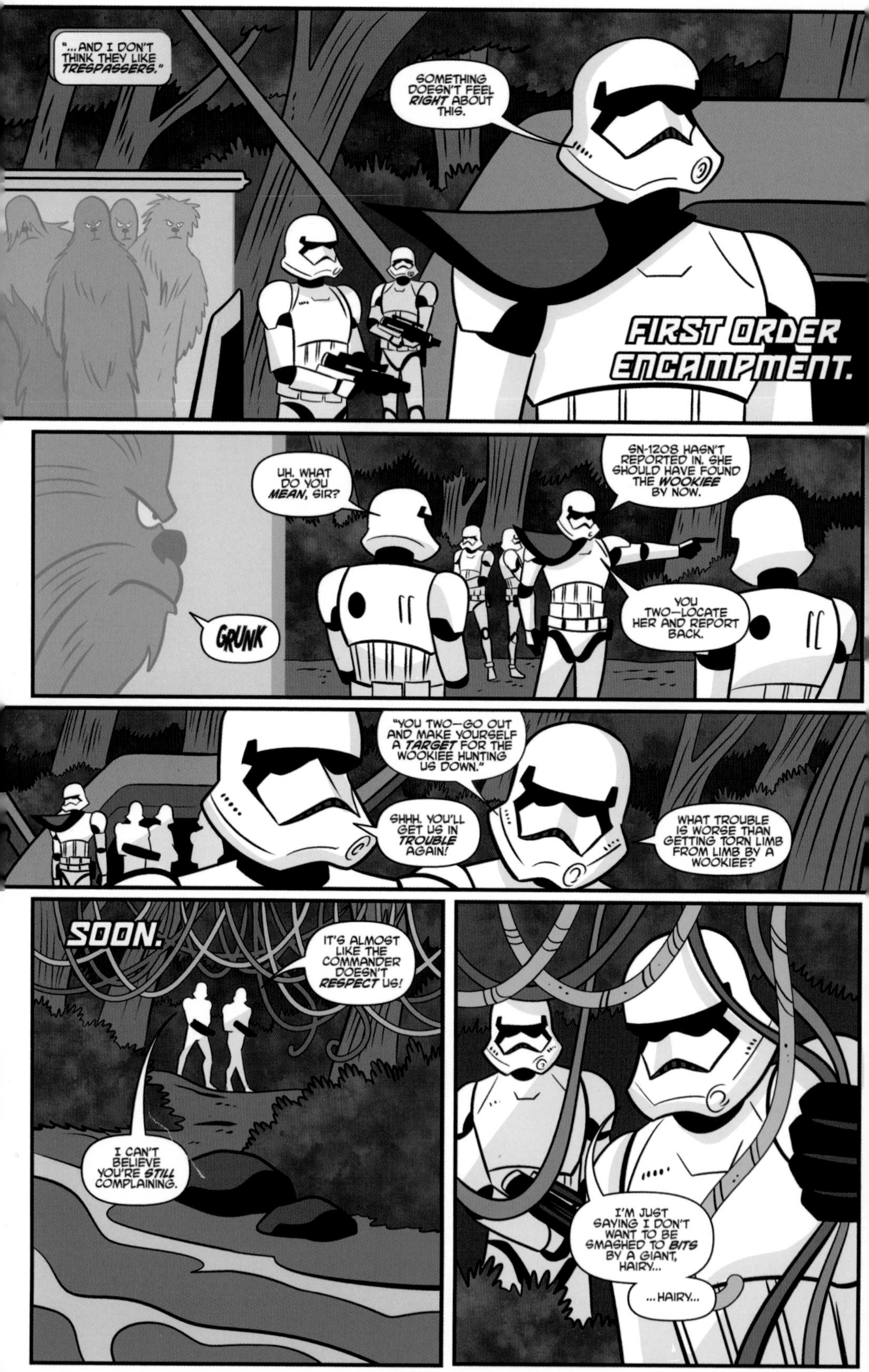
"...AND I DON'T THINK THEY LIKE TRESPASSERS."
SOMETHING DOESN'T FEEL RIGHT ABOUT THIS.
FIRST ORDER ENCAMPMENT.
UH. WHAT DO YOU MEAN, SIR?
SN-1208 HASN'T REPORTED IN. SHE SHOULD HAVE FOUND THE WOOKIEE BY NOW.
YOU TWO—LOCATE HER AND REPORT BACK.
GRUNK
"YOU TWO—GO OUT AND MAKE YOURSELF A TARGET FOR THE WOOKIEE HUNTING US DOWN."
SHHH. YOU'LL GET US IN TROUBLE AGAIN!
WHAT TROUBLE IS WORSE THAN GETTING TORN LIMB FROM LIMB BY A WOOKIEE?
SOON.
IT'S ALMOST LIKE THE COMMANDER DOESN'T RESPECT US!
I CAN'T BELIEVE YOU'RE STILL COMPLAINING.
I'M JUST SAYING I DON'T WANT TO BE SMASHED TO BITS BY A GIANT, HAIRY...
...HAIRY...

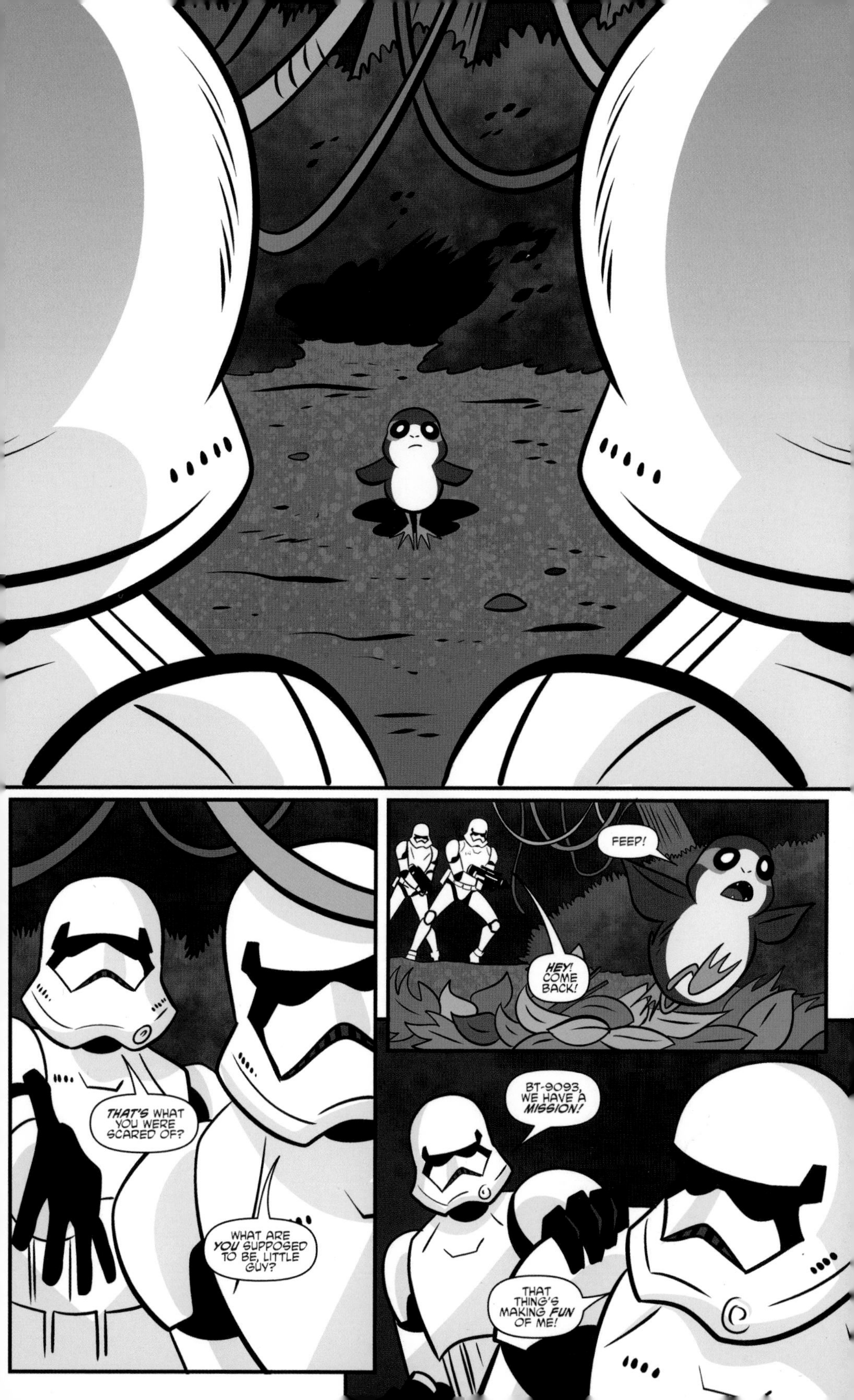
FEEP!
HEY! COME BACK!
THAT'S WHAT YOU WERE SCARED OF?
WHAT ARE YOU SUPPOSED TO BE, LITTLE GUY?
BT-9093, WE HAVE A MISSION!
THAT THING'S MAKING FUN OF ME!

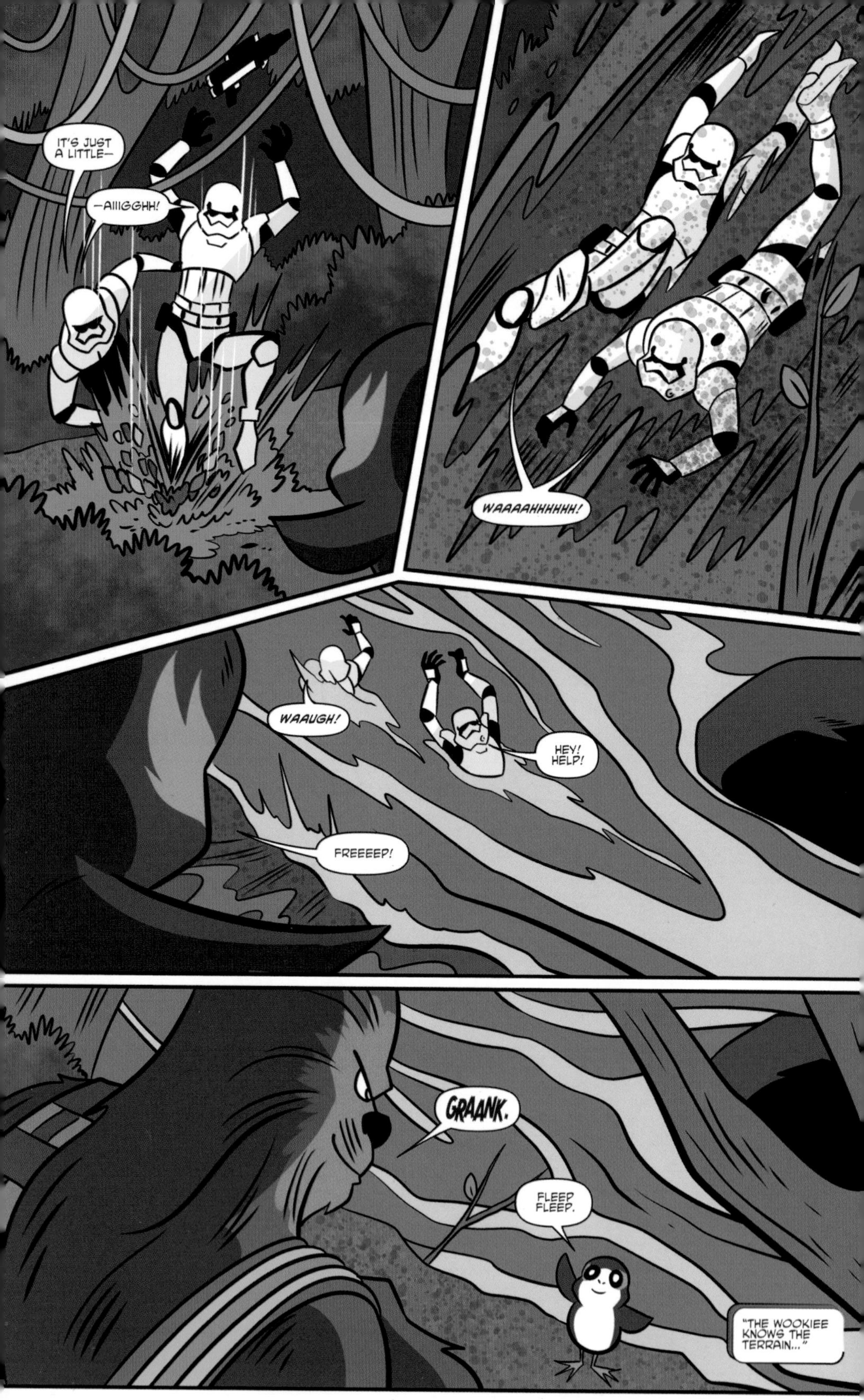
IT'S JUST A LITTLE—
—AIIIGGHH!
WAAAAHHHHHH!
WAAUGH!
HEY! HELP!
FREEEEP!
GRAANK.
FLEEP FLEEP.
"THE WOOKIEE KNOWS THE TERRAIN..."

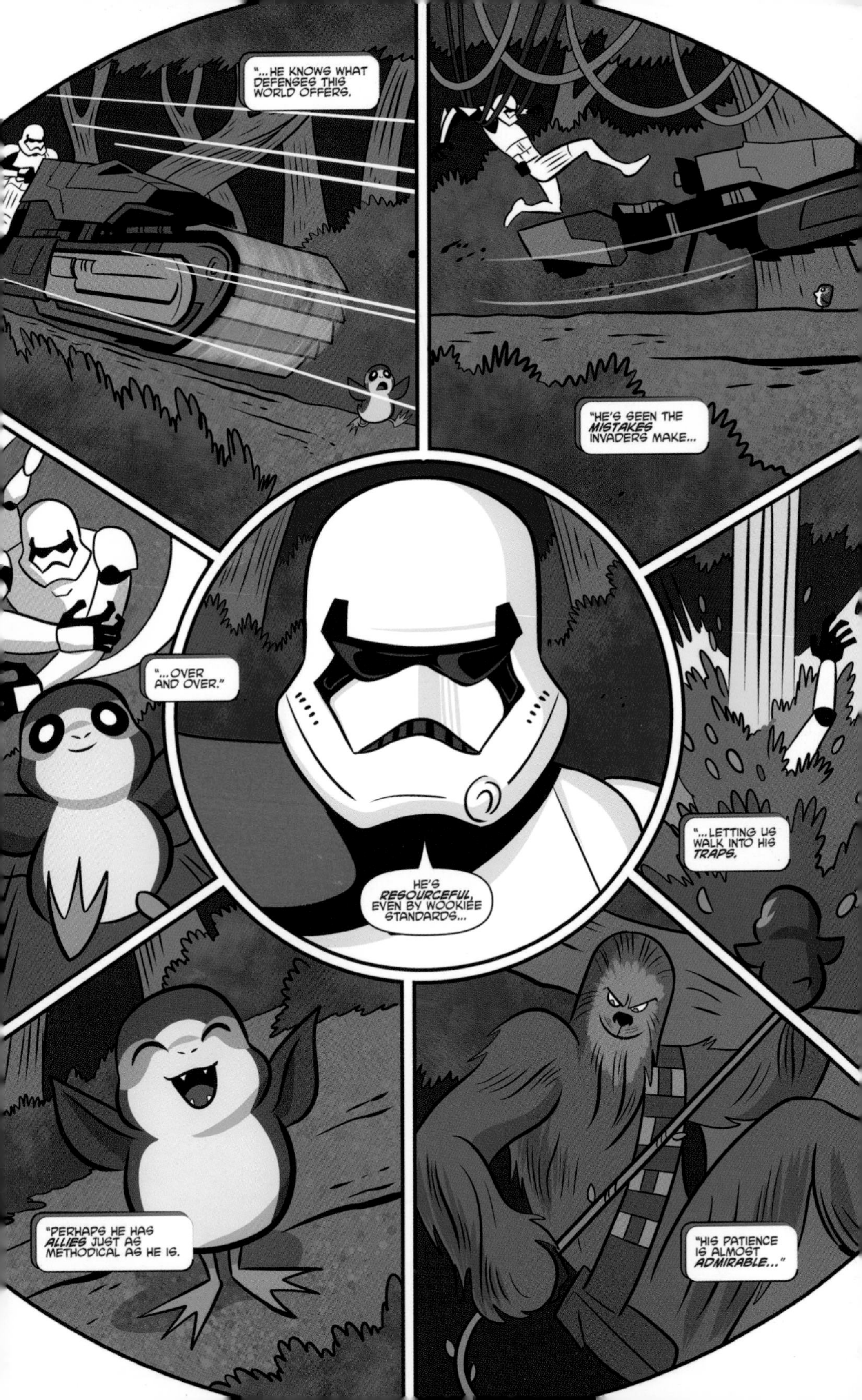
"...HE KNOWS WHAT DEFENSES THIS WORLD OFFERS.
"HE'S SEEN THE MISTAKES INVADERS MAKE...
"...OVER AND OVER."
HE'S RESOURCEFUL, EVEN BY WOOKIEE STANDARDS...
"...LETTING US WALK INTO HIS TRAPS.
"PERHAPS HE HAS ALLIES JUST AS METHODICAL AS HE IS.
"HIS PATIENCE IS ALMOST ADMIRABLE..."

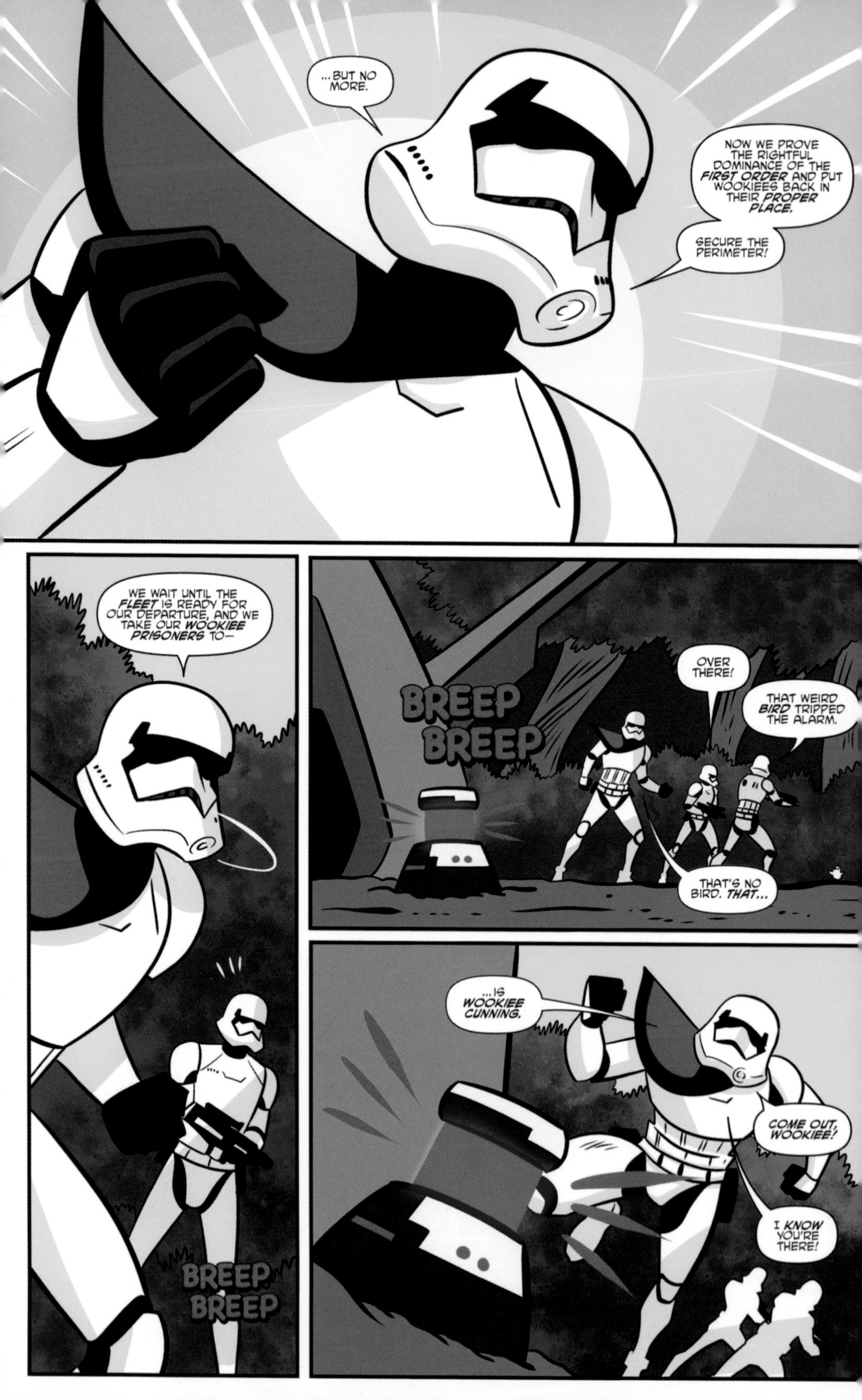
...BUT NO MORE.
NOW WE PROVE THE RIGHTFUL DOMINANCE OF THE FIRST ORDER AND PUT WOOKIEES BACK IN THEIR PROPER PLACE.
SECURE THE PERIMETER!
WE WAIT UNTIL THE FLEET IS READY FOR OUR DEPARTURE, AND WE TAKE OUR WOOKIEE PRISONERS TO—
BREEP BREEP
BREEP BREEP
OVER THERE!
THAT WEIRD BIRD TRIPPED THE ALARM.
THAT'S NO BIRD. THAT...
...IS WOOKIEE CUNNING.
COME OUT, WOOKIEE!
I KNOW YOU'RE THERE!

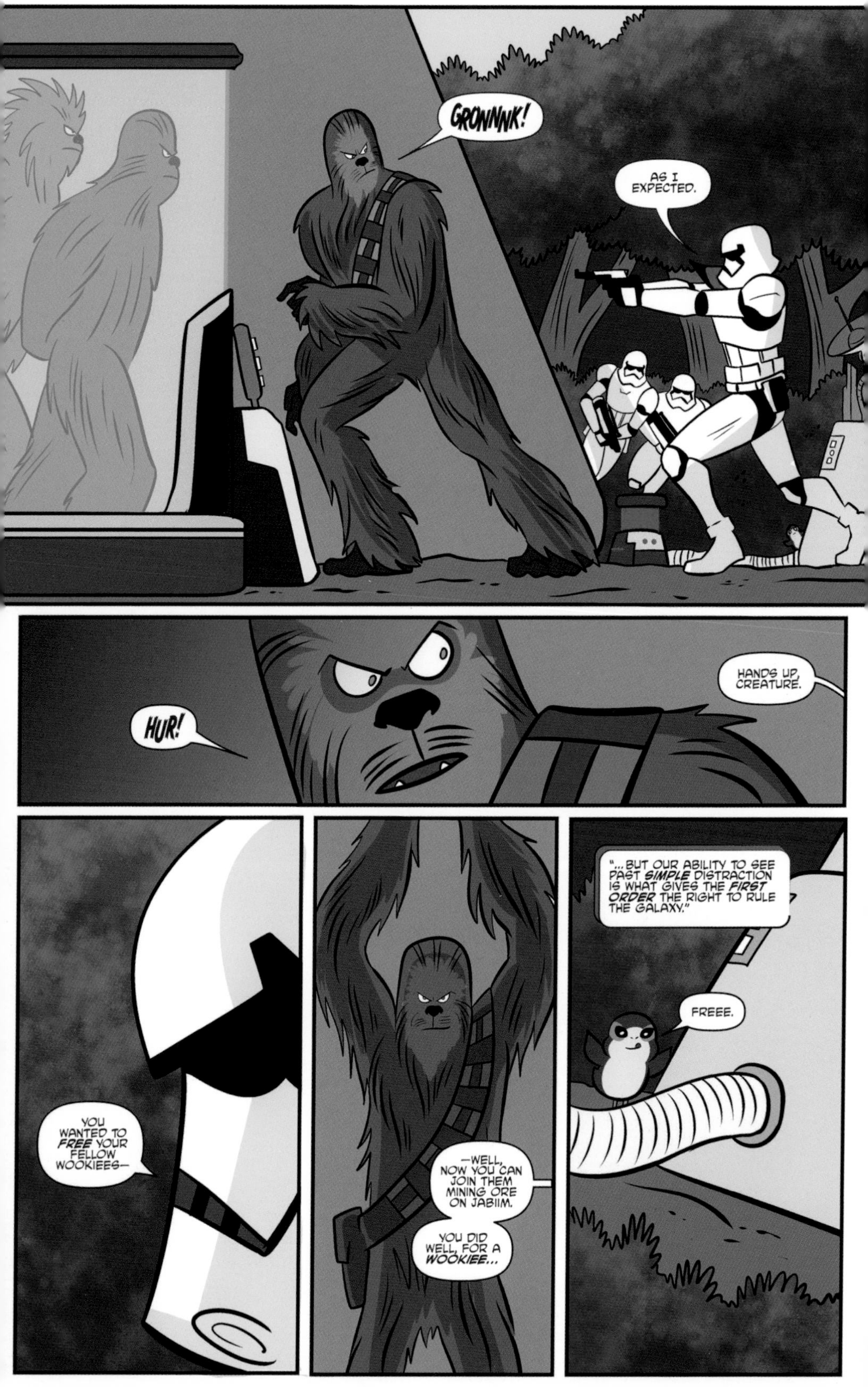
GRONNNK!
AS I EXPECTED.
HANDS UP, CREATURE.
HUR!
YOU WANTED TO FREE YOUR FELLOW WOOKIEES—
—WELL, NOW YOU CAN JOIN THEM MINING ORE ON JABIIM.
YOU DID WELL, FOR A WOOKIEE...
"...BUT OUR ABILITY TO SEE PAST SIMPLE DISTRACTION IS WHAT GIVES THE FIRST ORDER THE RIGHT TO RULE THE GALAXY."
FREEE.

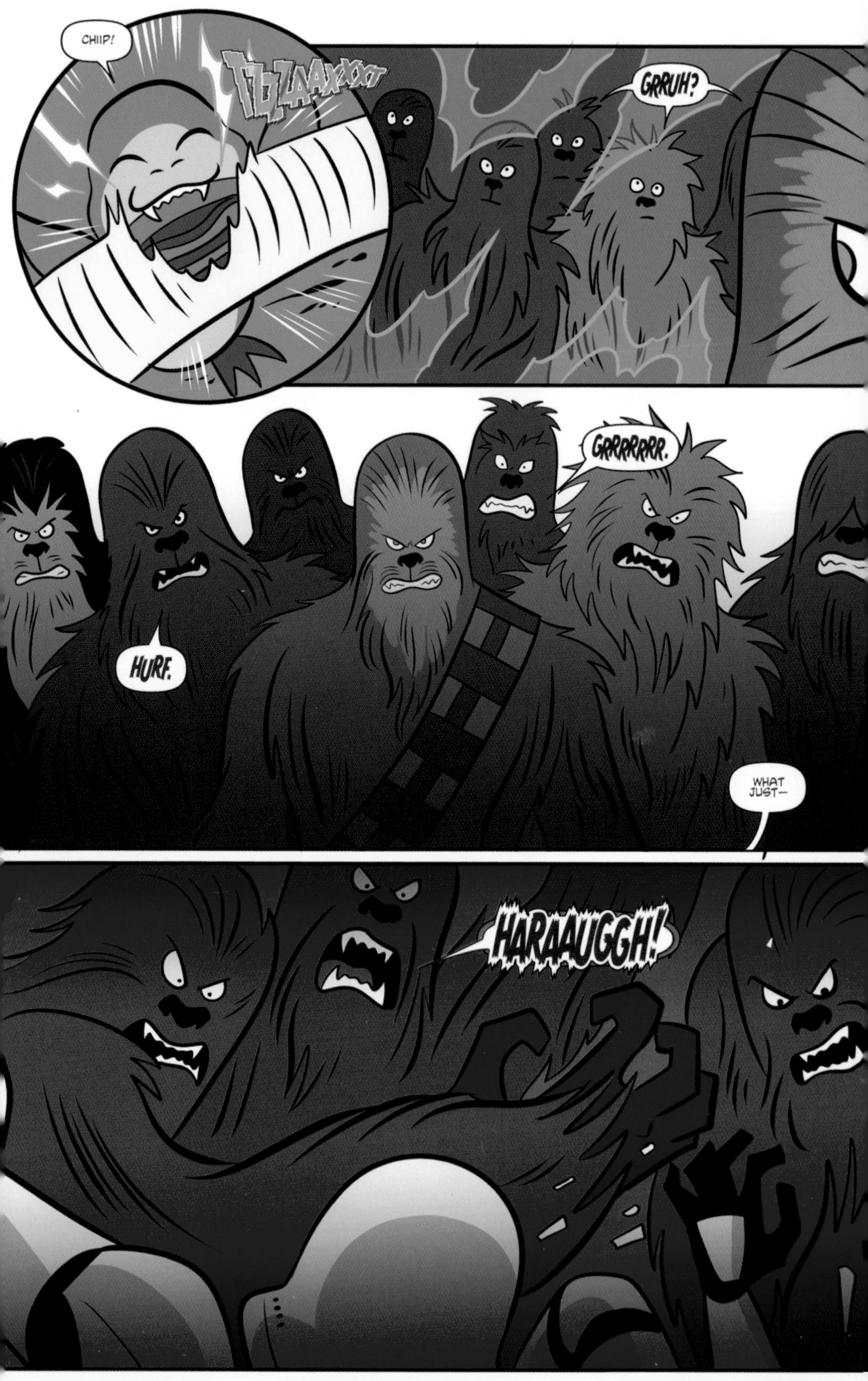
CHIIP!
TZZZAAXXXT
GRRUH?
GRRRRRRR.
HURF.
WHAT JUST—
HARAAUGGH!

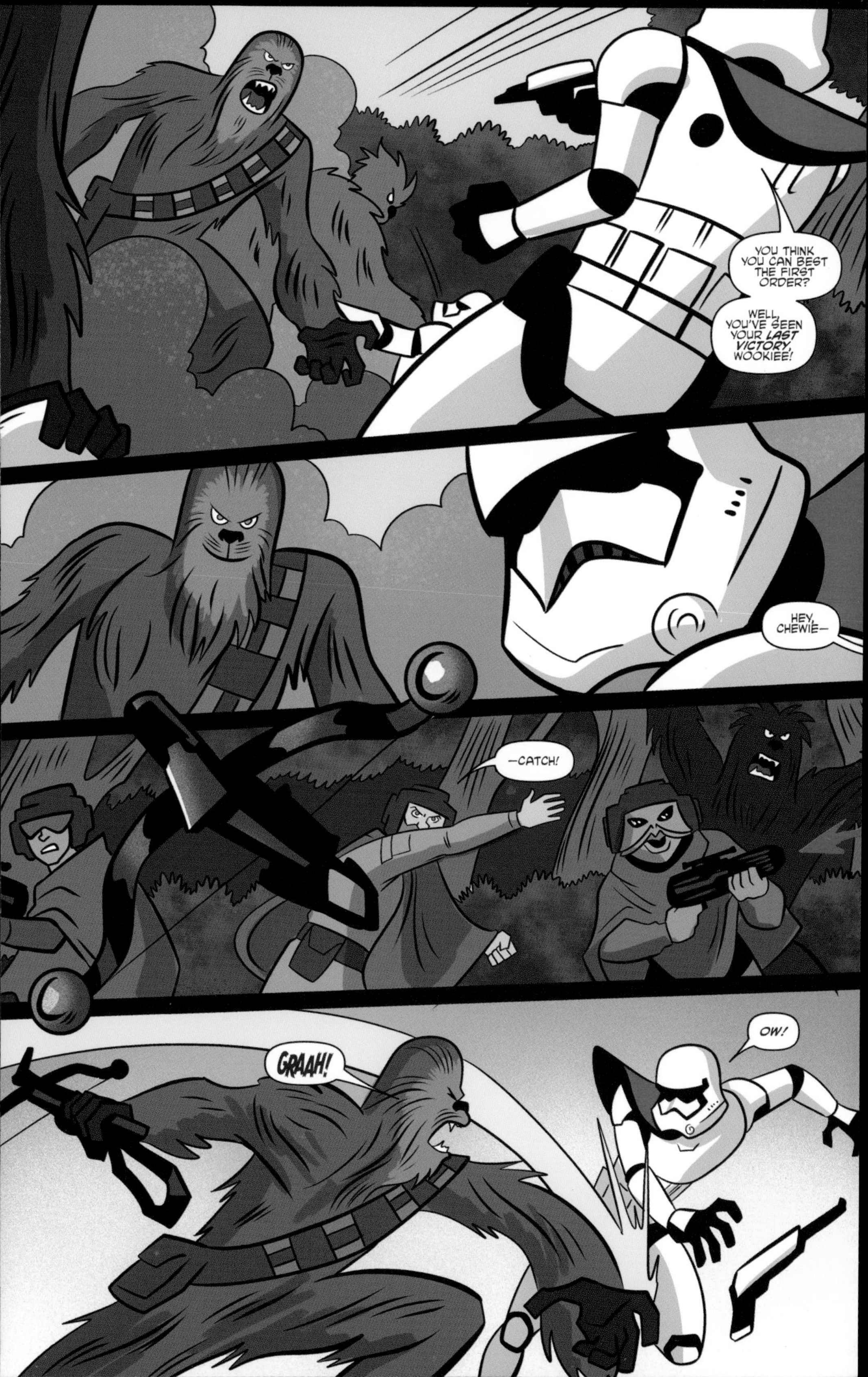

YOU THINK YOU CAN BEST THE FIRST ORDER?
WELL, YOU'VE SEEN YOUR *LAST VICTORY*, WOOKIEE!
HEY, CHEWIE—
—CATCH!
GRAAH!
OW!

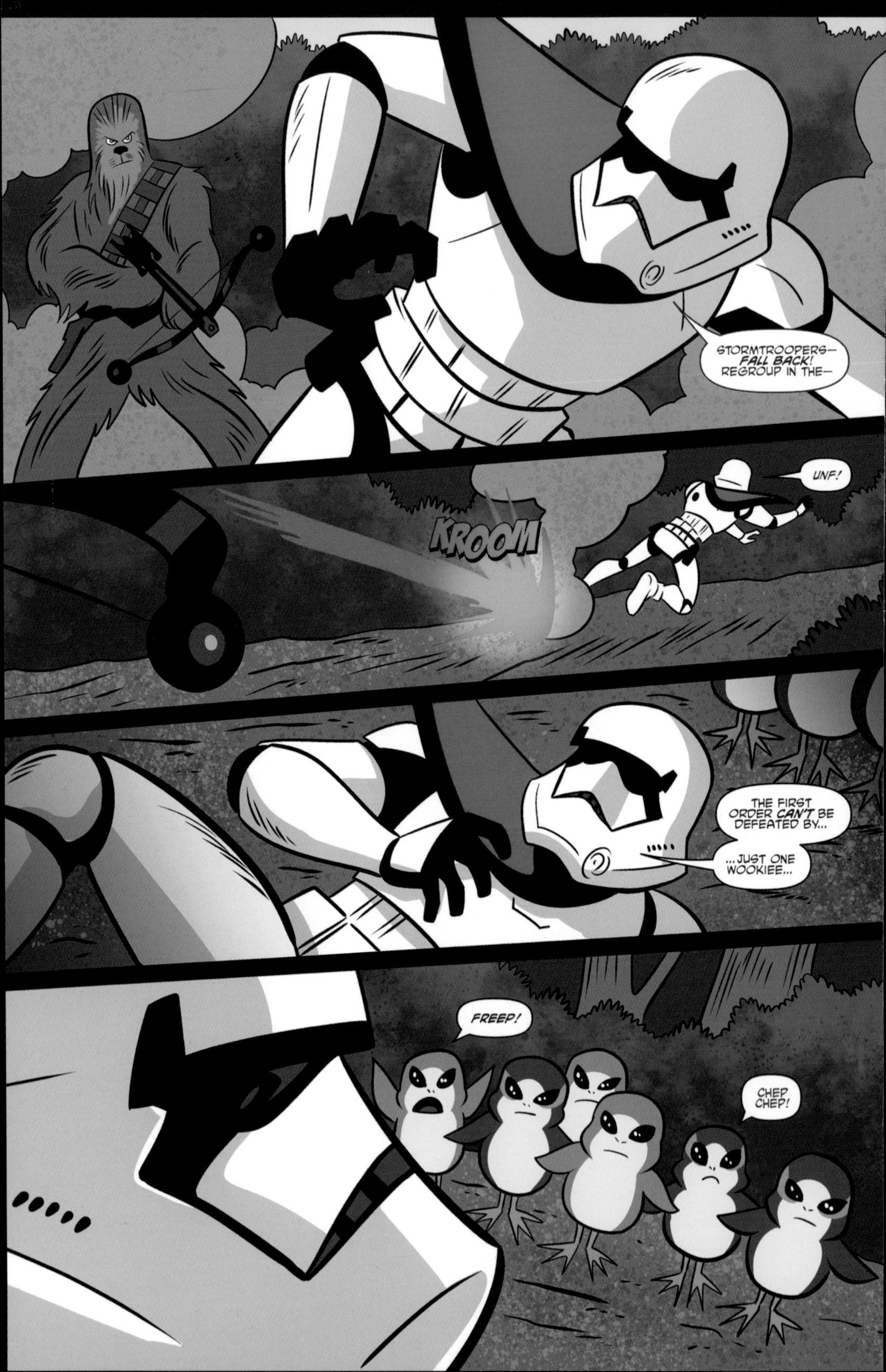
STORMTROOPERS—
FALL BACK!
REGROUP IN THE—
UNF!
KROOM
THE FIRST ORDER CAN'T BE DEFEATED BY...
...JUST ONE WOOKIEE...
FREEP!
CHEP CHEP!

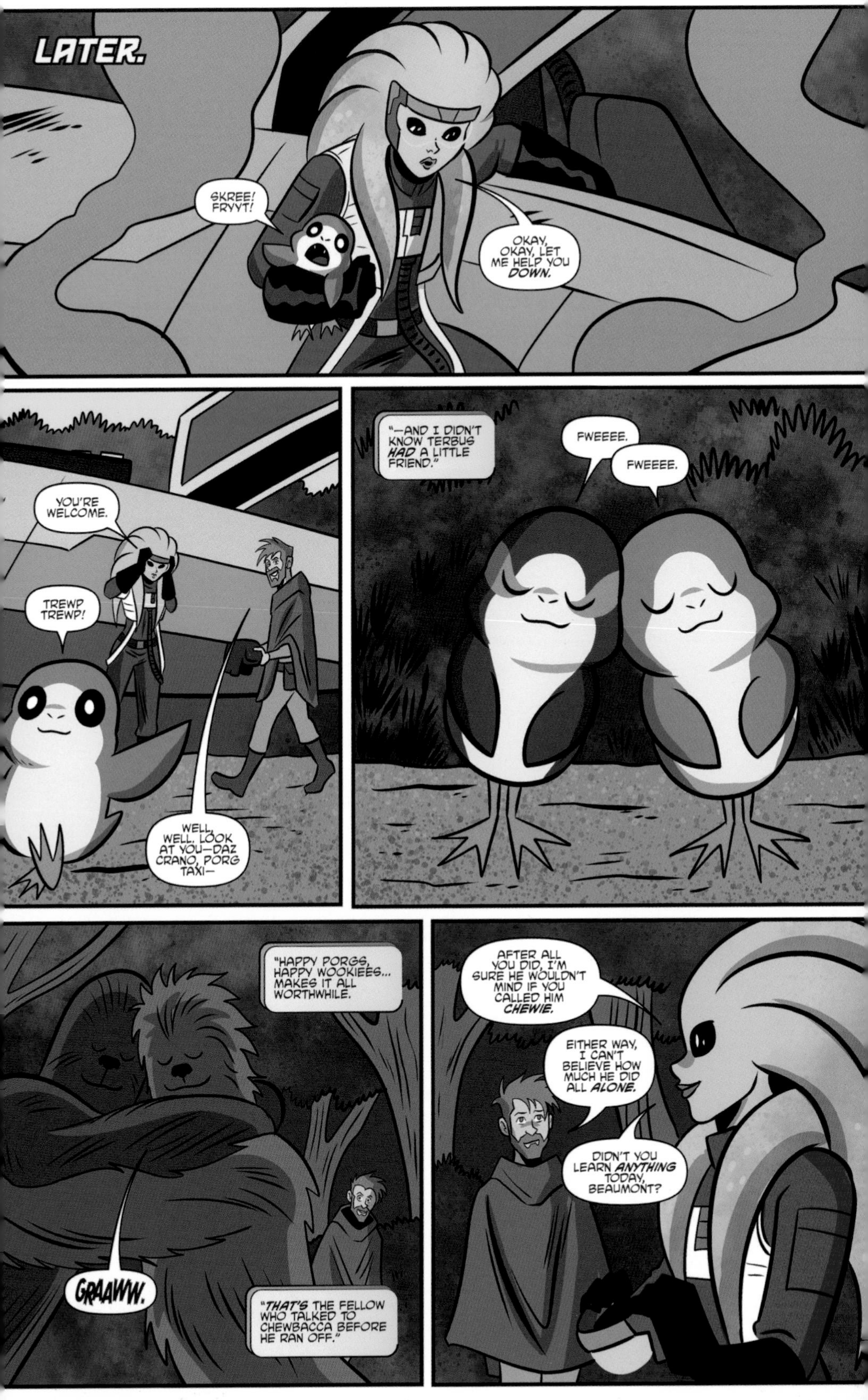
LATER.
SKREE! FRYYT!
OKAY, OKAY, LET ME HELP YOU *DOWN.*
YOU'RE WELCOME.
TREWP TREWP!
WELL, WELL. LOOK AT YOU—DAZ CRANO, PORG TAXI—
"—AND I DIDN'T KNOW TERBUS *HAD* A LITTLE FRIEND."
FWEEEE.
FWEEEE.
"HAPPY PORGS, HAPPY WOOKIEES... MAKES IT ALL WORTHWHILE.
GRAAWW.
"*THAT'S* THE FELLOW WHO TALKED TO CHEWBACCA BEFORE HE RAN OFF."
AFTER ALL YOU DID, I'M SURE HE WOULDN'T MIND IF YOU CALLED HIM *CHEWIE.*
EITHER WAY, I CAN'T BELIEVE HOW MUCH HE DID ALL *ALONE.*
DIDN'T YOU LEARN *ANYTHING* TODAY, BEAUMONT?

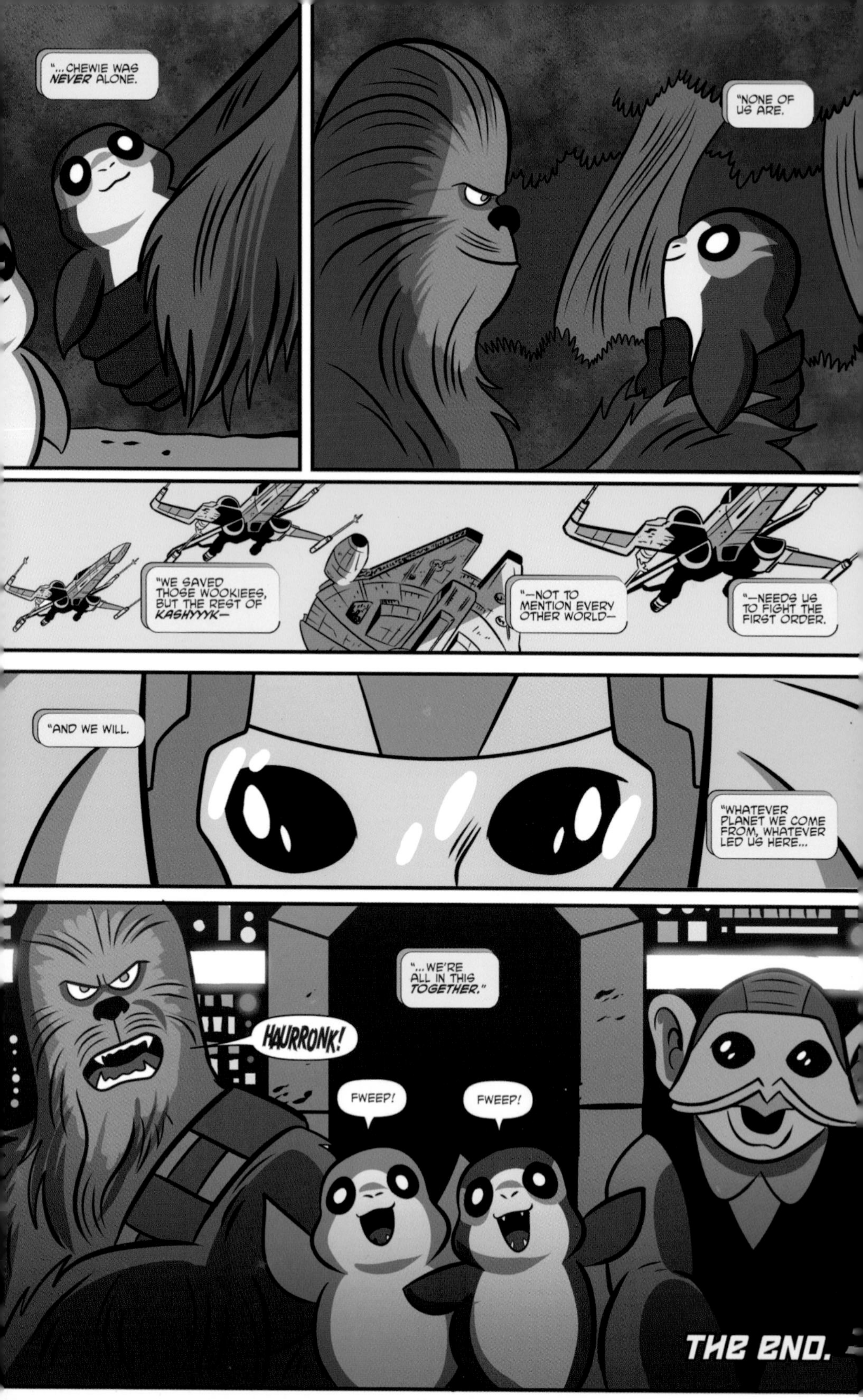
"...CHEWIE WAS NEVER ALONE.
"NONE OF US ARE.
"WE SAVED THOSE WOOKIEES, BUT THE REST OF KASHYYYK—
"—NOT TO MENTION EVERY OTHER WORLD—
"—NEEDS US TO FIGHT THE FIRST ORDER.
"AND WE WILL.
"WHATEVER PLANET WE COME FROM, WHATEVER LED US HERE...
"...WE'RE ALL IN THIS TOGETHER."
HAURRONK!
FWEEP!
FWEEP!
THE END.

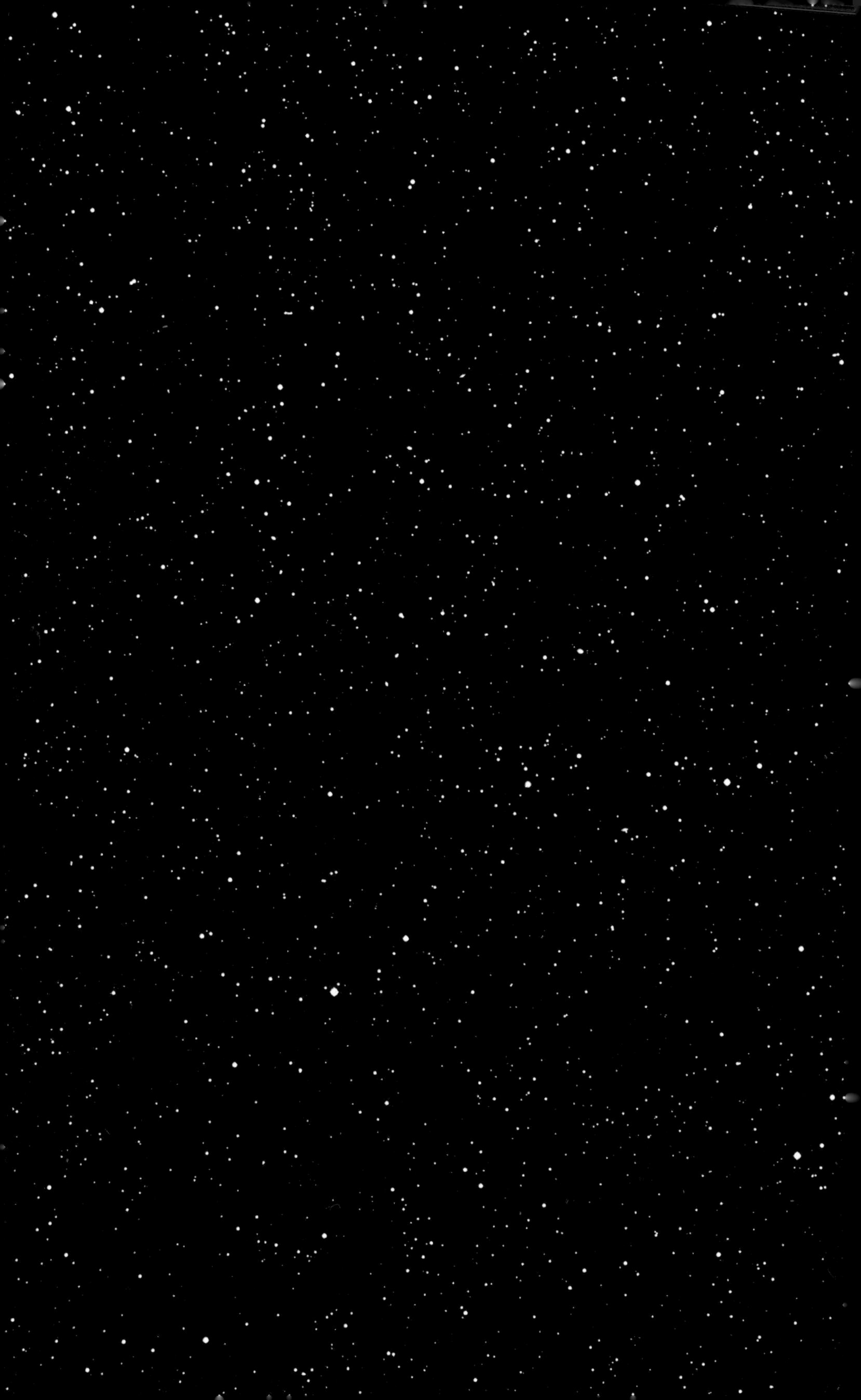

STAR WARS

ADVENTURES

Secret Agent Droids

WRITER
MICHAEL MORECI

ARTIST
TONY FLEECS

COLORIST
MATT HERMS

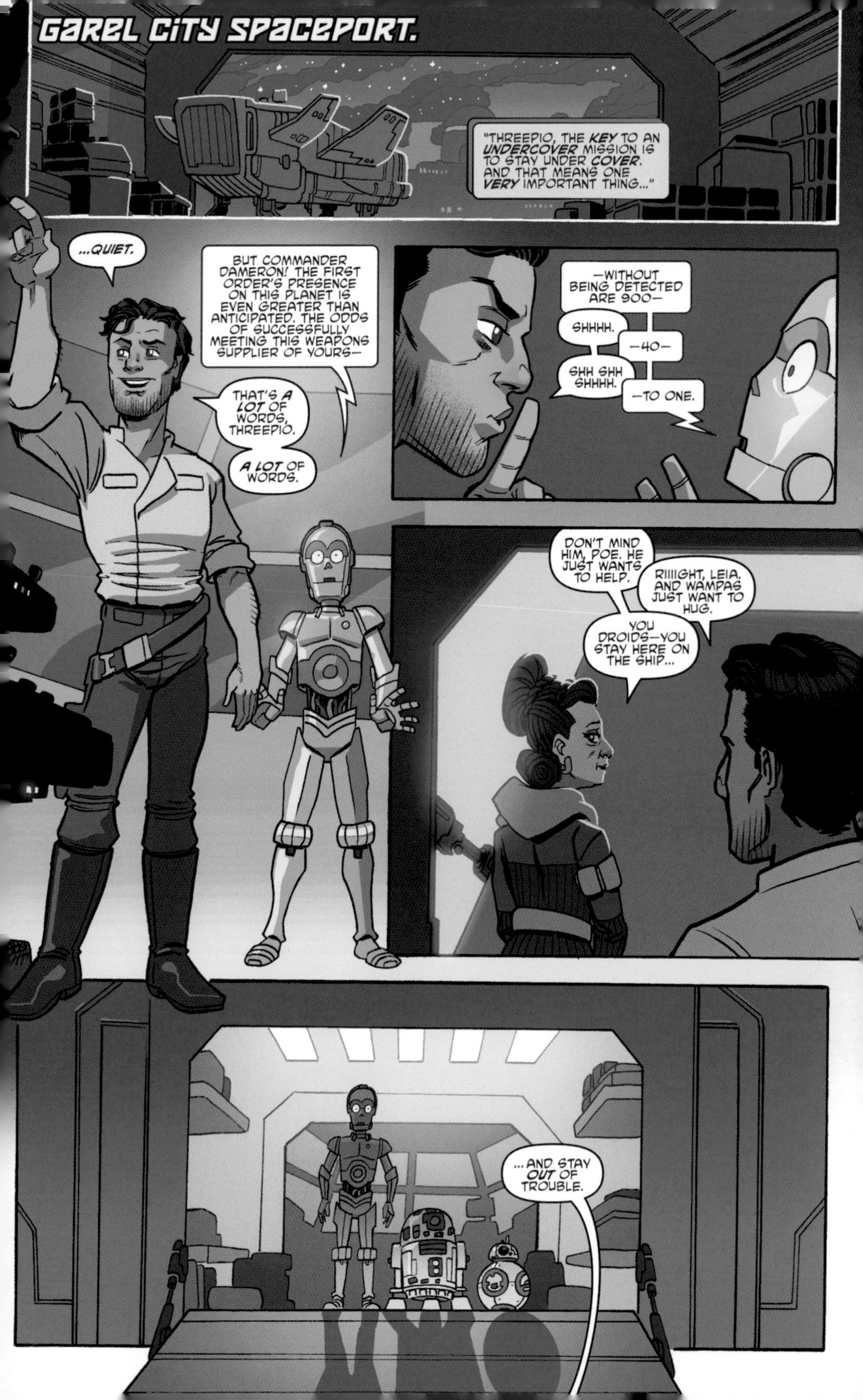
GAREL CITY SPACEPORT.
"THREEPIO, THE KEY TO AN UNDERCOVER MISSION IS TO STAY UNDER COVER. AND THAT MEANS ONE VERY IMPORTANT THING..."
...QUIET.
BUT COMMANDER DAMERON! THE FIRST ORDER'S PRESENCE ON THIS PLANET IS EVEN GREATER THAN ANTICIPATED. THE ODDS OF SUCCESSFULLY MEETING THIS WEAPONS SUPPLIER OF YOURS—
THAT'S A LOT OF WORDS, THREEPIO.
A LOT OF WORDS.
—WITHOUT BEING DETECTED ARE 900—
SHHHH.
—40—
SHH SHH SHHHH.
—TO ONE.
DON'T MIND HIM, POE. HE JUST WANTS TO HELP.
RIIIIGHT, LEIA. AND WAMPAS JUST WANT TO HUG.
YOU DROIDS—YOU STAY HERE ON THE SHIP...
...AND STAY OUT OF TROUBLE.

THEY NEVER LISTEN.

BWWP BORP BWWP

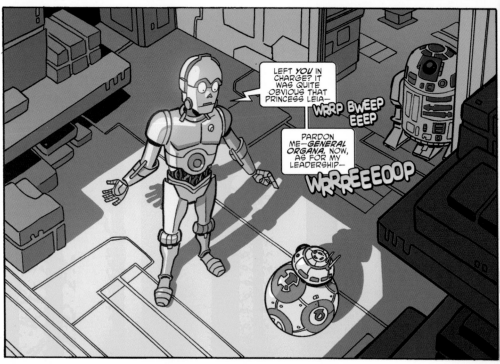

LEFT *YOU* IN CHARGE? IT WAS QUITE OBVIOUS THAT PRINCESS LEIA—

WRRP BWEEP EEEP

PARDON ME—*GENERAL ORGANA*, NOW, AS FOR MY LEADERSHIP—

WRRREEEOOP

A COMMUNICATION? WHAT COMMUNICATION?

BRRADWEEEP WEEP

YOU KNOW BETTER THAN TO OPEN STRANGE MESSAGES! WE COULDN'T POSSIBLY KNOW IF THE TRANSMISSION IS SECURE OR—

WHIRRRRR

MEMBERS OF THE RESISTANCE! I LEAD A TEAM OF SOLDIERS, ALL WILLING TO FIGHT THE FIR ⸗TSHHH⸗ ORDER. BUT I ⸗TSHHH⸗ ED *HELP.*

WE'RE TRAPPED, AND WE NEED TRAN ⸗TSHHH⸗ *OFF* OF GAREL.

FIND US AT THE COORDINATES I JUST SENT, AND WE WILL ⸗TSHHH⸗ FOR THE RESISTA—

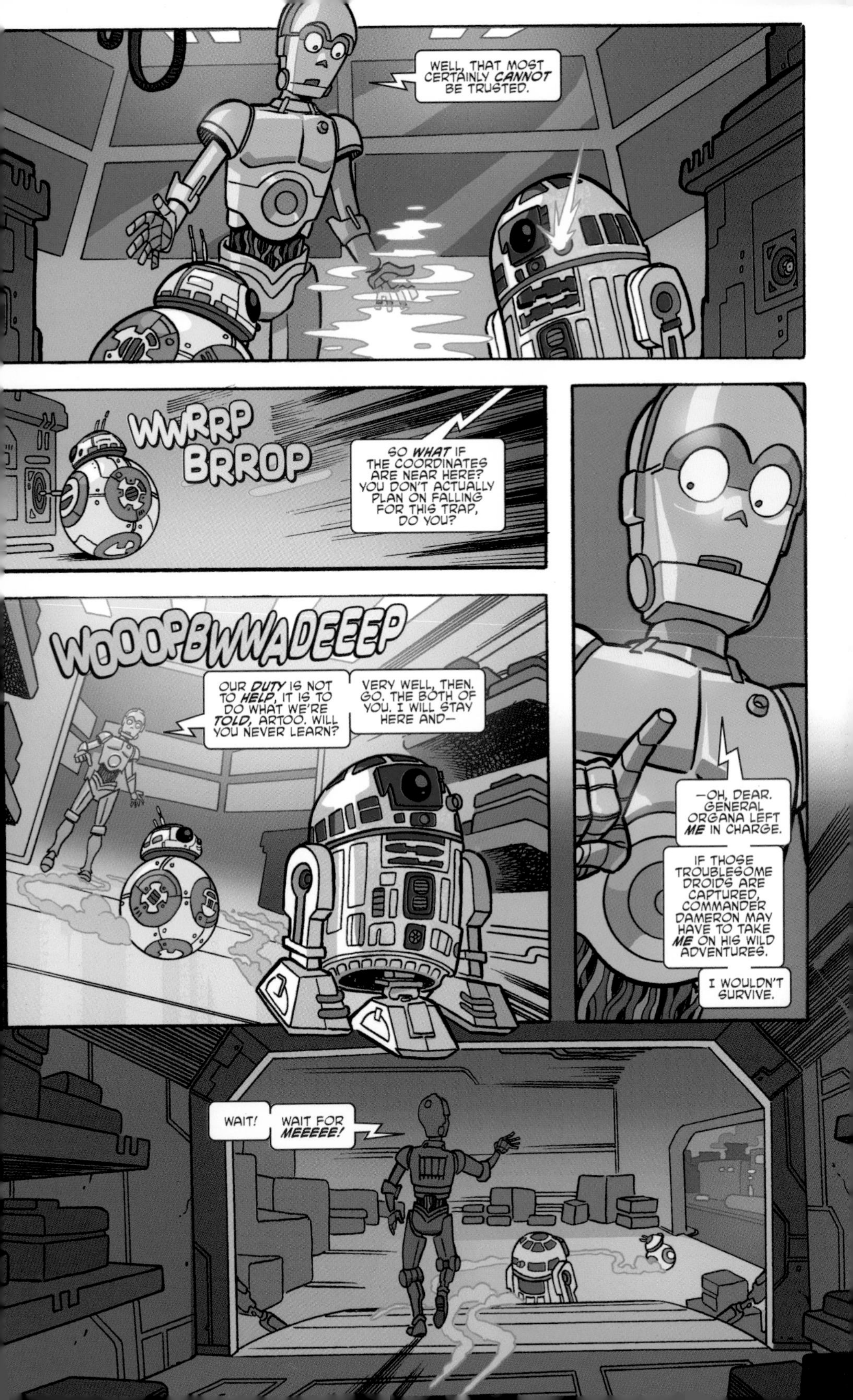
WELL, THAT MOST CERTAINLY CANNOT BE TRUSTED.
WWRRP BRROP
SO WHAT IF THE COORDINATES ARE NEAR HERE? YOU DON'T ACTUALLY PLAN ON FALLING FOR THIS TRAP, DO YOU?
WOOOPBWWADEEEP
OUR DUTY IS NOT TO HELP, IT IS TO DO WHAT WE'RE TOLD, ARTOO. WILL YOU NEVER LEARN?
VERY WELL, THEN. GO. THE BOTH OF YOU. I WILL STAY HERE AND—
—OH, DEAR. GENERAL ORGANA LEFT ME IN CHARGE.
IF THOSE TROUBLESOME DROIDS ARE CAPTURED, COMMANDER DAMERON MAY HAVE TO TAKE ME ON HIS WILD ADVENTURES.
I WOULDN'T SURVIVE.
WAIT!
WAIT FOR MEEEEE!

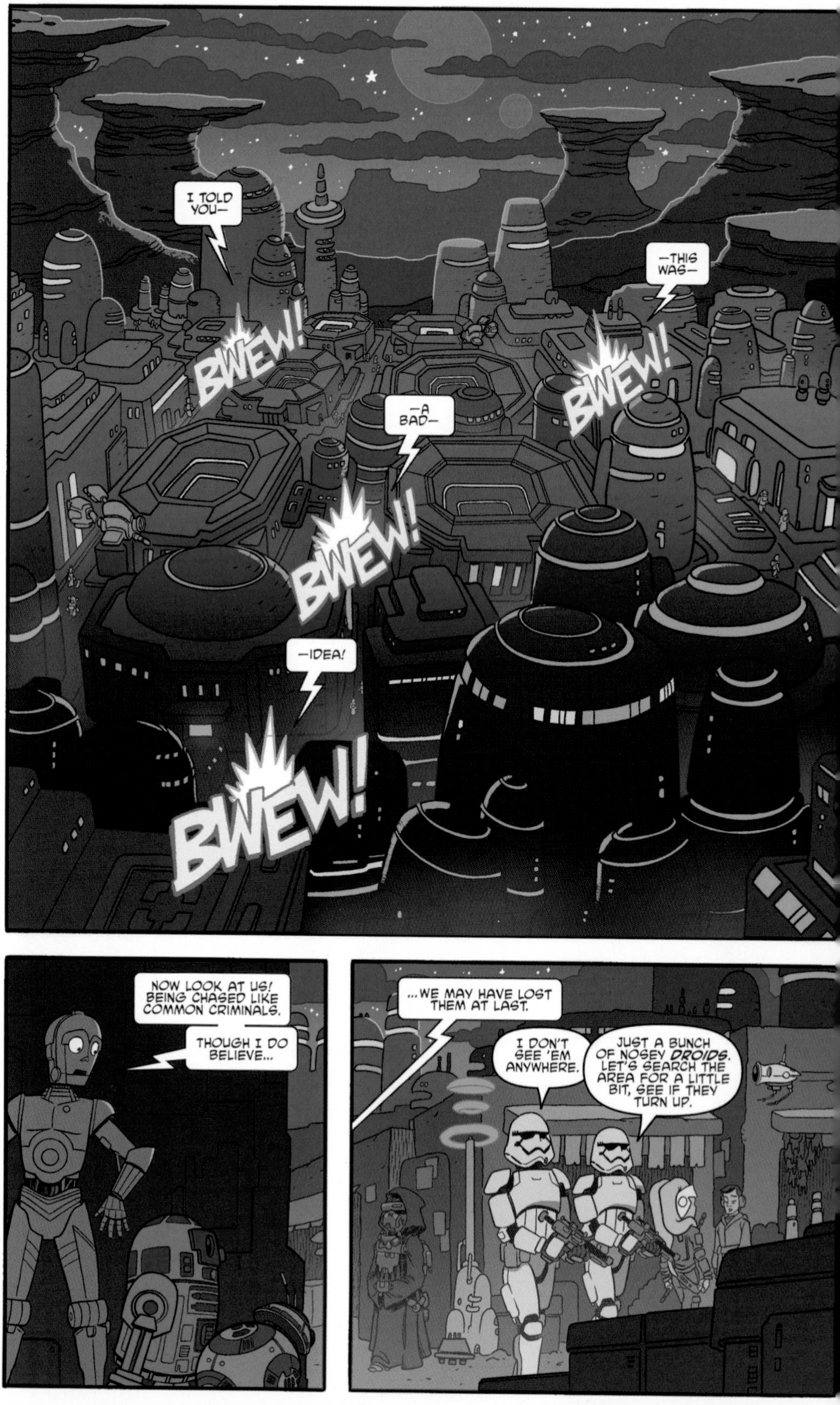
I TOLD YOU—
BWEW!
—THIS WAS—
BWEW!
—A BAD—
BWEW!
—IDEA!
BWEW!
NOW LOOK AT US! BEING CHASED LIKE COMMON CRIMINALS.
THOUGH I DO BELIEVE...
...WE MAY HAVE LOST THEM AT LAST.
I DON'T SEE 'EM ANYWHERE.
JUST A BUNCH OF NOSEY DROIDS. LET'S SEARCH THE AREA FOR A LITTLE BIT, SEE IF THEY TURN UP.

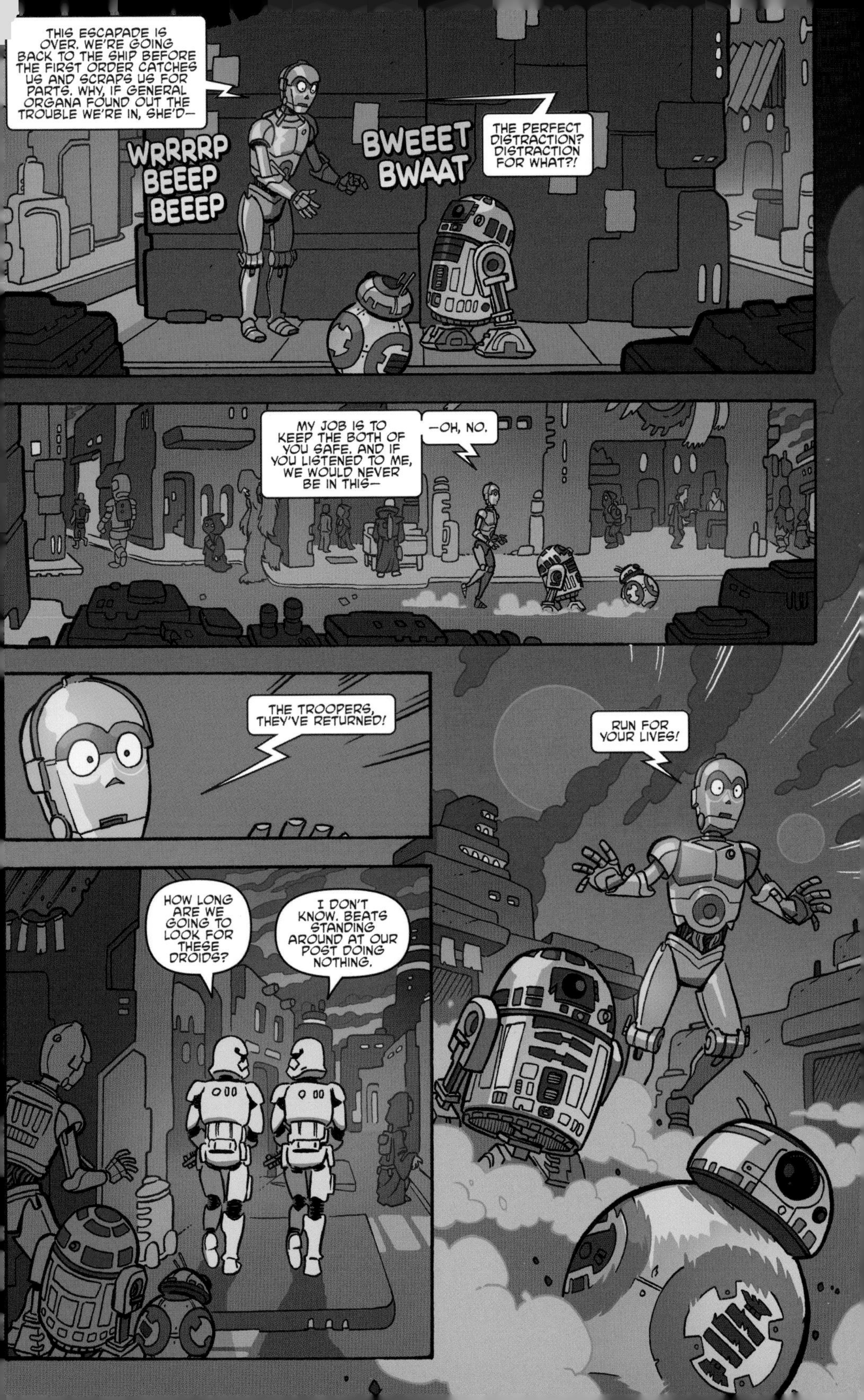
THIS ESCAPADE IS OVER. WE'RE GOING BACK TO THE SHIP BEFORE THE FIRST ORDER CATCHES US AND SCRAPS US FOR PARTS. WHY, IF GENERAL ORGANA FOUND OUT THE TROUBLE WE'RE IN, SHE'D—
WRRRRP BEEEP BEEEP
BWEEET BWAAT
THE PERFECT DISTRACTION? DISTRACTION FOR WHAT?!
MY JOB IS TO KEEP THE BOTH OF YOU SAFE. AND IF YOU LISTENED TO ME, WE WOULD NEVER BE IN THIS—
—OH, NO.
THE TROOPERS, THEY'VE RETURNED!
HOW LONG ARE WE GOING TO LOOK FOR THESE DROIDS?
I DON'T KNOW. BEATS STANDING AROUND AT OUR POST DOING NOTHING.
RUN FOR YOUR LIVES!

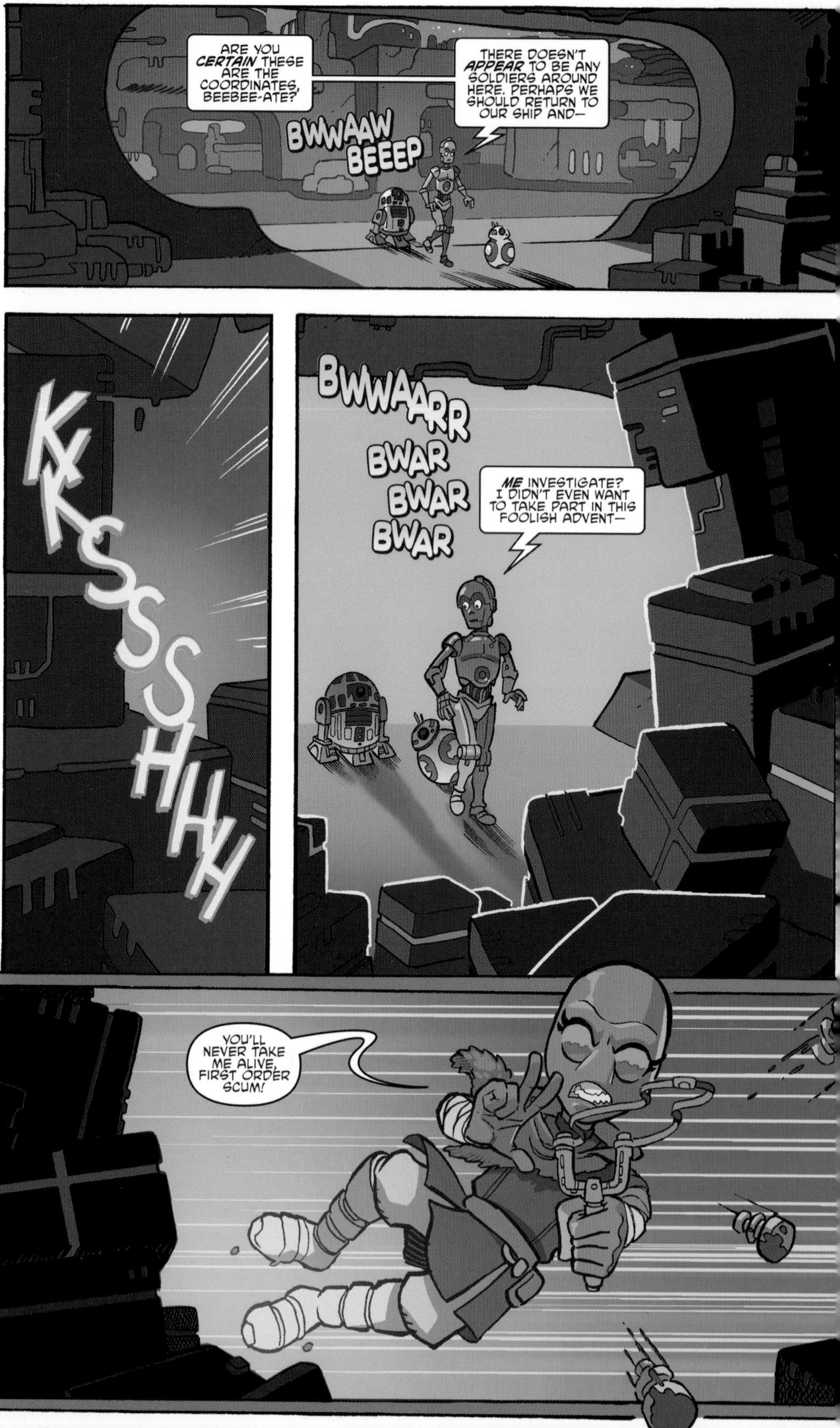
ARE YOU CERTAIN THESE ARE THE COORDINATES, BEEBEE-ATE?
THERE DOESN'T APPEAR TO BE ANY SOLDIERS AROUND HERE. PERHAPS WE SHOULD RETURN TO OUR SHIP AND—
BWWAAW BEEEP
KKKSSSSHHHH
BWWAARR BWAR BWAR BWAR
ME INVESTIGATE? I DIDN'T EVEN WANT TO TAKE PART IN THIS FOOLISH ADVENT—
YOU'LL NEVER TAKE ME ALIVE, FIRST ORDER SCUM!

SPTING

OH, MY!

PLEASE DON'T LET THERE BE A NEW DENT IN MY HEAD!

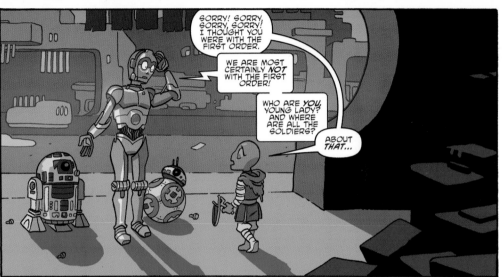

SORRY! SORRY, SORRY, SORRY! I THOUGHT YOU WERE WITH THE FIRST ORDER.

WE ARE MOST CERTAINLY *NOT* WITH THE FIRST ORDER!

WHO ARE *YOU*, YOUNG LADY? AND WHERE ARE ALL THE SOLDIERS?

ABOUT *THAT*...

...I *MIGHT* HAVE MADE THAT UP TO TRICK YOU INTO COMING HERE.

YOU *LIED?* WHY WOULD YOU DO SUCH A THING?

NEVER MIND—WE *MUST* RETURN TO OUR SHIP AT ONC—

WAIT, WAIT, WAIT! I SWEAR, I ONLY TRICKED YOU BECAUSE I *HAD* TO.

I NEED THE RESISTANCE'S *HELP*.

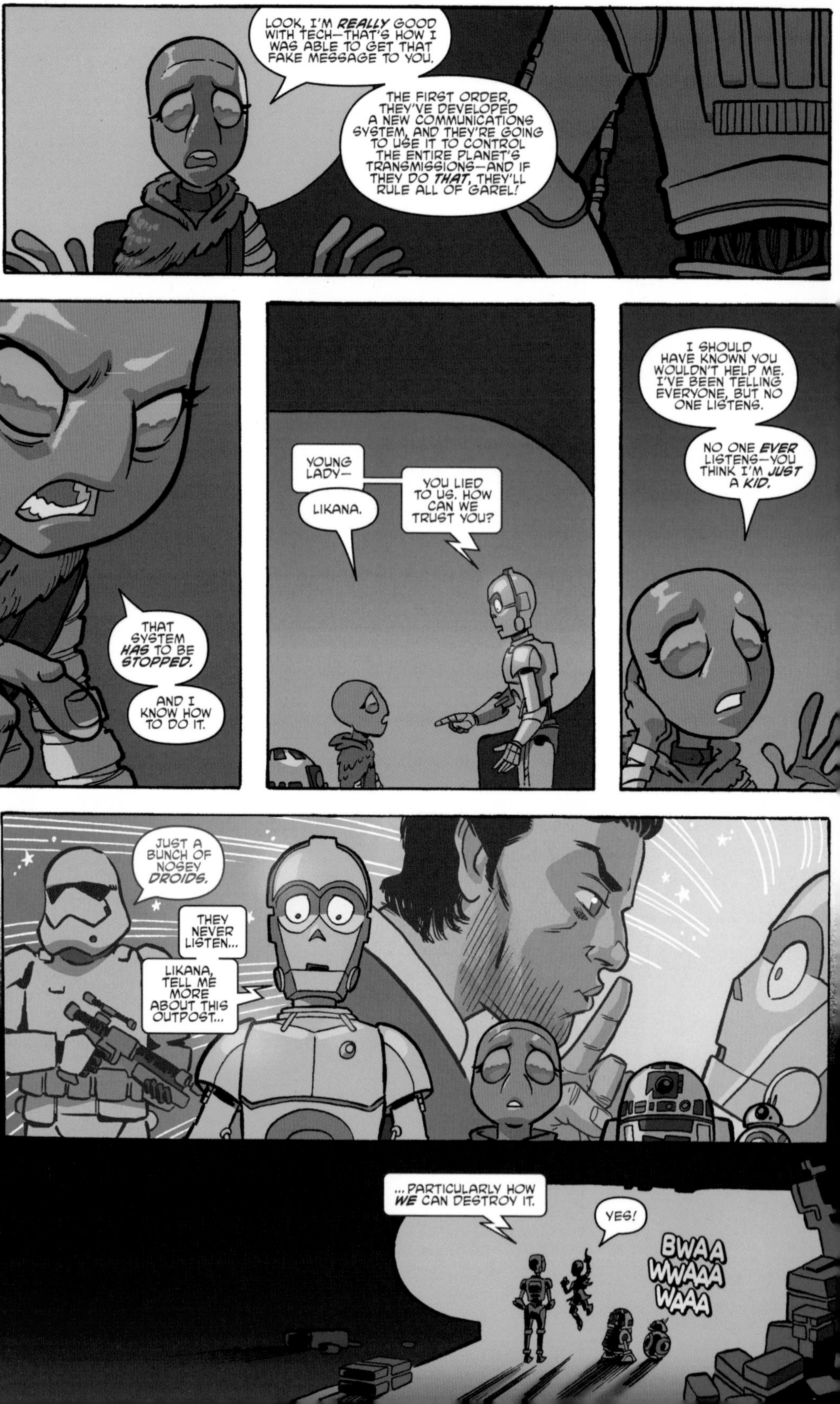
LOOK, I'M REALLY GOOD WITH TECH—THAT'S HOW I WAS ABLE TO GET THAT FAKE MESSAGE TO YOU.
THE FIRST ORDER, THEY'VE DEVELOPED A NEW COMMUNICATIONS SYSTEM, AND THEY'RE GOING TO USE IT TO CONTROL THE ENTIRE PLANET'S TRANSMISSIONS—AND IF THEY DO THAT, THEY'LL RULE ALL OF GAREL!
THAT SYSTEM HAS TO BE STOPPED.
AND I KNOW HOW TO DO IT.
YOUNG LADY—
LIKANA.
YOU LIED TO US. HOW CAN WE TRUST YOU?
I SHOULD HAVE KNOWN YOU WOULDN'T HELP ME. I'VE BEEN TELLING EVERYONE, BUT NO ONE LISTENS.
NO ONE EVER LISTENS—YOU THINK I'M JUST A KID.
JUST A BUNCH OF NOSEY DROIDS.
THEY NEVER LISTEN...
LIKANA, TELL ME MORE ABOUT THIS OUTPOST...
...PARTICULARLY HOW WE CAN DESTROY IT.
YES!
BWAA WWAAA WAAA

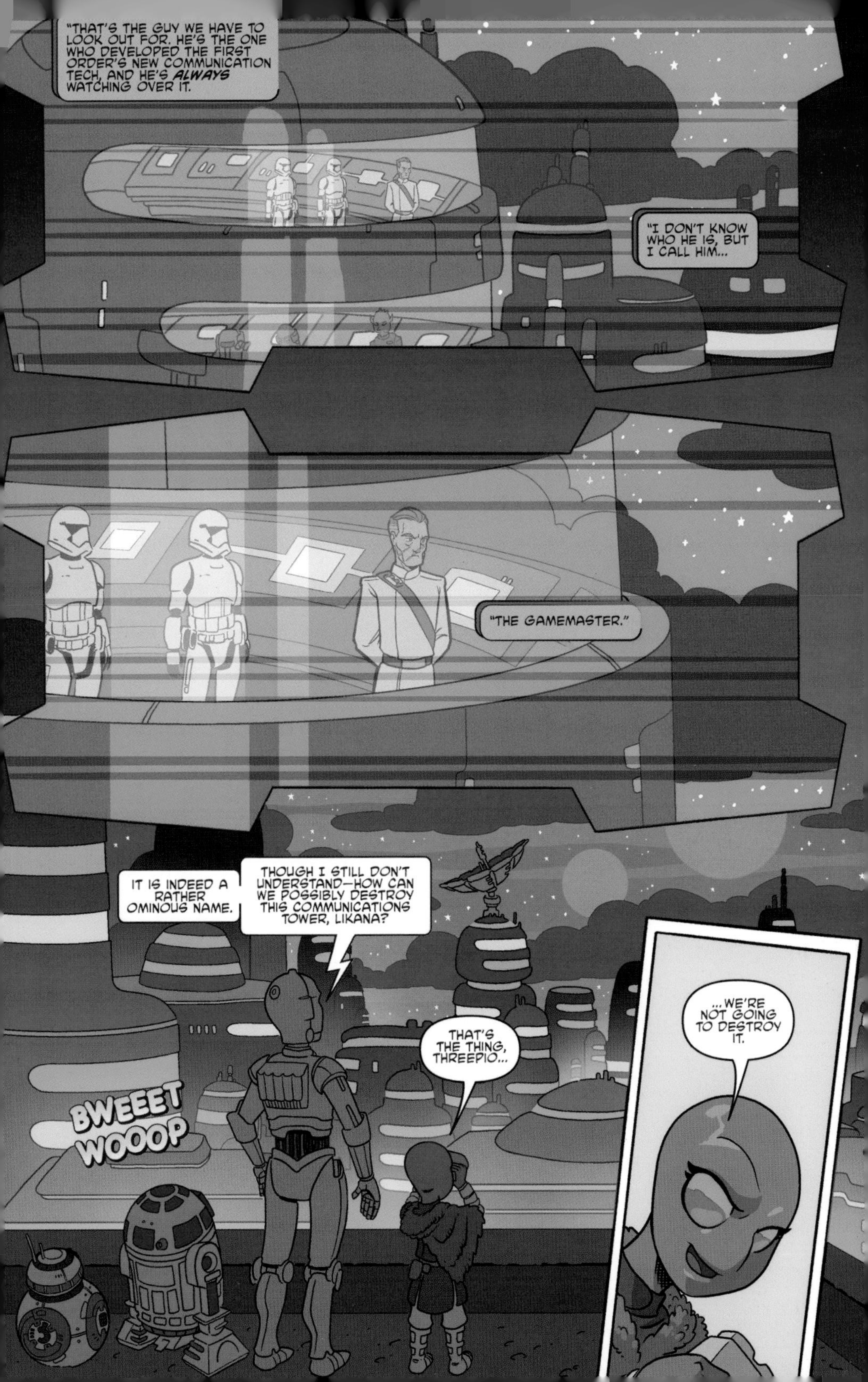
"THAT'S THE GUY WE HAVE TO LOOK OUT FOR. HE'S THE ONE WHO DEVELOPED THE FIRST ORDER'S NEW COMMUNICATION TECH, AND HE'S *ALWAYS* WATCHING OVER IT.
"I DON'T KNOW WHO HE IS, BUT I CALL HIM...
"THE GAMEMASTER."
IT IS INDEED A RATHER OMINOUS NAME.
THOUGH I STILL DON'T UNDERSTAND—HOW CAN WE POSSIBLY DESTROY THIS COMMUNICATIONS TOWER, LIKANA?
BWEEET WOOOP
THAT'S THE THING, THREEPIO...
...WE'RE NOT GOING TO DESTROY IT.

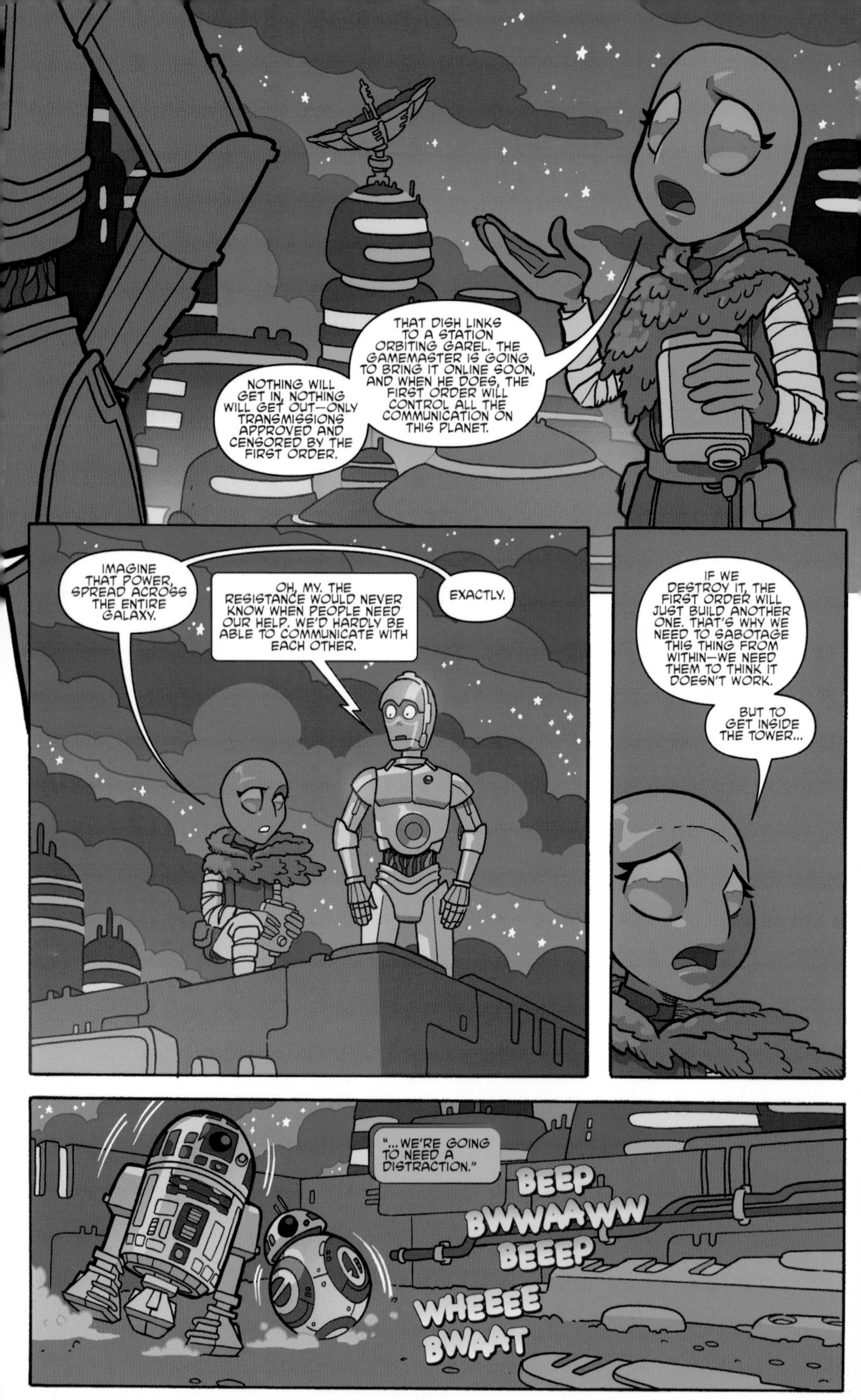
NOTHING WILL GET IN, NOTHING WILL GET OUT—ONLY TRANSMISSIONS APPROVED AND CENSORED BY THE FIRST ORDER.
THAT DISH LINKS TO A STATION ORBITING GAREL. THE GAMEMASTER IS GOING TO BRING IT ONLINE SOON, AND WHEN HE DOES, THE FIRST ORDER WILL CONTROL ALL THE COMMUNICATION ON THIS PLANET.
IMAGINE THAT POWER, SPREAD ACROSS THE ENTIRE GALAXY.
OH, MY. THE RESISTANCE WOULD NEVER KNOW WHEN PEOPLE NEED OUR HELP. WE'D HARDLY BE ABLE TO COMMUNICATE WITH EACH OTHER.
EXACTLY.
IF WE DESTROY IT, THE FIRST ORDER WILL JUST BUILD ANOTHER ONE. THAT'S WHY WE NEED TO SABOTAGE THIS THING FROM WITHIN—WE NEED THEM TO THINK IT DOESN'T WORK.
BUT TO GET INSIDE THE TOWER...
"...WE'RE GOING TO NEED A DISTRACTION."
BEEP
BWWAAWW
BEEEP
WHEEEE
BWAAT

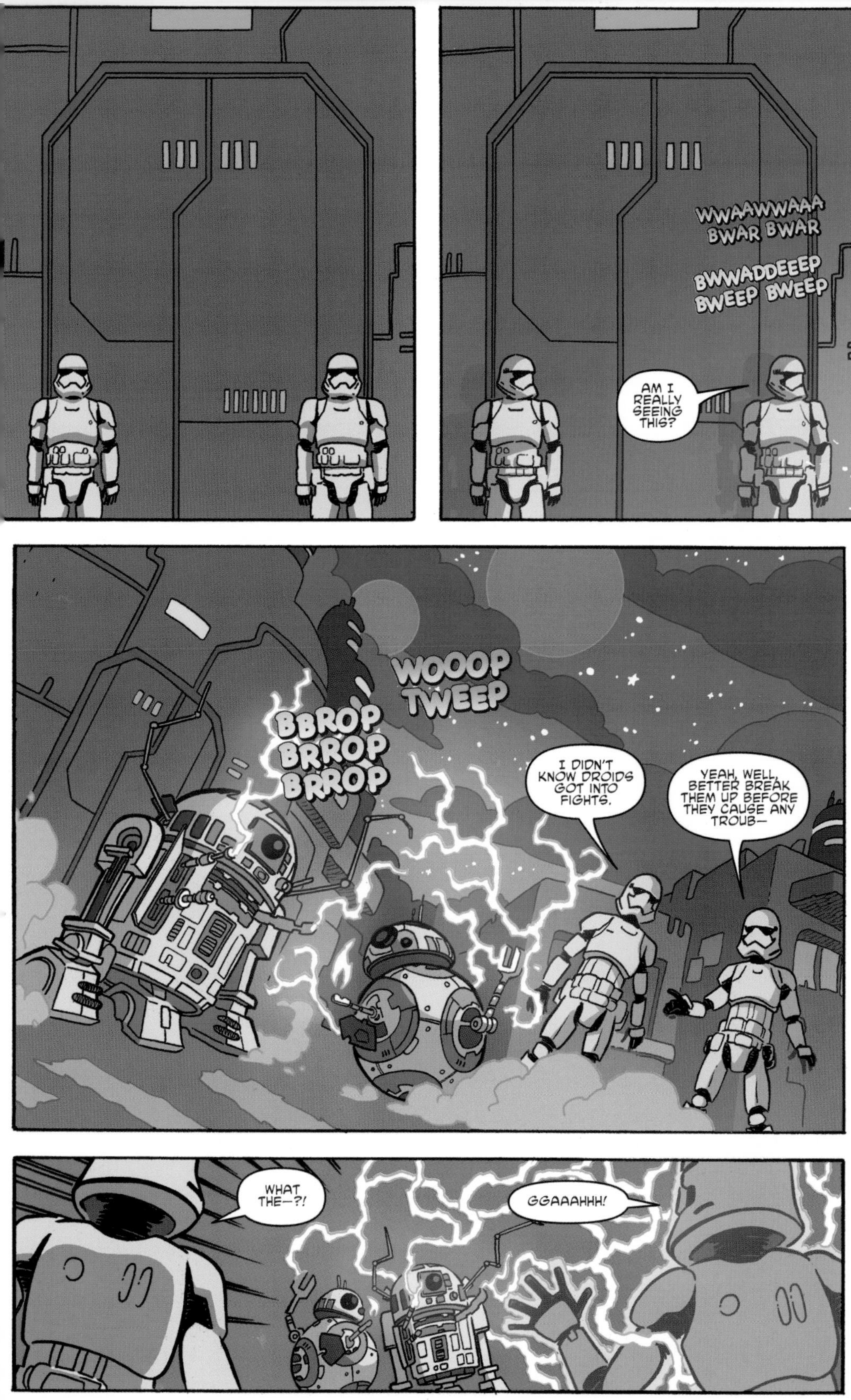
WWAAWWAAA BWAR BWAR
BWWADDEEEP BWEEP BWEEP
AM I REALLY SEEING THIS?
WOOOP TWEEP
BBROP BRROP BRROP
I DIDN'T KNOW DROIDS GOT INTO FIGHTS.
YEAH, WELL, BETTER BREAK THEM UP BEFORE THEY CAUSE ANY TROUB—
WHAT THE—?!
GGAAAHHH!

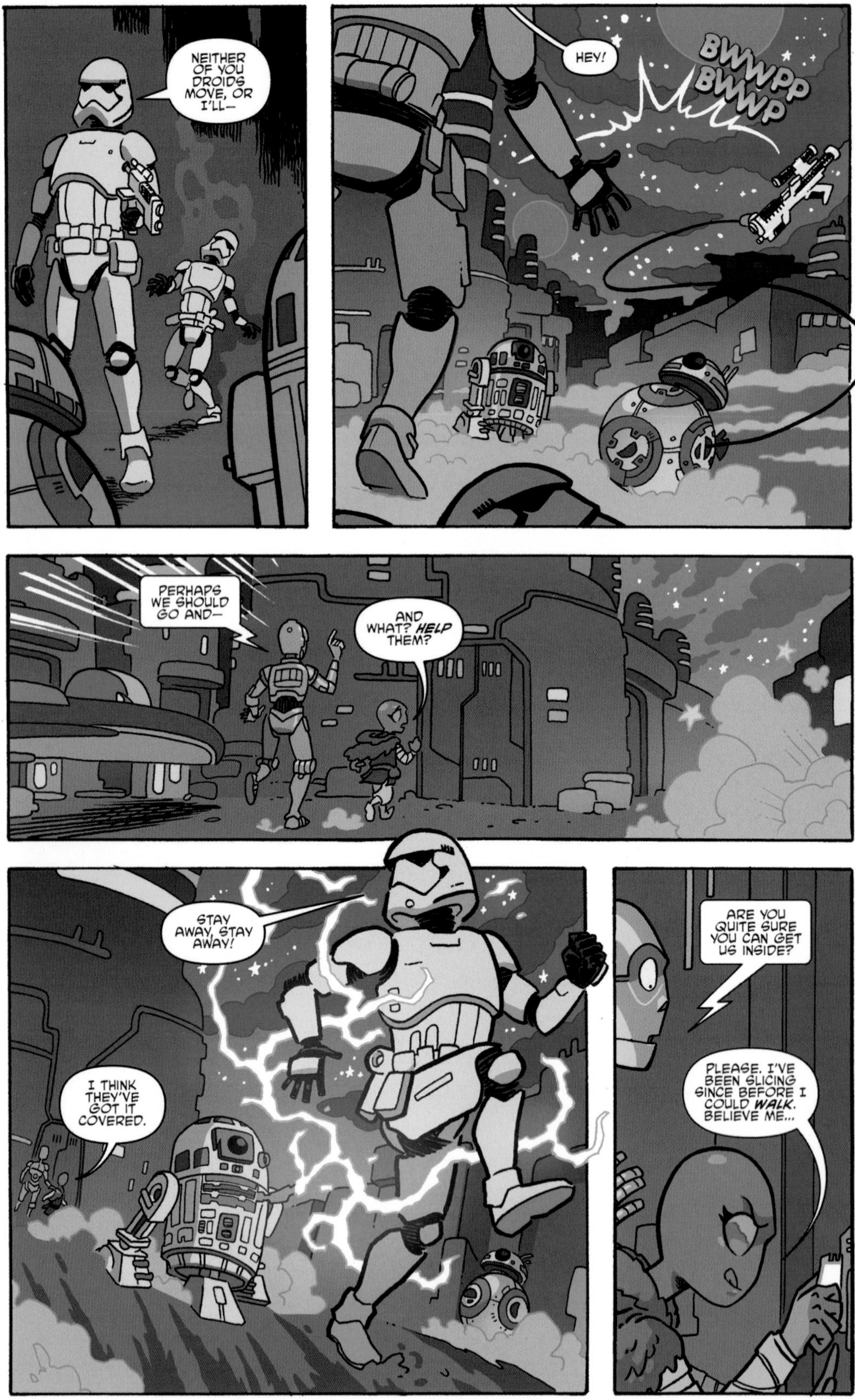
NEITHER OF YOU DROIDS MOVE, OR I'LL—
HEY!
BWWPP BWWP
PERHAPS WE SHOULD GO AND—
AND WHAT? *HELP* THEM?
STAY AWAY, STAY AWAY!
I THINK THEY'VE GOT IT COVERED.
ARE YOU QUITE SURE YOU CAN GET US INSIDE?
PLEASE. I'VE BEEN SLICING SINCE BEFORE I COULD *WALK*. BELIEVE ME...

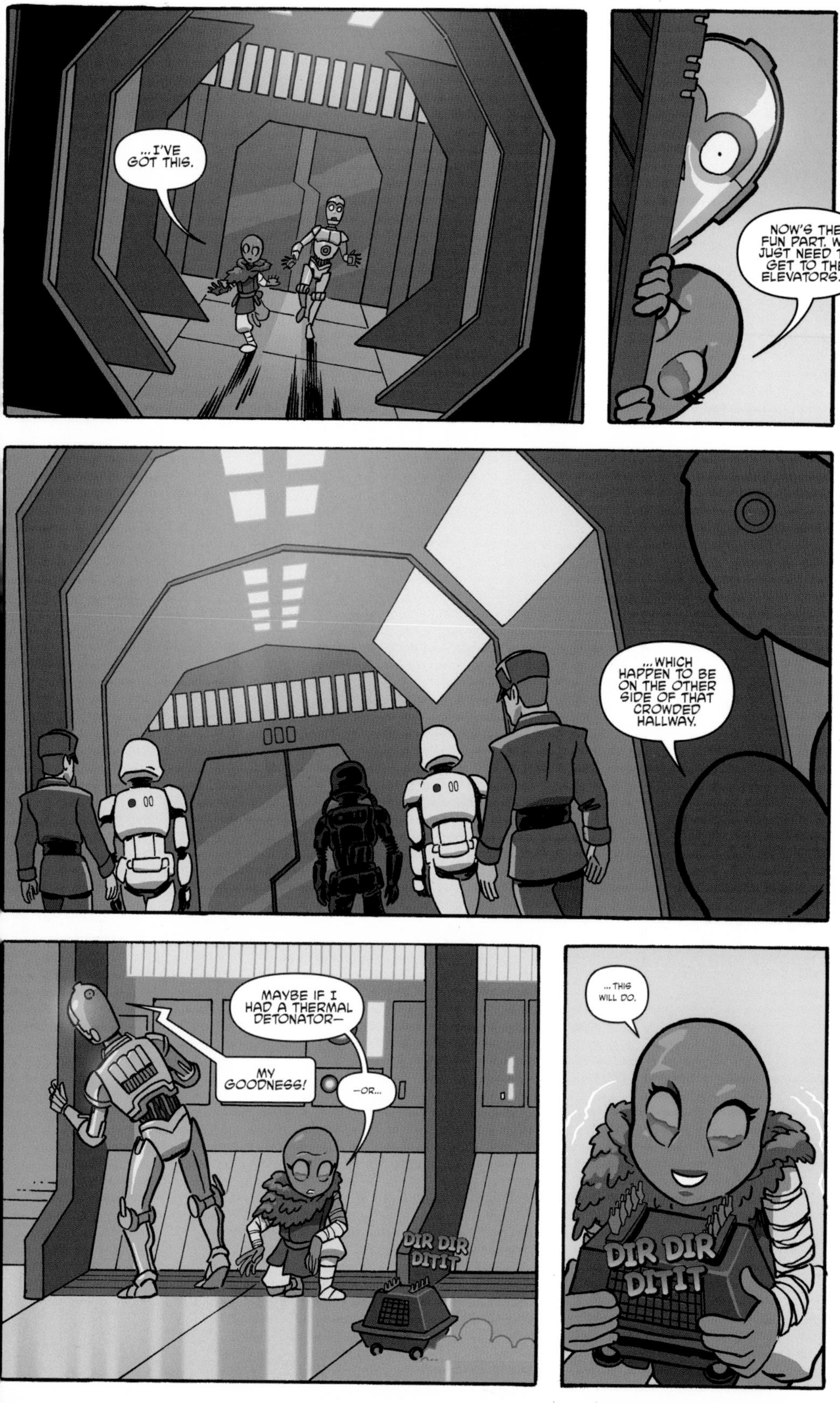
...I'VE GOT THIS.
NOW'S THE FUN PART. WE JUST NEED TO GET TO THE ELEVATORS...
...WHICH HAPPEN TO BE ON THE OTHER SIDE OF THAT CROWDED HALLWAY.
MAYBE IF I HAD A THERMAL DETONATOR—
MY GOODNESS!
—OR...
DIR DIR DITIT
...THIS WILL DO.
DIR DIR DITIT

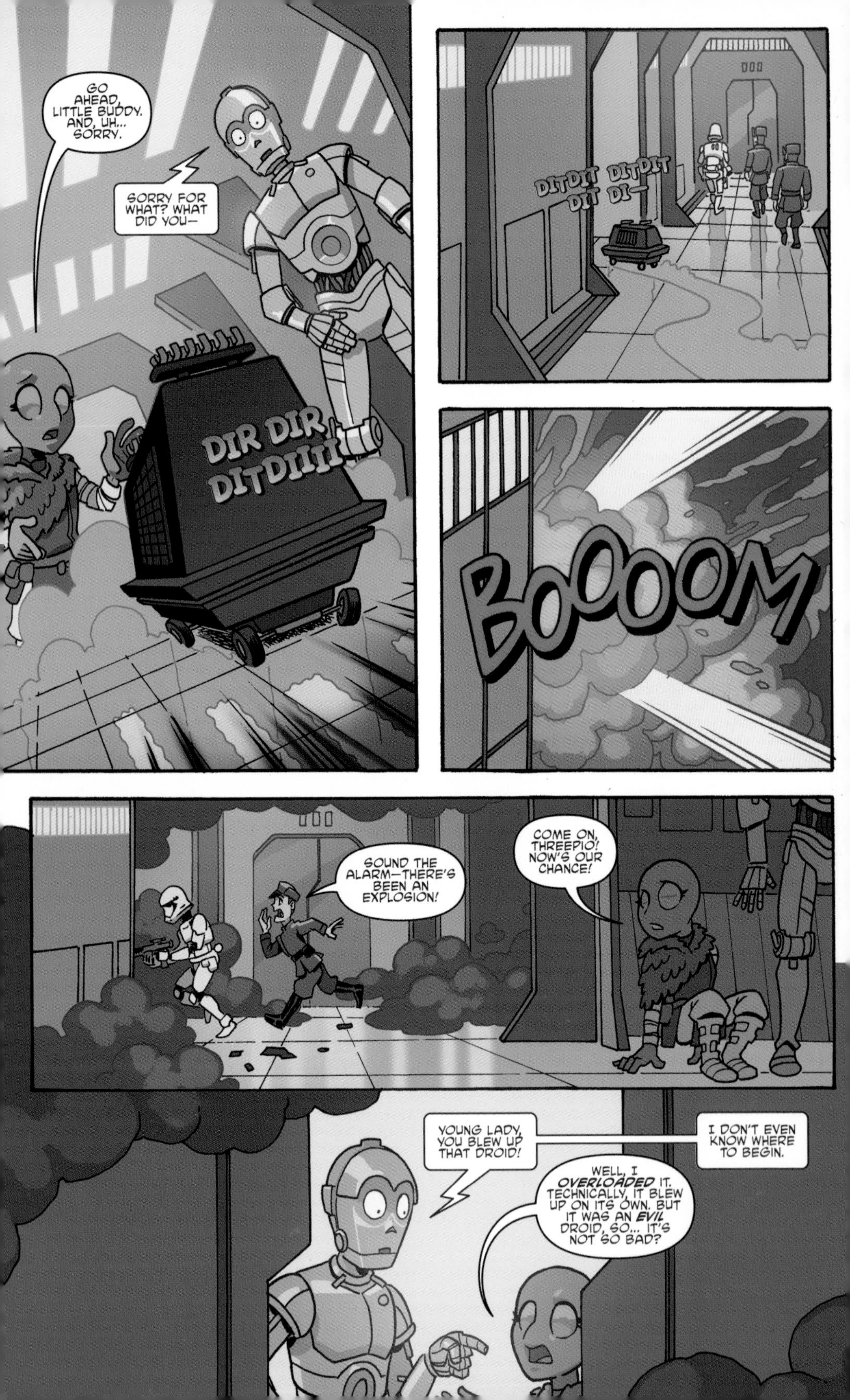
GO AHEAD, LITTLE BUDDY. AND, UH... SORRY.
SORRY FOR WHAT? WHAT DID YOU—
DIR DIR DITDIIII
DITDIT DITDIT DIT DI—
BOOOOM
SOUND THE ALARM—THERE'S BEEN AN EXPLOSION!
COME ON, THREEPIO! NOW'S OUR CHANCE!
YOUNG LADY, YOU BLEW UP THAT DROID!
I DON'T EVEN KNOW WHERE TO BEGIN.
WELL, I OVERLOADED IT. TECHNICALLY, IT BLEW UP ON ITS OWN. BUT IT WAS AN EVIL DROID, SO... IT'S NOT SO BAD?

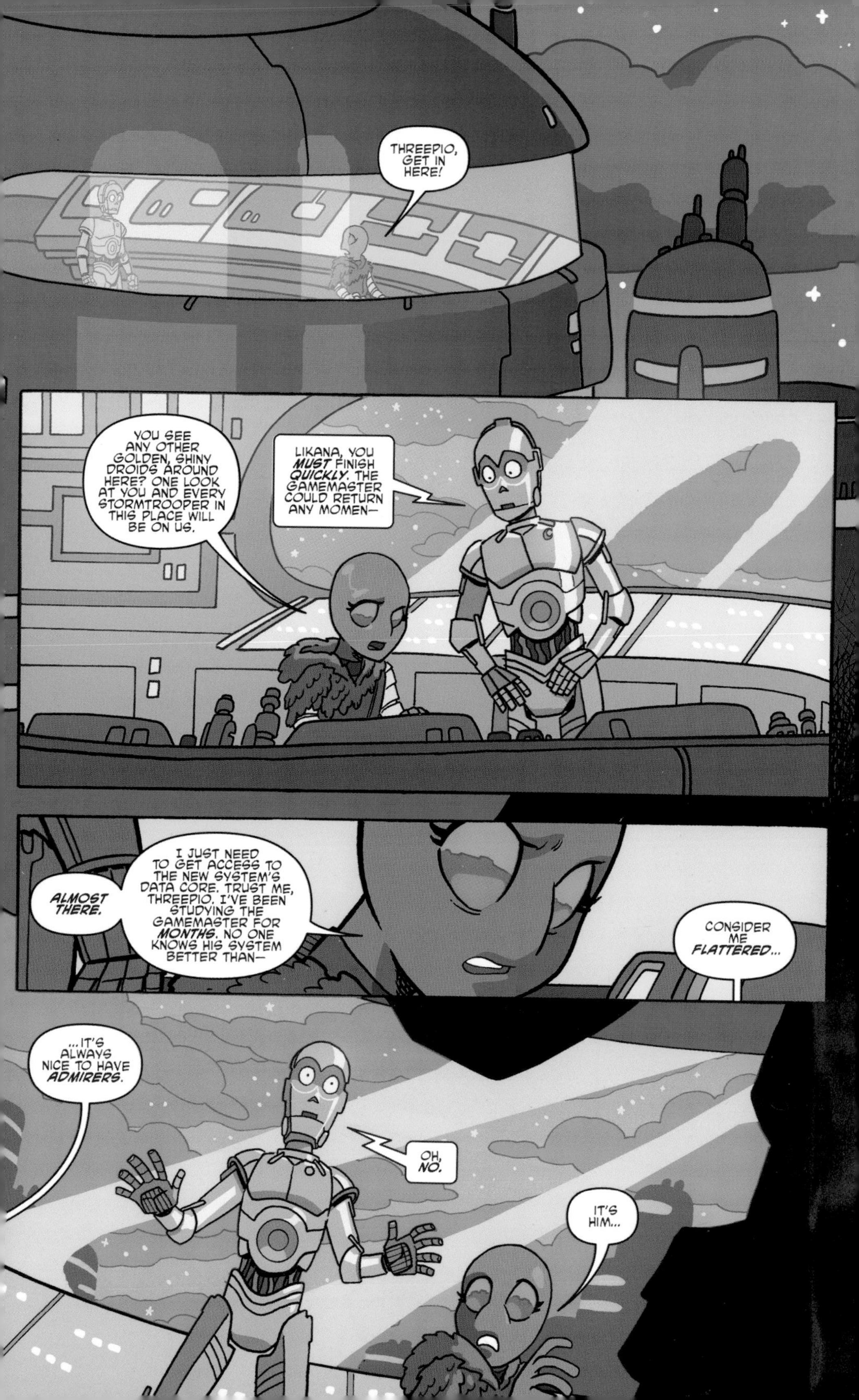
THREEPIO, GET IN HERE!
LIKANA, YOU MUST FINISH QUICKLY. THE GAMEMASTER COULD RETURN ANY MOMEN—
YOU SEE ANY OTHER GOLDEN, SHINY DROIDS AROUND HERE? ONE LOOK AT YOU AND EVERY STORMTROOPER IN THIS PLACE WILL BE ON US.
ALMOST THERE.
I JUST NEED TO GET ACCESS TO THE NEW SYSTEM'S DATA CORE. TRUST ME, THREEPIO. I'VE BEEN STUDYING THE GAMEMASTER FOR MONTHS. NO ONE KNOWS HIS SYSTEM BETTER THAN—
CONSIDER ME FLATTERED...
...IT'S ALWAYS NICE TO HAVE ADMIRERS.
OH, NO.
IT'S HIM...

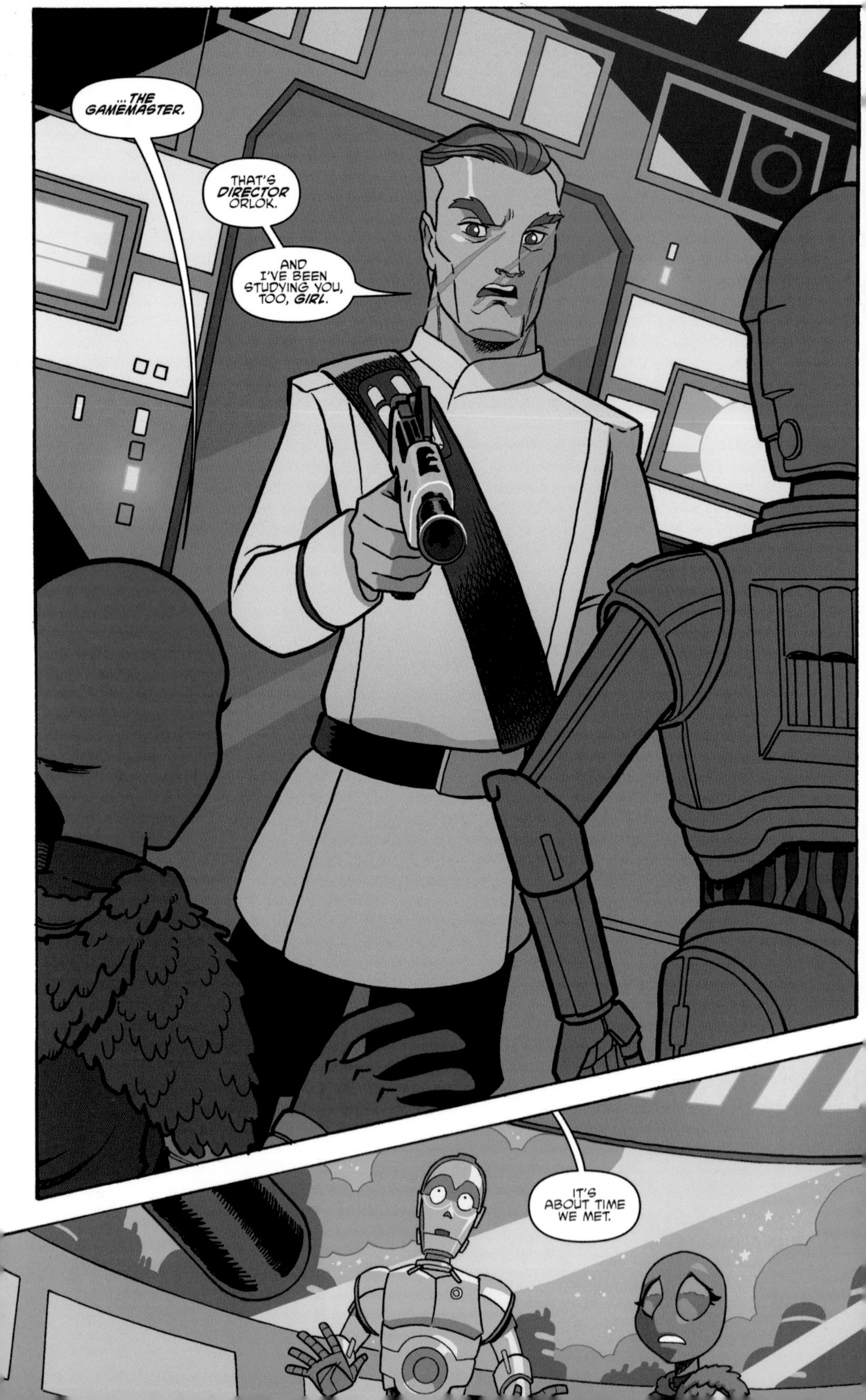
...THE GAMEMASTER.
THAT'S DIRECTOR ORLOK.
AND I'VE BEEN STUDYING YOU, TOO, GIRL.
IT'S ABOUT TIME WE MET.

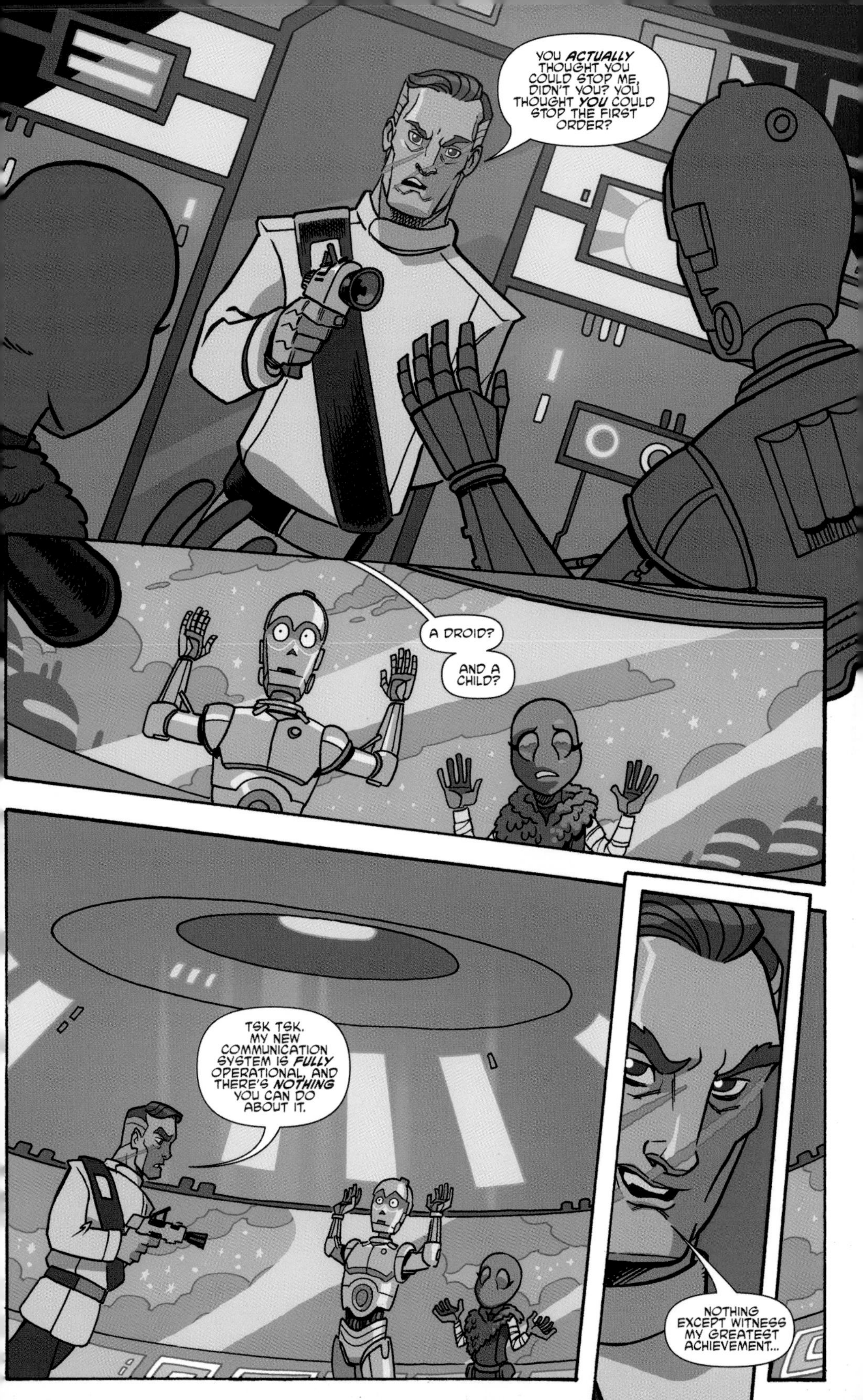
YOU ACTUALLY THOUGHT YOU COULD STOP ME, DIDN'T YOU? YOU THOUGHT YOU COULD STOP THE FIRST ORDER?
A DROID?
AND A CHILD?
TSK TSK. MY NEW COMMUNICATION SYSTEM IS FULLY OPERATIONAL, AND THERE'S NOTHING YOU CAN DO ABOUT IT.
NOTHING EXCEPT WITNESS MY GREATEST ACHIEVEMENT...

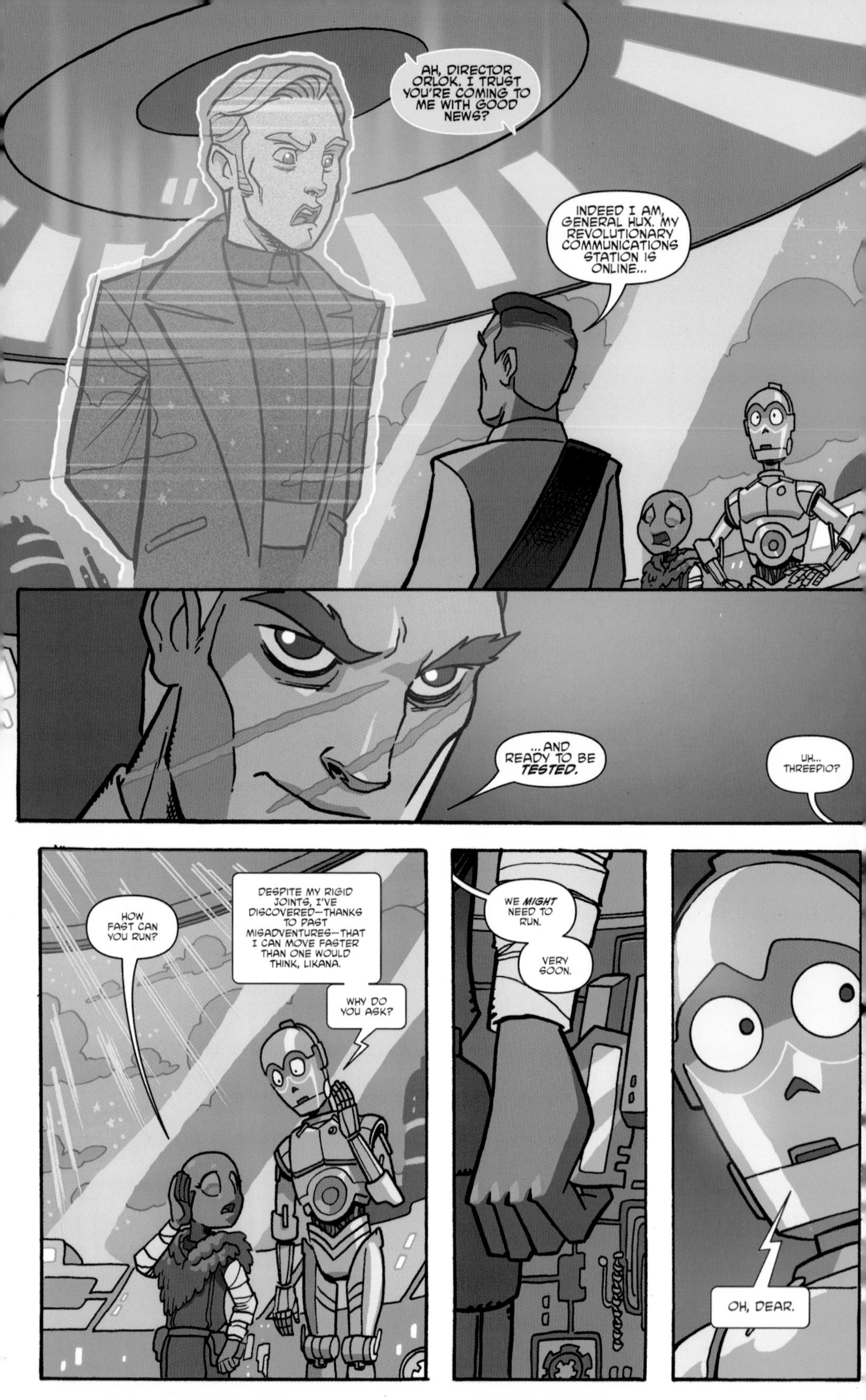
AH, DIRECTOR ORLOK. I TRUST YOU'RE COMING TO ME WITH GOOD NEWS?
INDEED I AM, GENERAL HUX. MY REVOLUTIONARY COMMUNICATIONS STATION IS ONLINE...
...AND READY TO BE *TESTED.*
UH... THREEPIO?
HOW FAST CAN YOU RUN?
DESPITE MY RIGID JOINTS, I'VE DISCOVERED—THANKS TO PAST MISADVENTURES—THAT I CAN MOVE FASTER THAN ONE WOULD THINK, LIKANA.
WHY DO YOU ASK?
WE *MIGHT* NEED TO RUN.
VERY SOON.
OH, DEAR.

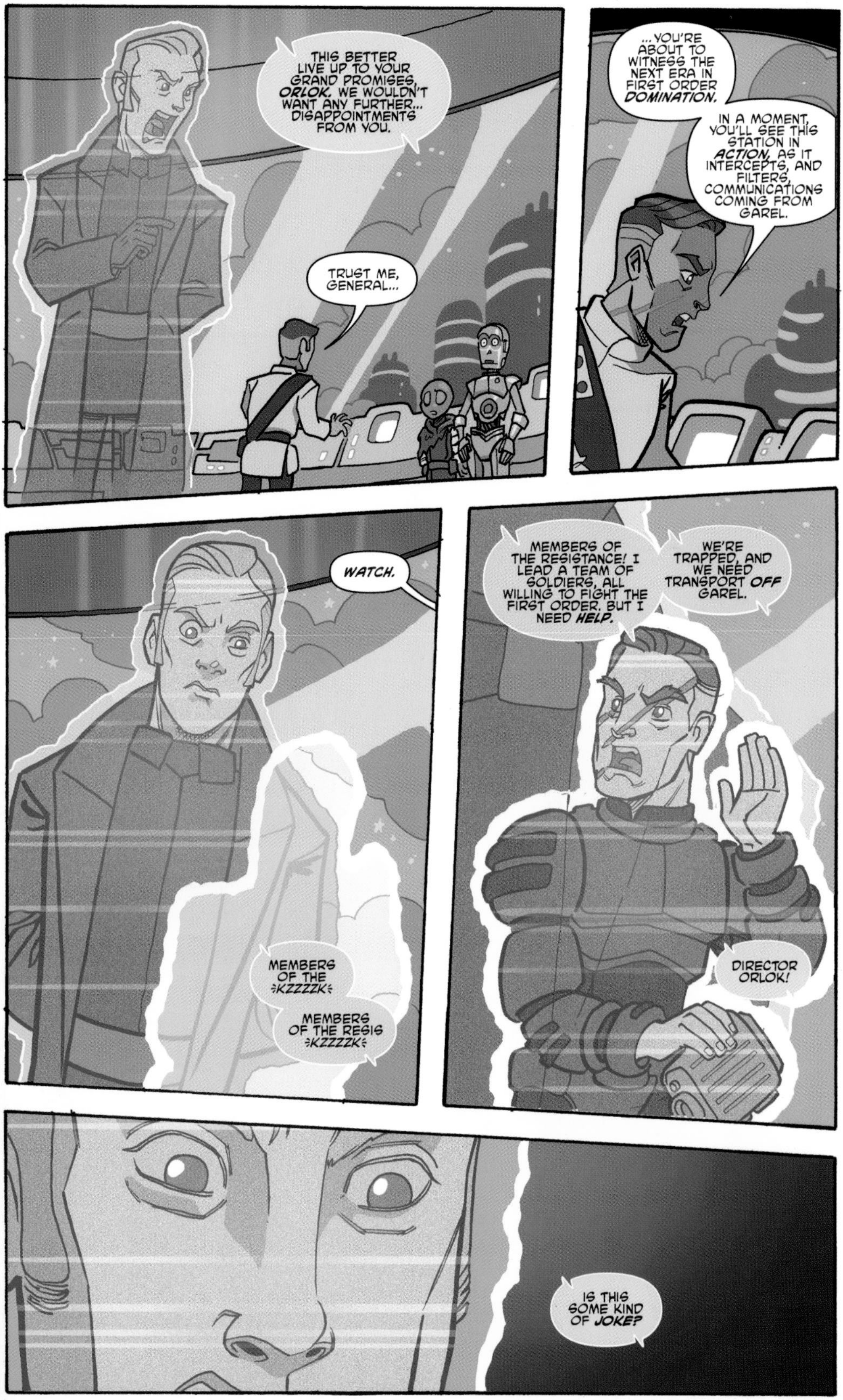
THIS BETTER LIVE UP TO YOUR GRAND PROMISES, ORLOK. WE WOULDN'T WANT ANY FURTHER... DISAPPOINTMENTS FROM YOU.
TRUST ME, GENERAL...
...YOU'RE ABOUT TO WITNESS THE NEXT ERA IN FIRST ORDER DOMINATION.
IN A MOMENT, YOU'LL SEE THIS STATION IN ACTION, AS IT INTERCEPTS, AND FILTERS, COMMUNICATIONS COMING FROM GAREL.
WATCH.
MEMBERS OF THE KZZZZK
MEMBERS OF THE RESIS KZZZZK
MEMBERS OF THE RESISTANCE! I LEAD A TEAM OF SOLDIERS, ALL WILLING TO FIGHT THE FIRST ORDER. BUT I NEED HELP.
WE'RE TRAPPED, AND WE NEED TRANSPORT OFF GAREL.
DIRECTOR ORLOK!
IS THIS SOME KIND OF JOKE?

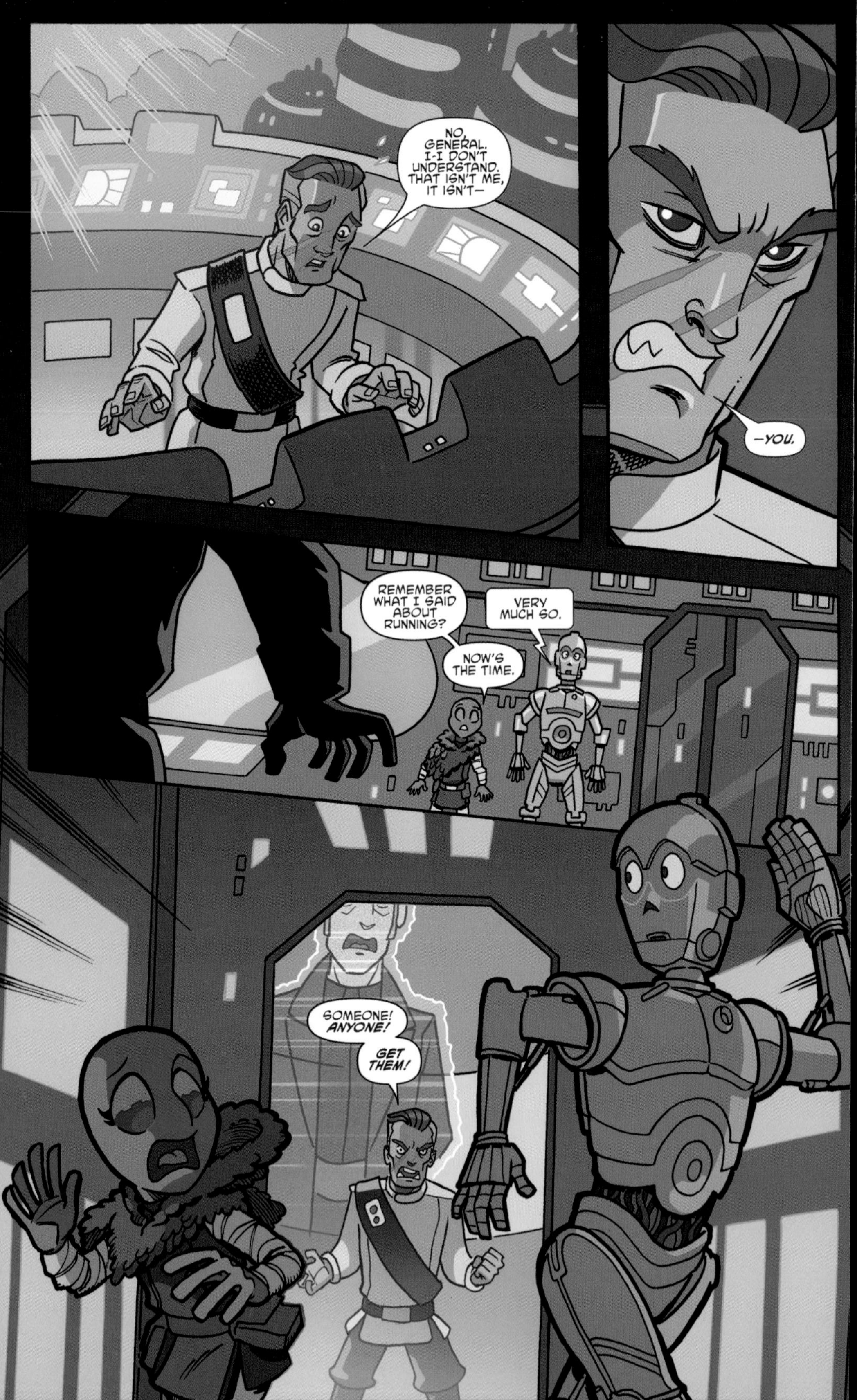
NO, GENERAL. I-I DON'T UNDERSTAND. THAT ISN'T ME, IT ISN'T—
—YOU.
REMEMBER WHAT I SAID ABOUT RUNNING?
VERY MUCH SO.
NOW'S THE TIME.
SOMEONE! ANYONE!
GET THEM!

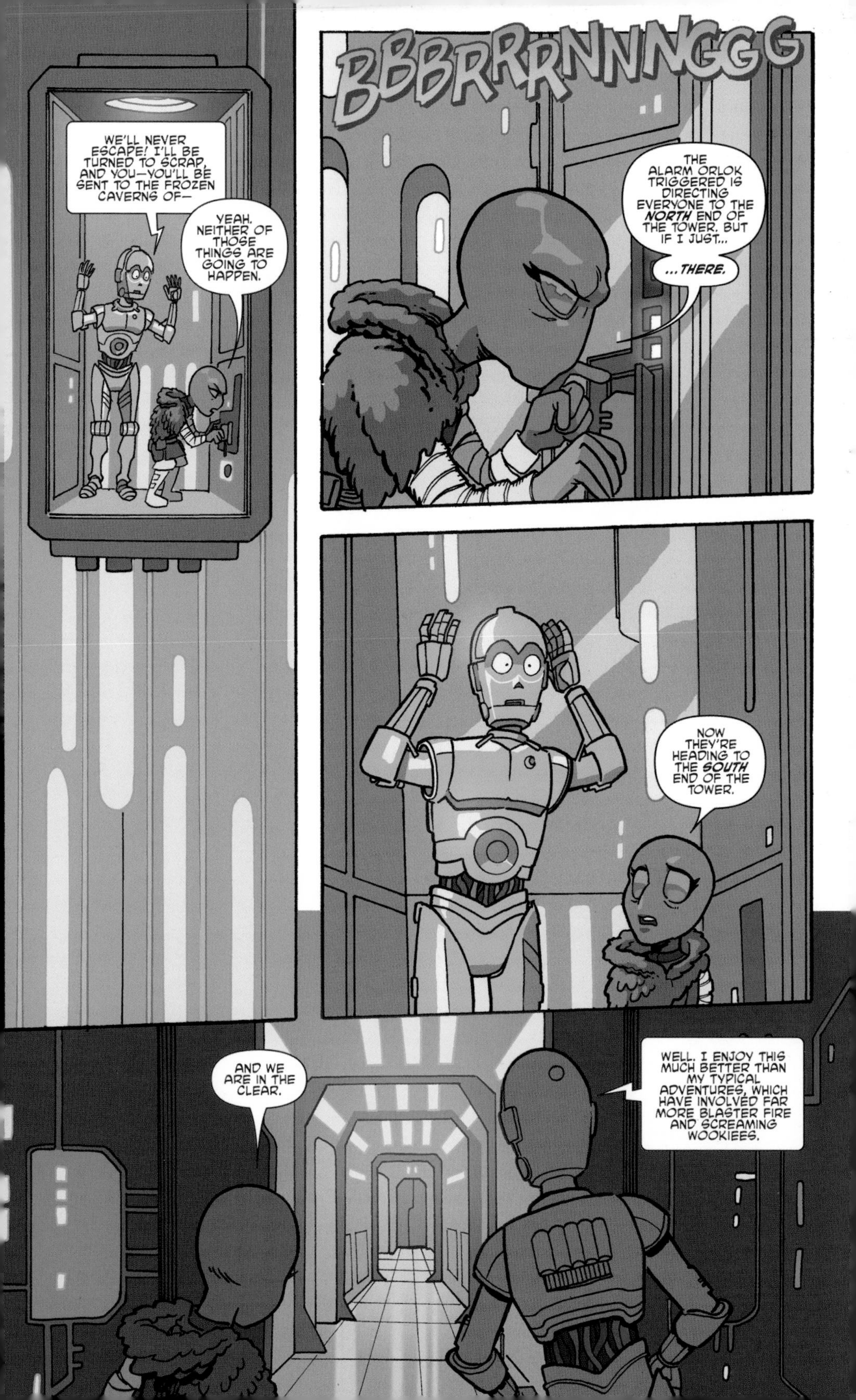
WE'LL NEVER ESCAPE! I'LL BE TURNED TO SCRAP, AND YOU—YOU'LL BE SENT TO THE FROZEN CAVERNS OF—
YEAH. NEITHER OF THOSE THINGS ARE GOING TO HAPPEN.
BBBRRRNNNGGG
THE ALARM ORLOK TRIGGERED IS DIRECTING EVERYONE TO THE NORTH END OF THE TOWER. BUT IF I JUST...
...THERE.
NOW THEY'RE HEADING TO THE SOUTH END OF THE TOWER.
AND WE ARE IN THE CLEAR.
WELL. I ENJOY THIS MUCH BETTER THAN MY TYPICAL ADVENTURES, WHICH HAVE INVOLVED FAR MORE BLASTER FIRE AND SCREAMING WOOKIEES.

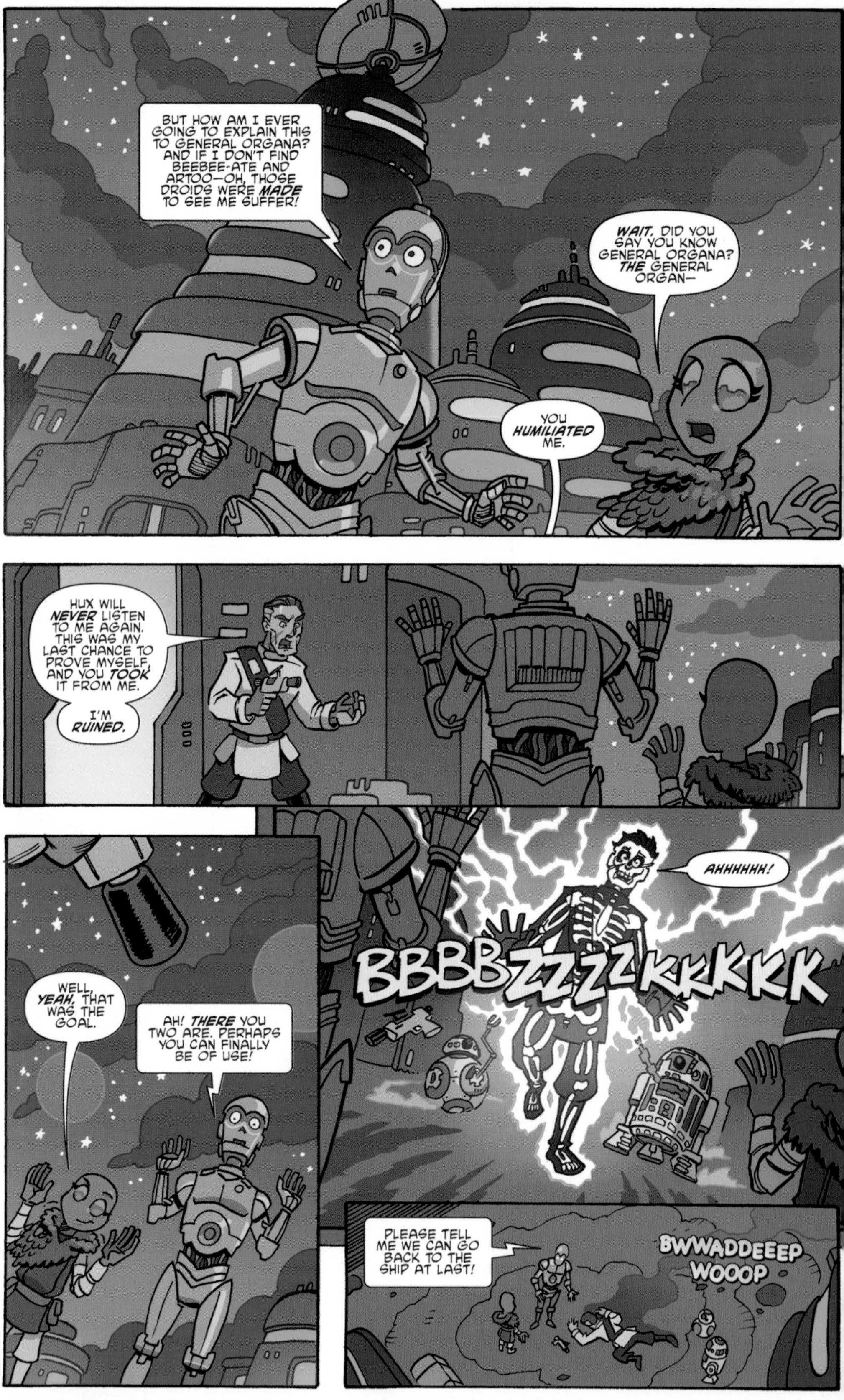
BUT HOW AM I EVER GOING TO EXPLAIN THIS TO GENERAL ORGANA? AND IF I DON'T FIND BEEBEE-ATE AND ARTOO—OH, THOSE DROIDS WERE *MADE* TO SEE ME SUFFER!
WAIT. DID YOU SAY YOU KNOW GENERAL ORGANA? *THE* GENERAL ORGAN—
YOU *HUMILIATED* ME.
HUX WILL *NEVER* LISTEN TO ME AGAIN. THIS WAS MY LAST CHANCE TO PROVE MYSELF, AND YOU *TOOK* IT FROM ME.
I'M *RUINED.*
AHHHHHH!
BBBBZZZZKKKKK
WELL, *YEAH,* THAT WAS THE GOAL.
AH! *THERE* YOU TWO ARE. PERHAPS YOU CAN FINALLY BE OF USE!
PLEASE TELL ME WE CAN GO BACK TO THE SHIP AT LAST!
BWWADDEEEP WOOOP

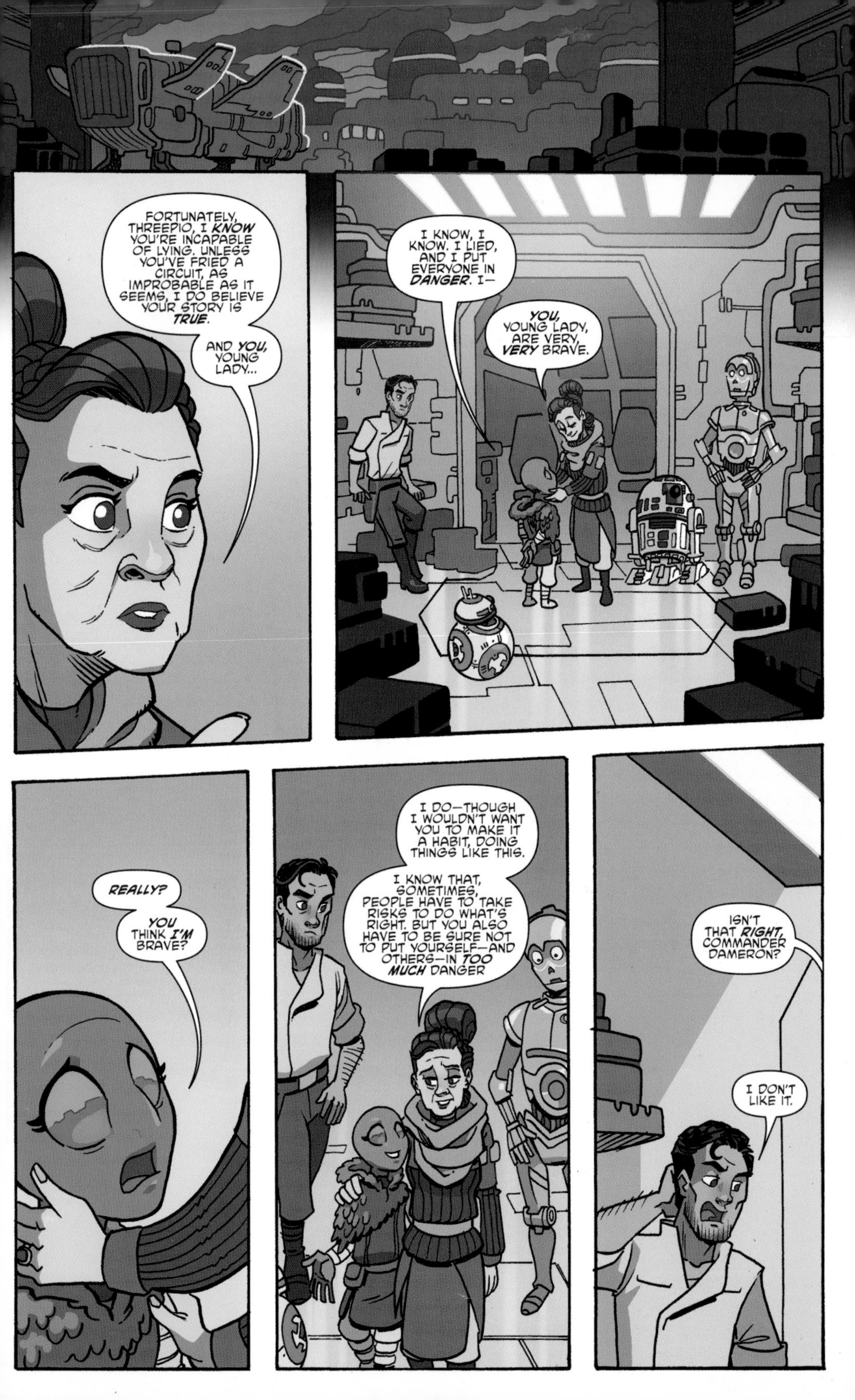
FORTUNATELY, THREEPIO, I KNOW YOU'RE INCAPABLE OF LYING. UNLESS YOU'VE FRIED A CIRCUIT, AS IMPROBABLE AS IT SEEMS, I DO BELIEVE YOUR STORY IS TRUE.
AND YOU, YOUNG LADY...
I KNOW, I KNOW. I LIED, AND I PUT EVERYONE IN DANGER. I—
YOU, YOUNG LADY, ARE VERY, VERY BRAVE.
REALLY?
YOU THINK I'M BRAVE?
I DO—THOUGH I WOULDN'T WANT YOU TO MAKE IT A HABIT, DOING THINGS LIKE THIS.
I KNOW THAT, SOMETIMES, PEOPLE HAVE TO TAKE RISKS TO DO WHAT'S RIGHT. BUT YOU ALSO HAVE TO BE SURE NOT TO PUT YOURSELF—AND OTHERS—IN TOO MUCH DANGER
ISN'T THAT RIGHT, COMMANDER DAMERON?
I DON'T LIKE IT.

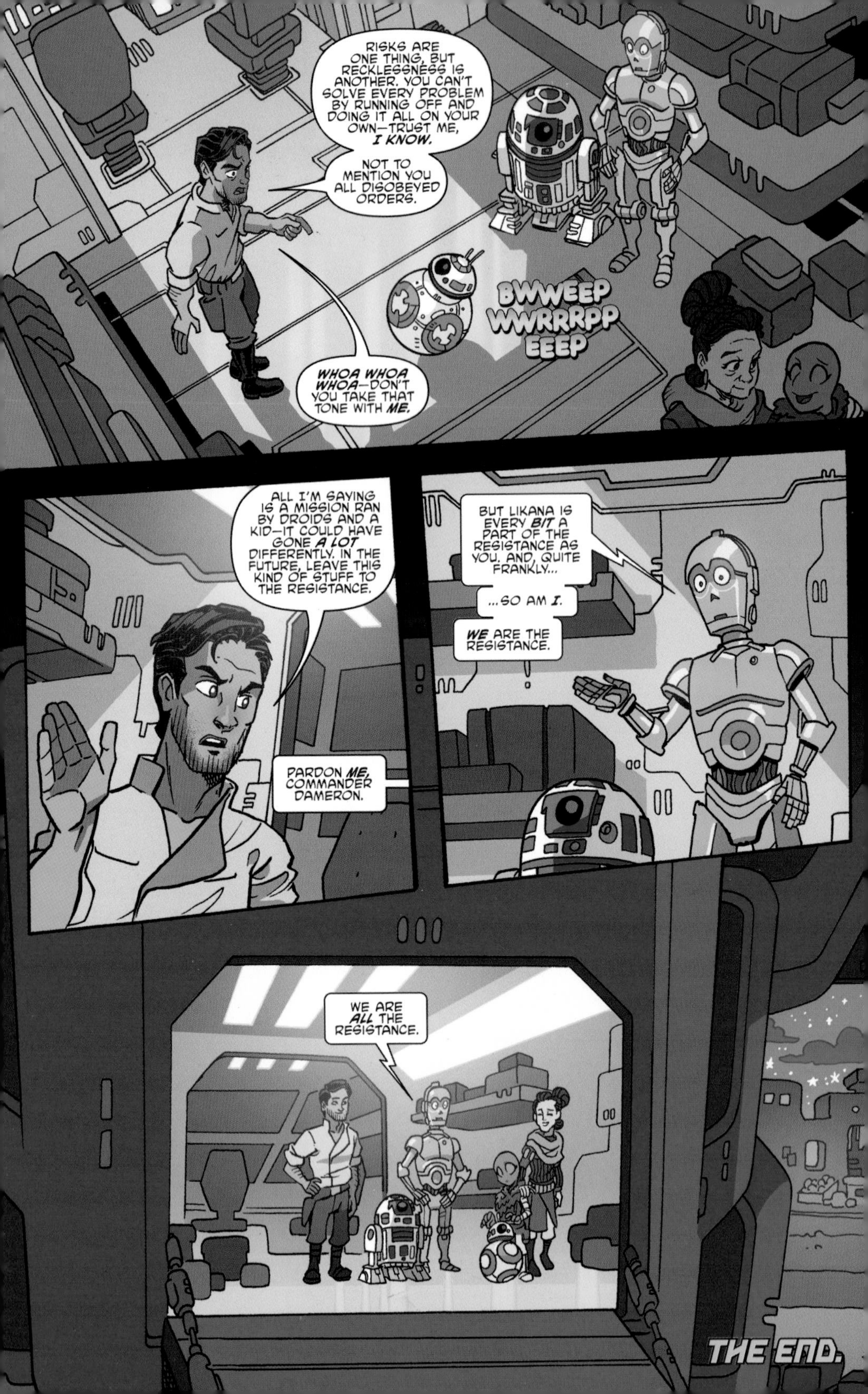
RISKS ARE ONE THING, BUT RECKLESSNESS IS ANOTHER. YOU CAN'T SOLVE EVERY PROBLEM BY RUNNING OFF AND DOING IT ALL ON YOUR OWN—TRUST ME, I KNOW.
NOT TO MENTION YOU ALL DISOBEYED ORDERS.
BWWEEP WWRRRPP EEEP
WHOA WHOA WHOA—DON'T YOU TAKE THAT TONE WITH ME.
ALL I'M SAYING IS A MISSION RAN BY DROIDS AND A KID—IT COULD HAVE GONE A LOT DIFFERENTLY. IN THE FUTURE, LEAVE THIS KIND OF STUFF TO THE RESISTANCE.
PARDON ME, COMMANDER DAMERON.
BUT LIKANA IS EVERY BIT A PART OF THE RESISTANCE AS YOU. AND, QUITE FRANKLY...
...SO AM I.
WE ARE THE RESISTANCE.
WE ARE ALL THE RESISTANCE.
THE END.

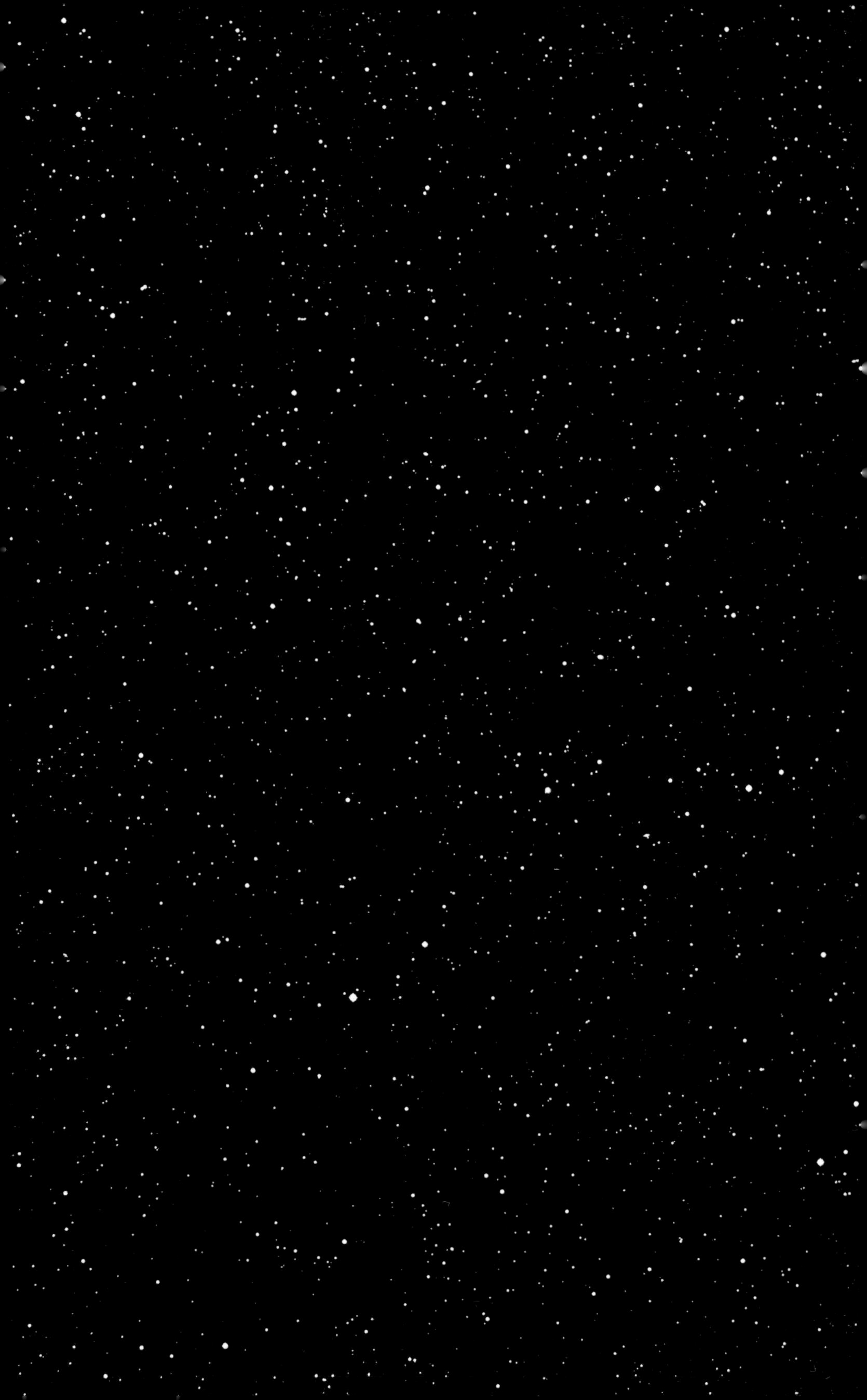

TALES FROM WILD SPACE

The Lost Stories

WRITER
CAVAN SCOTT

ARTIST
DAVID M. BUISAN

COLORIST
CHARLIE KIRCHOFF

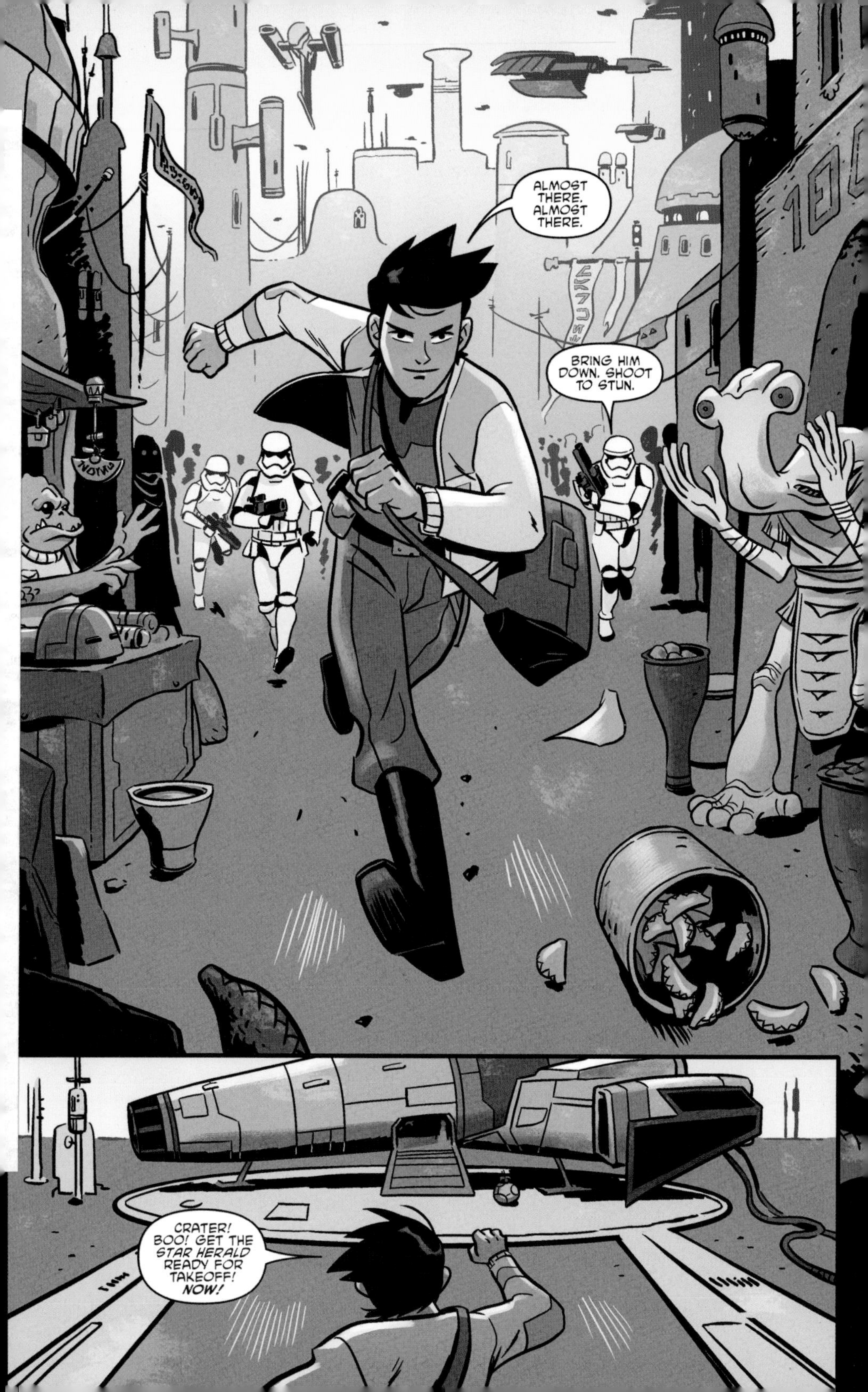
ALMOST THERE. ALMOST THERE.
BRING HIM DOWN. SHOOT TO STUN.
CRATER! BOO! GET THE *STAR HERALD* READY FOR TAKEOFF! *NOW!*

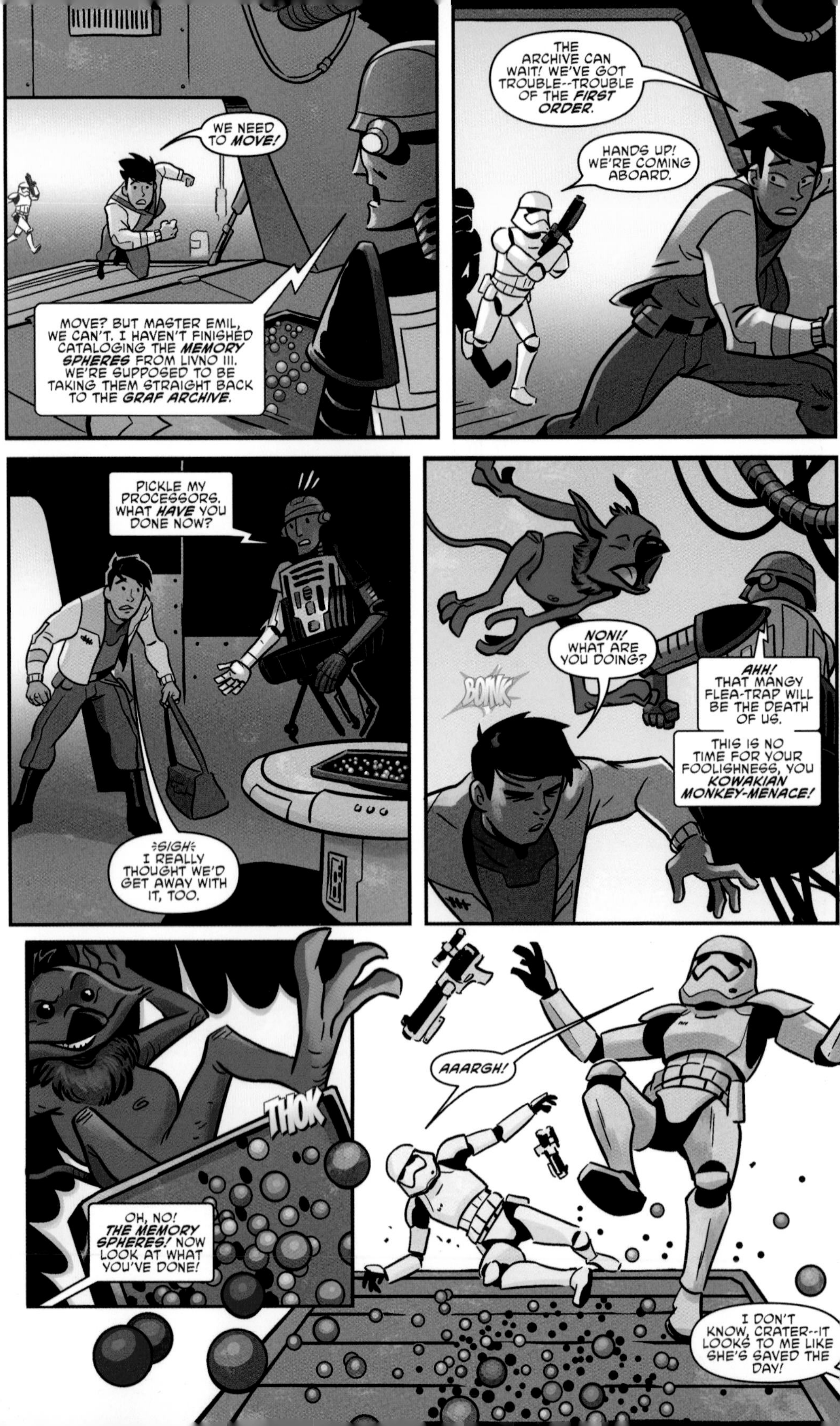
WE NEED TO *MOVE!*
MOVE? BUT MASTER EMIL, WE CAN'T. I HAVEN'T FINISHED CATALOGING THE *MEMORY SPHERES* FROM LIVNO III. WE'RE SUPPOSED TO BE TAKING THEM STRAIGHT BACK TO THE *GRAF ARCHIVE*.
THE ARCHIVE CAN WAIT! WE'VE GOT TROUBLE--TROUBLE OF THE *FIRST ORDER*.
HANDS UP! WE'RE COMING ABOARD.
PICKLE MY PROCESSORS. WHAT *HAVE* YOU DONE NOW?
SIGH I REALLY THOUGHT WE'D GET AWAY WITH IT, TOO.
NONI! WHAT ARE YOU DOING?
BONK
AHH! THAT MANGY FLEA-TRAP WILL BE THE DEATH OF US.
THIS IS NO TIME FOR YOUR FOOLISHNESS, YOU *KOWAKIAN MONKEY-MENACE!*
THOK
OH, NO! *THE MEMORY SPHERES!* NOW LOOK AT WHAT YOU'VE DONE!
AAARGH!
I DON'T KNOW, CRATER--IT LOOKS TO ME LIKE SHE'S SAVED THE DAY!

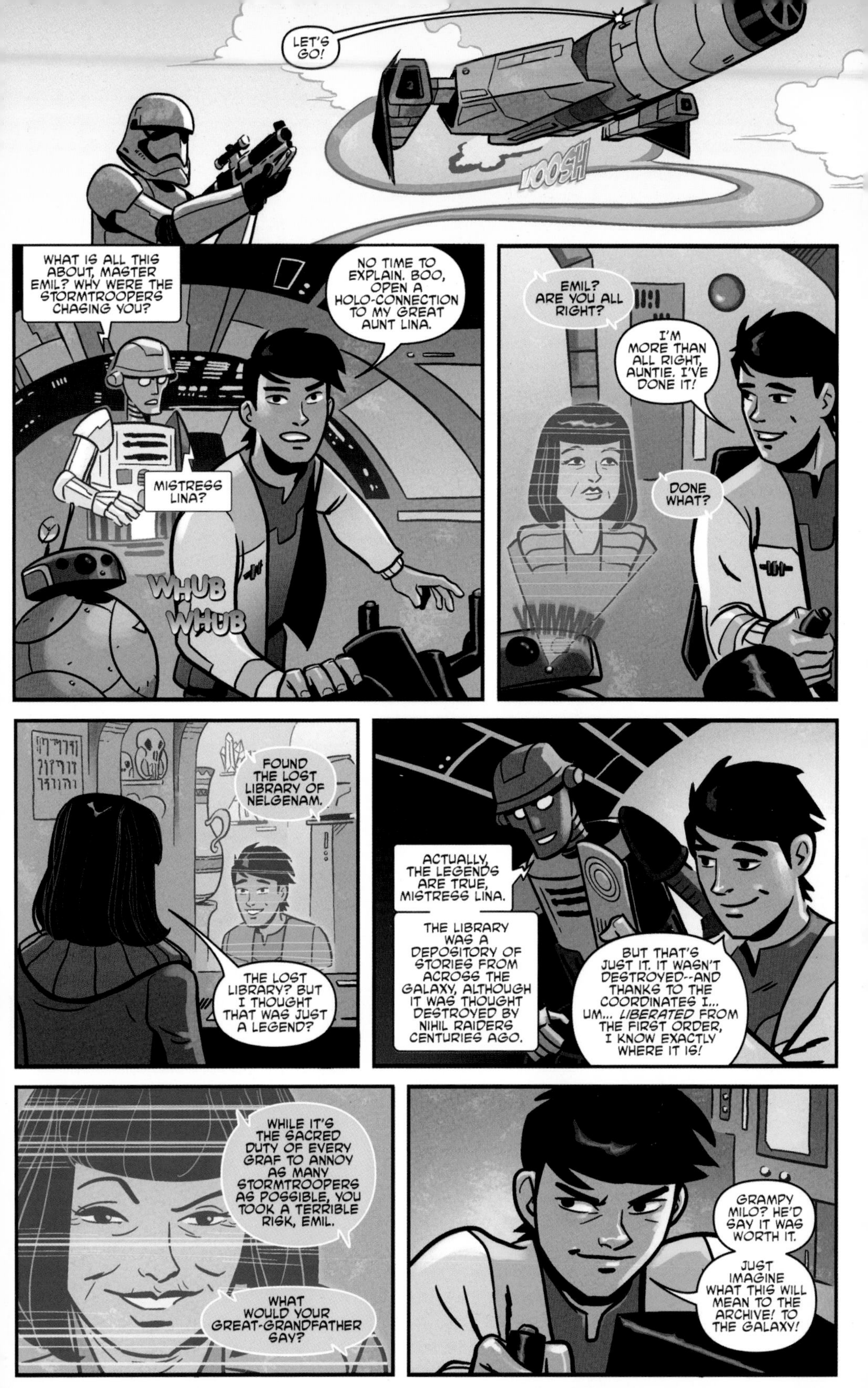
LET'S GO!
KOOSH
WHAT IS ALL THIS ABOUT, MASTER EMIL? WHY WERE THE STORMTROOPERS CHASING YOU?
NO TIME TO EXPLAIN. BOO, OPEN A HOLO-CONNECTION TO MY GREAT AUNT LINA.
MISTRESS LINA?
WHUB WHUB
EMIL? ARE YOU ALL RIGHT?
I'M MORE THAN ALL RIGHT, AUNTIE. I'VE DONE IT!
DONE WHAT?
FOUND THE LOST LIBRARY OF NELGENAM.
THE LOST LIBRARY? BUT I THOUGHT THAT WAS JUST A LEGEND?
ACTUALLY, THE LEGENDS ARE TRUE, MISTRESS LINA.
THE LIBRARY WAS A DEPOSITORY OF STORIES FROM ACROSS THE GALAXY, ALTHOUGH IT WAS THOUGHT DESTROYED BY NIHIL RAIDERS CENTURIES AGO.
BUT THAT'S JUST IT. IT WASN'T DESTROYED--AND THANKS TO THE COORDINATES I... UM... *LIBERATED* FROM THE FIRST ORDER, I KNOW EXACTLY WHERE IT IS!
WHILE IT'S THE SACRED DUTY OF EVERY GRAF TO ANNOY AS MANY STORMTROOPERS AS POSSIBLE, YOU TOOK A TERRIBLE RISK, EMIL.
WHAT WOULD YOUR GREAT-GRANDFATHER SAY?
GRAMPY MILO? HE'D SAY IT WAS WORTH IT.
JUST IMAGINE WHAT THIS WILL MEAN TO THE ARCHIVE! TO THE GALAXY!

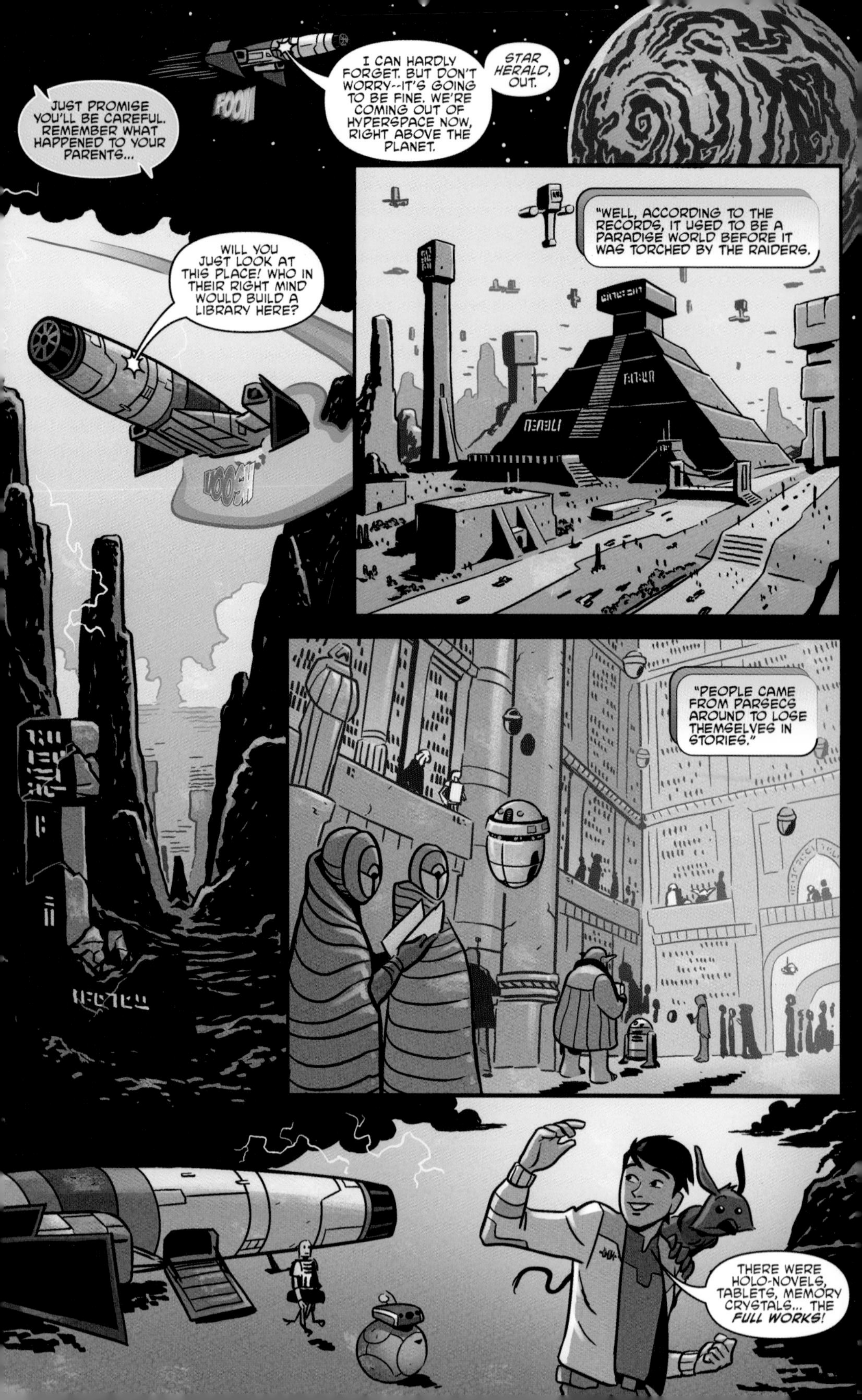
JUST PROMISE YOU'LL BE CAREFUL. REMEMBER WHAT HAPPENED TO YOUR PARENTS...
FOOM
I CAN HARDLY FORGET. BUT DON'T WORRY--IT'S GOING TO BE FINE. WE'RE COMING OUT OF HYPERSPACE NOW, RIGHT ABOVE THE PLANET.
STAR HERALD, OUT.
WILL YOU JUST LOOK AT THIS PLACE! WHO IN THEIR RIGHT MIND WOULD BUILD A LIBRARY HERE?
VOOSH
"WELL, ACCORDING TO THE RECORDS, IT USED TO BE A PARADISE WORLD BEFORE IT WAS TORCHED BY THE RAIDERS.
"PEOPLE CAME FROM PARSECS AROUND TO LOSE THEMSELVES IN STORIES."
THERE WERE HOLO-NOVELS, TABLETS, MEMORY CRYSTALS... THE ***FULL WORKS!***

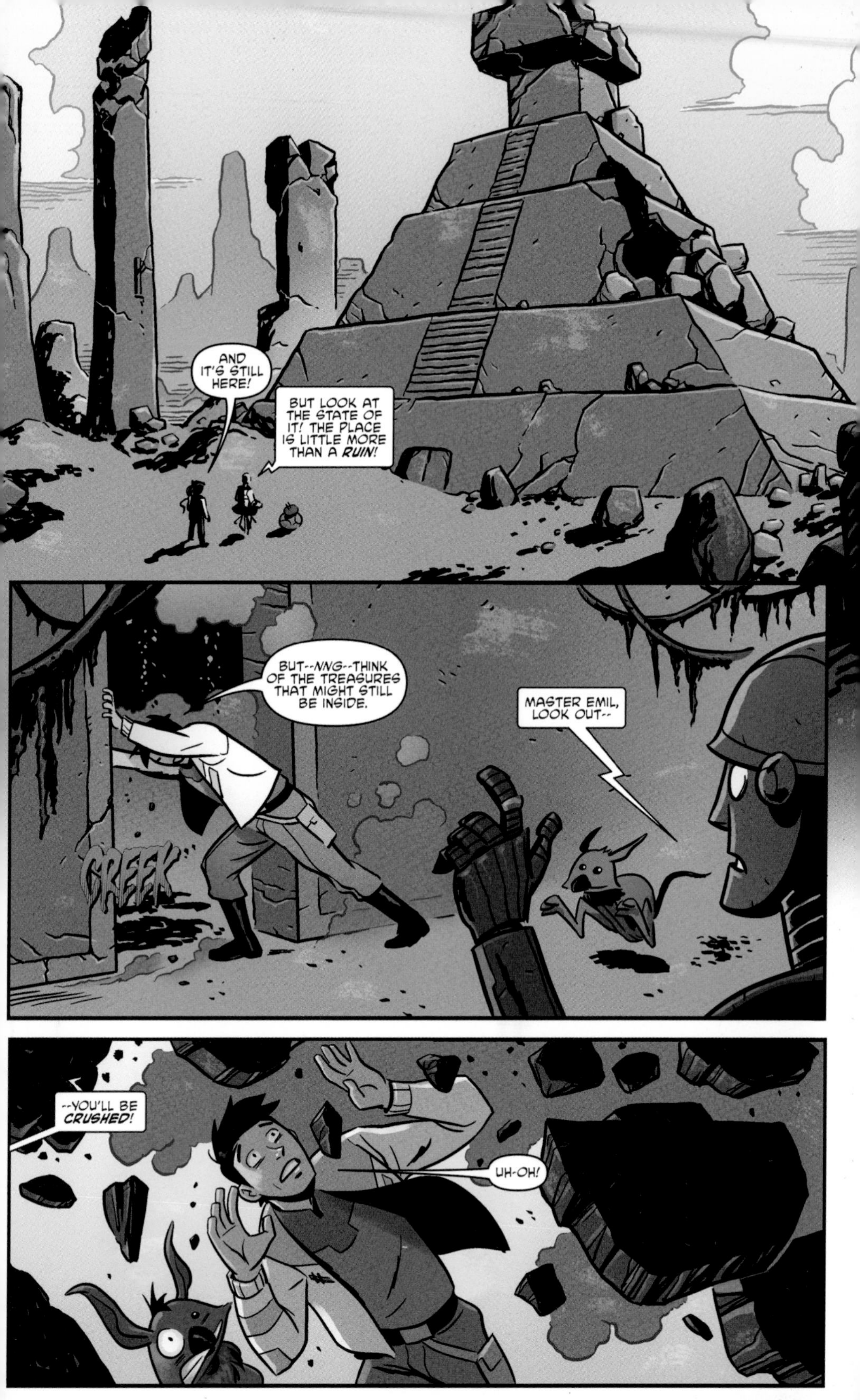
AND IT'S STILL HERE!
BUT LOOK AT THE STATE OF IT! THE PLACE IS LITTLE MORE THAN A *RUIN!*
CREEK
BUT--*NNG*--THINK OF THE TREASURES THAT MIGHT STILL BE INSIDE.
MASTER EMIL, LOOK OUT--
--YOU'LL BE *CRUSHED!*
UH-OH!

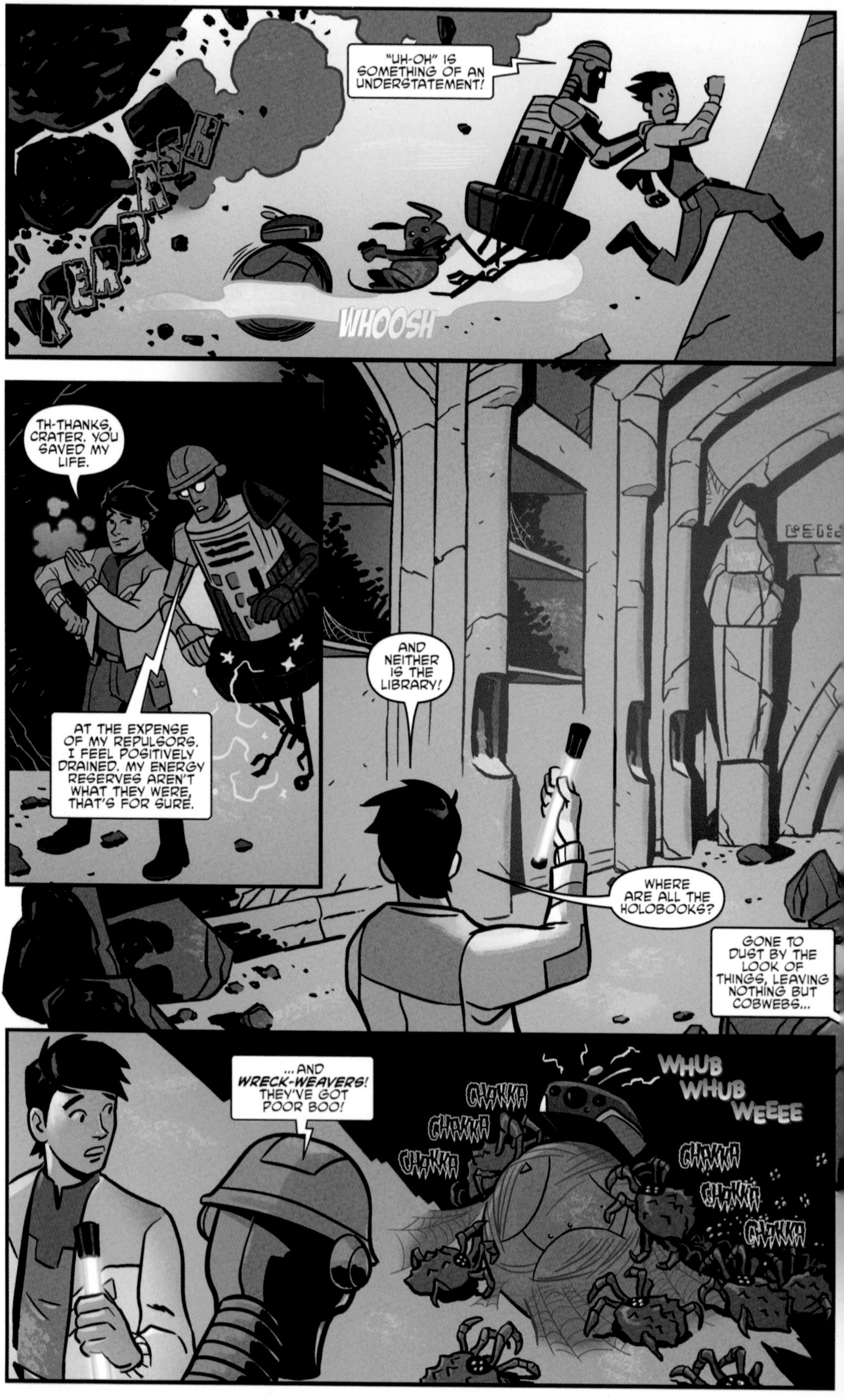
KERRASH
"UH-OH" IS SOMETHING OF AN UNDERSTATEMENT!
WHOOSH
TH-THANKS, CRATER. YOU SAVED MY LIFE.
AT THE EXPENSE OF MY REPULSORS. I FEEL POSITIVELY DRAINED. MY ENERGY RESERVES AREN'T WHAT THEY WERE, THAT'S FOR SURE.
AND NEITHER IS THE LIBRARY!
WHERE ARE ALL THE HOLOBOOKS?
GONE TO DUST BY THE LOOK OF THINGS, LEAVING NOTHING BUT COBWEBS...
...AND WRECK-WEAVERS! THEY'VE GOT POOR BOO!
WHUB WHUB WEEEE
CHAKKA
CHAKKA
CHAKKA
CHAKKA
CHAKKA
CHAKKA

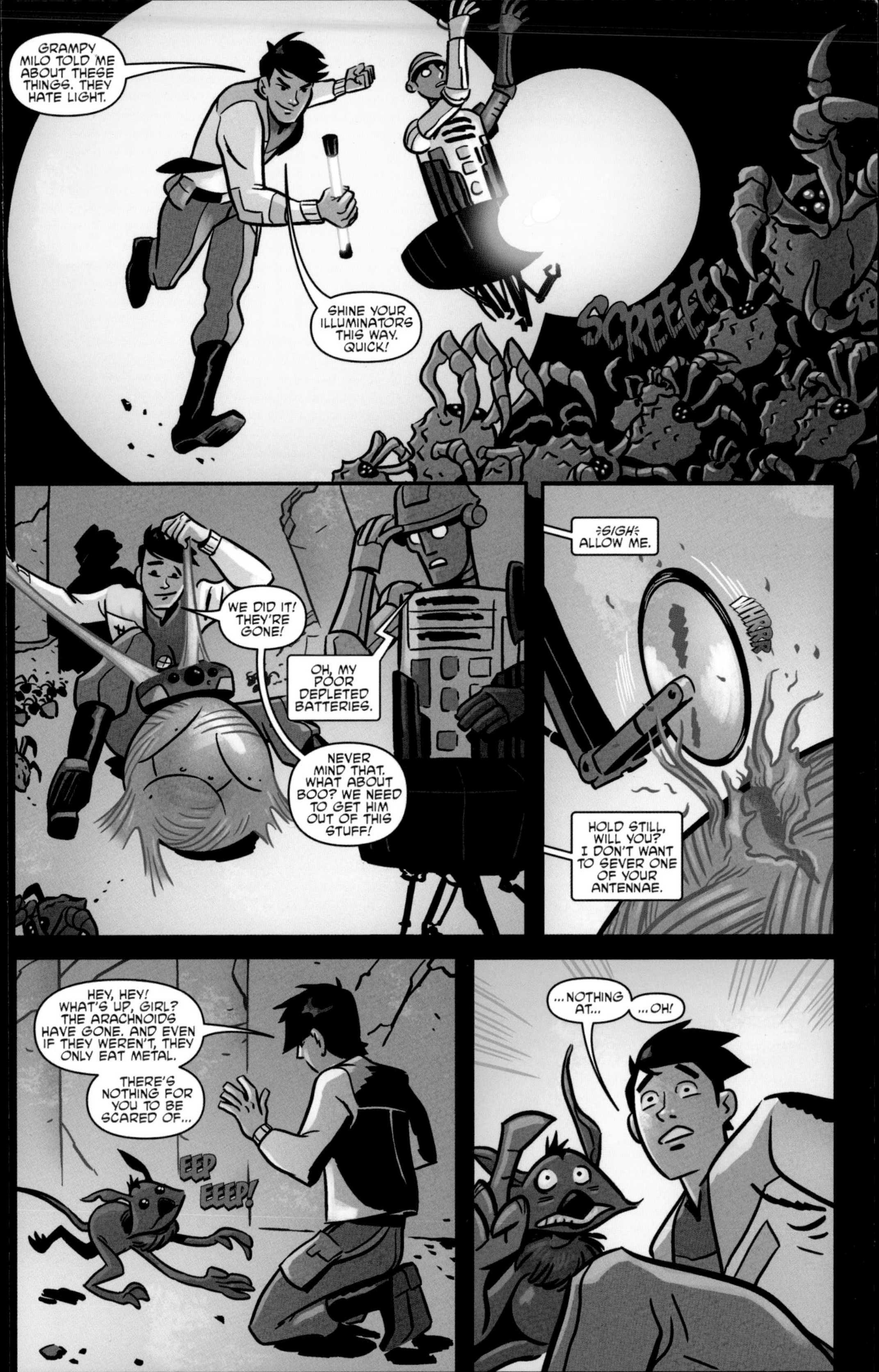
GRAMPY MILO TOLD ME ABOUT THESE THINGS. THEY HATE LIGHT.
SHINE YOUR ILLUMINATORS THIS WAY. QUICK!
SCREEE!
WE DID IT! THEY'RE GONE!
OH, MY POOR DEPLETED BATTERIES.
NEVER MIND THAT. WHAT ABOUT BOO? WE NEED TO GET HIM OUT OF THIS STUFF!
SIGH ALLOW ME.
WHRRR
HOLD STILL, WILL YOU? I DON'T WANT TO SEVER ONE OF YOUR ANTENNAE.
HEY, HEY! WHAT'S UP, GIRL? THE ARACHNOIDS HAVE GONE. AND EVEN IF THEY WEREN'T, THEY ONLY EAT METAL.
THERE'S NOTHING FOR YOU TO BE SCARED OF...
EEP EEEP!
...NOTHING AT...
...OH!

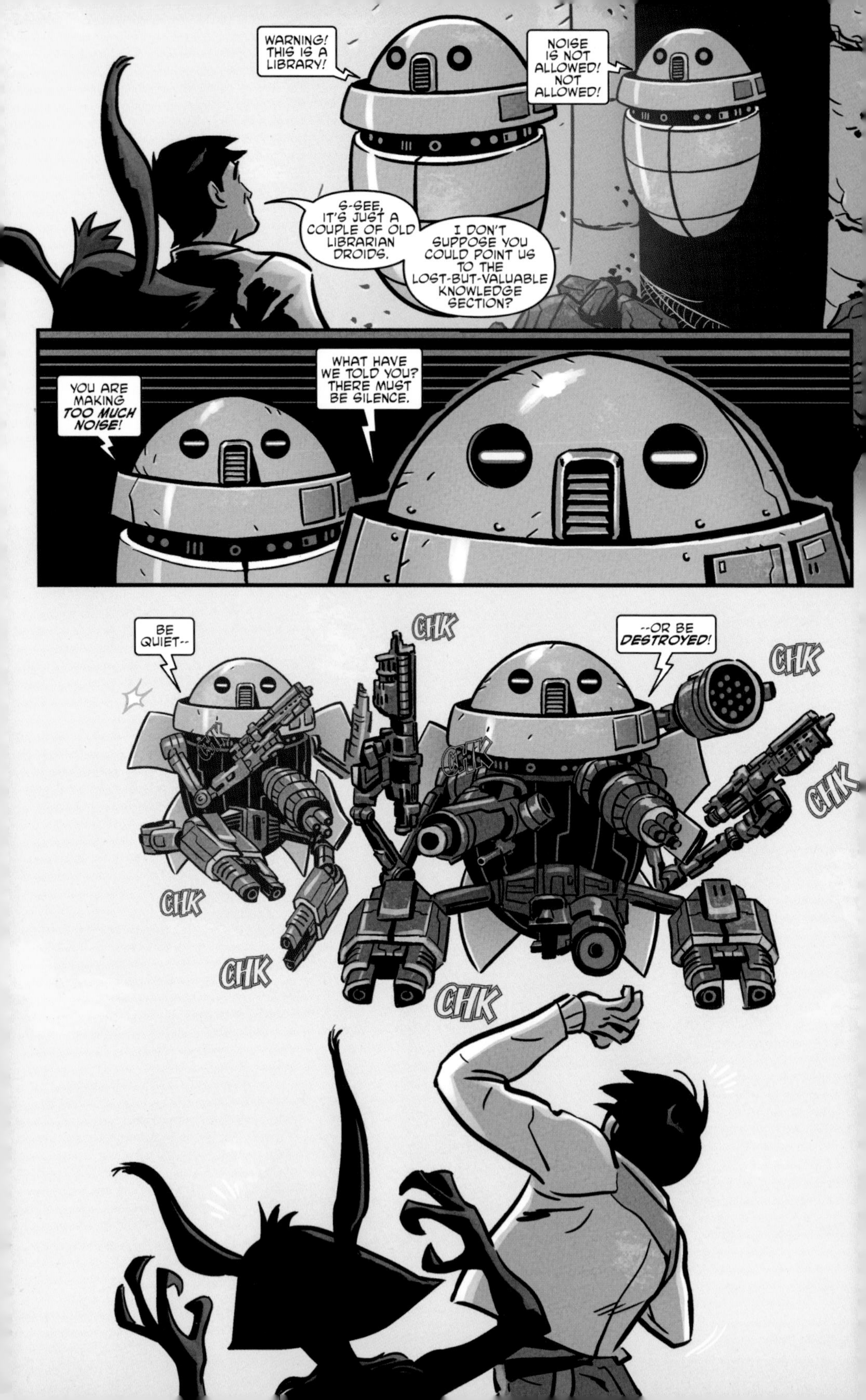
WARNING! THIS IS A LIBRARY!
NOISE IS NOT ALLOWED! NOT ALLOWED!
S-SEE, IT'S JUST A COUPLE OF OLD LIBRARIAN DROIDS.
I DON'T SUPPOSE YOU COULD POINT US TO THE LOST-BUT-VALUABLE KNOWLEDGE SECTION?
YOU ARE MAKING TOO MUCH NOISE!
WHAT HAVE WE TOLD YOU? THERE MUST BE SILENCE.
BE QUIET--
CHK
--OR BE DESTROYED!
CHK
CHK
CHK
CHK
CHK
CHK
CHK

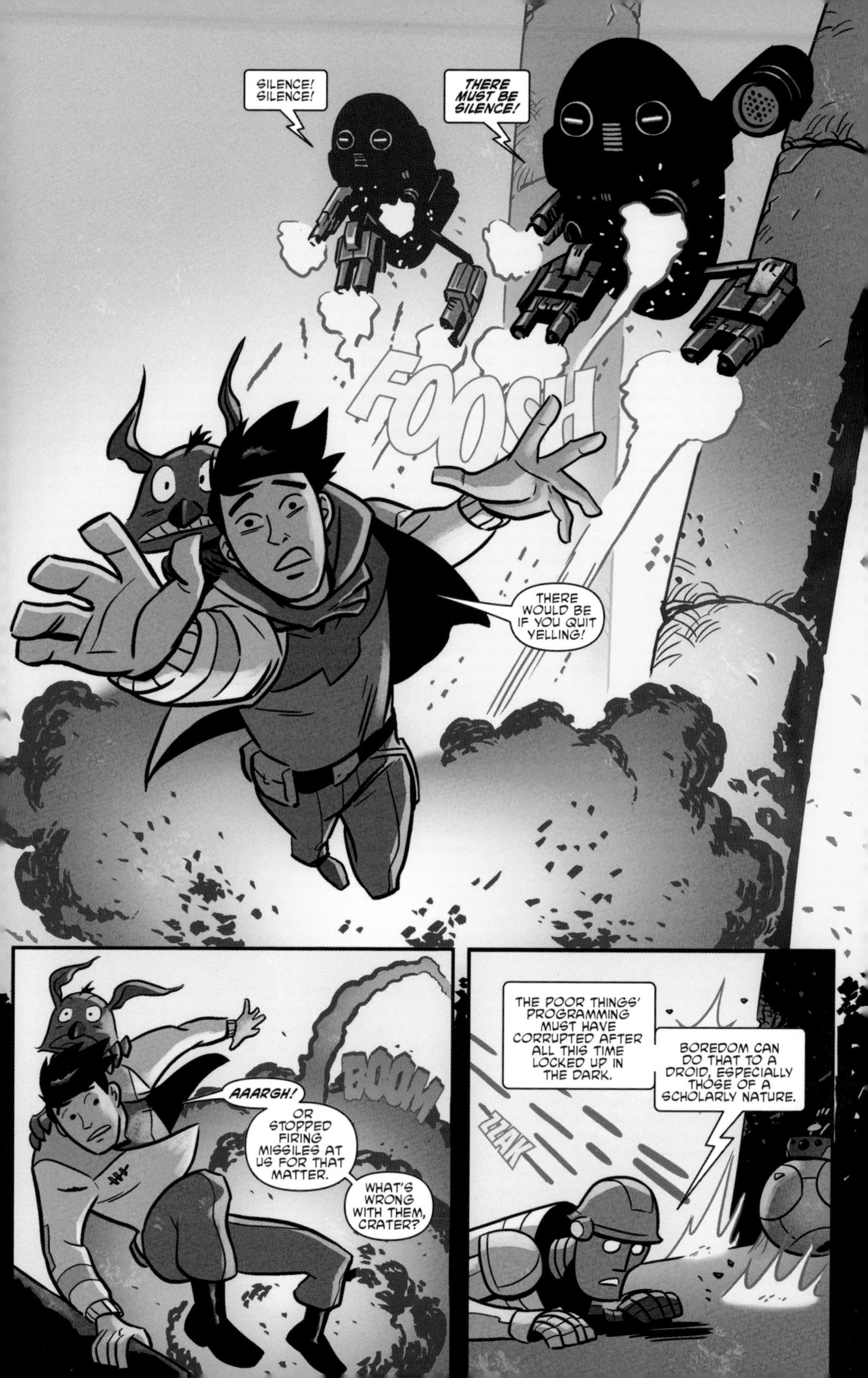
SILENCE! SILENCE!
THERE MUST BE SILENCE!
FOOSH
THERE WOULD BE IF YOU QUIT YELLING!
BOOM
AAARGH!
OR STOPPED FIRING MISSILES AT US FOR THAT MATTER.
WHAT'S WRONG WITH THEM, CRATER?
ZZAK
THE POOR THINGS' PROGRAMMING MUST HAVE CORRUPTED AFTER ALL THIS TIME LOCKED UP IN THE DARK.
BOREDOM CAN DO THAT TO A DROID, ESPECIALLY THOSE OF A SCHOLARLY NATURE.

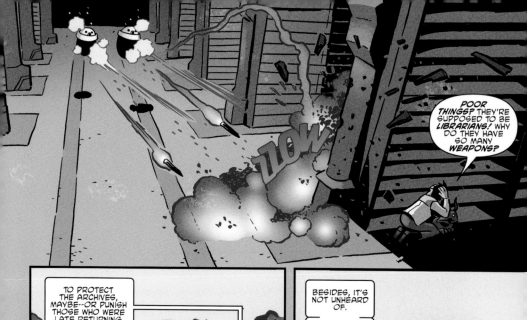

POOR *THINGS?* THEY'RE SUPPOSED TO BE *LIBRARIANS!* WHY DO THEY HAVE SO MANY *WEAPONS?*

TO PROTECT THE ARCHIVES, MAYBE--OR PUNISH THOSE WHO WERE LATE RETURNING THEIR HOLO-NOVELS?

THIS IS NO TIME TO DEVELOP A SENSE OF HUMOR, CRATER!

HUMOR? ME? PERISH THE THOUGHT.

BESIDES, IT'S NOT UNHEARD OF.

(ENGAGING LECTURE MODE)

THE LIBRARIAN MONKS OF ANCIENT CHAZWA WERE PARTICULARLY VENGEFUL. THEY ONCE THREW A RIKADIAN PRINCE TO A SARLACC FOR LEAVING STICKY FINGERPRINTS ON A TEXT-READER.

AND YOU SHOULD HAVE SEEN WHAT THEY DID TO ANYONE WHO MIGHT ACCIDENTALLY *CRACK A SCREEN!*

CRACK A SCREEN? *CRACK A SCREEN?*

TO EVEN IMAGINE SUCH A THING IS A *CRIME!*

YOU MUST BE SILENCED... *FOREVER!*

NOT HELPFUL, CRATE!

YES--IT SEEMS TO HAVE RILED THEM SOMEWHAT.

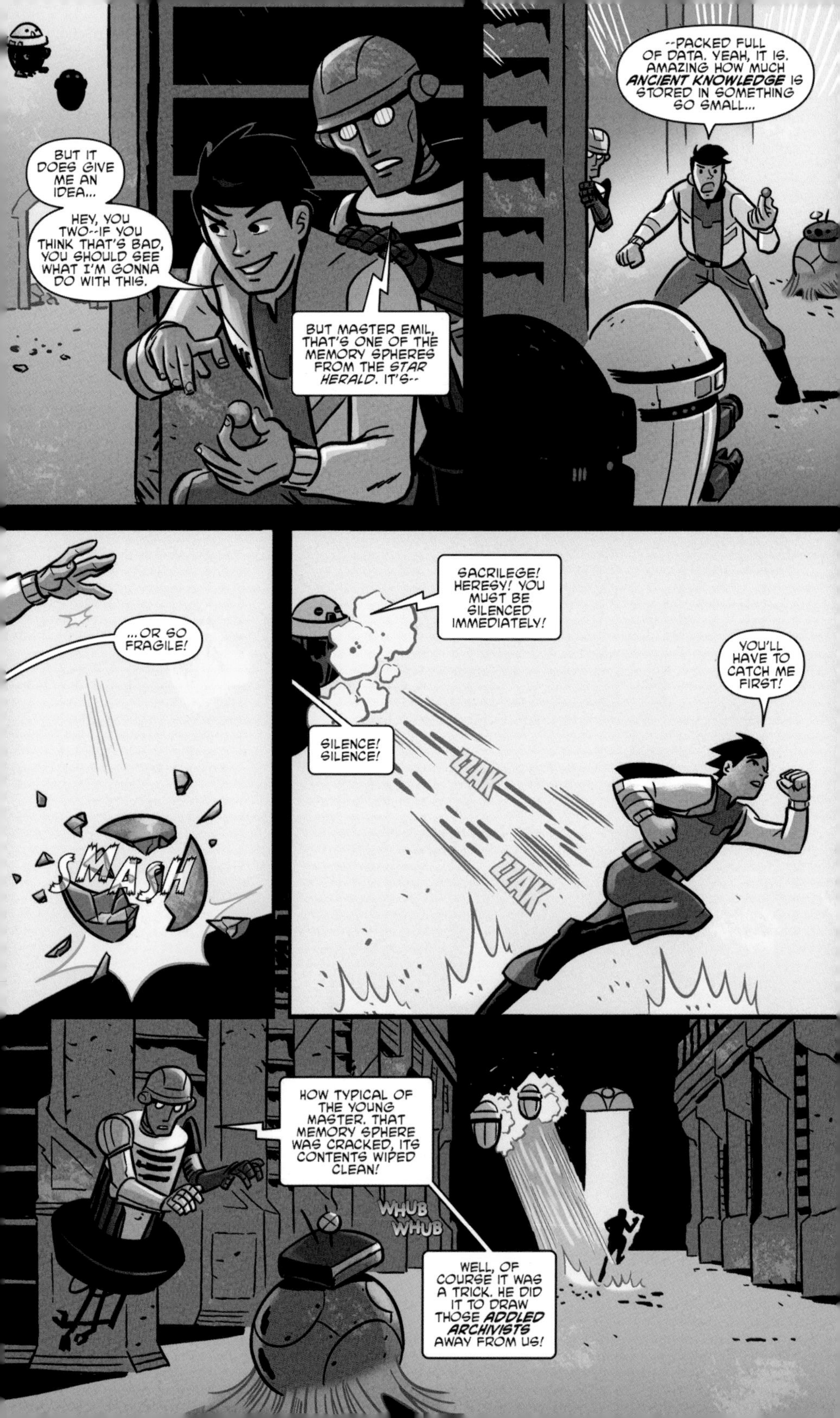
BUT IT DOES GIVE ME AN IDEA...
HEY, YOU TWO--IF YOU THINK THAT'S BAD, YOU SHOULD SEE WHAT I'M GONNA DO WITH THIS.
BUT MASTER EMIL, THAT'S ONE OF THE MEMORY SPHERES FROM THE STAR HERALD. IT'S--
--PACKED FULL OF DATA. YEAH, IT IS. AMAZING HOW MUCH ANCIENT KNOWLEDGE IS STORED IN SOMETHING SO SMALL...
...OR SO FRAGILE!
SMASH
SACRILEGE! HERESY! YOU MUST BE SILENCED IMMEDIATELY!
SILENCE! SILENCE!
YOU'LL HAVE TO CATCH ME FIRST!
ZZAK
ZZAK
HOW TYPICAL OF THE YOUNG MASTER. THAT MEMORY SPHERE WAS CRACKED, ITS CONTENTS WIPED CLEAN!
WHUB WHUB
WELL, OF COURSE IT WAS A TRICK. HE DID IT TO DRAW THOSE ADDLED ARCHIVISTS AWAY FROM US!

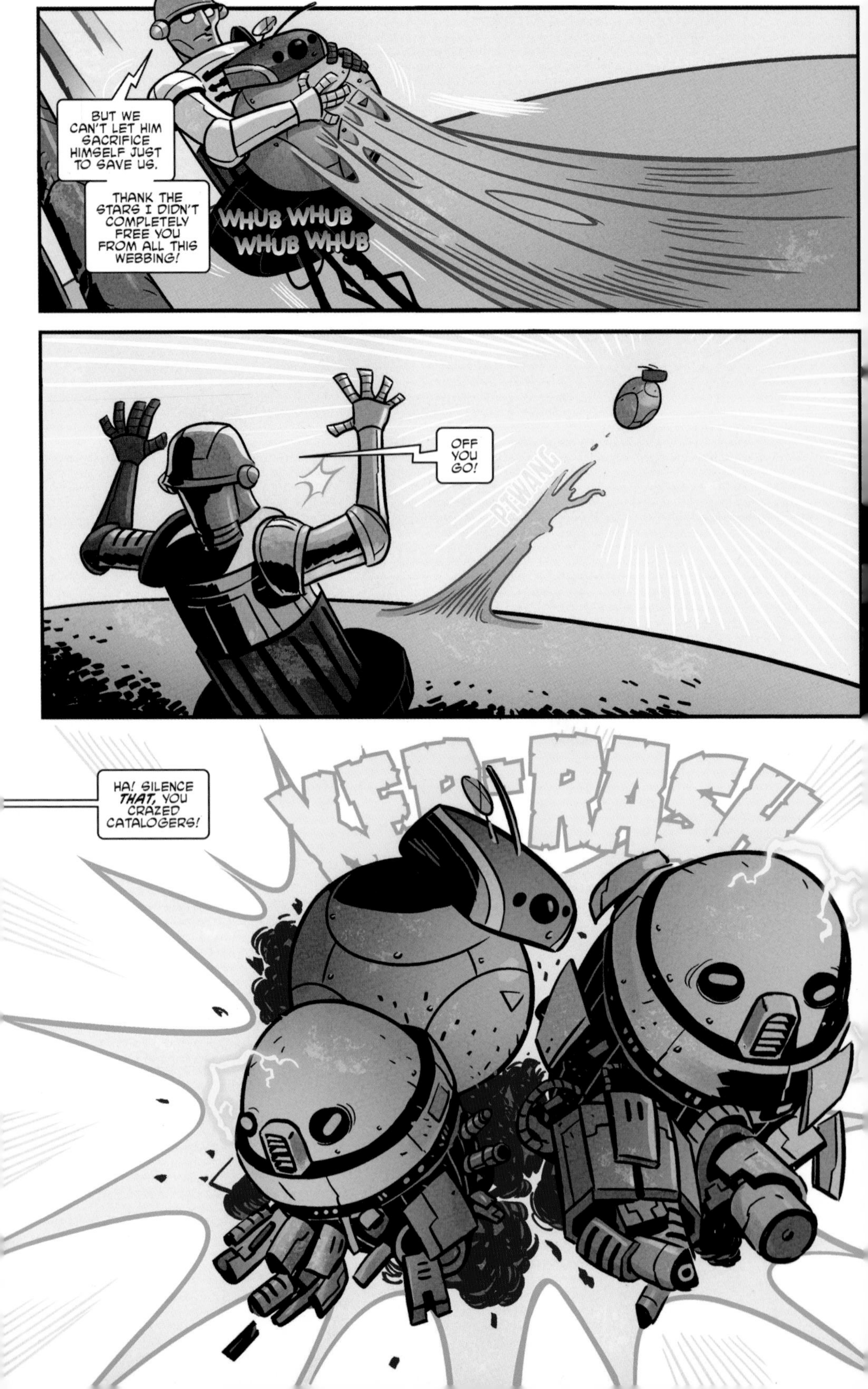
BUT WE CAN'T LET HIM SACRIFICE HIMSELF JUST TO SAVE US.
THANK THE STARS I DIDN'T COMPLETELY FREE YOU FROM ALL THIS WEBBING!
WHUB WHUB WHUB WHUB
OFF YOU GO!
P-TWANG
HA! SILENCE *THAT,* YOU CRAZED CATALOGERS!
KER-RASH

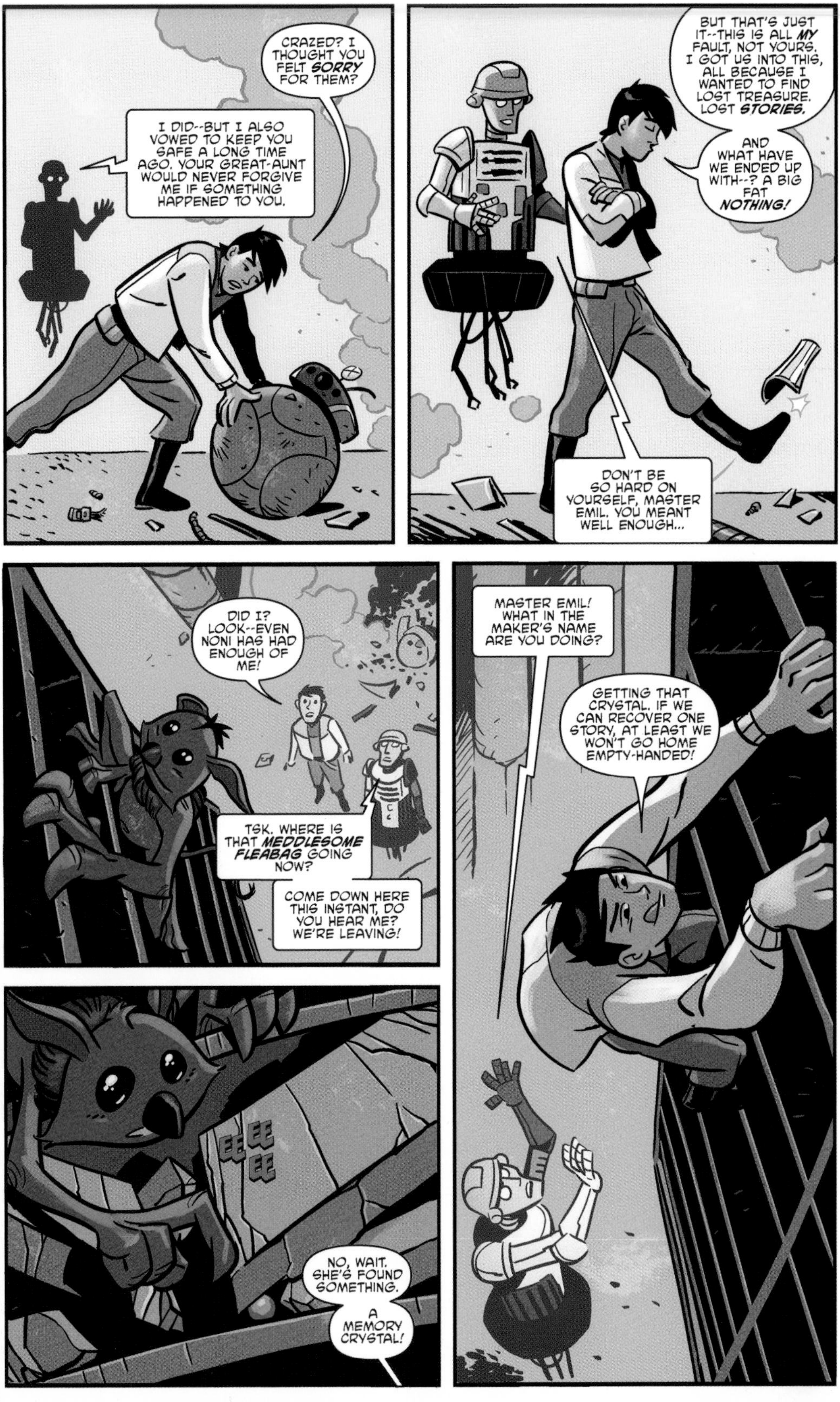

CRAZED? I THOUGHT YOU FELT SORRY FOR THEM?
I DID--BUT I ALSO VOWED TO KEEP YOU SAFE A LONG TIME AGO. YOUR GREAT-AUNT WOULD NEVER FORGIVE ME IF SOMETHING HAPPENED TO YOU.
BUT THAT'S JUST IT--THIS IS ALL MY FAULT, NOT YOURS. I GOT US INTO THIS, ALL BECAUSE I WANTED TO FIND LOST TREASURE. LOST STORIES.
AND WHAT HAVE WE ENDED UP WITH--? A BIG FAT NOTHING!
DON'T BE SO HARD ON YOURSELF, MASTER EMIL. YOU MEANT WELL ENOUGH...
DID I? LOOK--EVEN NONI HAS HAD ENOUGH OF ME!
TSK. WHERE IS THAT MEDDLESOME FLEABAG GOING NOW?
COME DOWN HERE THIS INSTANT, DO YOU HEAR ME? WE'RE LEAVING!
NO, WAIT. SHE'S FOUND SOMETHING.
A MEMORY CRYSTAL!
MASTER EMIL! WHAT IN THE MAKER'S NAME ARE YOU DOING?
GETTING THAT CRYSTAL. IF WE CAN RECOVER ONE STORY, AT LEAST WE WON'T GO HOME EMPTY-HANDED!

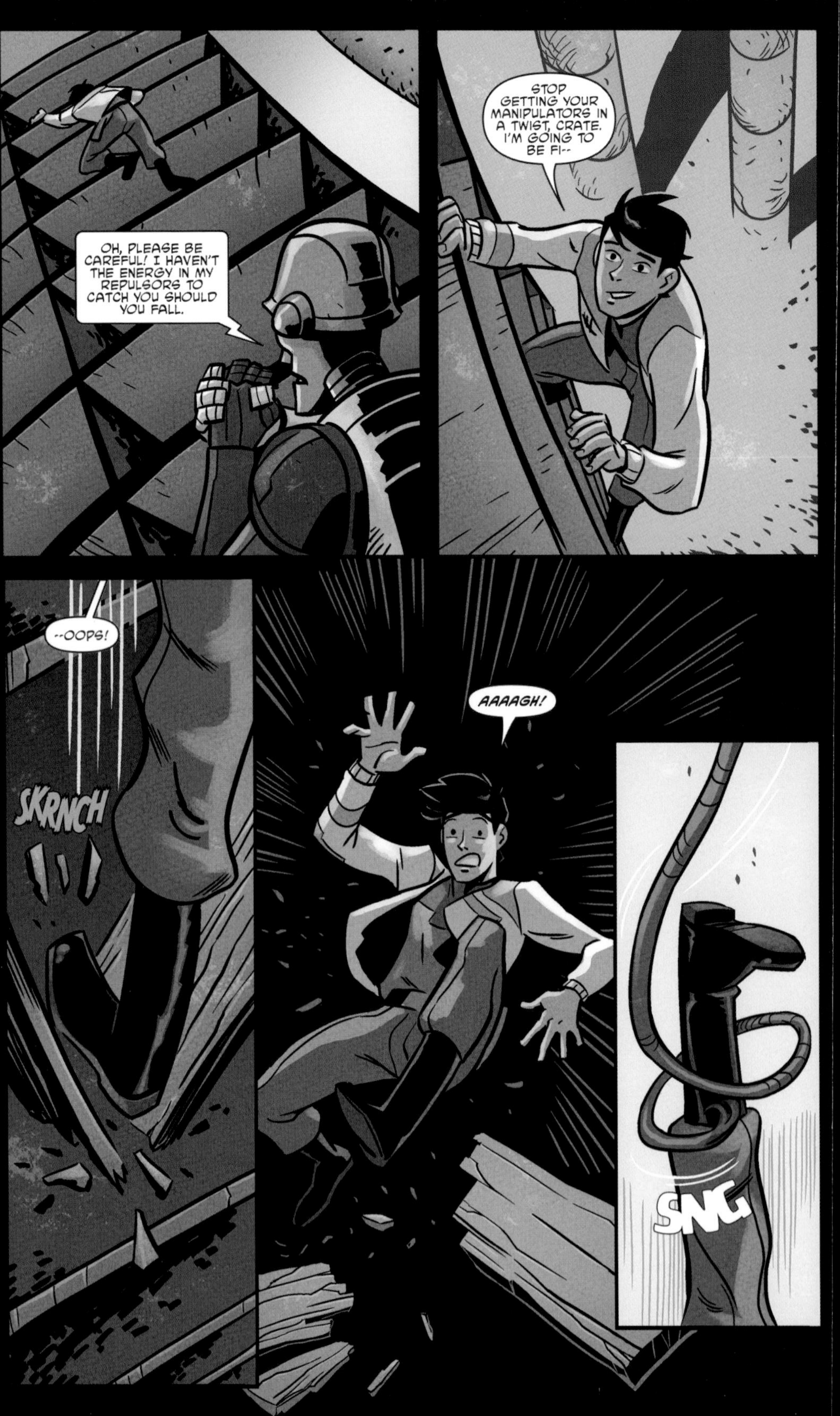
OH, PLEASE BE CAREFUL! I HAVEN'T THE ENERGY IN MY REPULSORS TO CATCH YOU SHOULD YOU FALL.
STOP GETTING YOUR MANIPULATORS IN A TWIST, CRATE. I'M GOING TO BE FI--
--OOPS!
SKRNCH
AAAAGH!
SNG

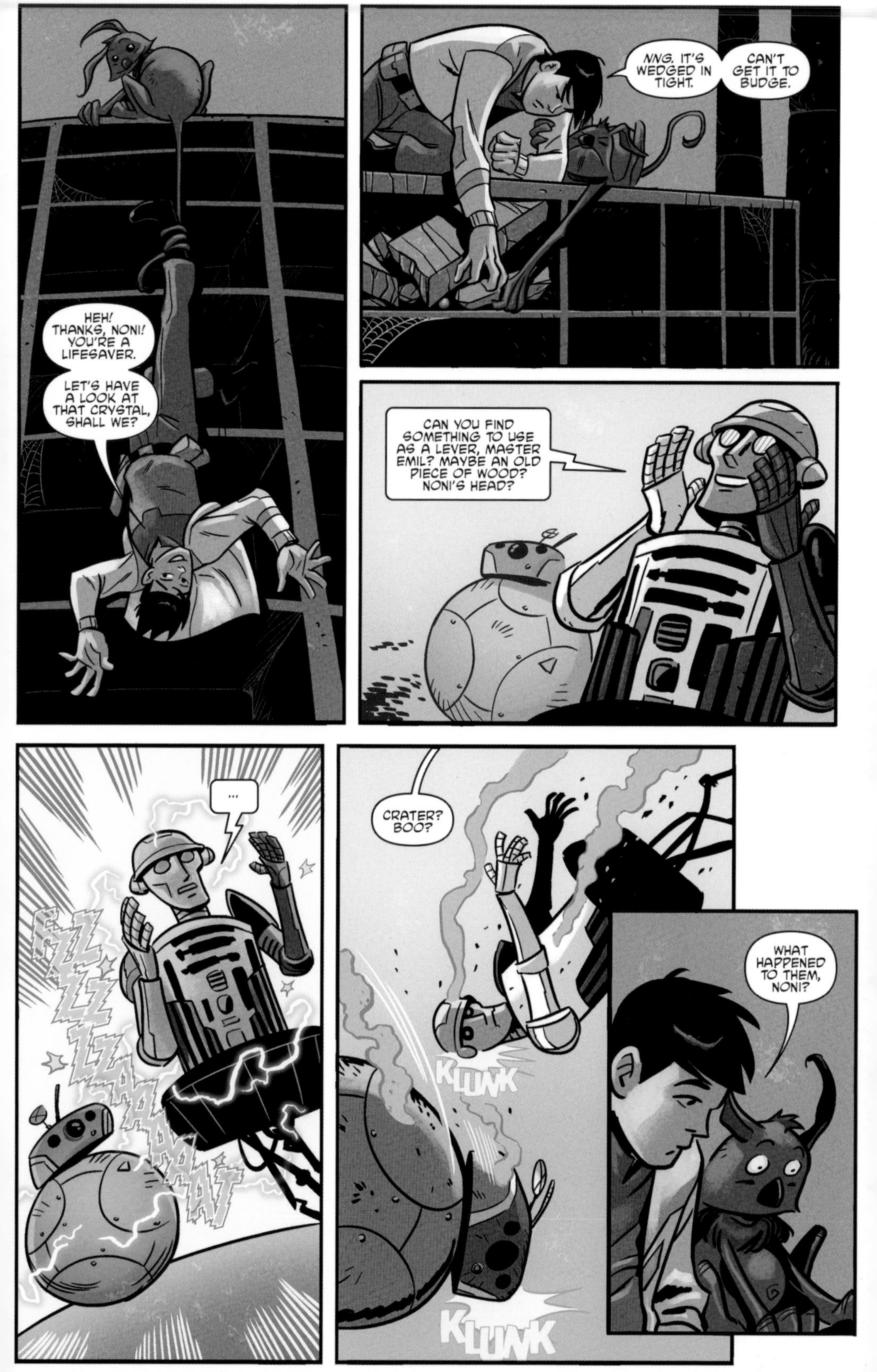
HEH! THANKS, NONI! YOU'RE A LIFESAVER.
LET'S HAVE A LOOK AT THAT CRYSTAL, SHALL WE?
NNG. IT'S WEDGED IN TIGHT.
CAN'T GET IT TO BUDGE.
CAN YOU FIND SOMETHING TO USE AS A LEVER, MASTER EMIL? MAYBE AN OLD PIECE OF WOOD? NONI'S HEAD?
...
CRATER? BOO?
KLUNK
KLUNK
WHAT HAPPENED TO THEM, NONI?

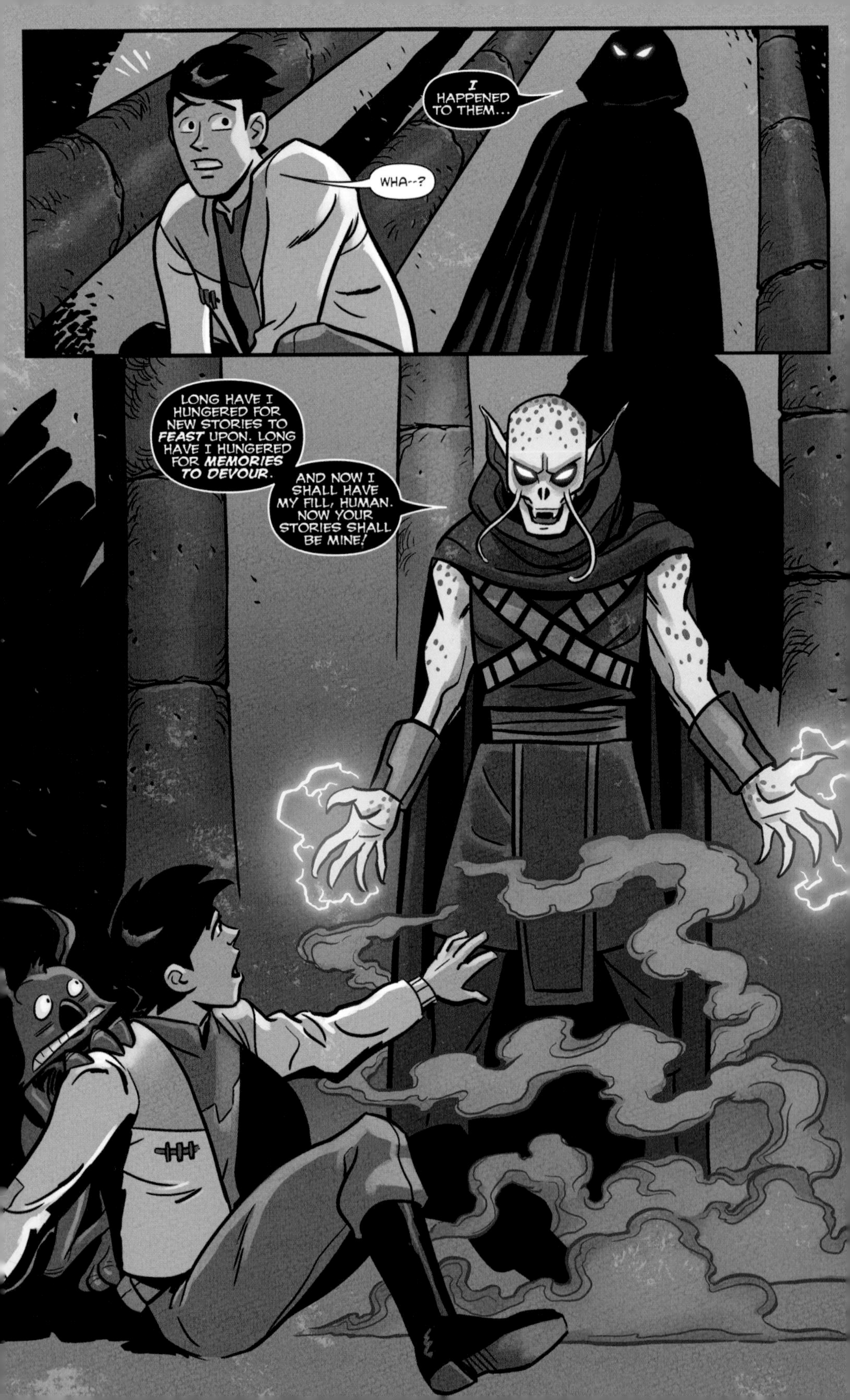
I HAPPENED TO THEM...
WHA--?
LONG HAVE I HUNGERED FOR NEW STORIES TO FEAST UPON. LONG HAVE I HUNGERED FOR MEMORIES TO DEVOUR.
AND NOW I SHALL HAVE MY FILL, HUMAN. NOW YOUR STORIES SHALL BE MINE!

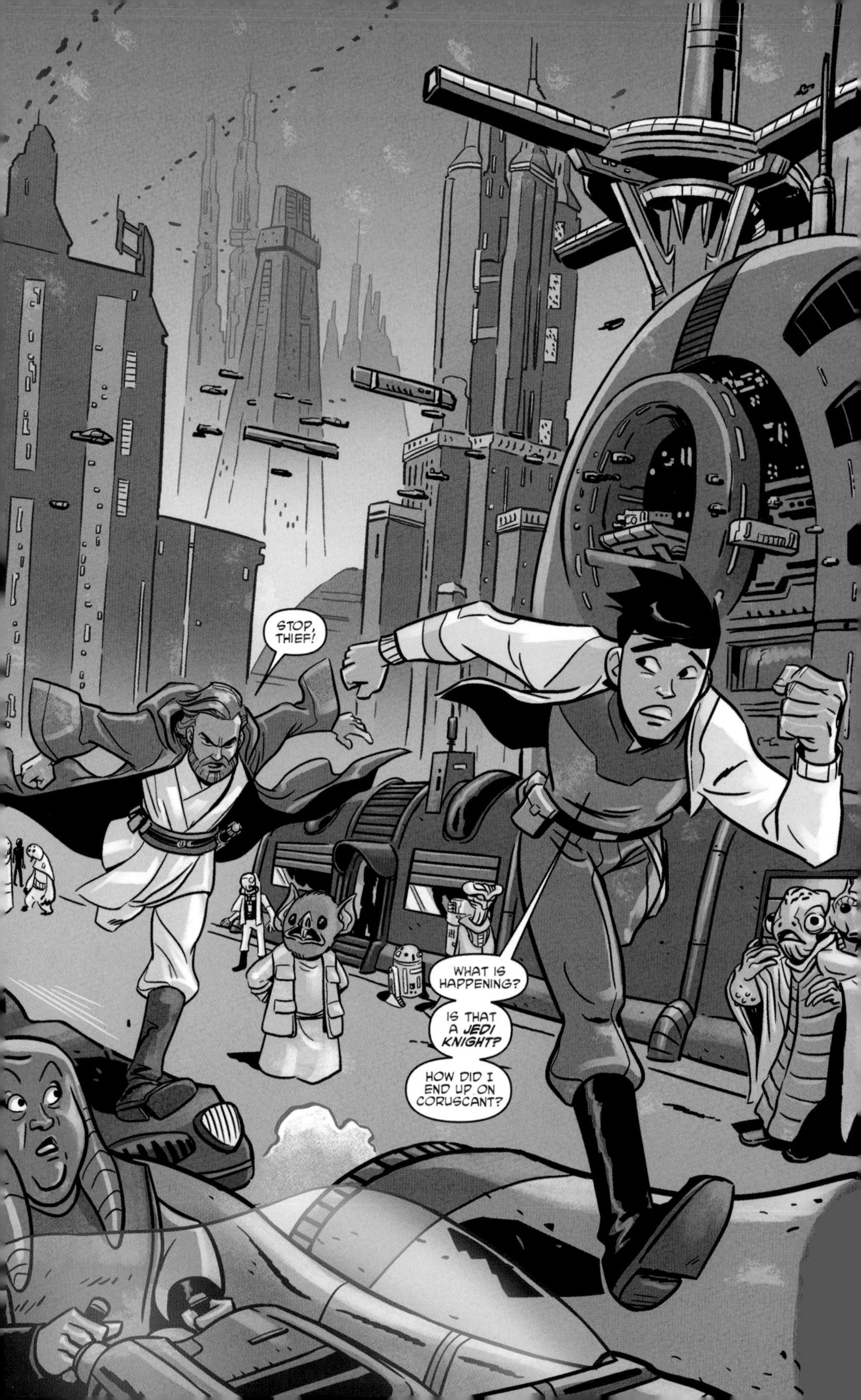
STOP, THIEF!
WHAT IS HAPPENING?
IS THAT A JEDI KNIGHT?
HOW DID I END UP ON CORUSCANT?

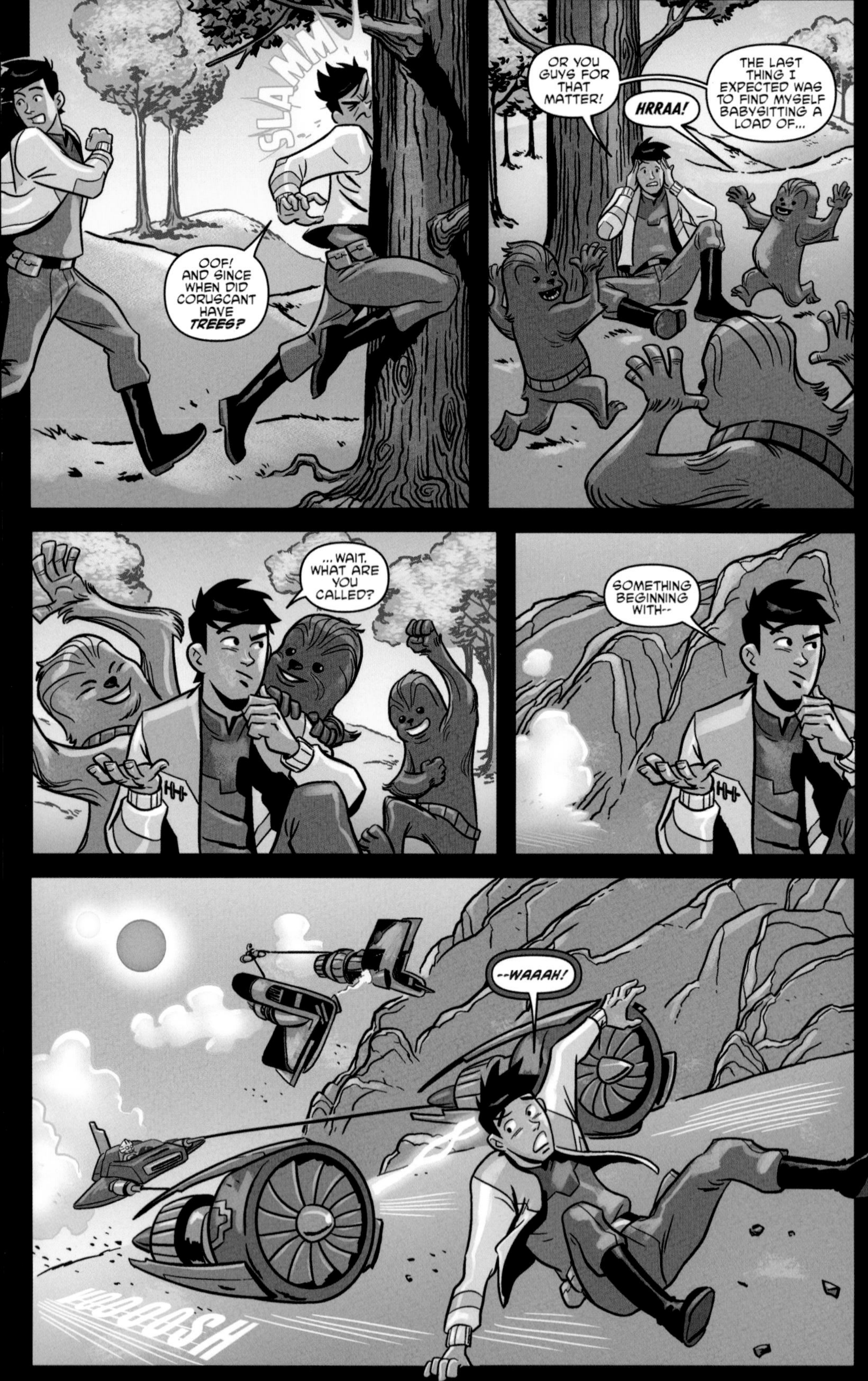
SLAMM
OOF! AND SINCE WHEN DID CORUSCANT HAVE *TREES?*
THE LAST THING I EXPECTED WAS TO FIND MYSELF BABYSITTING A LOAD OF...
HRRAA!
OR YOU GUYS FOR THAT MATTER!
...WAIT. WHAT ARE YOU CALLED?
SOMETHING BEGINNING WITH--
--WAAAH!
WHOOOSH

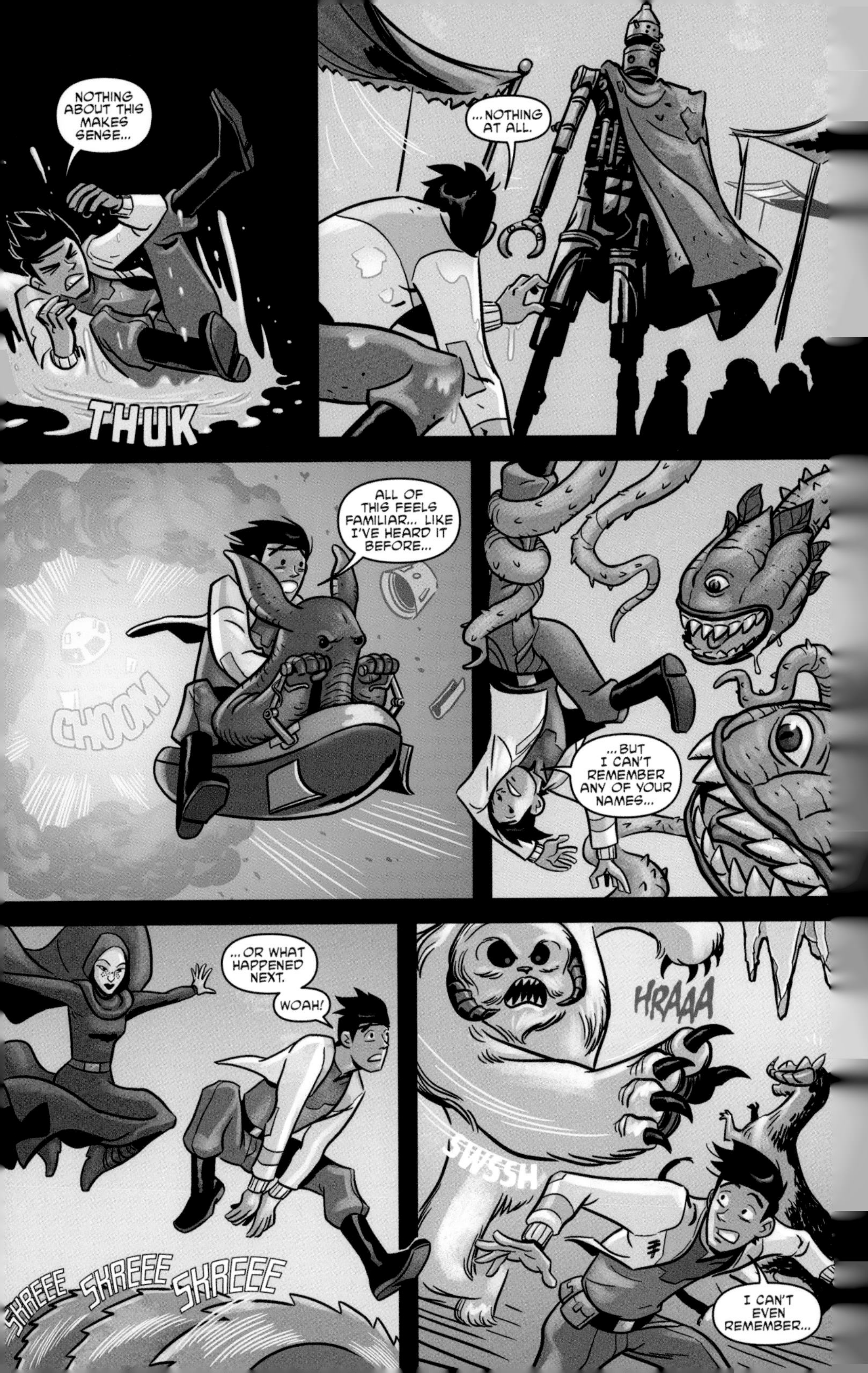
NOTHING ABOUT THIS MAKES SENSE...
THUK
...NOTHING AT ALL.
ALL OF THIS FEELS FAMILIAR... LIKE I'VE HEARD IT BEFORE...
CHOOM
...BUT I CAN'T REMEMBER ANY OF YOUR NAMES...
...OR WHAT HAPPENED NEXT.
WOAH!
SKREEE SKREEE SKREEE
HRAAA
SWSSH
I CAN'T EVEN REMEMBER...

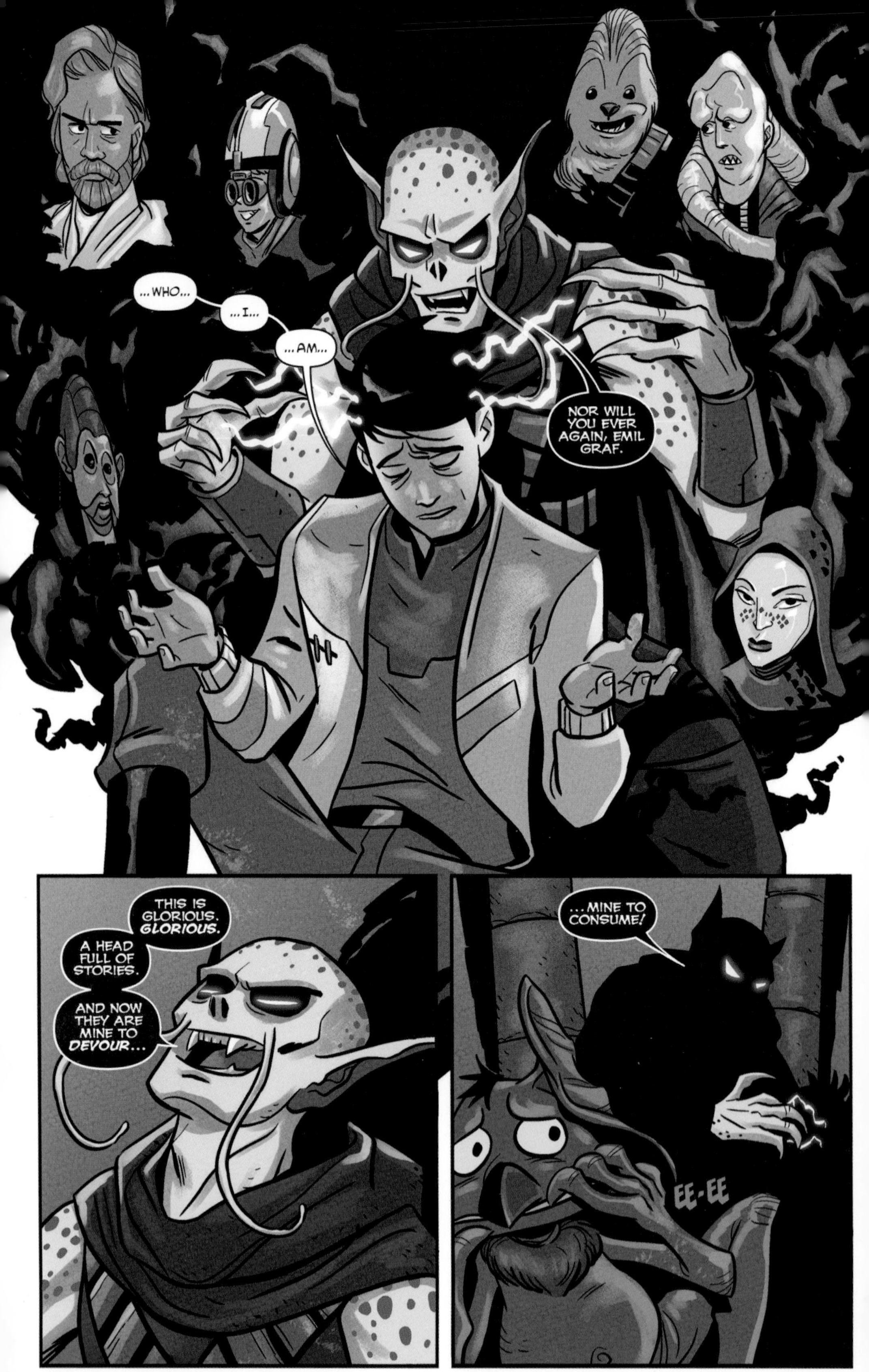
...WHO...
...I...
...AM...
NOR WILL YOU EVER AGAIN, EMIL GRAF.
THIS IS GLORIOUS. GLORIOUS.
A HEAD FULL OF STORIES.
AND NOW THEY ARE MINE TO DEVOUR...
...MINE TO CONSUME!
EE-EE

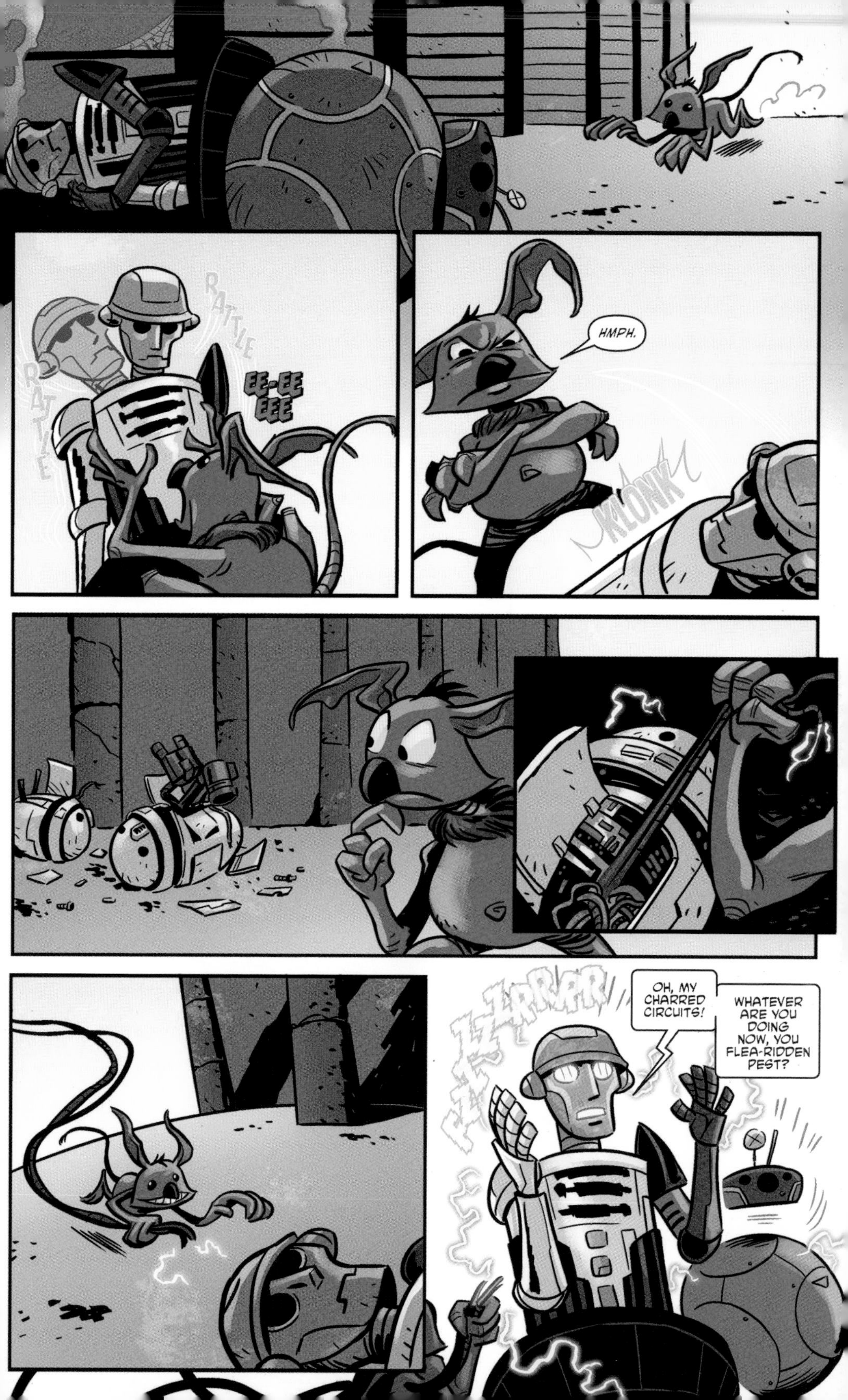
RATTLE
RATTLE
EE-EE
EEE
HMPH.
KLONK
OH, MY CHARRED CIRCUITS!
WHATEVER ARE YOU DOING NOW, YOU FLEA-RIDDEN PEST?

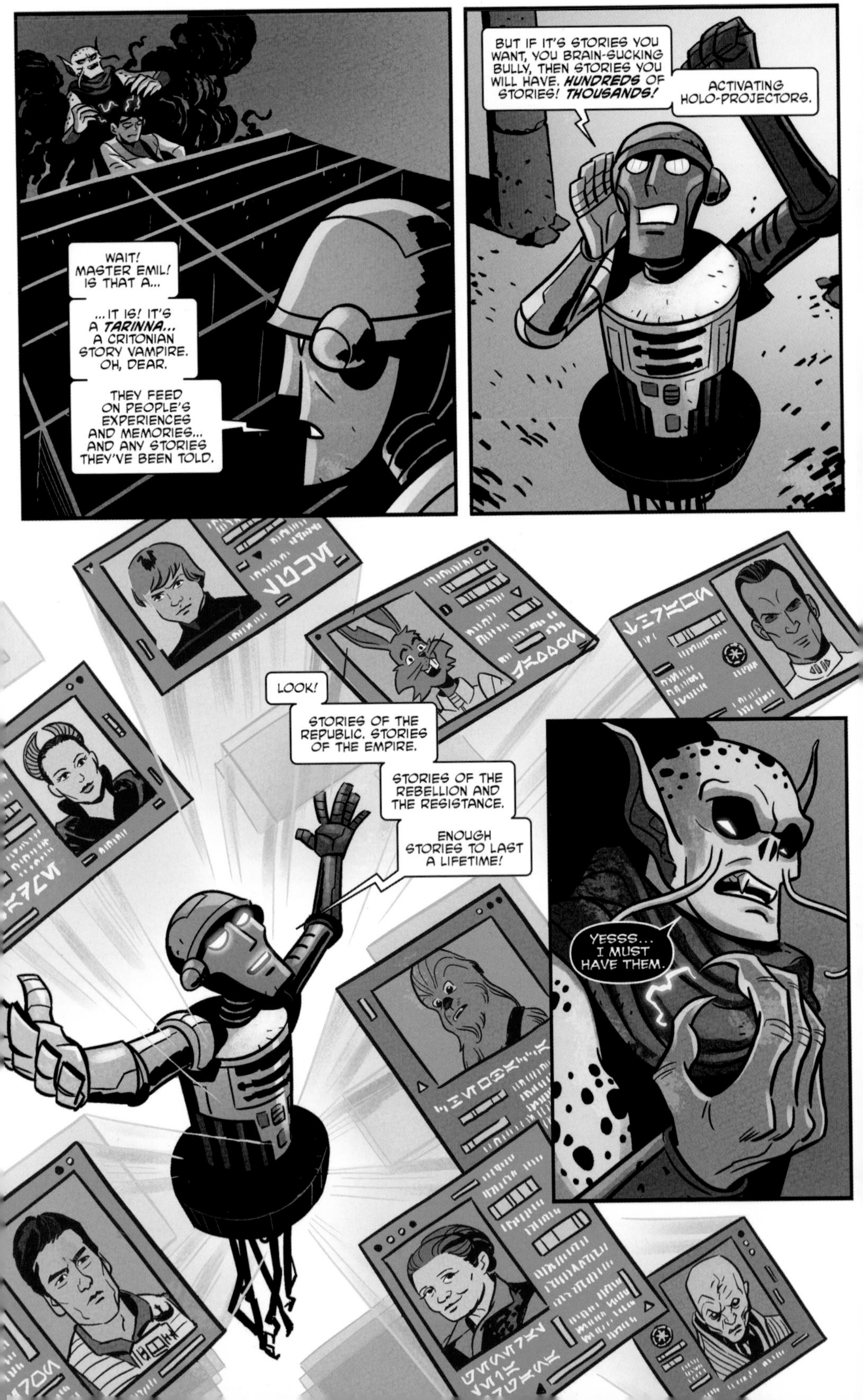
WAIT! MASTER EMIL! IS THAT A...
...IT IS! IT'S A *TARINNA...* A CRITONIAN STORY VAMPIRE. OH, DEAR.
THEY FEED ON PEOPLE'S EXPERIENCES AND MEMORIES... AND ANY STORIES THEY'VE BEEN TOLD.
BUT IF IT'S STORIES YOU WANT, YOU BRAIN-SUCKING BULLY, THEN STORIES YOU WILL HAVE. *HUNDREDS* OF STORIES! *THOUSANDS!*
ACTIVATING HOLO-PROJECTORS.
LOOK!
STORIES OF THE REPUBLIC. STORIES OF THE EMPIRE.
STORIES OF THE REBELLION AND THE RESISTANCE.
ENOUGH STORIES TO LAST A LIFETIME!
YESSS... I MUST HAVE THEM.

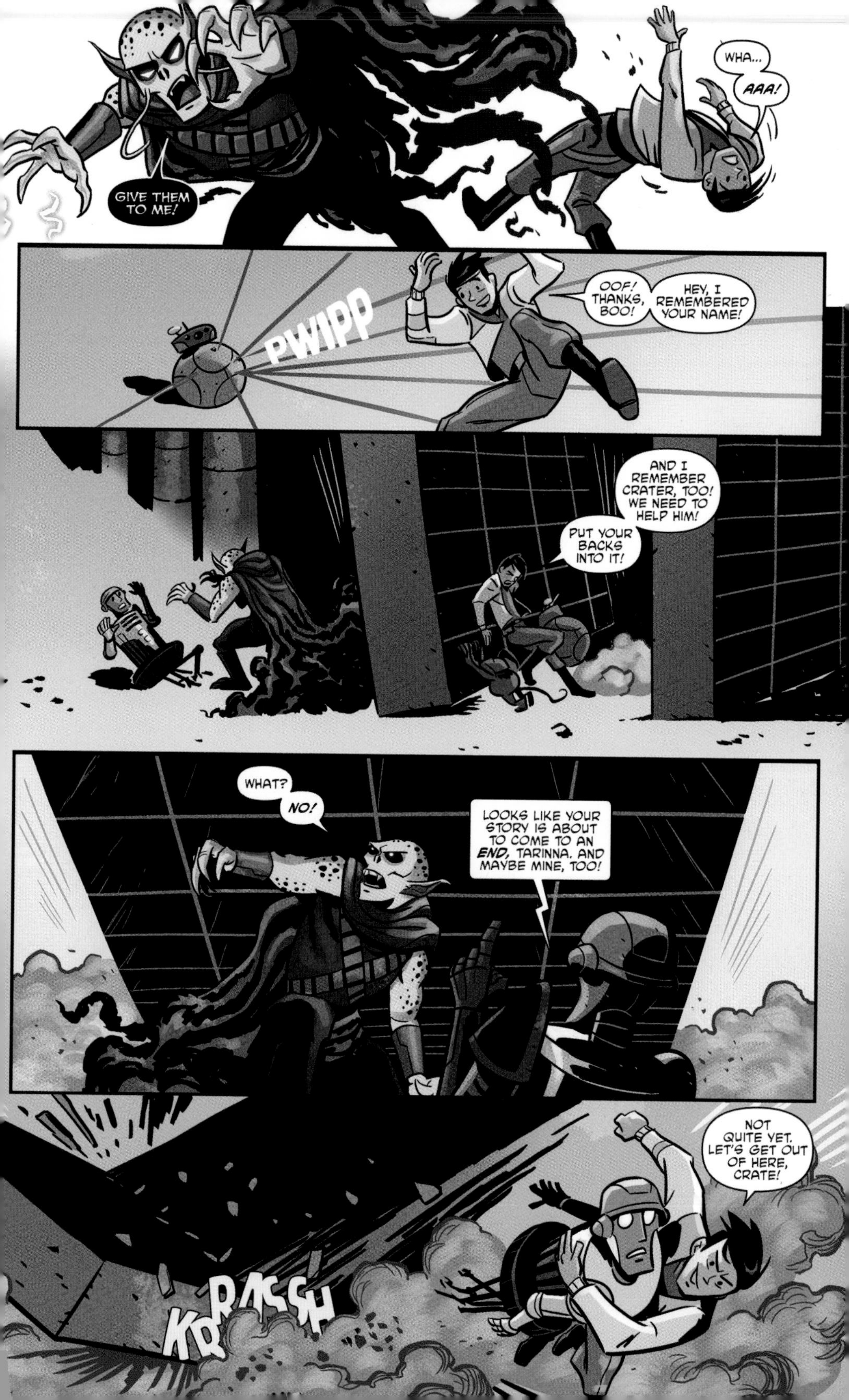
WHA...
AAA!
GIVE THEM TO ME!
PWIPP
OOF! THANKS, BOO!
HEY, I REMEMBERED YOUR NAME!
AND I REMEMBER CRATER, TOO! WE NEED TO HELP HIM!
PUT YOUR BACKS INTO IT!
WHAT?
NO!
LOOKS LIKE YOUR STORY IS ABOUT TO COME TO AN END, TARINNA. AND MAYBE MINE, TOO!
NOT QUITE YET. LET'S GET OUT OF HERE, CRATE!
KRASSH

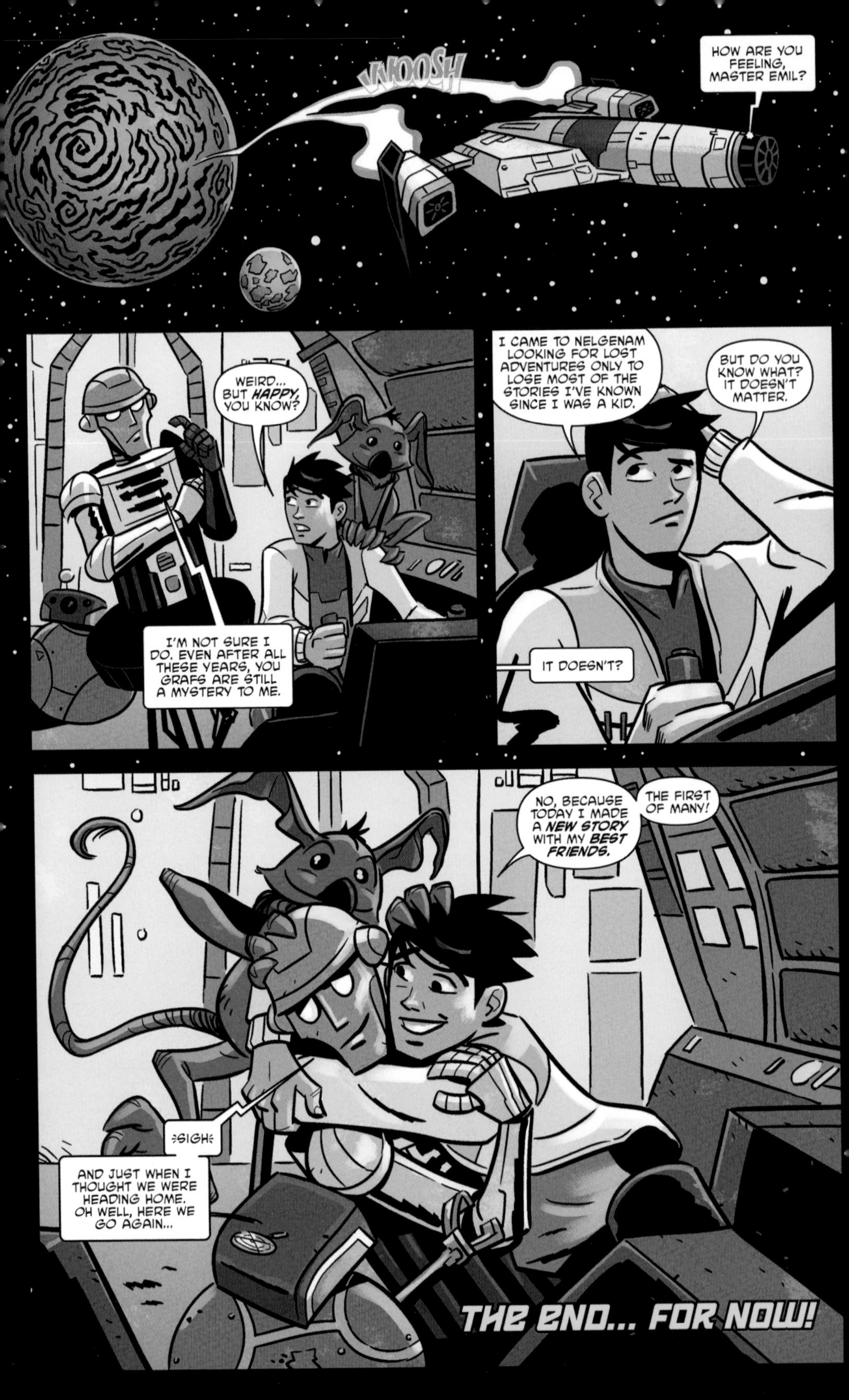

WHOOSH
HOW ARE YOU FEELING, MASTER EMIL?
WEIRD... BUT HAPPY, YOU KNOW?
I'M NOT SURE I DO. EVEN AFTER ALL THESE YEARS, YOU GRAFS ARE STILL A MYSTERY TO ME.
I CAME TO NELGENAM LOOKING FOR LOST ADVENTURES ONLY TO LOSE MOST OF THE STORIES I'VE KNOWN SINCE I WAS A KID.
BUT DO YOU KNOW WHAT? IT DOESN'T MATTER.
IT DOESN'T?
NO, BECAUSE TODAY I MADE A NEW STORY WITH MY BEST FRIENDS.
THE FIRST OF MANY!
SIGH
AND JUST WHEN I THOUGHT WE WERE HEADING HOME. OH WELL, HERE WE GO AGAIN...
THE END... FOR NOW!

STAR WARS ADVENTURES

Loyalty Test

WRITER
MICHAEL MORECI

ARTIST
ARIANNA FLOREAN

LAYOUT ASSISTANT
MARIO DEL PENNINO

COLORIST
VALENTINA TADDEO

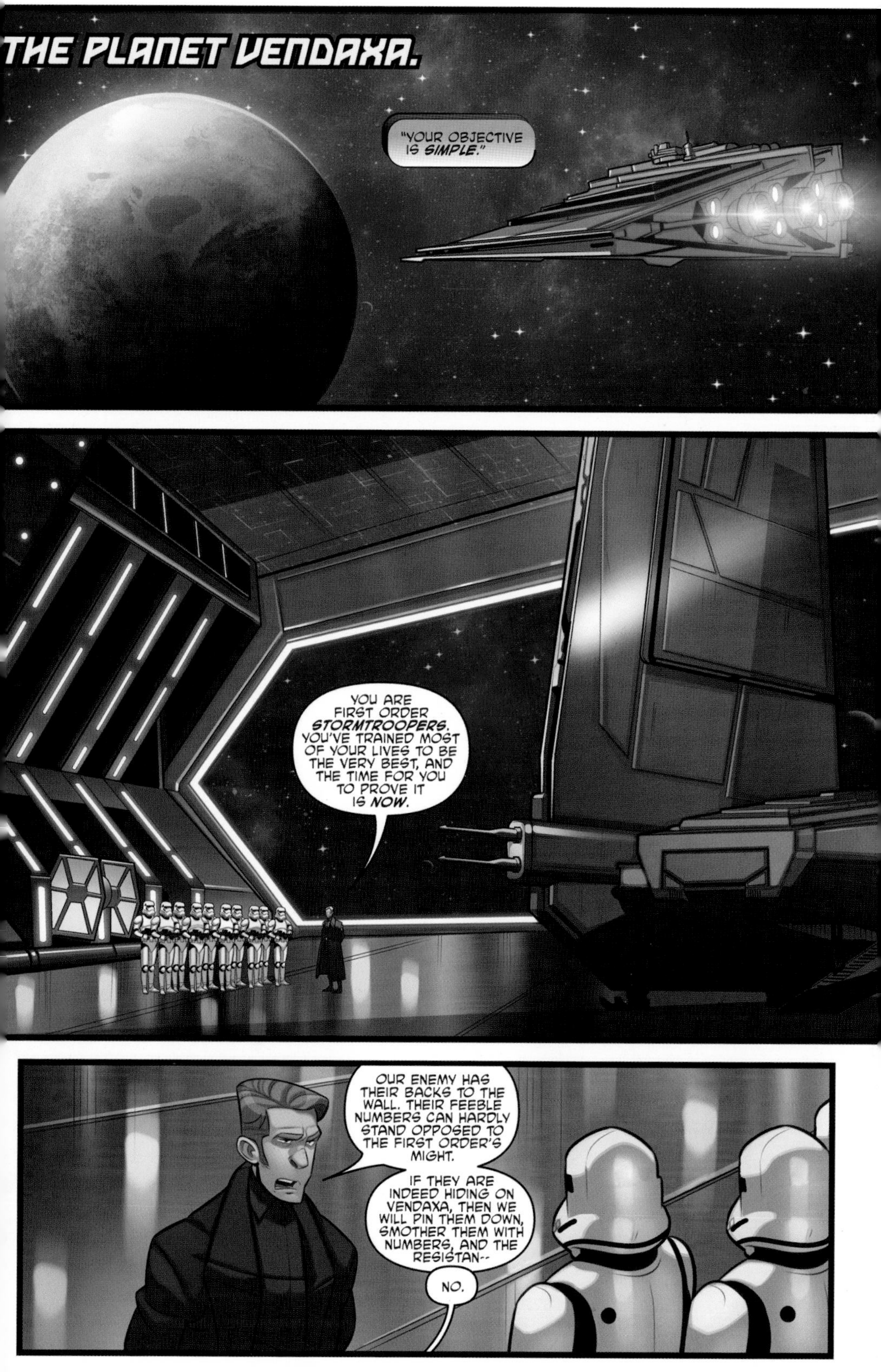
THE PLANET VENDAXA.
"YOUR OBJECTIVE IS SIMPLE."
YOU ARE FIRST ORDER STORMTROOPERS. YOU'VE TRAINED MOST OF YOUR LIVES TO BE THE VERY BEST, AND THE TIME FOR YOU TO PROVE IT IS NOW.
OUR ENEMY HAS THEIR BACKS TO THE WALL. THEIR FEEBLE NUMBERS CAN HARDLY STAND OPPOSED TO THE FIRST ORDER'S MIGHT.
IF THEY ARE INDEED HIDING ON VENDAXA, THEN WE WILL PIN THEM DOWN, SMOTHER THEM WITH NUMBERS, AND THE RESISTAN--
NO.

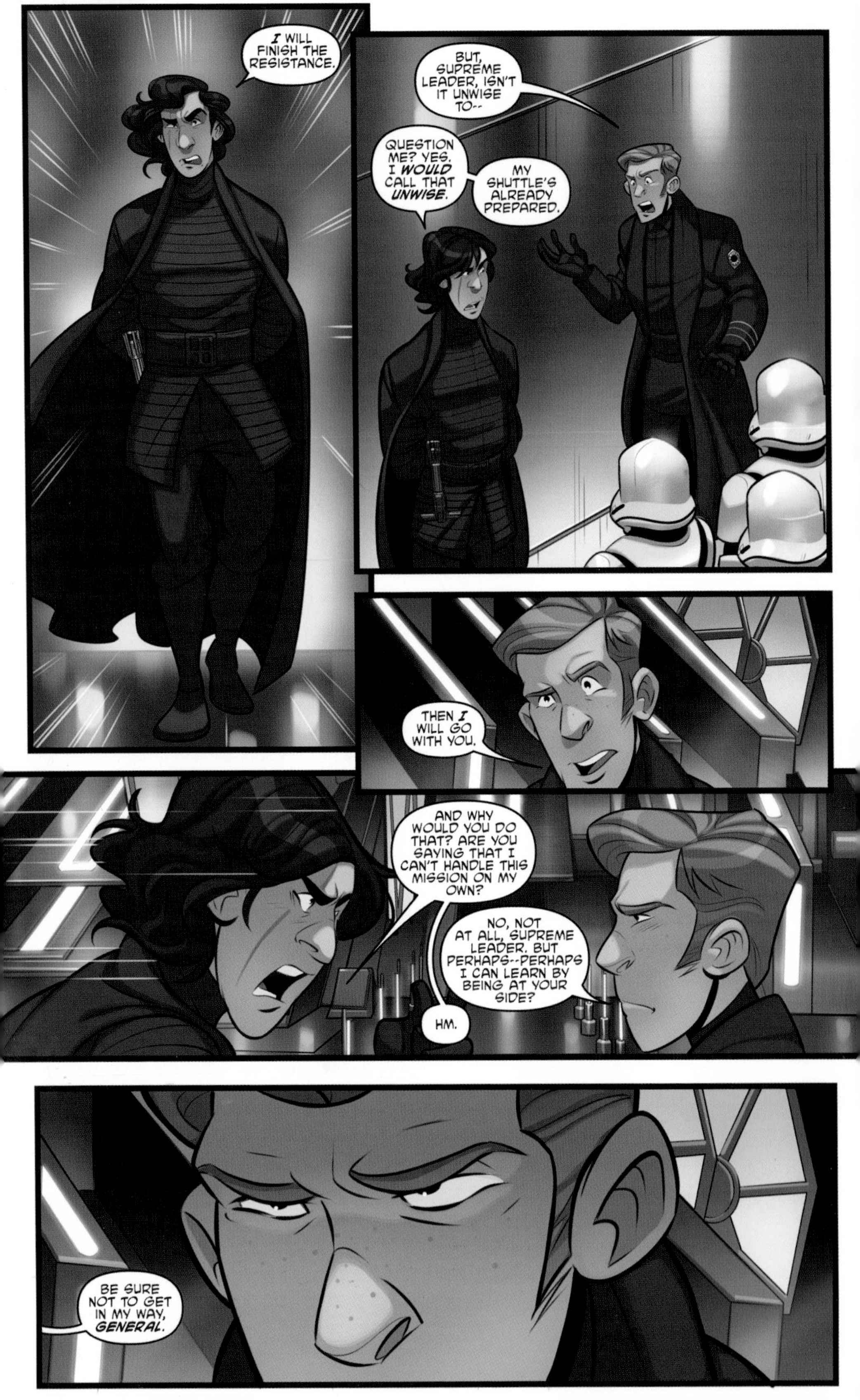
I WILL FINISH THE RESISTANCE.
BUT, SUPREME LEADER, ISN'T IT UNWISE TO--
QUESTION ME? YES. I WOULD CALL THAT UNWISE.
MY SHUTTLE'S ALREADY PREPARED.
THEN I WILL GO WITH YOU.
AND WHY WOULD YOU DO THAT? ARE YOU SAYING THAT I CAN'T HANDLE THIS MISSION ON MY OWN?
NO, NOT AT ALL, SUPREME LEADER. BUT PERHAPS--PERHAPS I CAN LEARN BY BEING AT YOUR SIDE?
HM.
BE SURE NOT TO GET IN MY WAY, GENERAL.

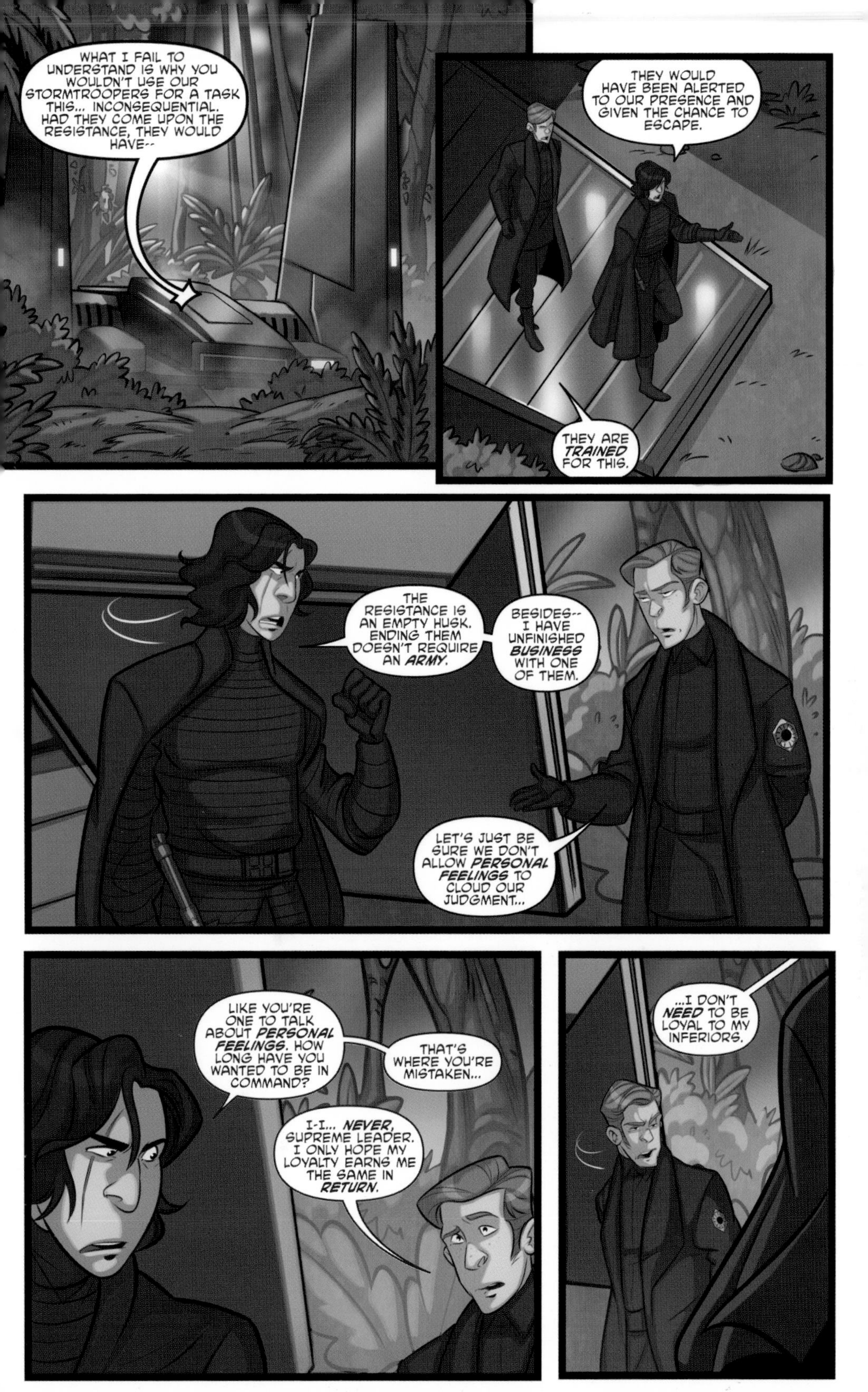
WHAT I FAIL TO UNDERSTAND IS WHY YOU WOULDN'T USE OUR STORMTROOPERS FOR A TASK THIS... INCONSEQUENTIAL. HAD THEY COME UPON THE RESISTANCE, THEY WOULD HAVE--
THEY WOULD HAVE BEEN ALERTED TO OUR PRESENCE AND GIVEN THE CHANCE TO ESCAPE.
THEY ARE *TRAINED* FOR THIS.
THE RESISTANCE IS AN EMPTY HUSK. ENDING THEM DOESN'T REQUIRE AN *ARMY*.
BESIDES-- I HAVE UNFINISHED *BUSINESS* WITH ONE OF THEM.
LET'S JUST BE SURE WE DON'T ALLOW *PERSONAL FEELINGS* TO CLOUD OUR JUDGMENT...
LIKE YOU'RE ONE TO TALK ABOUT *PERSONAL FEELINGS*. HOW LONG HAVE YOU WANTED TO BE IN COMMAND?
I-I... *NEVER*, SUPREME LEADER. I ONLY HOPE MY LOYALTY EARNS ME THE SAME IN *RETURN*.
THAT'S WHERE YOU'RE MISTAKEN...
...I DON'T *NEED* TO BE LOYAL TO MY INFERIORS.

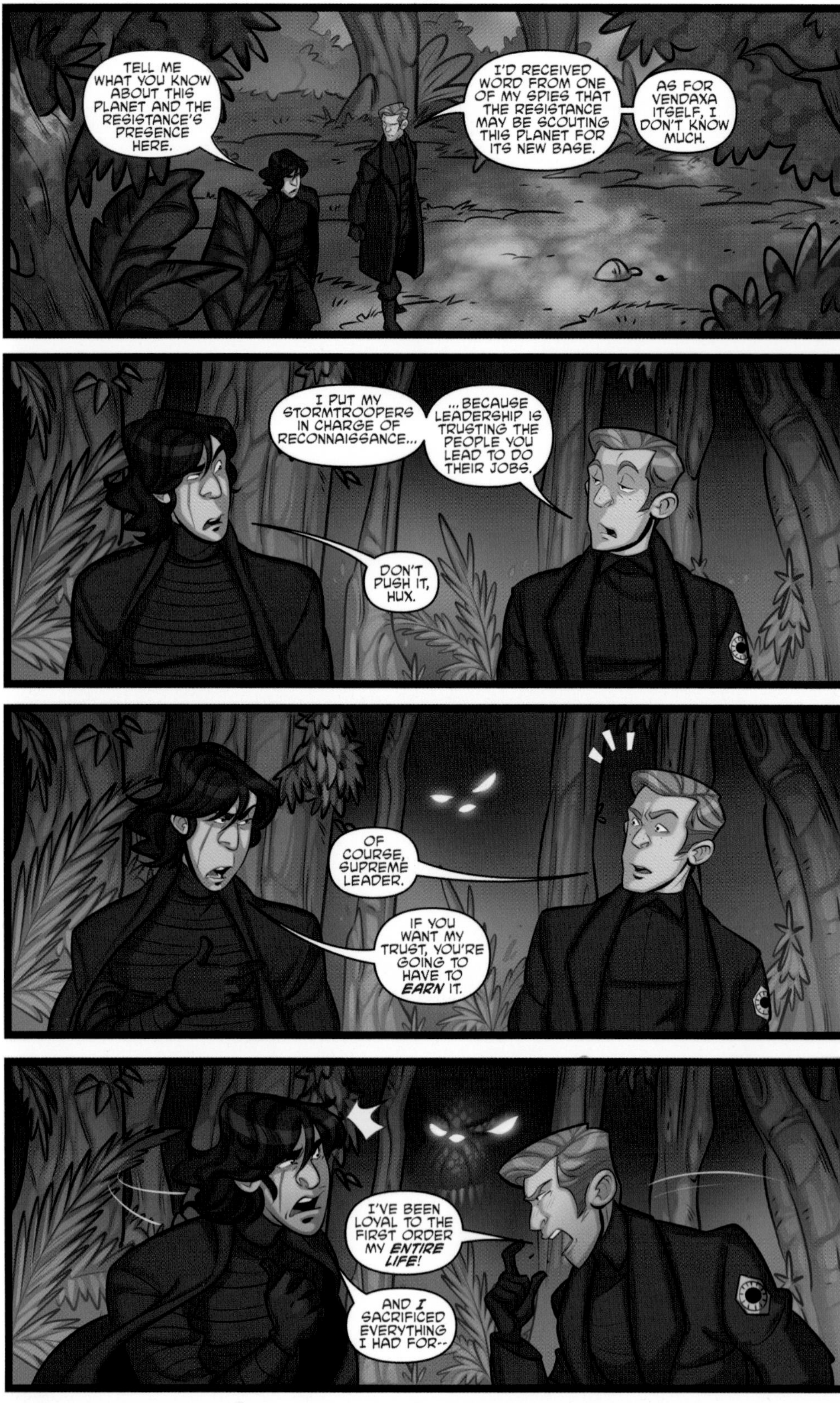
TELL ME WHAT YOU KNOW ABOUT THIS PLANET AND THE RESISTANCE'S PRESENCE HERE.
I'D RECEIVED WORD FROM ONE OF MY SPIES THAT THE RESISTANCE MAY BE SCOUTING THIS PLANET FOR ITS NEW BASE.
AS FOR VENDAXA ITSELF, I DON'T KNOW MUCH.
I PUT MY STORMTROOPERS IN CHARGE OF RECONNAISSANCE...
...BECAUSE LEADERSHIP IS TRUSTING THE PEOPLE YOU LEAD TO DO THEIR JOBS.
DON'T PUSH IT, HUX.
OF COURSE, SUPREME LEADER.
IF YOU WANT MY TRUST, YOU'RE GOING TO HAVE TO *EARN* IT.
I'VE BEEN LOYAL TO THE FIRST ORDER MY *ENTIRE LIFE*!
AND *I* SACRIFICED EVERYTHING I HAD FOR--

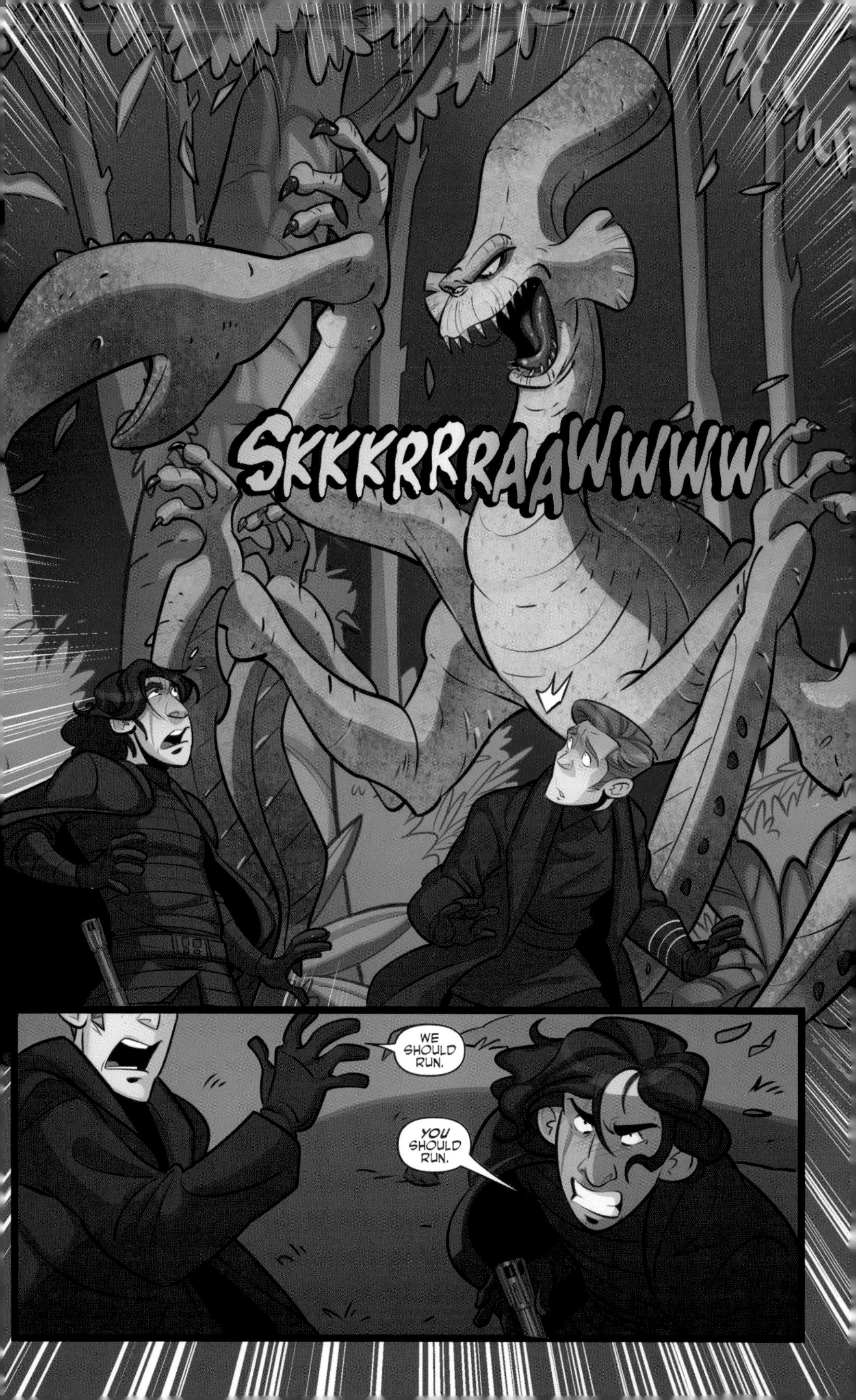
SKKKRRRAAWWWW
WE SHOULD RUN.
YOU SHOULD RUN.

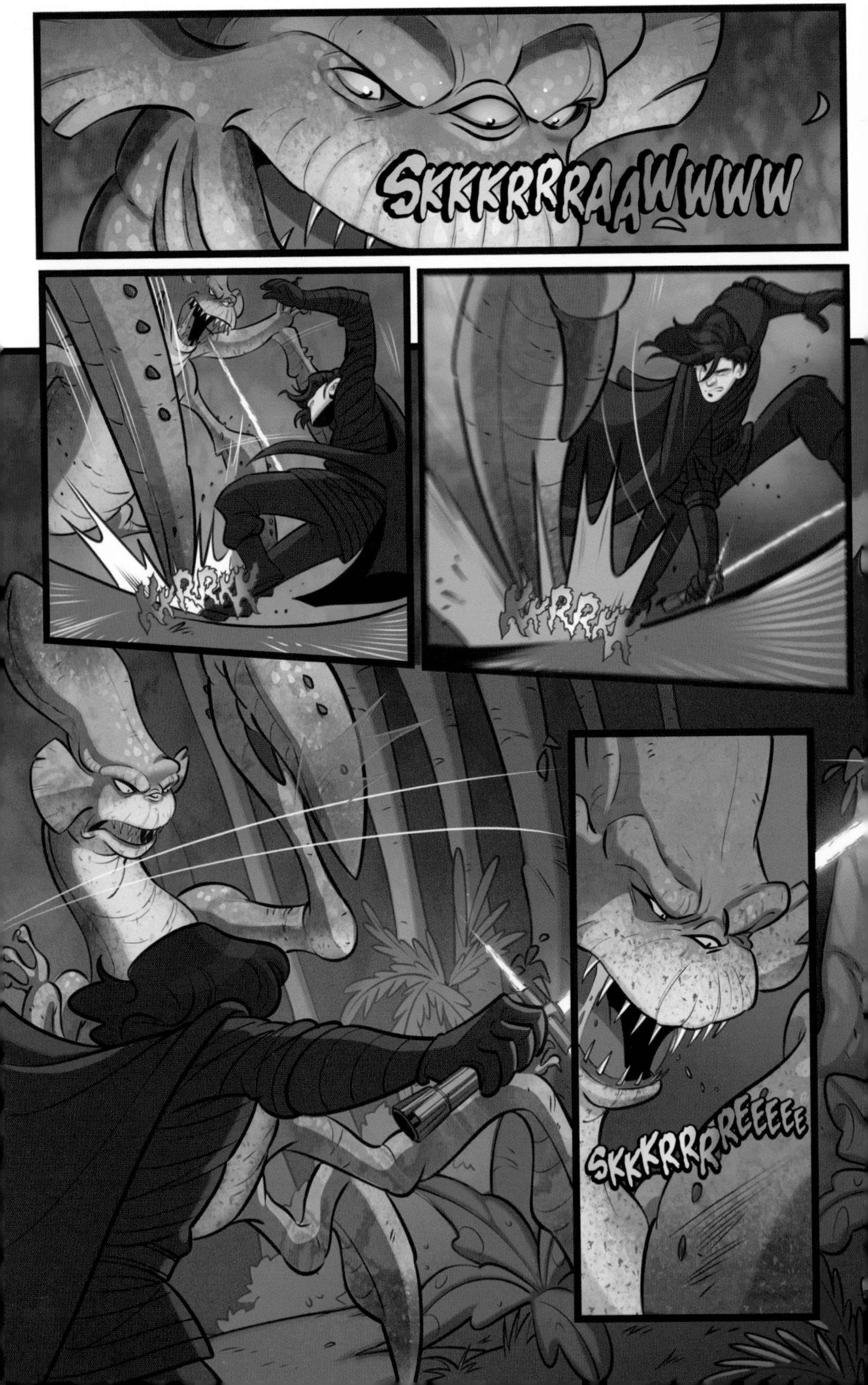
SKKKRRRRAAWWWW
SKKRRRREEEEE

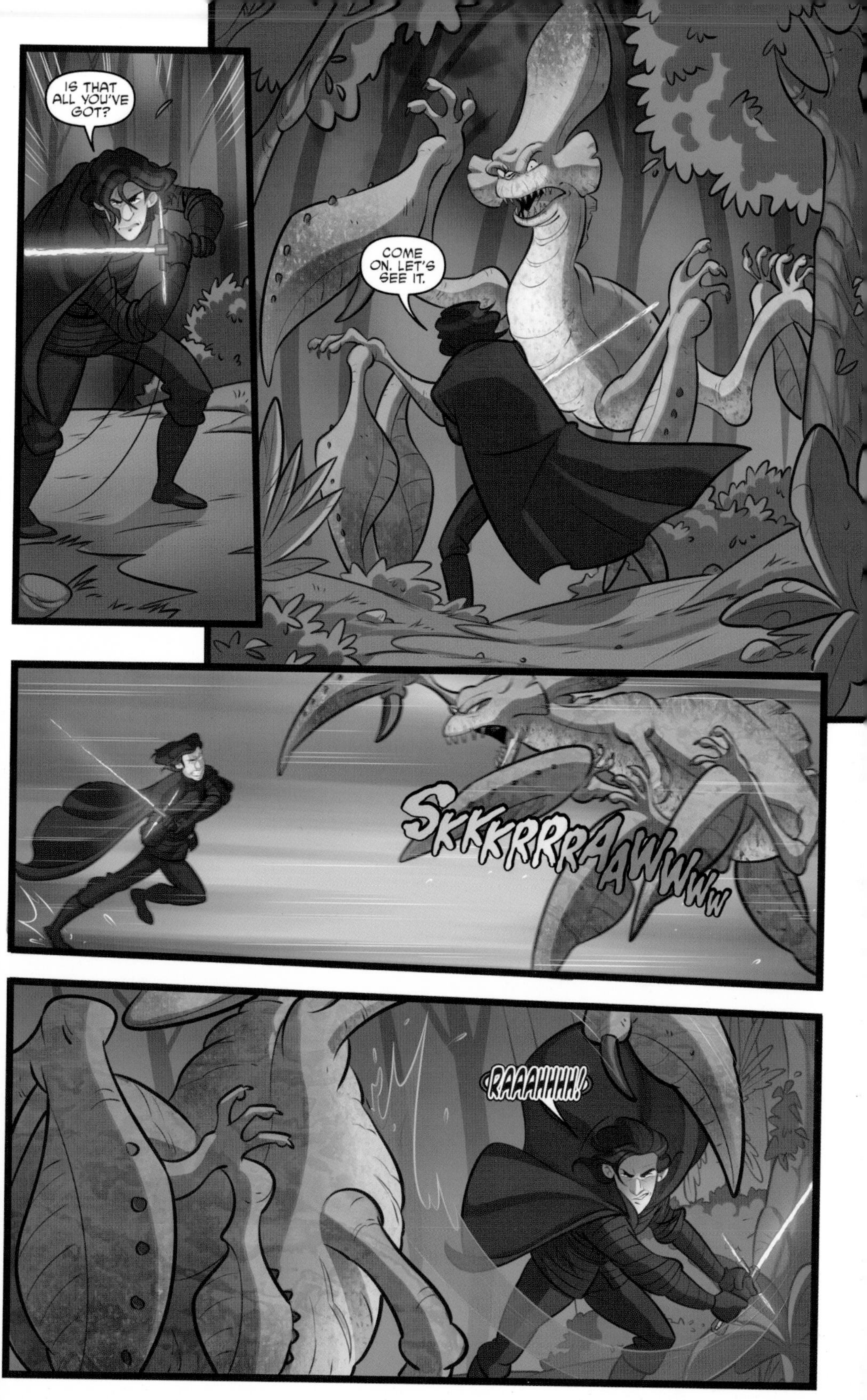
IS THAT ALL YOU'VE GOT?
COME ON. LET'S SEE IT.
SKKKRRRRAAWWWW
RAAAHHHH!

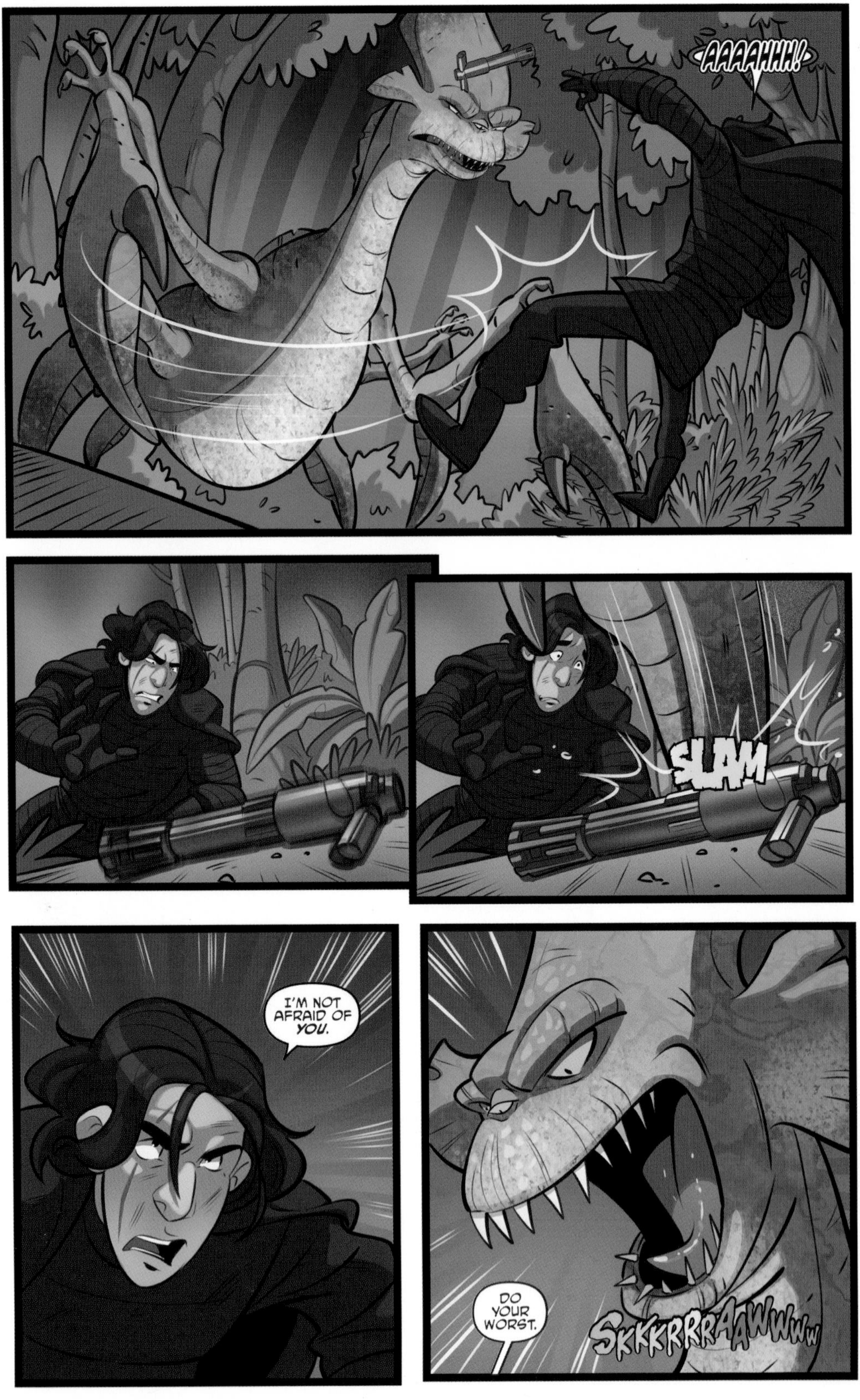
AAAAHHH!
SLAM
I'M NOT AFRAID OF YOU.
DO YOUR WORST.
SKKKRRRAAWWWW

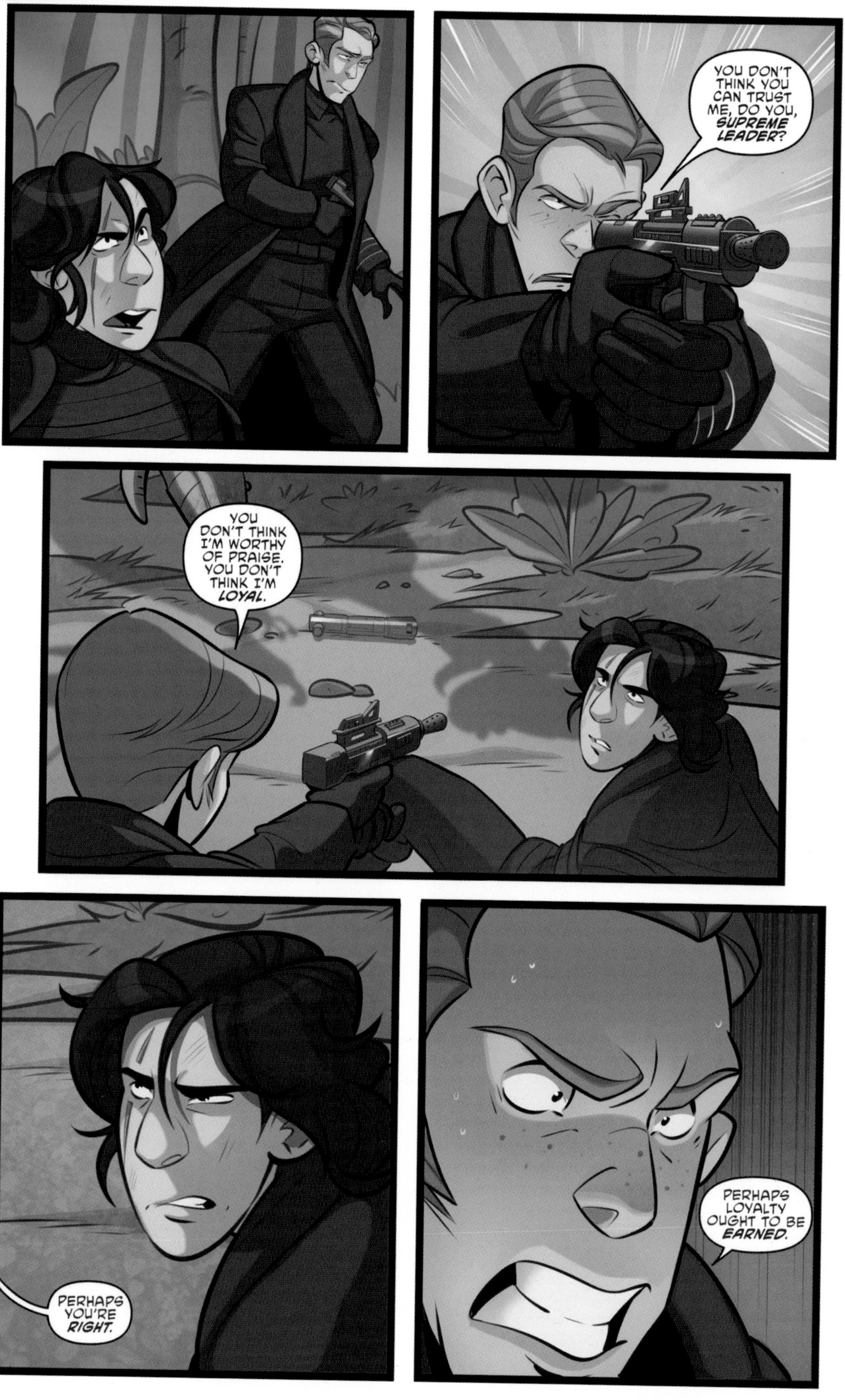
YOU DON'T THINK YOU CAN TRUST ME, DO YOU, SUPREME LEADER?
YOU DON'T THINK I'M WORTHY OF PRAISE. YOU DON'T THINK I'M LOYAL.
PERHAPS YOU'RE RIGHT.
PERHAPS LOYALTY OUGHT TO BE EARNED.

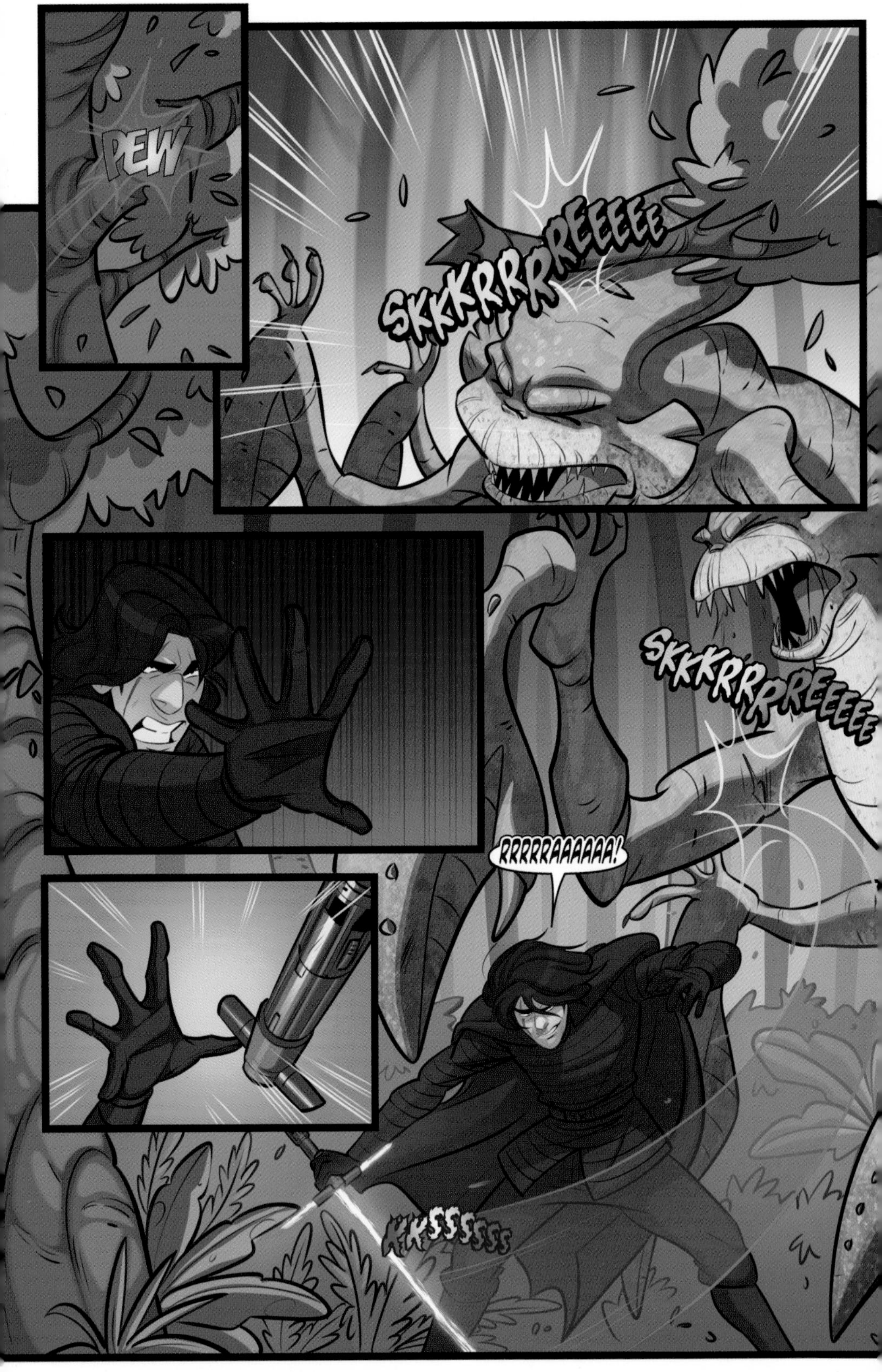
PEW
SKKRRRREEEEE
SKKKRRRREEEEEE
RRRRRAAAAAAA!
KKSSSSSSS

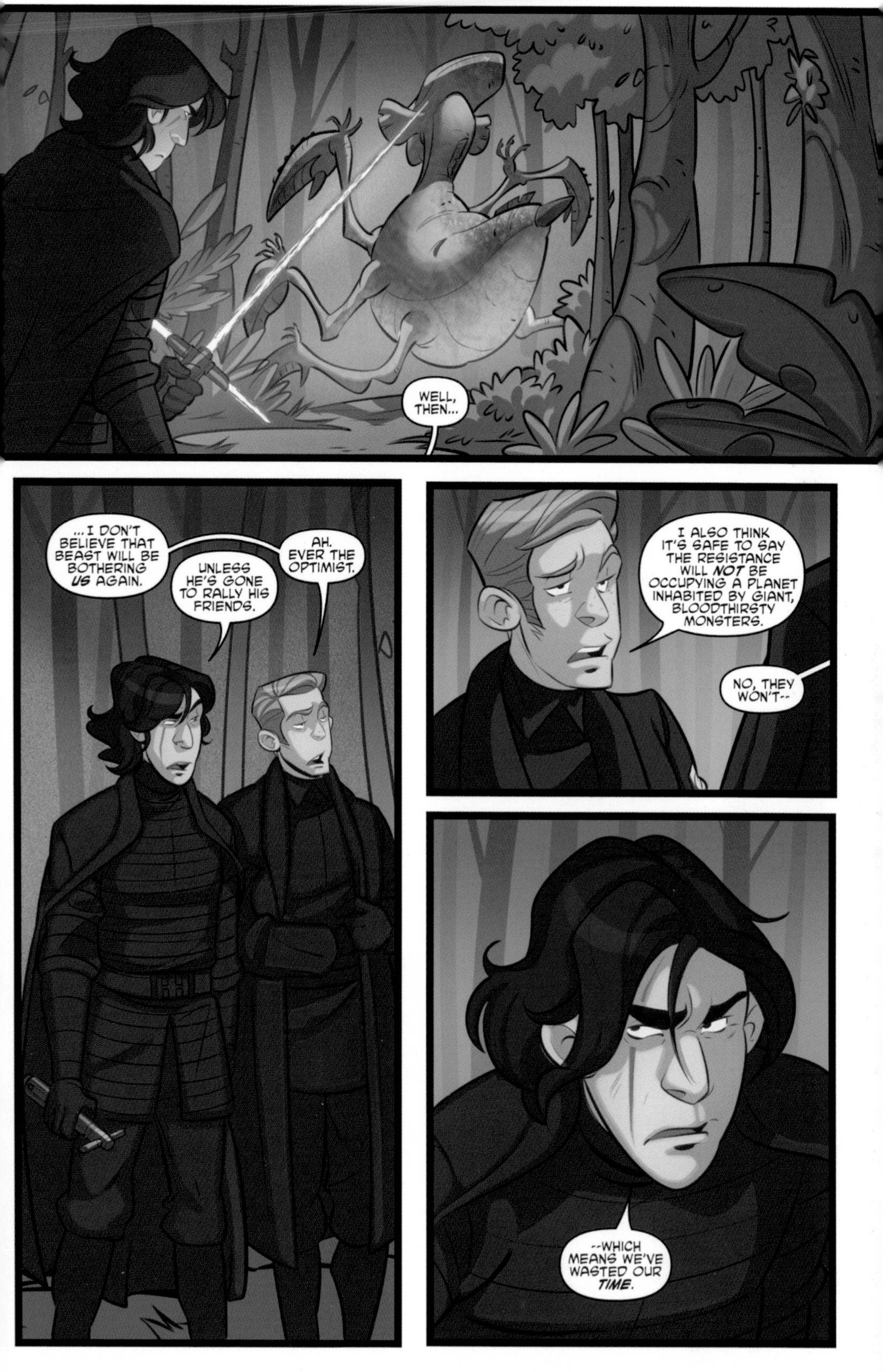
WELL, THEN...
...I DON'T BELIEVE THAT BEAST WILL BE BOTHERING US AGAIN.
UNLESS HE'S GONE TO RALLY HIS FRIENDS.
AH. EVER THE OPTIMIST.
I ALSO THINK IT'S SAFE TO SAY THE RESISTANCE WILL NOT BE OCCUPYING A PLANET INHABITED BY GIANT, BLOODTHIRSTY MONSTERS.
NO, THEY WON'T--
--WHICH MEANS WE'VE WASTED OUR TIME.

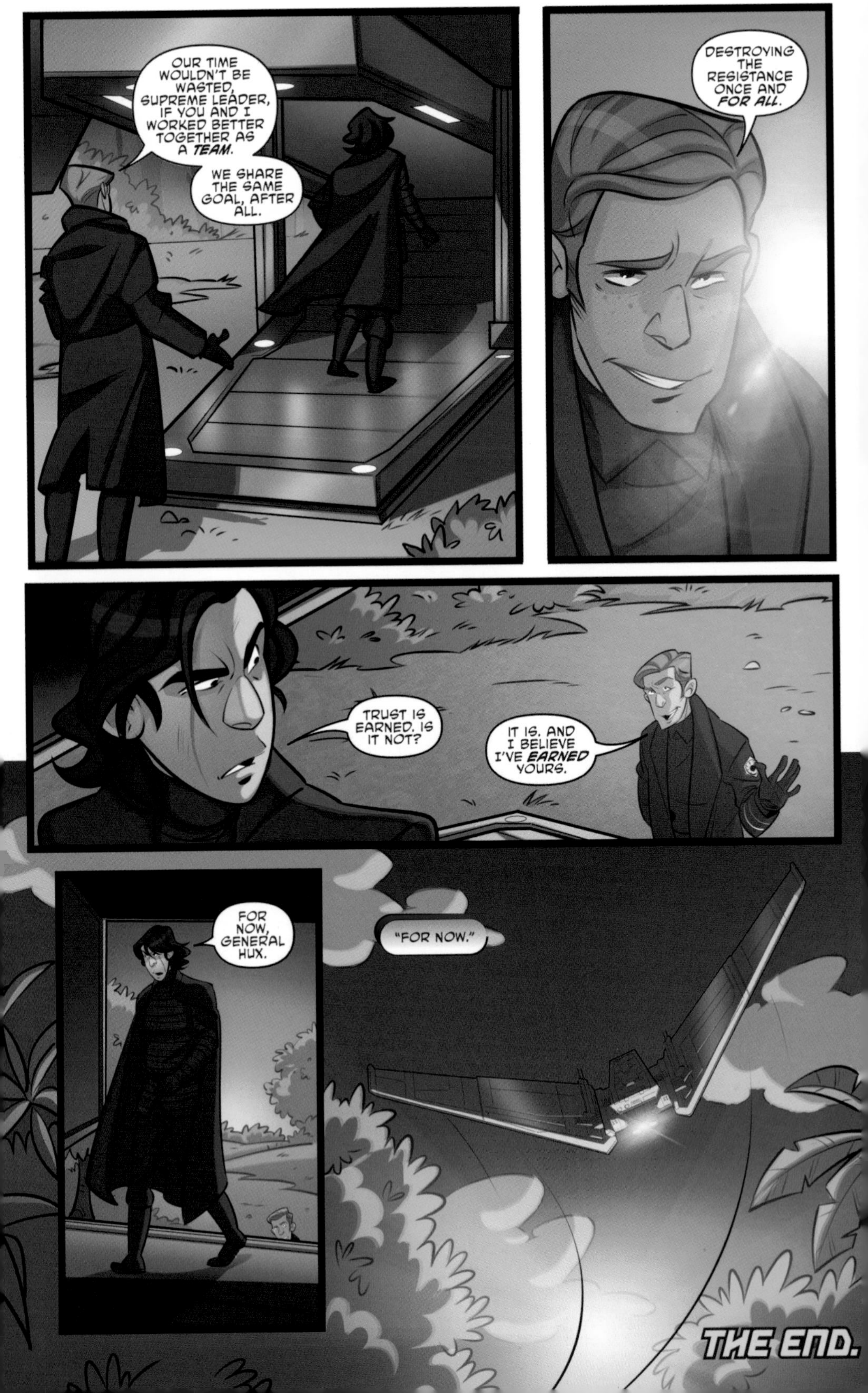
OUR TIME WOULDN'T BE WASTED, SUPREME LEADER, IF YOU AND I WORKED BETTER TOGETHER AS A TEAM.
WE SHARE THE SAME GOAL, AFTER ALL.
DESTROYING THE RESISTANCE ONCE AND FOR ALL.
TRUST IS EARNED. IS IT NOT?
IT IS. AND I BELIEVE I'VE EARNED YOURS.
FOR NOW, GENERAL HUX.
"FOR NOW."
THE END.

STAR WARS
ADVENTURES

Squad Goals

WRITER
MICHAEL MORECI

ARTIST
ARIANNA FLOREAN

COLORIST
VALENTINA TADDEO

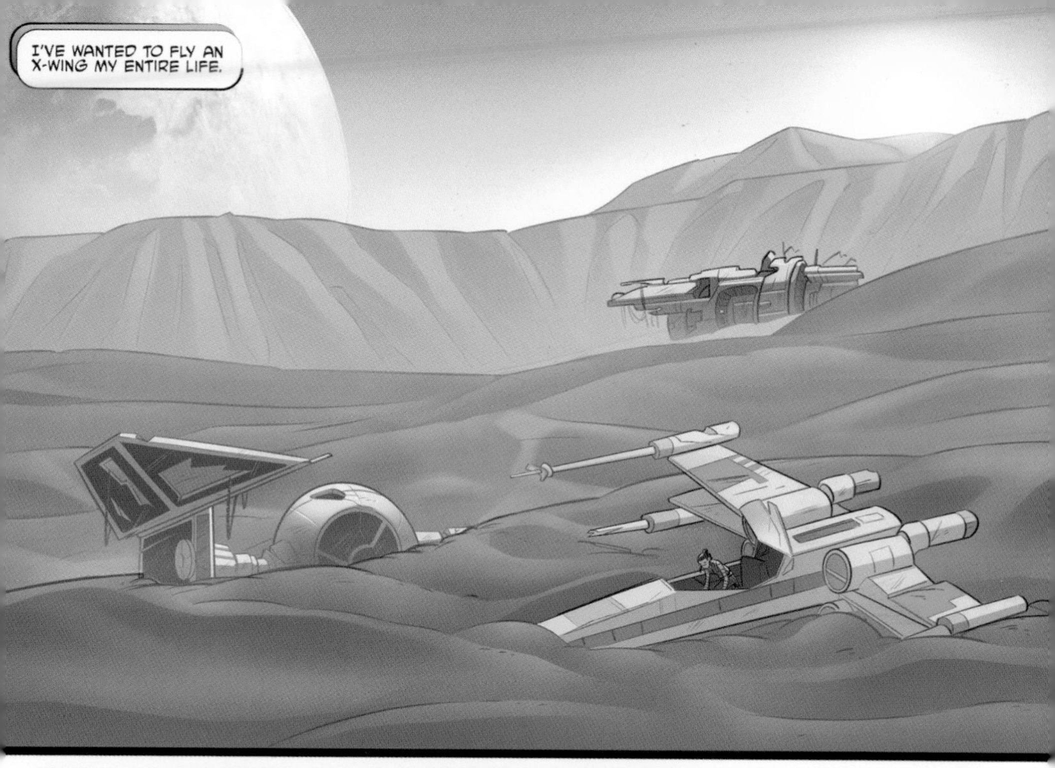
I'VE WANTED TO FLY AN X-WING MY ENTIRE LIFE.

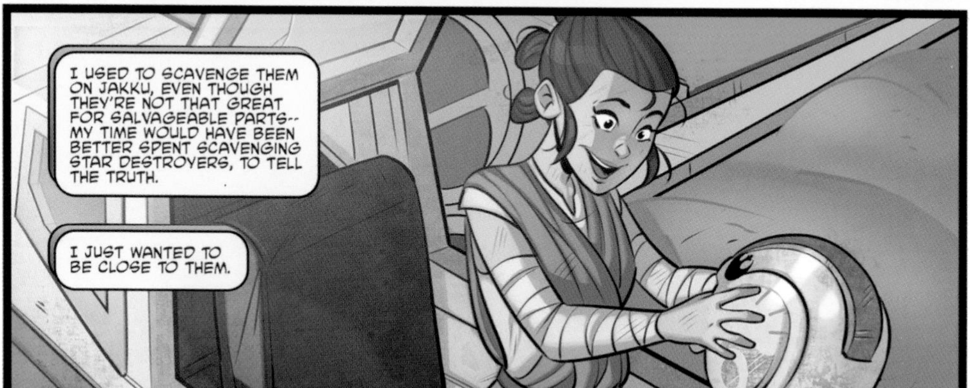
I USED TO SCAVENGE THEM ON JAKKU, EVEN THOUGH THEY'RE NOT THAT GREAT FOR SALVAGEABLE PARTS-- MY TIME WOULD HAVE BEEN BETTER SPENT SCAVENGING STAR DESTROYERS, TO TELL THE TRUTH.
I JUST WANTED TO BE CLOSE TO THEM.

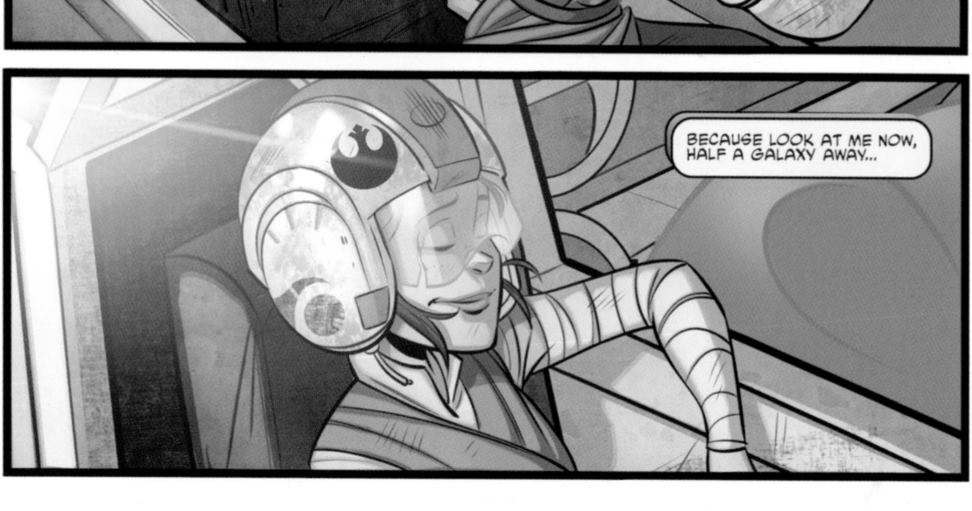
BECAUSE LOOK AT ME NOW, HALF A GALAXY AWAY...

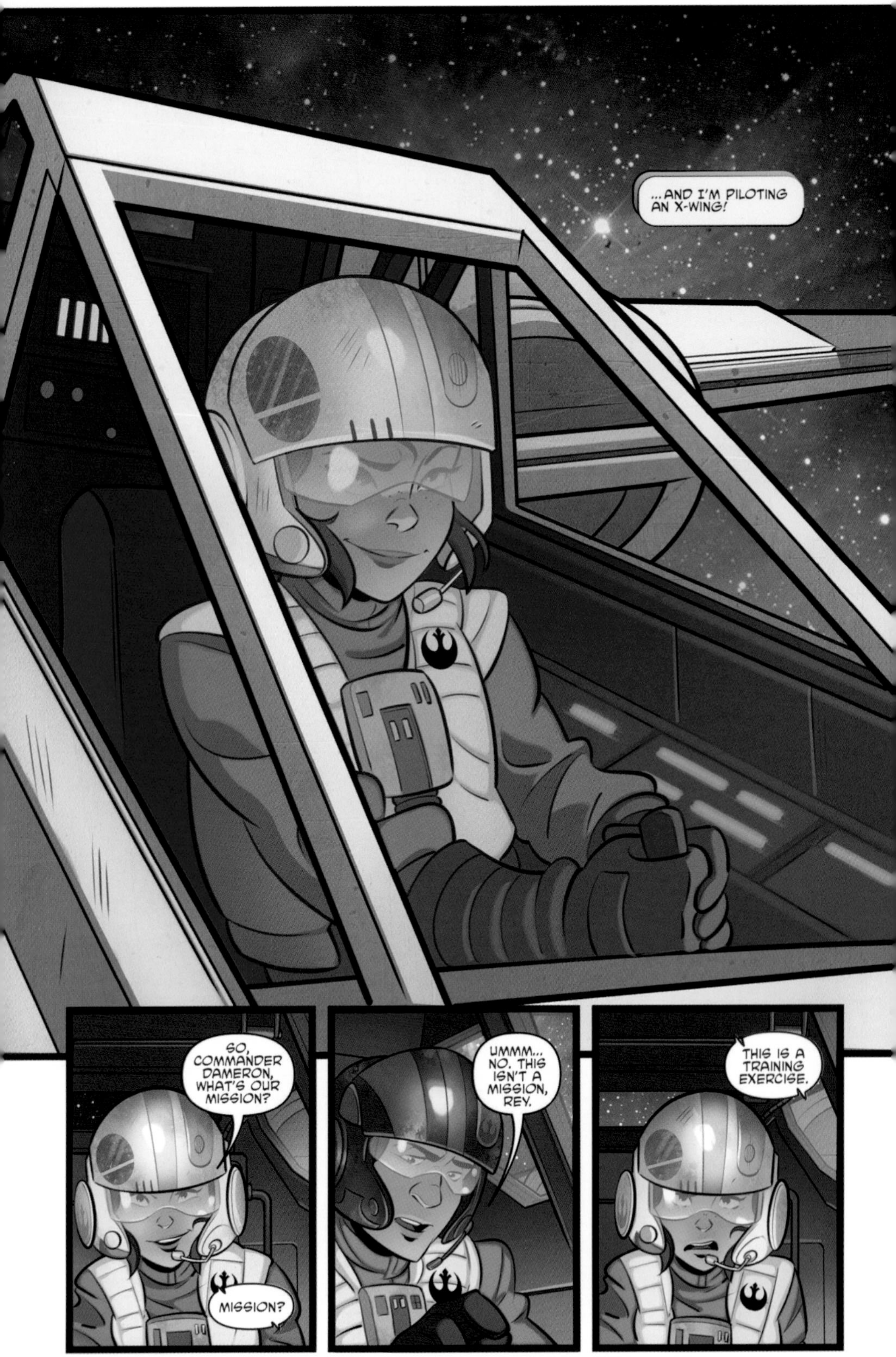
...AND I'M PILOTING AN X-WING!
SO, COMMANDER DAMERON, WHAT'S OUR MISSION?
MISSION?
UMMM... NO. THIS ISN'T A MISSION, REY.
THIS IS A TRAINING EXERCISE.

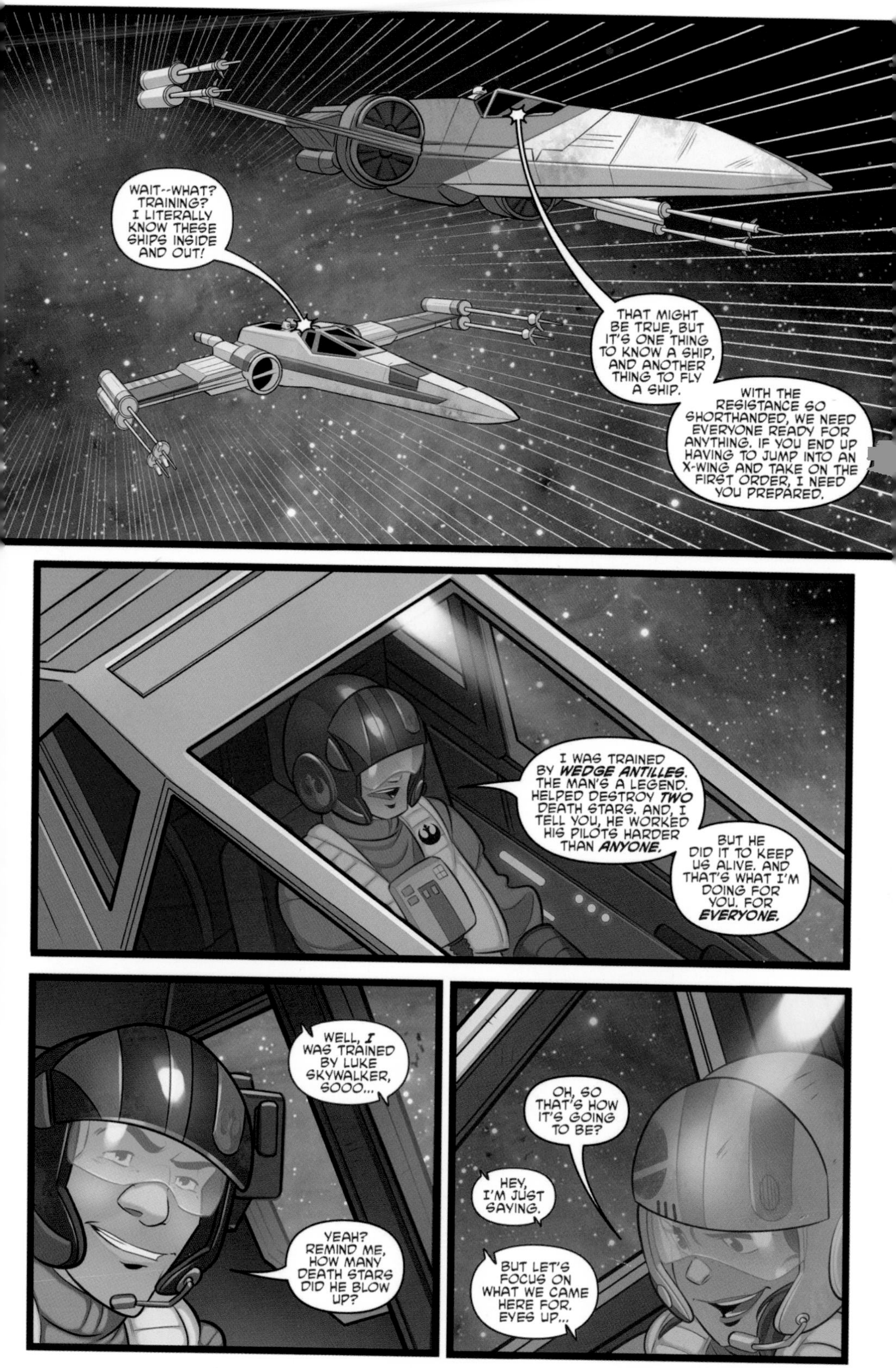
WAIT--WHAT? TRAINING? I LITERALLY KNOW THESE SHIPS INSIDE AND OUT!
THAT MIGHT BE TRUE, BUT IT'S ONE THING TO KNOW A SHIP, AND ANOTHER THING TO FLY A SHIP.
WITH THE RESISTANCE SO SHORTHANDED, WE NEED EVERYONE READY FOR ANYTHING. IF YOU END UP HAVING TO JUMP INTO AN X-WING AND TAKE ON THE FIRST ORDER, I NEED YOU PREPARED.
I WAS TRAINED BY WEDGE ANTILLES. THE MAN'S A LEGEND. HELPED DESTROY TWO DEATH STARS. AND, I TELL YOU, HE WORKED HIS PILOTS HARDER THAN ANYONE.
BUT HE DID IT TO KEEP US ALIVE. AND THAT'S WHAT I'M DOING FOR YOU. FOR EVERYONE.
WELL, I WAS TRAINED BY LUKE SKYWALKER, SOOO...
YEAH? REMIND ME, HOW MANY DEATH STARS DID HE BLOW UP?
OH, SO THAT'S HOW IT'S GOING TO BE?
HEY, I'M JUST SAYING.
BUT LET'S FOCUS ON WHAT WE CAME HERE FOR. EYES UP...

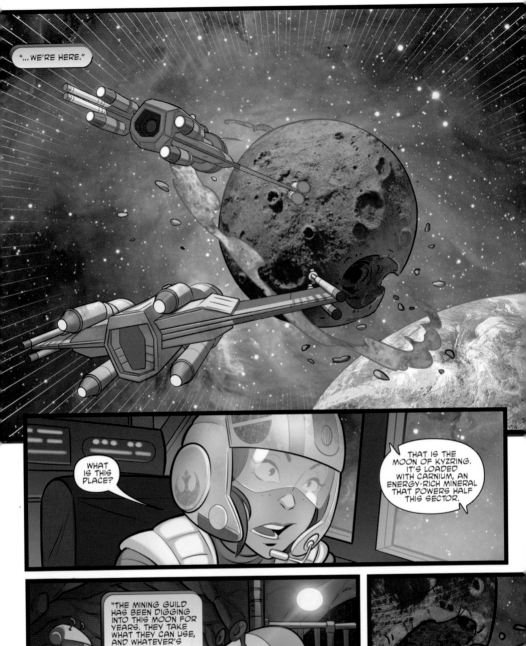

"...WE'RE HERE."

WHAT IS THIS PLACE?

THAT IS THE MOON OF KYZRING. IT'S LOADED WITH CARNIUM, AN ENERGY-RICH MINERAL THAT POWERS HALF THIS SECTOR.

"THE MINING GUILD HAS BEEN DIGGING INTO THIS MOON FOR YEARS. THEY TAKE WHAT THEY CAN USE, AND WHATEVER'S LEFT, WELL..."

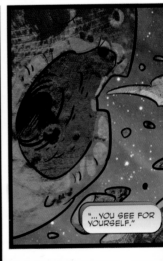

"...YOU SEE FOR YOURSELF."

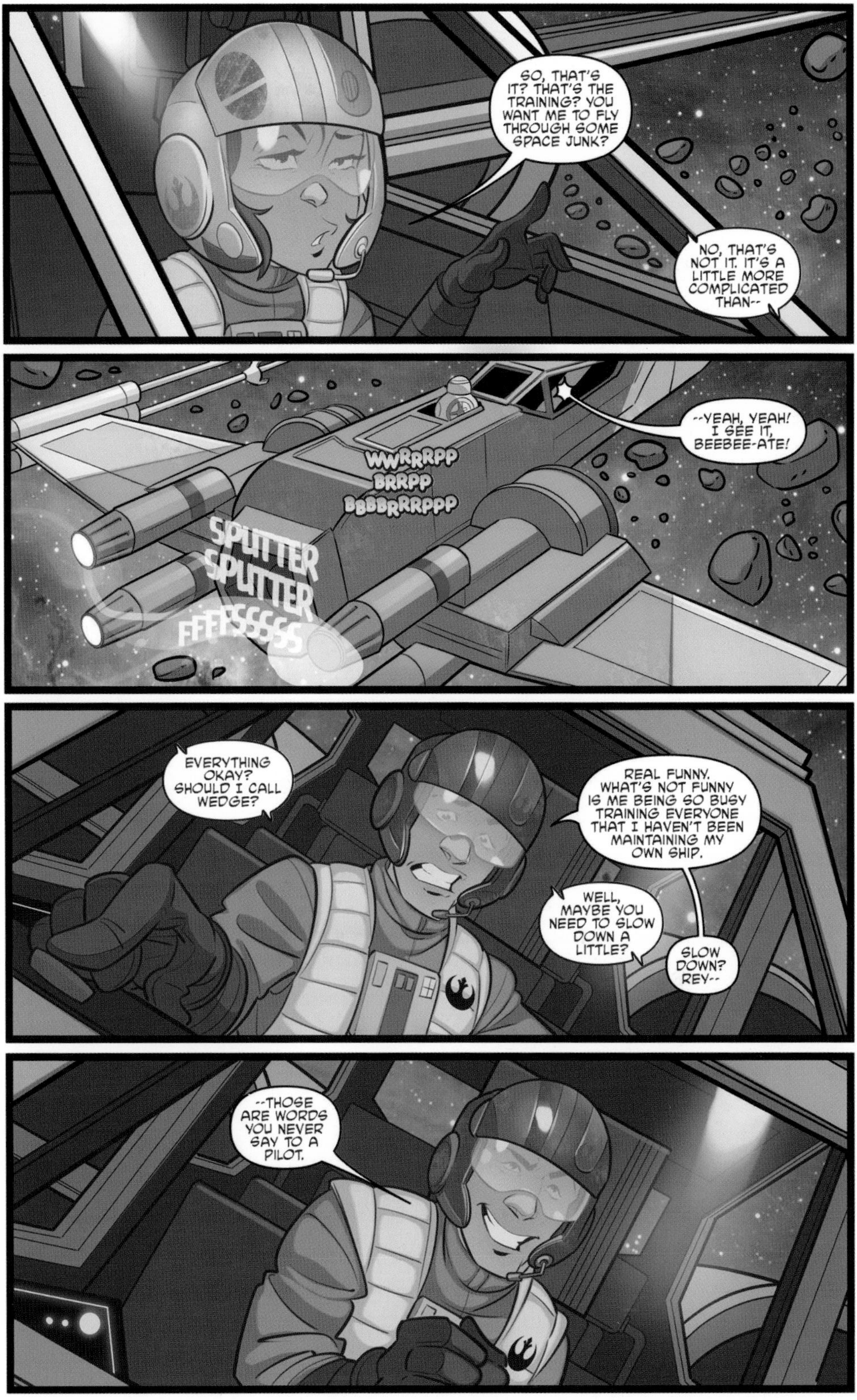
SO, THAT'S IT? THAT'S THE TRAINING? YOU WANT ME TO FLY THROUGH SOME SPACE JUNK?
NO, THAT'S NOT IT. IT'S A LITTLE MORE COMPLICATED THAN--
--YEAH, YEAH! I SEE IT, BEEBEE-ATE!
WWRRRPP
BRRPP
BBBBRRRPPP
SPUTTER
SPUTTER
FFFSSSSS
EVERYTHING OKAY? SHOULD I CALL WEDGE?
REAL FUNNY. WHAT'S NOT FUNNY IS ME BEING SO BUSY TRAINING EVERYONE THAT I HAVEN'T BEEN MAINTAINING MY OWN SHIP.
WELL, MAYBE YOU NEED TO SLOW DOWN A LITTLE?
SLOW DOWN? REY--
--THOSE ARE WORDS YOU NEVER SAY TO A PILOT.

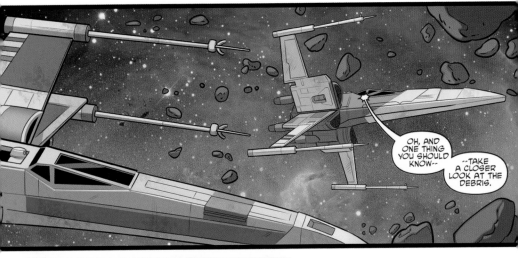

OH, AND ONE THING YOU SHOULD KNOW--

--TAKE A CLOSER LOOK AT THE DEBRIS.

CLOSER LOOK AT THE DEBRIS... CLOSER LOOK...

...AND WHAT AM I LOOKING FO--

"--EW! WHAT ARE THOSE THINGS?!"

BUZZ DROIDS. NASTY LITTLE RELICS FROM THE CLONE WARS. THEY'VE BEEN MODIFIED BY THE GUILD TO BREAK DOWN THE DEBRIS.

BUT WHAT THEY REALLY LOVE ARE SHIPS. TEARING THEM UP, RIPPING THEM APART. YOU LET THESE THINGS ANYWHERE NEAR YOUR SHIP, YOU BETTER GET REAL CLEVER REAL FAST.

"THEY MIGHT NOT LOOK LIKE MUCH, BUT THESE THINGS WILL HAVE YOUR X-WING FOR LUNCH, SO FOLLOW MY LEAD--AND STAY SHARP."

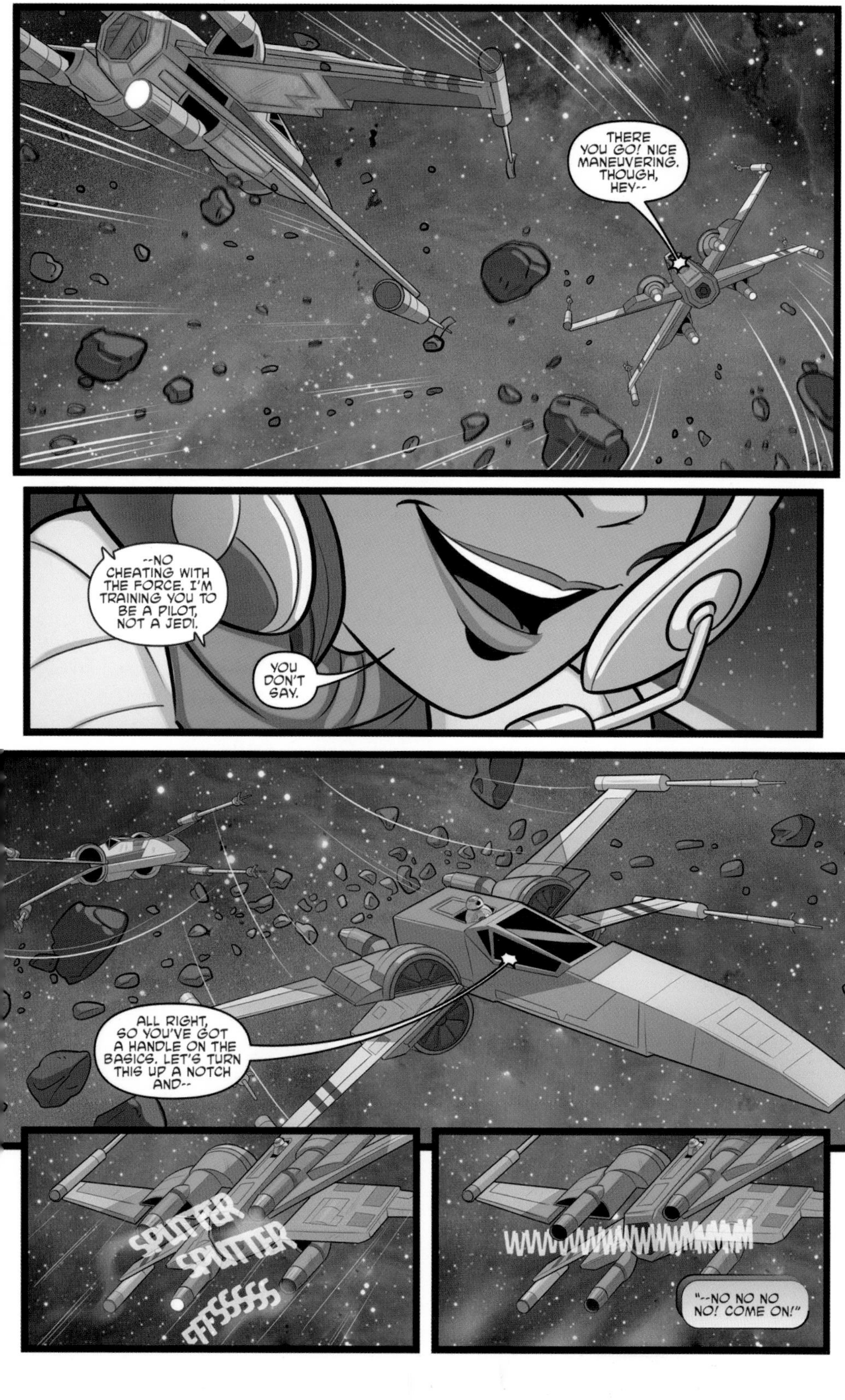
THERE YOU GO! NICE MANEUVERING. THOUGH, HEY--
--NO CHEATING WITH THE FORCE. I'M TRAINING YOU TO BE A PILOT, NOT A JEDI.
YOU DON'T SAY.
ALL RIGHT, SO YOU'VE GOT A HANDLE ON THE BASICS. LET'S TURN THIS UP A NOTCH AND--
SPLUTTER
SPLUTTER
FFSSSSS
WWWWWWWWWWMMMM
"--NO NO NO NO! COME ON!"

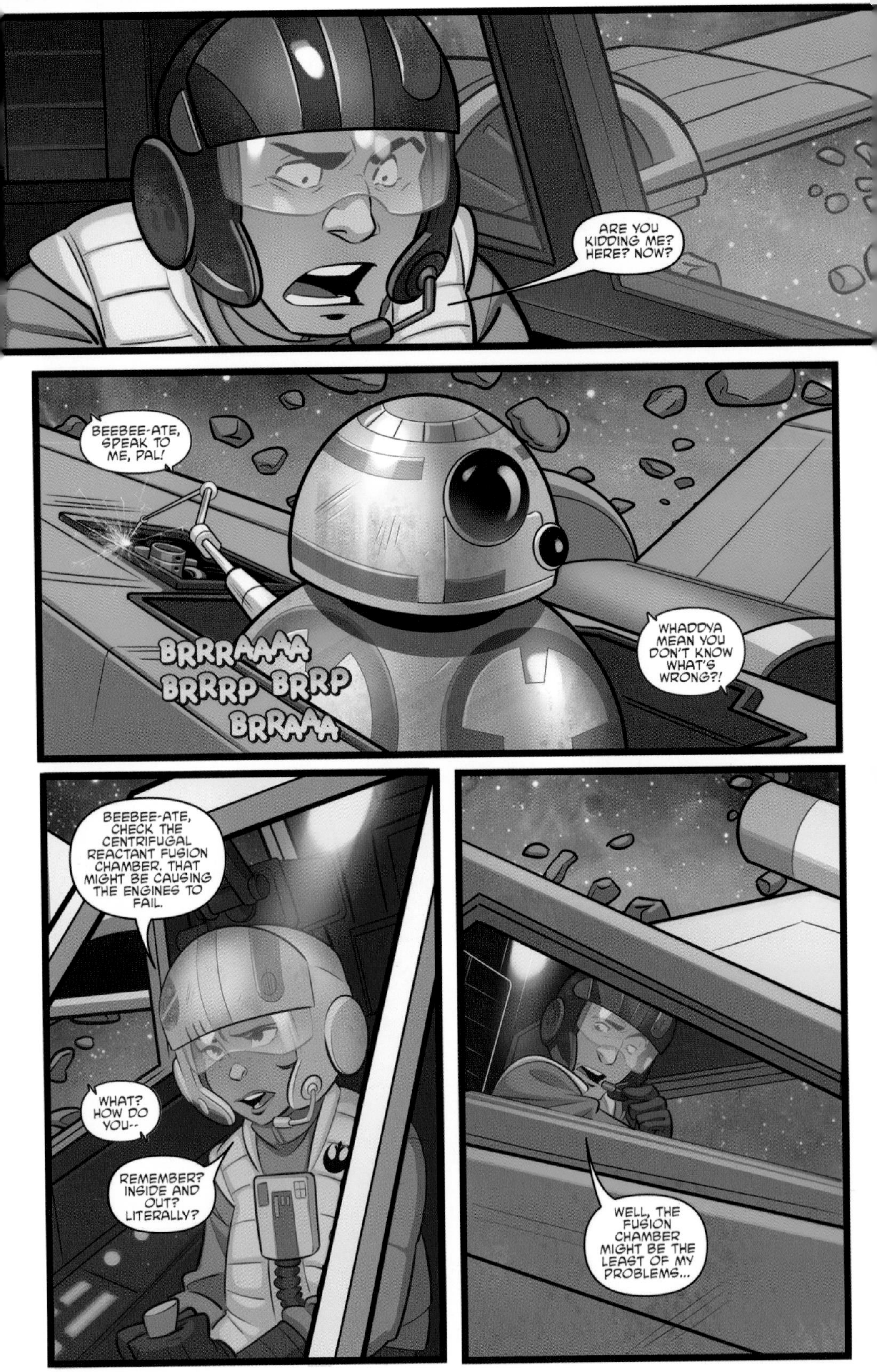
ARE YOU KIDDING ME? HERE? NOW?
BEEBEE-ATE, SPEAK TO ME, PAL!
BRRRAAAA BRRRP BRRP BRRAAA
WHADDYA MEAN YOU DON'T KNOW WHAT'S WRONG?!
BEEBEE-ATE, CHECK THE CENTRIFUGAL REACTANT FUSION CHAMBER. THAT MIGHT BE CAUSING THE ENGINES TO FAIL.
WHAT? HOW DO YOU--
REMEMBER? INSIDE AND OUT? LITERALLY?
WELL, THE FUSION CHAMBER MIGHT BE THE LEAST OF MY PROBLEMS...

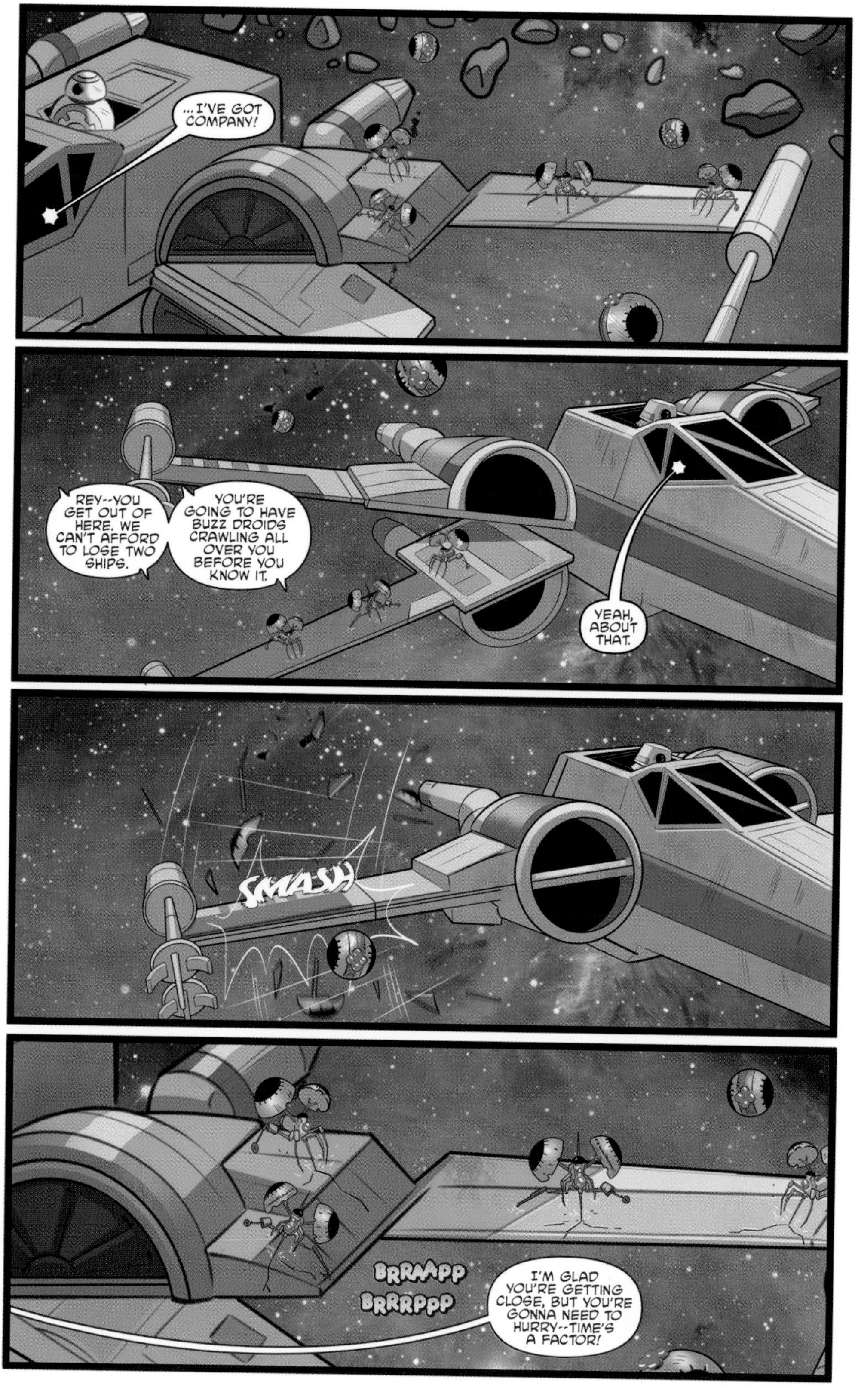
...I'VE GOT COMPANY!
REY--YOU GET OUT OF HERE. WE CAN'T AFFORD TO LOSE TWO SHIPS.
YOU'RE GOING TO HAVE BUZZ DROIDS CRAWLING ALL OVER YOU BEFORE YOU KNOW IT.
YEAH, ABOUT THAT.
SMASH
BRRAAPP
BRRRPPP
I'M GLAD YOU'RE GETTING CLOSE, BUT YOU'RE GONNA NEED TO HURRY--TIME'S A FACTOR!

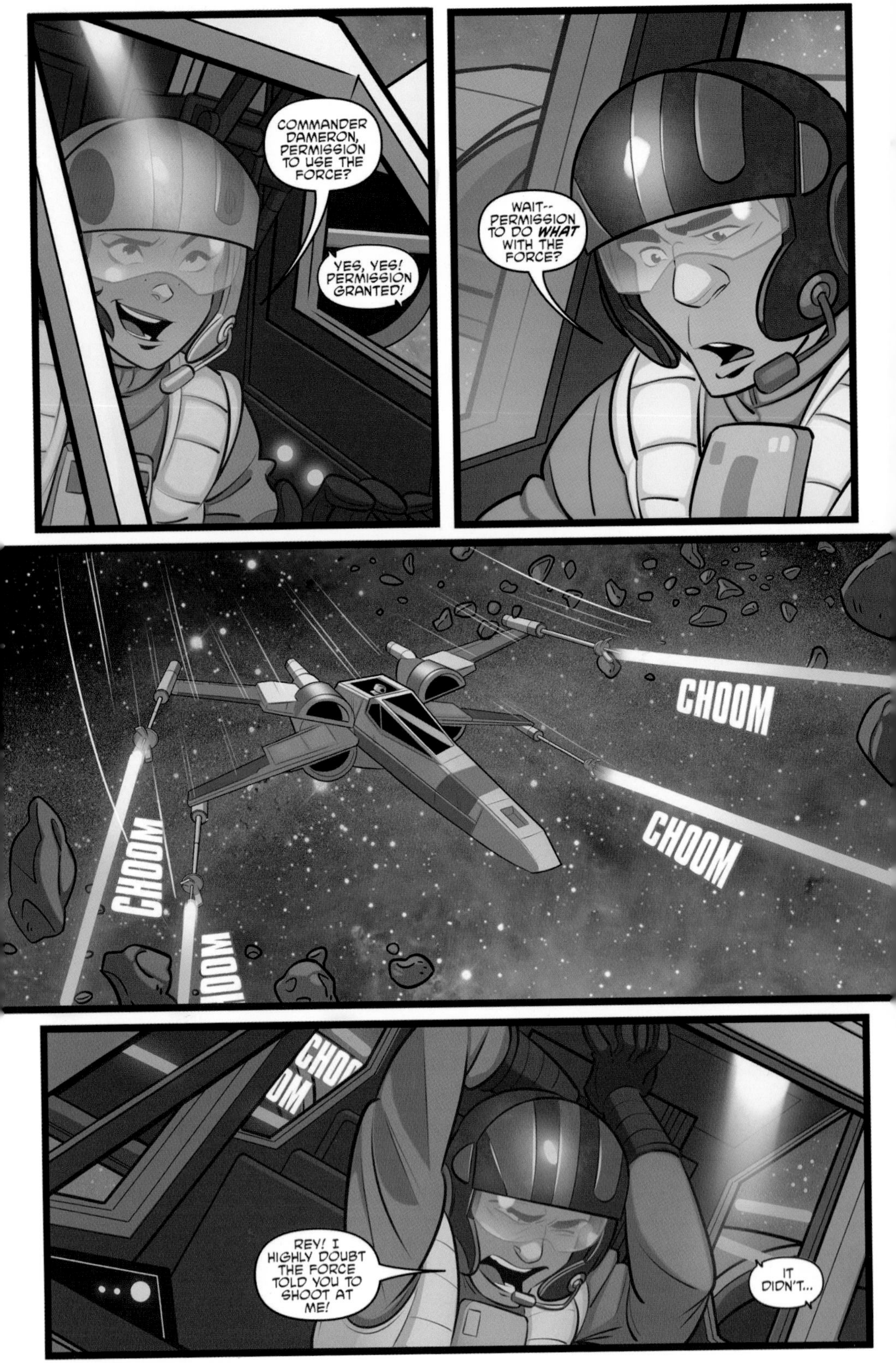

COMMANDER DAMERON, PERMISSION TO USE THE FORCE?
YES, YES! PERMISSION GRANTED!
WAIT-- PERMISSION TO DO ***WHAT*** WITH THE FORCE?
CHOOM
CHOOM
CHOOM
REY! I HIGHLY DOUBT THE FORCE TOLD YOU TO SHOOT AT ME!
IT DIDN'T...

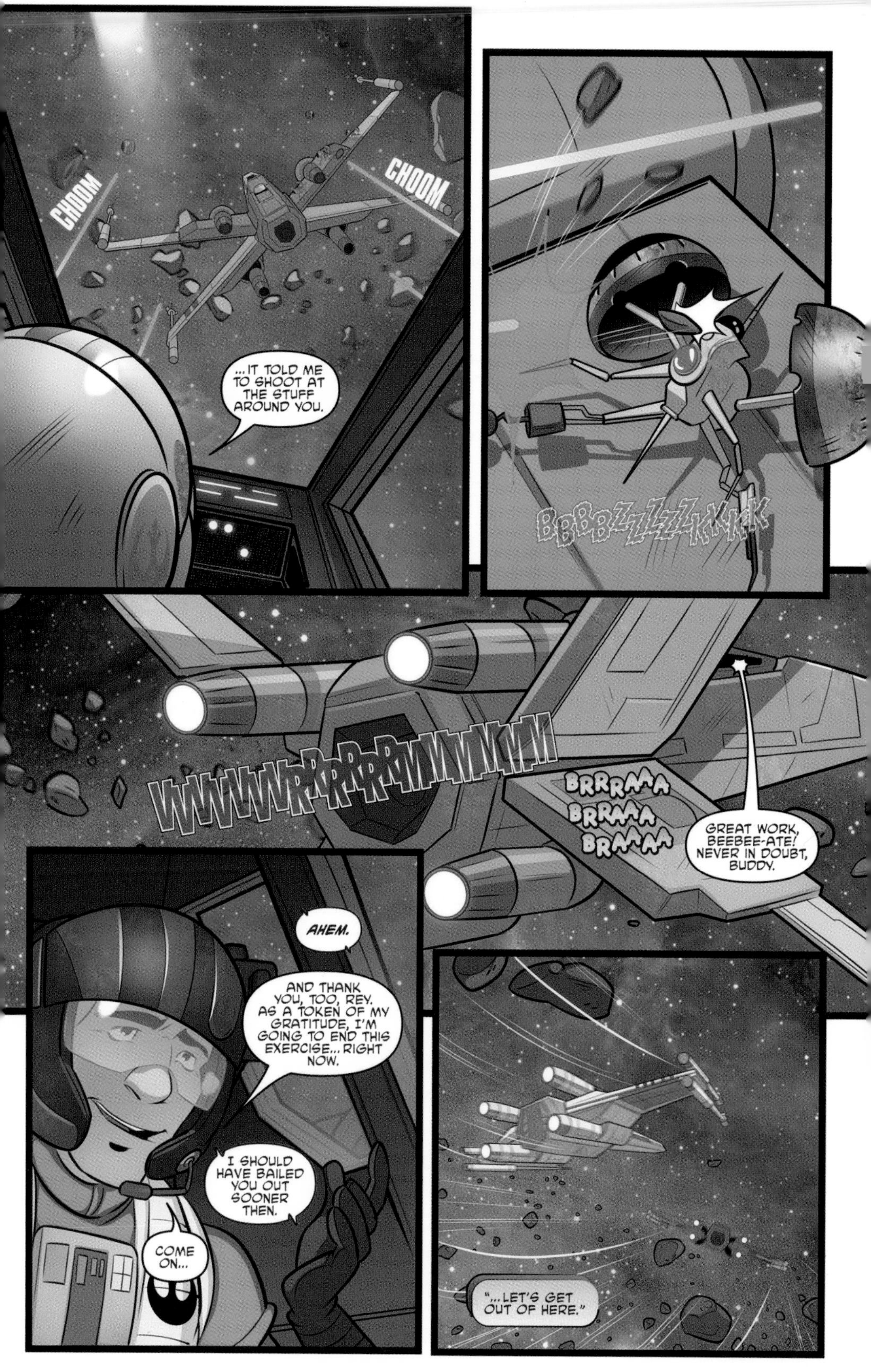
CHOOM
CHOOM
...IT TOLD ME TO SHOOT AT THE STUFF AROUND YOU.
BBBBZZZZZKKKKK
VVVVVVVVRRRRRRRMMMMMMM
BRRRAAAA BRRAAAA BRAAAA
GREAT WORK, BEEBEE-ATE! NEVER IN DOUBT, BUDDY.
AHEM.
AND THANK YOU, TOO, REY. AS A TOKEN OF MY GRATITUDE, I'M GOING TO END THIS EXERCISE... RIGHT NOW.
I SHOULD HAVE BAILED YOU OUT SOONER THEN.
COME ON...
"...LET'S GET OUT OF HERE."

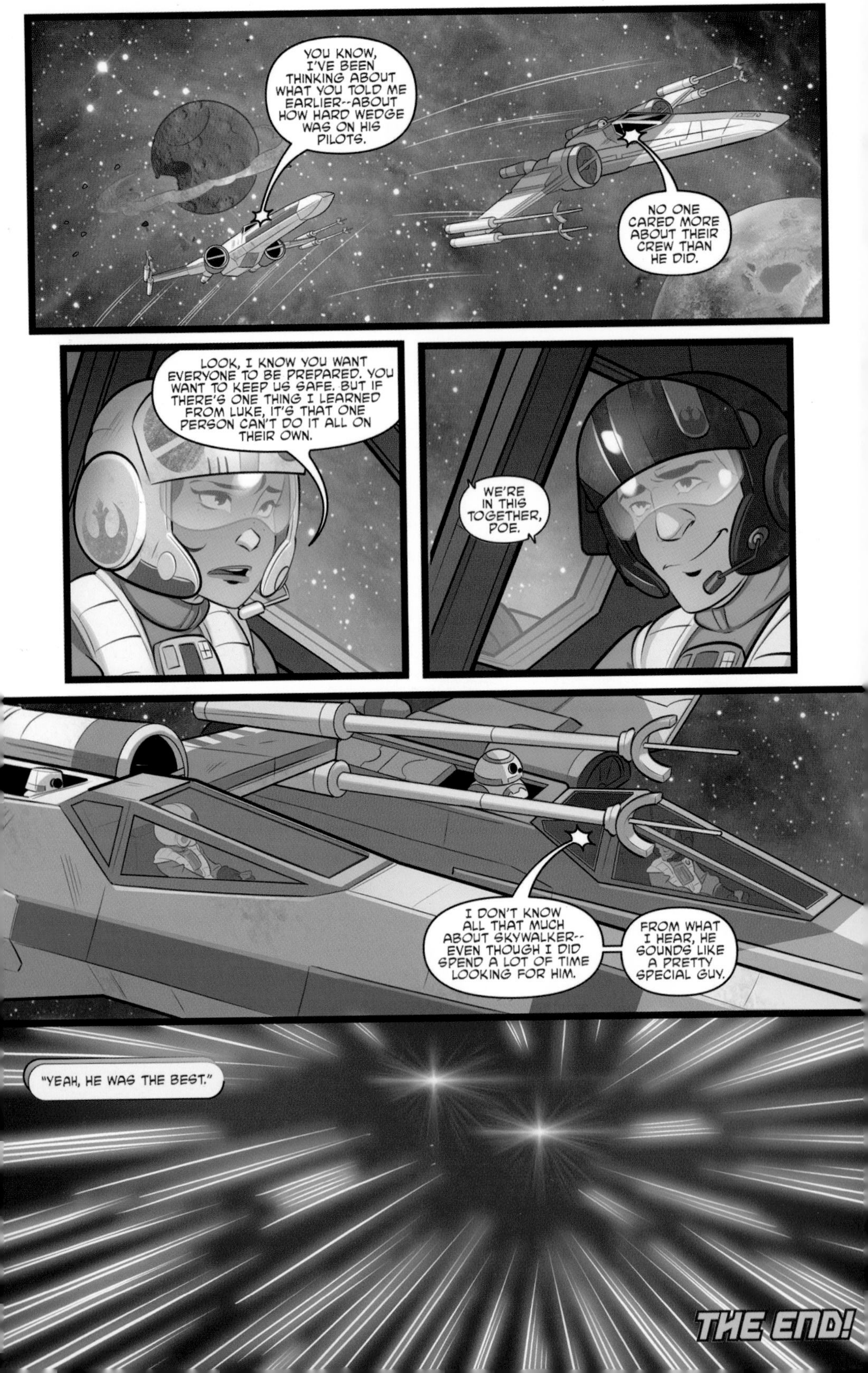
YOU KNOW, I'VE BEEN THINKING ABOUT WHAT YOU TOLD ME EARLIER--ABOUT HOW HARD WEDGE WAS ON HIS PILOTS.
NO ONE CARED MORE ABOUT THEIR CREW THAN HE DID.
LOOK, I KNOW YOU WANT EVERYONE TO BE PREPARED. YOU WANT TO KEEP US SAFE. BUT IF THERE'S ONE THING I LEARNED FROM LUKE, IT'S THAT ONE PERSON CAN'T DO IT ALL ON THEIR OWN.
WE'RE IN THIS TOGETHER, POE.
I DON'T KNOW ALL THAT MUCH ABOUT SKYWALKER--EVEN THOUGH I DID SPEND A LOT OF TIME LOOKING FOR HIM.
FROM WHAT I HEAR, HE SOUNDS LIKE A PRETTY SPECIAL GUY.
"YEAH, HE WAS THE BEST."
THE END!

STAR WARS
ADVENTURES

The Battle for Horizon Base

WRITER
MICHAEL MORECI

ARTIST
ARIANNA FLOREAN

ASSISTANT ARTIST
MARIO DEL PENNINO

COLORIST
VALENTINA TADDEO

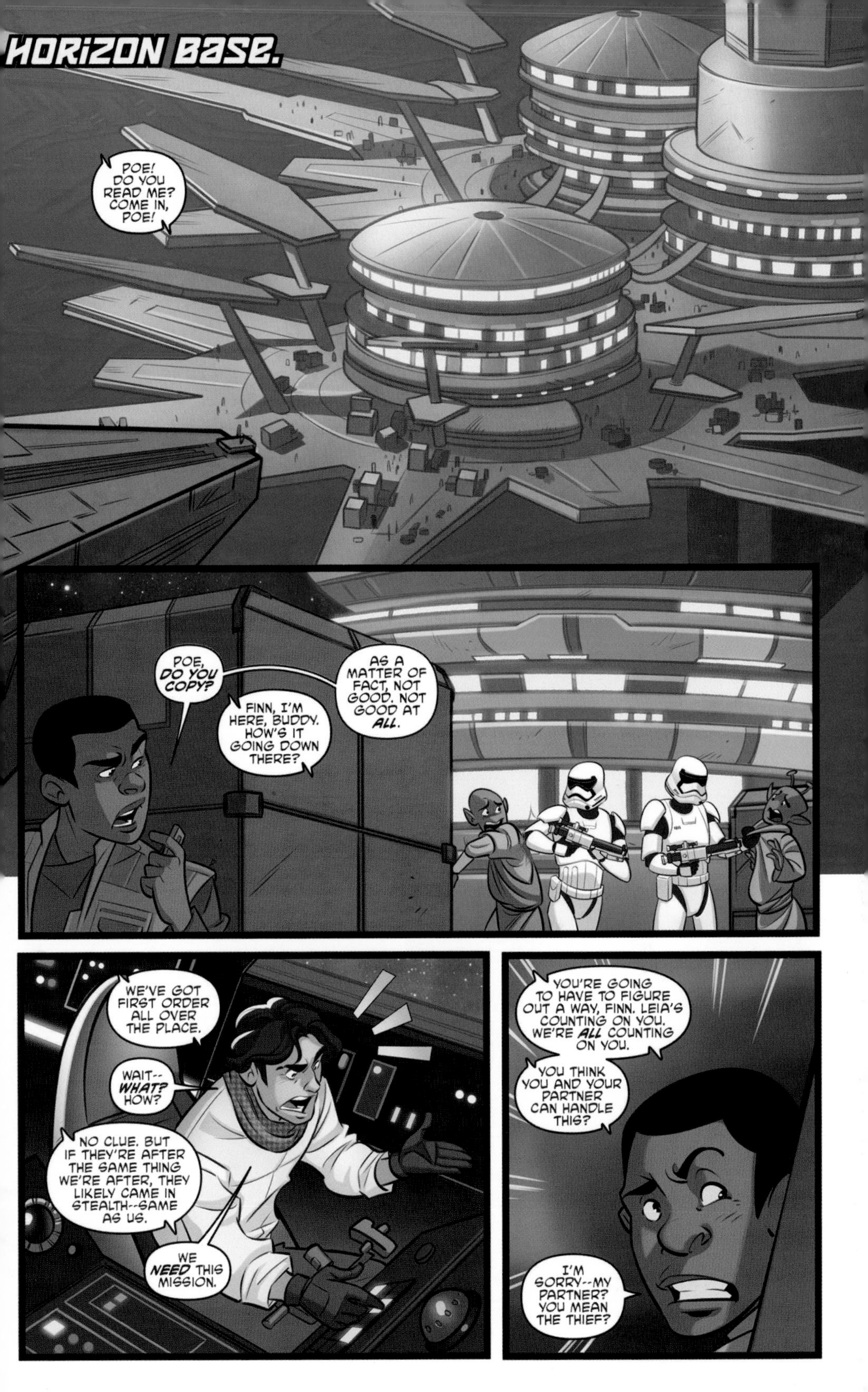
HORIZON BASE.
POE! DO YOU READ ME? COME IN, POE!
POE, DO YOU COPY?
FINN, I'M HERE, BUDDY. HOW'S IT GOING DOWN THERE?
AS A MATTER OF FACT, NOT GOOD. NOT GOOD AT ALL.
WE'VE GOT FIRST ORDER ALL OVER THE PLACE.
WAIT-- WHAT? HOW?
NO CLUE. BUT IF THEY'RE AFTER THE SAME THING WE'RE AFTER, THEY LIKELY CAME IN STEALTH--SAME AS US.
WE NEED THIS MISSION.
YOU'RE GOING TO HAVE TO FIGURE OUT A WAY, FINN. LEIA'S COUNTING ON YOU. WE'RE ALL COUNTING ON YOU.
YOU THINK YOU AND YOUR PARTNER CAN HANDLE THIS?
I'M SORRY--MY PARTNER? YOU MEAN THE THIEF?

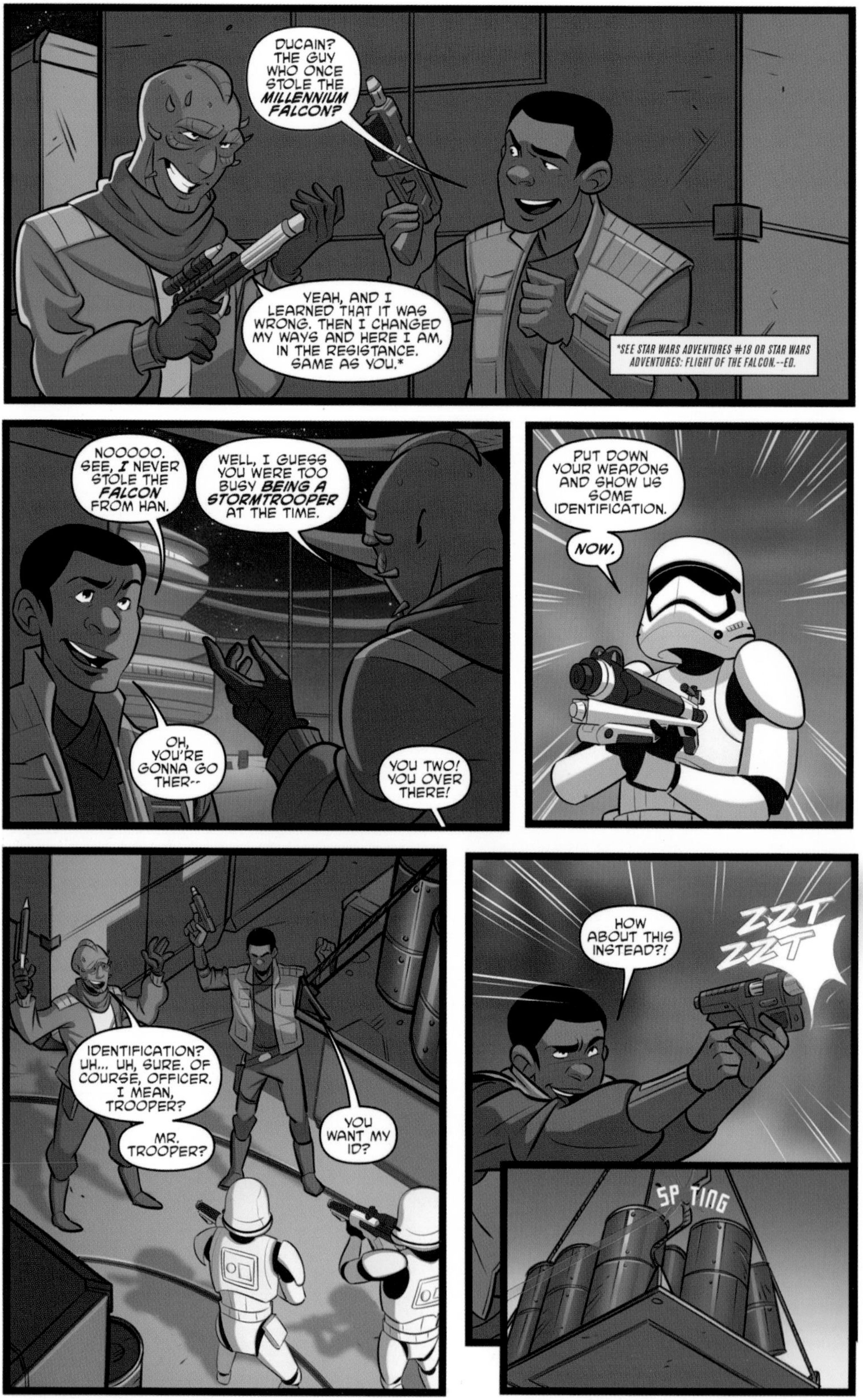
DUCAIN? THE GUY WHO ONCE STOLE THE *MILLENNIUM FALCON?*
YEAH, AND I LEARNED THAT IT WAS WRONG. THEN I CHANGED MY WAYS AND HERE I AM, IN THE RESISTANCE. SAME AS YOU.*
*SEE STAR WARS ADVENTURES #18 OR STAR WARS ADVENTURES: FLIGHT OF THE FALCON.--ED.
NOOOOO. SEE, *I* NEVER STOLE THE *FALCON* FROM HAN.
WELL, I GUESS YOU WERE TOO BUSY *BEING A STORMTROOPER* AT THE TIME.
OH, YOU'RE GONNA GO THER--
YOU TWO! YOU OVER THERE!
PUT DOWN YOUR WEAPONS AND SHOW US SOME IDENTIFICATION.
NOW.
IDENTIFICATION? UH... UH, SURE. OF COURSE, OFFICER. I MEAN, TROOPER?
MR. TROOPER?
YOU WANT MY ID?
HOW ABOUT THIS INSTEAD?!
ZZT
ZZT
SP TING

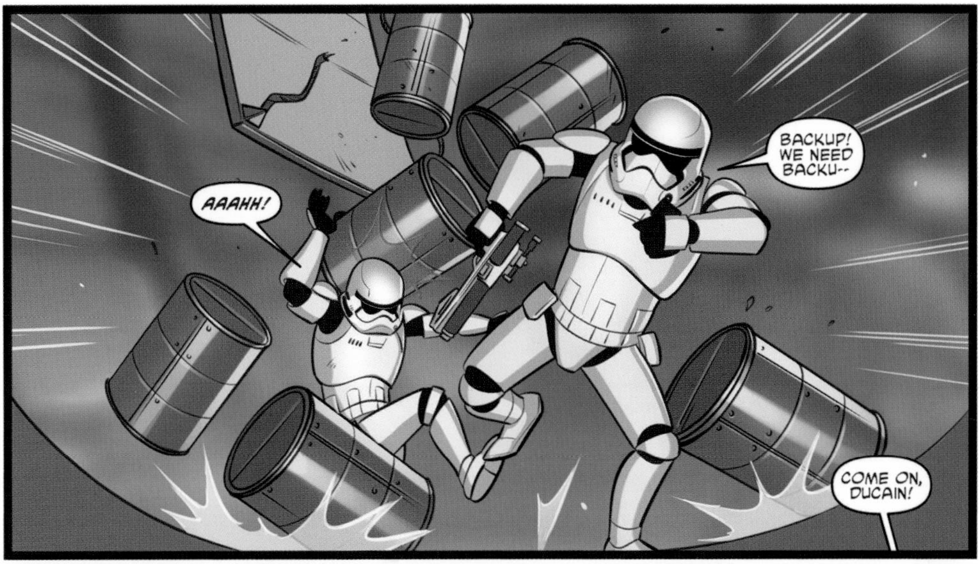
AAAHH!
BACKUP! WE NEED BACKU--
COME ON, DUCAIN!

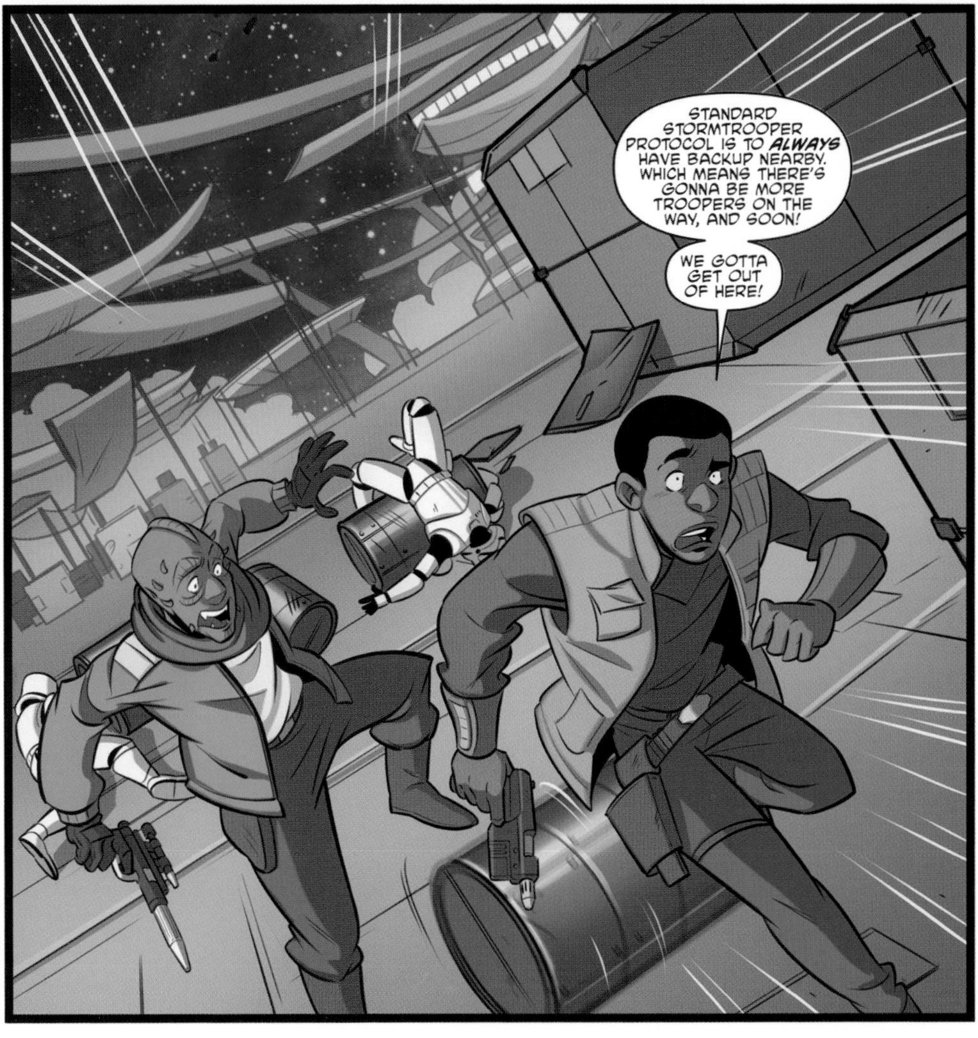
STANDARD STORMTROOPER PROTOCOL IS TO ALWAYS HAVE BACKUP NEARBY. WHICH MEANS THERE'S GONNA BE MORE TROOPERS ON THE WAY, AND SOON!
WE GOTTA GET OUT OF HERE!

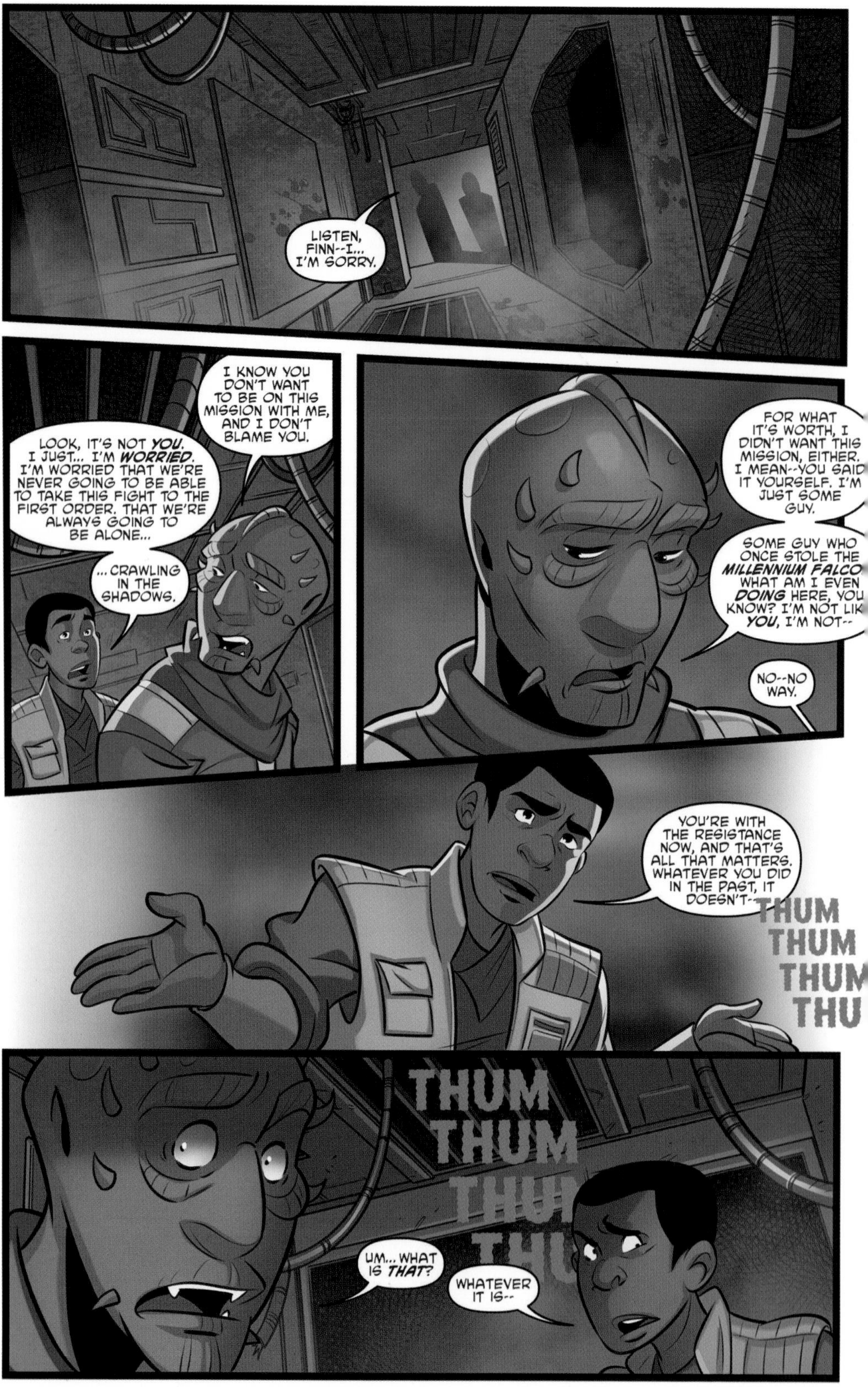
LISTEN, FINN--I... I'M SORRY.
I KNOW YOU DON'T WANT TO BE ON THIS MISSION WITH ME, AND I DON'T BLAME YOU.
LOOK, IT'S NOT *YOU*. I JUST... I'M *WORRIED*. I'M WORRIED THAT WE'RE NEVER GOING TO BE ABLE TO TAKE THIS FIGHT TO THE FIRST ORDER. THAT WE'RE ALWAYS GOING TO BE ALONE...
...CRAWLING IN THE SHADOWS.
FOR WHAT IT'S WORTH, I DIDN'T WANT THIS MISSION, EITHER. I MEAN--YOU SAID IT YOURSELF. I'M JUST SOME GUY.
SOME GUY WHO ONCE STOLE THE *MILLENNIUM FALCO* WHAT AM I EVEN *DOING* HERE, YOU KNOW? I'M NOT LIK *YOU*, I'M NOT--
NO--NO WAY.
YOU'RE WITH THE RESISTANCE NOW, AND THAT'S ALL THAT MATTERS. WHATEVER YOU DID IN THE PAST, IT DOESN'T--
THUM THUM THUM THU
THUM THUM THU THU
UM... WHAT IS *THAT*?
WHATEVER IT IS--

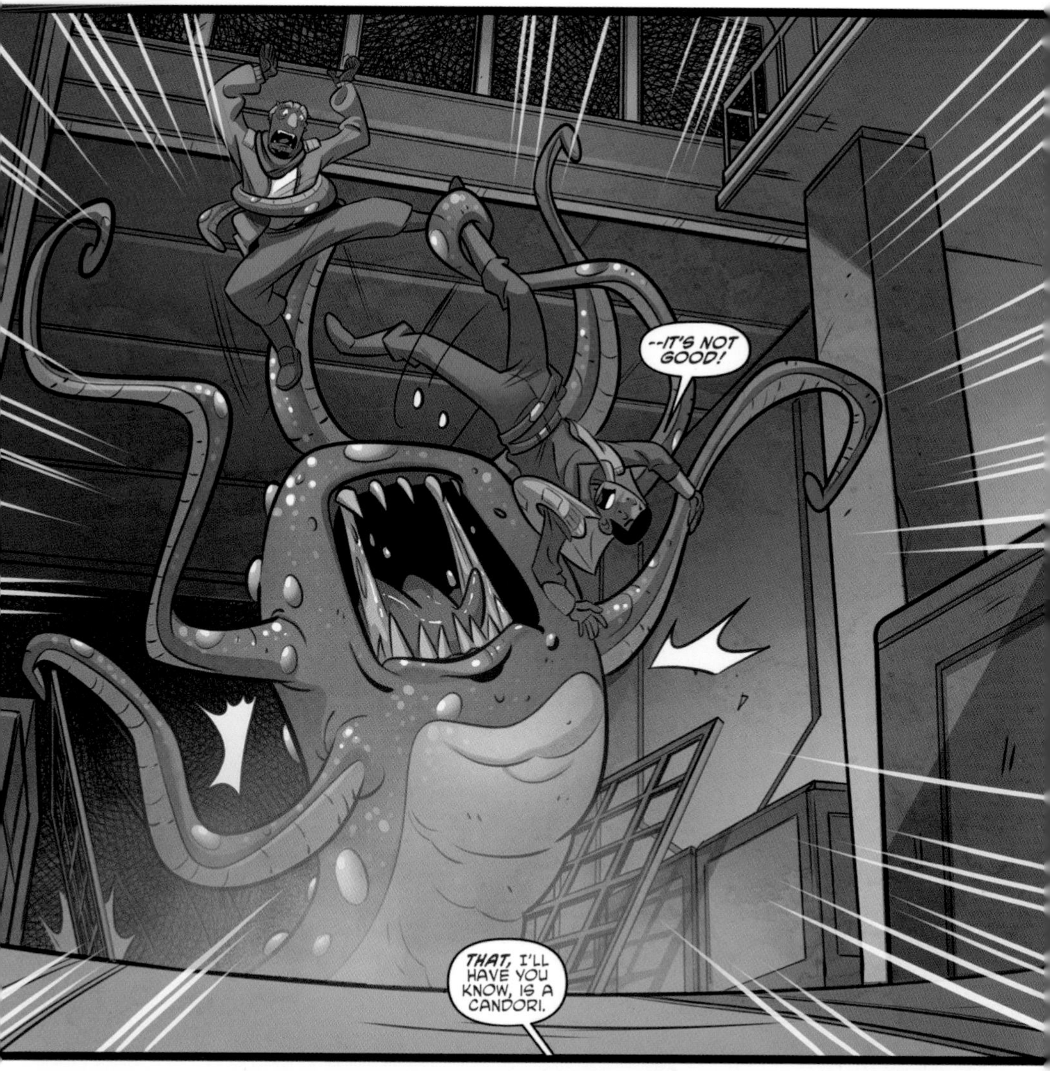
--IT'S NOT GOOD!
THAT, I'LL HAVE YOU KNOW, IS A CANDORI.
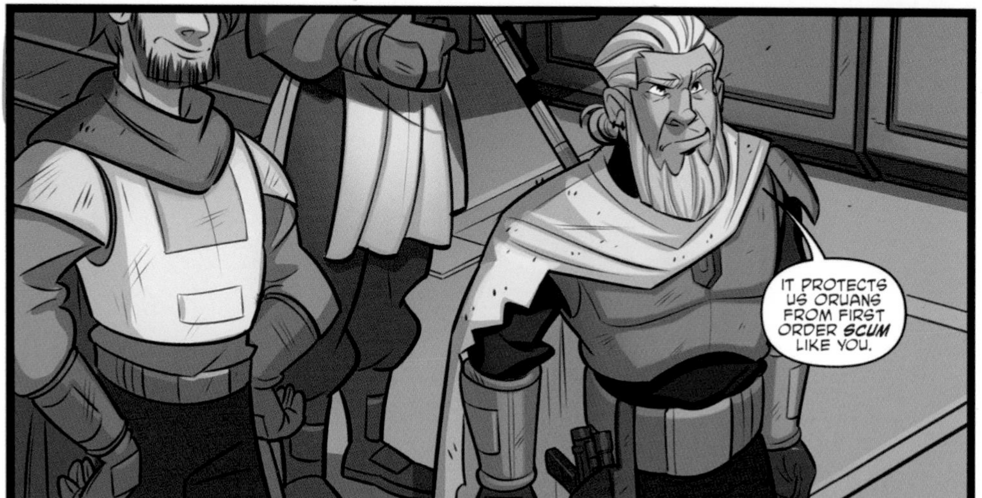
IT PROTECTS US ORUANS FROM FIRST ORDER SCUM LIKE YOU.

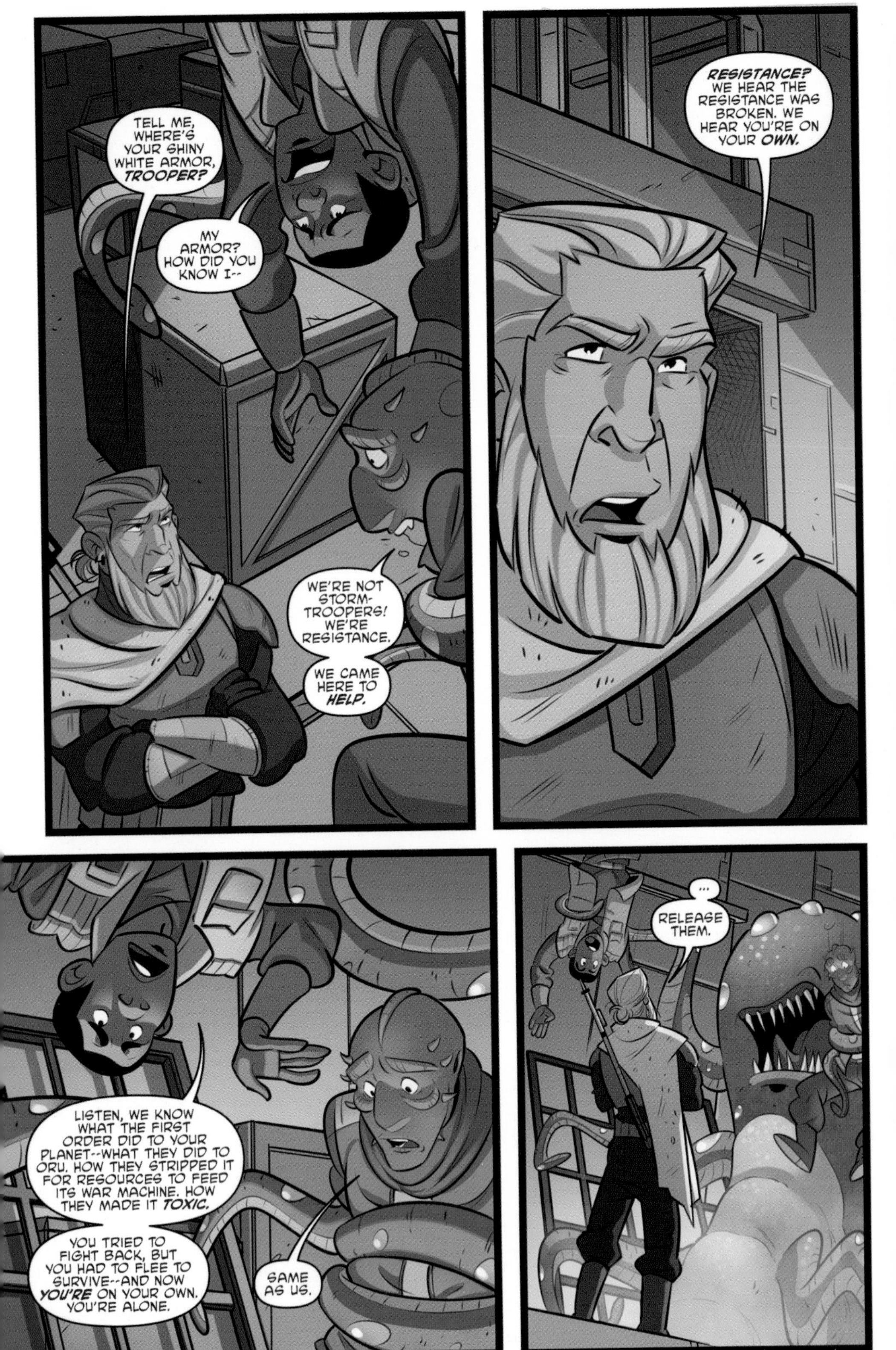
TELL ME, WHERE'S YOUR SHINY WHITE ARMOR, *TROOPER?*
MY ARMOR? HOW DID YOU KNOW I--
WE'RE NOT STORM-TROOPERS! WE'RE RESISTANCE.
WE CAME HERE TO *HELP.*
RESISTANCE? WE HEAR THE RESISTANCE WAS BROKEN. WE HEAR YOU'RE ON YOUR *OWN.*
LISTEN, WE KNOW WHAT THE FIRST ORDER DID TO YOUR PLANET--WHAT THEY DID TO ORU. HOW THEY STRIPPED IT FOR RESOURCES TO FEED ITS WAR MACHINE. HOW THEY MADE IT *TOXIC.*
YOU TRIED TO FIGHT BACK, BUT YOU HAD TO FLEE TO SURVIVE--AND NOW *YOU'RE* ON YOUR OWN. YOU'RE ALONE.
SAME AS US.
...
RELEASE THEM.

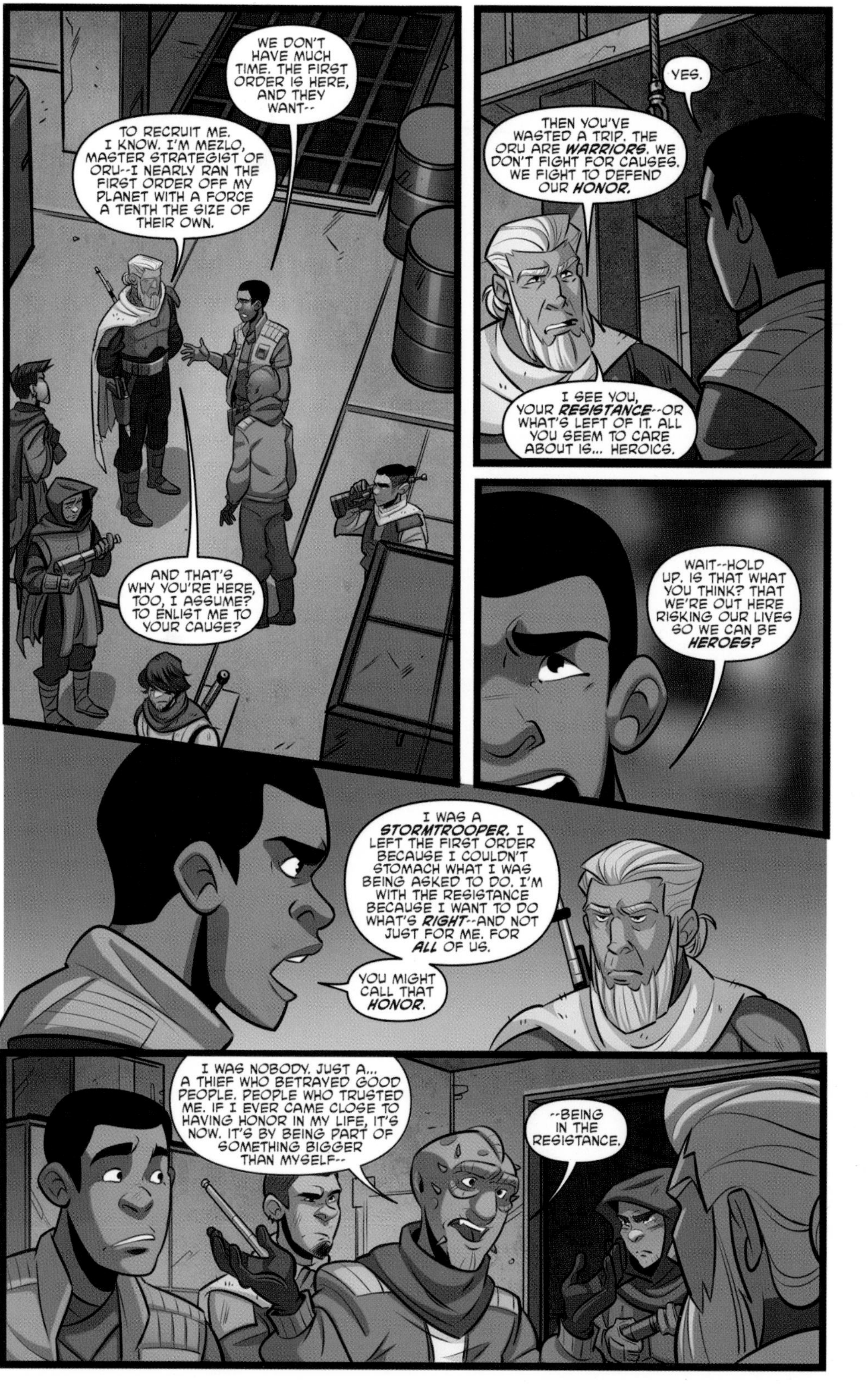
WE DON'T HAVE MUCH TIME. THE FIRST ORDER IS HERE, AND THEY WANT--
TO RECRUIT ME. I KNOW. I'M MEZLO, MASTER STRATEGIST OF ORU--I NEARLY RAN THE FIRST ORDER OFF MY PLANET WITH A FORCE A TENTH THE SIZE OF THEIR OWN.
AND THAT'S WHY YOU'RE HERE, TOO, I ASSUME? TO ENLIST ME TO YOUR CAUSE?
YES.
THEN YOU'VE WASTED A TRIP. THE ORU ARE WARRIORS. WE DON'T FIGHT FOR CAUSES. WE FIGHT TO DEFEND OUR HONOR.
I SEE YOU, YOUR RESISTANCE--OR WHAT'S LEFT OF IT. ALL YOU SEEM TO CARE ABOUT IS... HEROICS.
WAIT--HOLD UP. IS THAT WHAT YOU THINK? THAT WE'RE OUT HERE RISKING OUR LIVES SO WE CAN BE HEROES?
I WAS A STORMTROOPER. I LEFT THE FIRST ORDER BECAUSE I COULDN'T STOMACH WHAT I WAS BEING ASKED TO DO. I'M WITH THE RESISTANCE BECAUSE I WANT TO DO WHAT'S RIGHT--AND NOT JUST FOR ME. FOR ALL OF US.
YOU MIGHT CALL THAT HONOR.
I WAS NOBODY. JUST A... A THIEF WHO BETRAYED GOOD PEOPLE. PEOPLE WHO TRUSTED ME. IF I EVER CAME CLOSE TO HAVING HONOR IN MY LIFE, IT'S NOW. IT'S BY BEING PART OF SOMETHING BIGGER THAN MYSELF--
--BEING IN THE RESISTANCE.

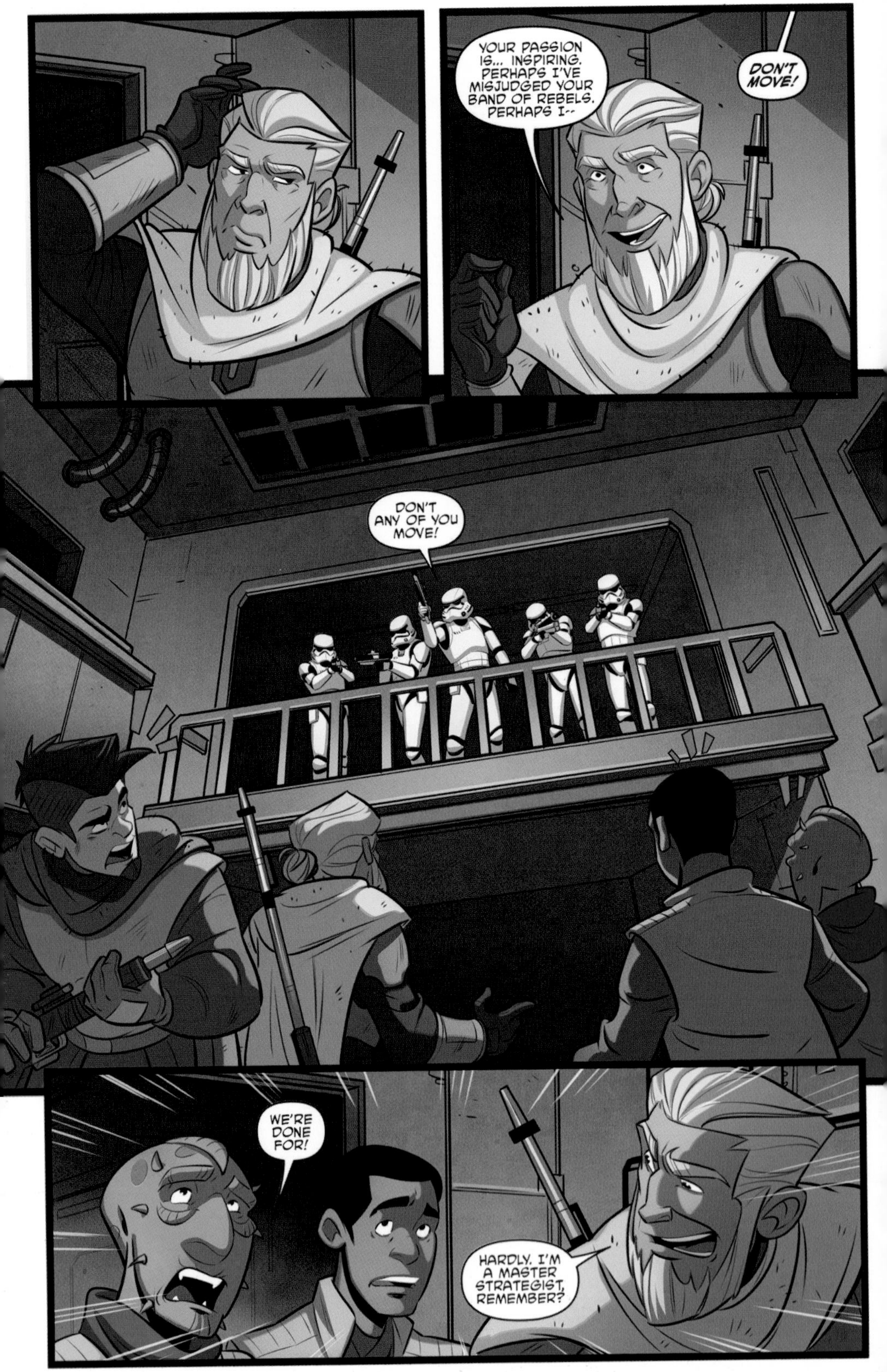
YOUR PASSION IS... INSPIRING. PERHAPS I'VE MISJUDGED YOUR BAND OF REBELS. PERHAPS I--
DON'T MOVE!
DON'T ANY OF YOU MOVE!
WE'RE DONE FOR!
HARDLY. I'M A MASTER STRATEGIST, REMEMBER?

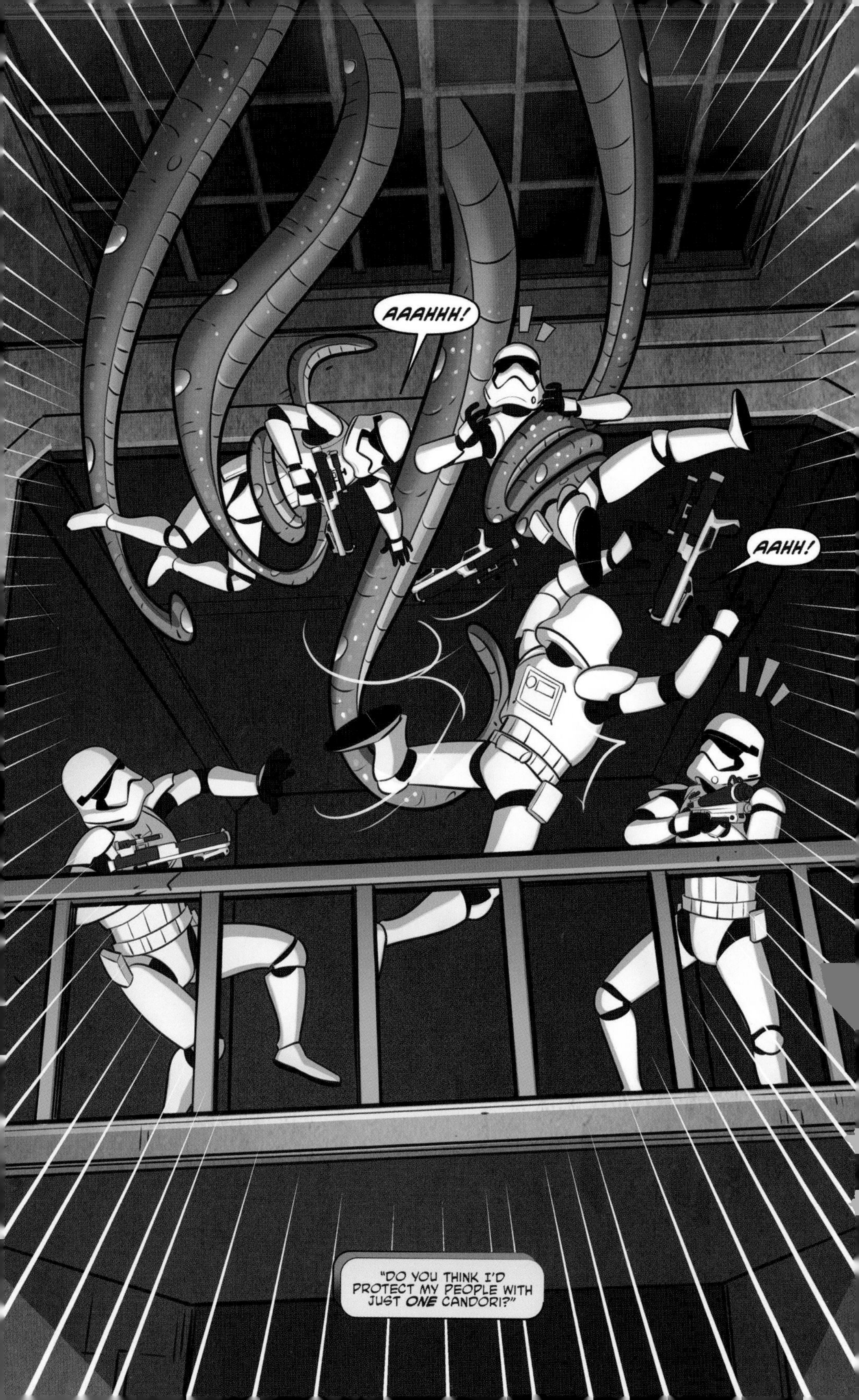
AAAHHH!
AAHH!
"DO YOU THINK I'D PROTECT MY PEOPLE WITH JUST *ONE* CANDORI?"

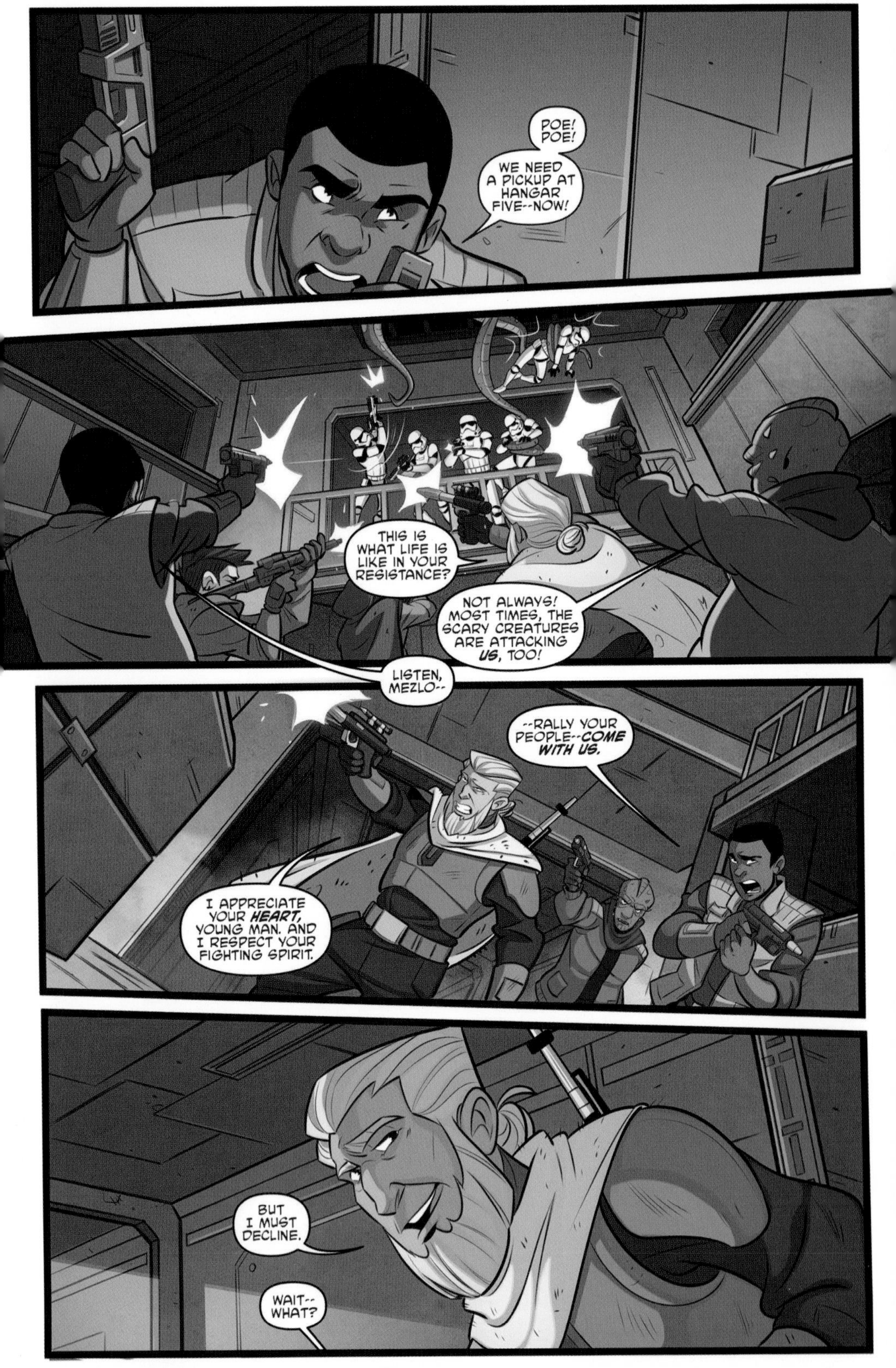
POE! POE!
WE NEED A PICKUP AT HANGAR FIVE--NOW!
THIS IS WHAT LIFE IS LIKE IN YOUR RESISTANCE?
NOT ALWAYS! MOST TIMES, THE SCARY CREATURES ARE ATTACKING *US*, TOO!
LISTEN, MEZLO--
--RALLY YOUR PEOPLE--*COME WITH US.*
I APPRECIATE YOUR *HEART,* YOUNG MAN. AND I RESPECT YOUR FIGHTING SPIRIT.
BUT I MUST DECLINE.
WAIT-- WHAT?

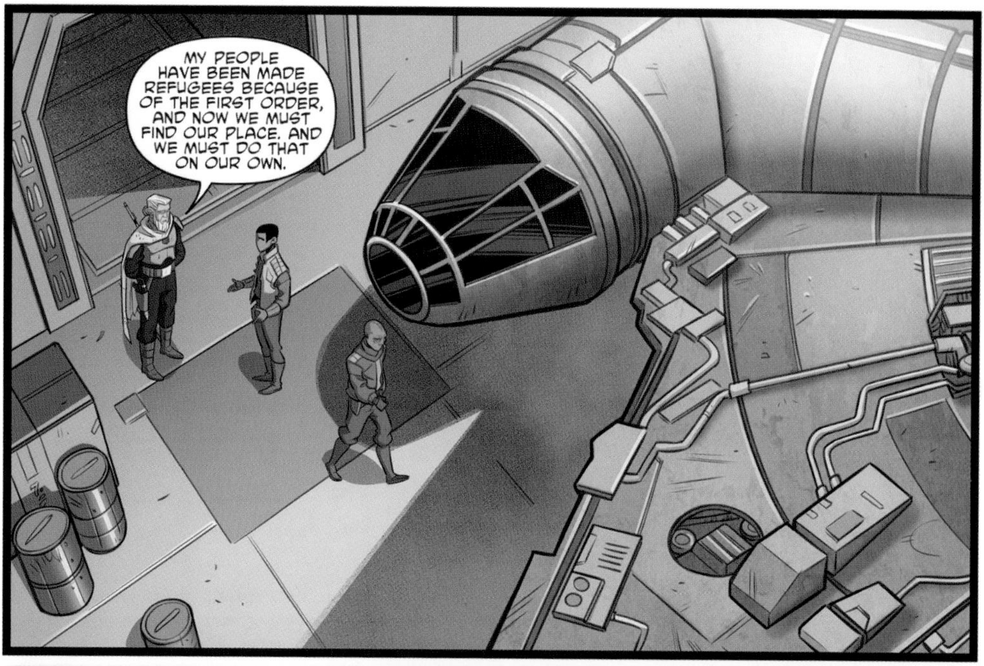
MY PEOPLE HAVE BEEN MADE REFUGEES BECAUSE OF THE FIRST ORDER, AND NOW WE MUST FIND OUR PLACE. AND WE MUST DO THAT ON OUR OWN.

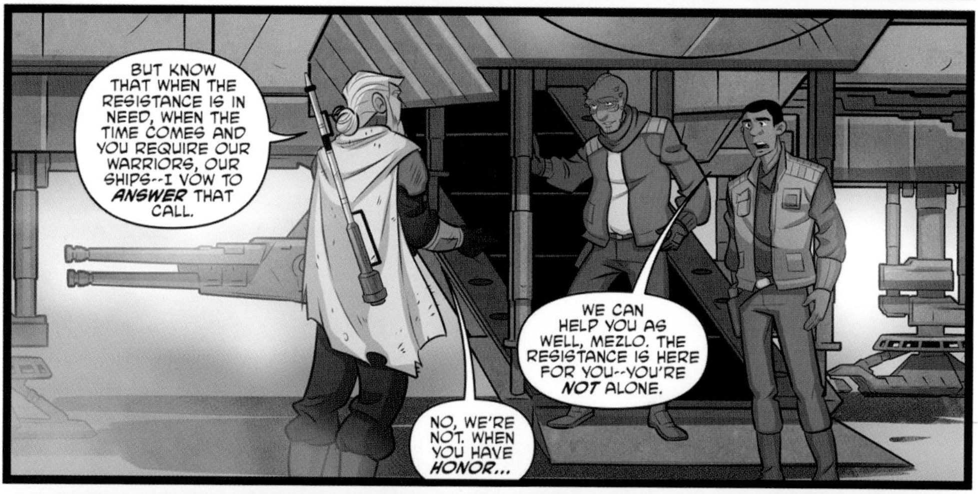
BUT KNOW THAT WHEN THE RESISTANCE IS IN NEED, WHEN THE TIME COMES AND YOU REQUIRE OUR WARRIORS, OUR SHIPS--I VOW TO ANSWER THAT CALL.
WE CAN HELP YOU AS WELL, MEZLO. THE RESISTANCE IS HERE FOR YOU--YOU'RE NOT ALONE.
NO, WE'RE NOT. WHEN YOU HAVE HONOR...

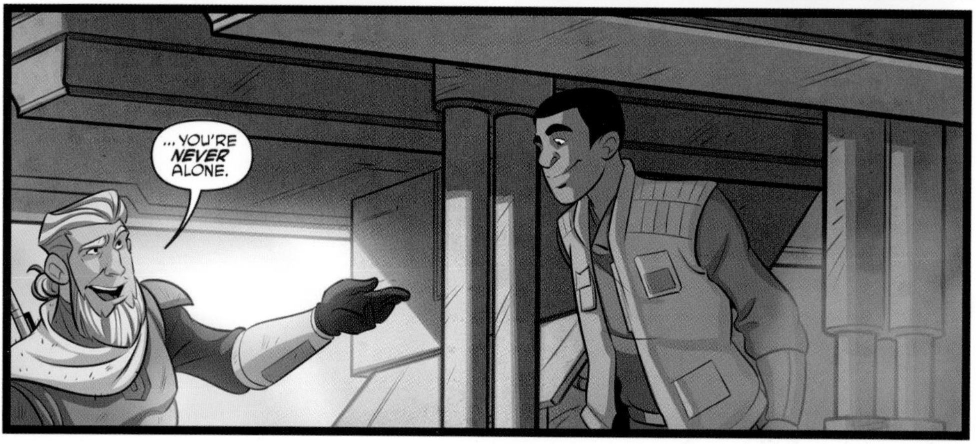
...YOU'RE NEVER ALONE.

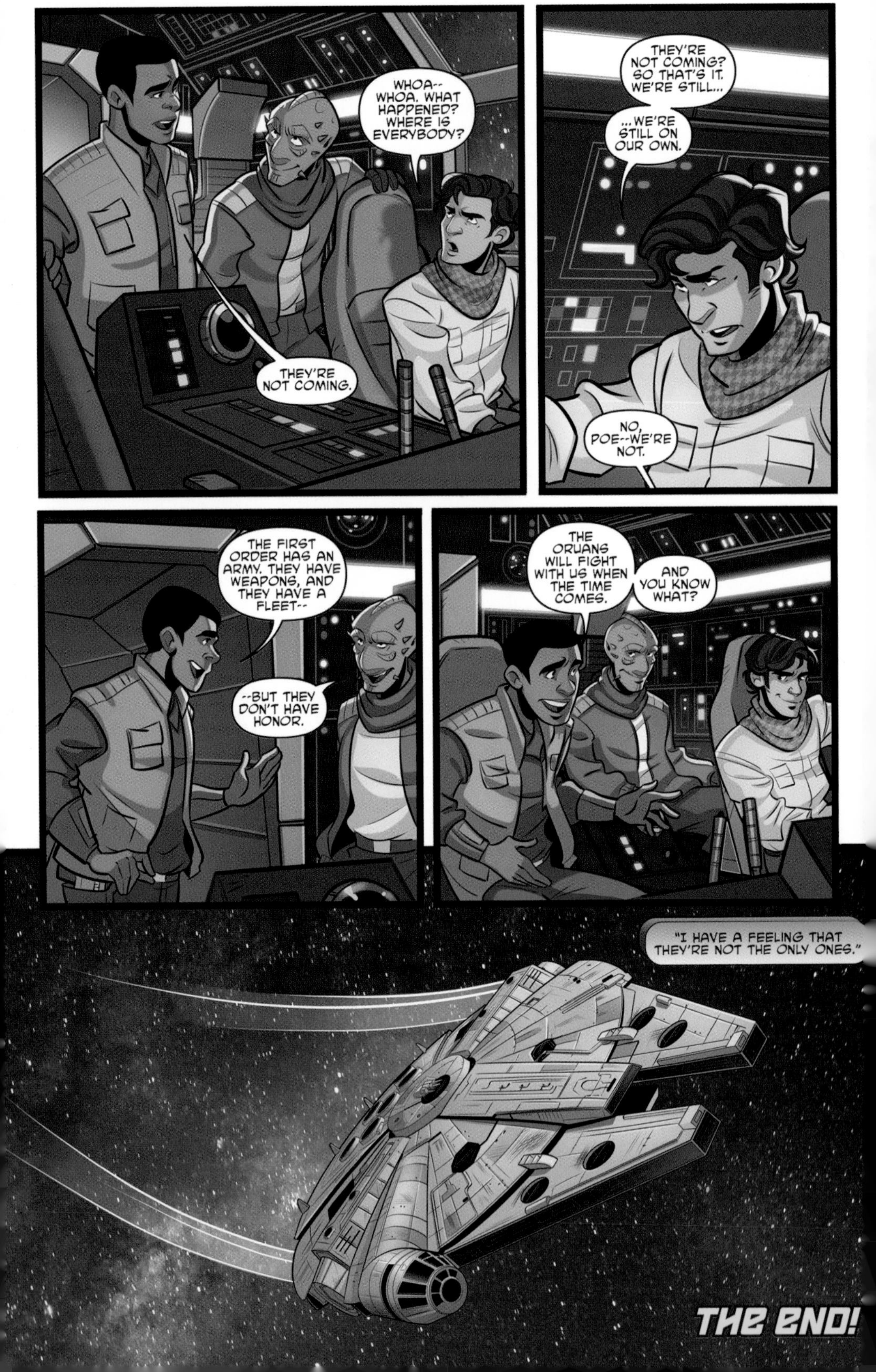
WHOA--
WHOA. WHAT HAPPENED? WHERE IS EVERYBODY?
THEY'RE NOT COMING.
THEY'RE NOT COMING? SO THAT'S IT. WE'RE STILL...
...WE'RE STILL ON OUR OWN.
NO, POE--WE'RE NOT.
THE FIRST ORDER HAS AN ARMY. THEY HAVE WEAPONS, AND THEY HAVE A FLEET--
--BUT THEY DON'T HAVE HONOR.
THE ORUANS WILL FIGHT WITH US WHEN THE TIME COMES.
AND YOU KNOW WHAT?
"I HAVE A FEELING THAT THEY'RE NOT THE ONLY ONES."
THE END!

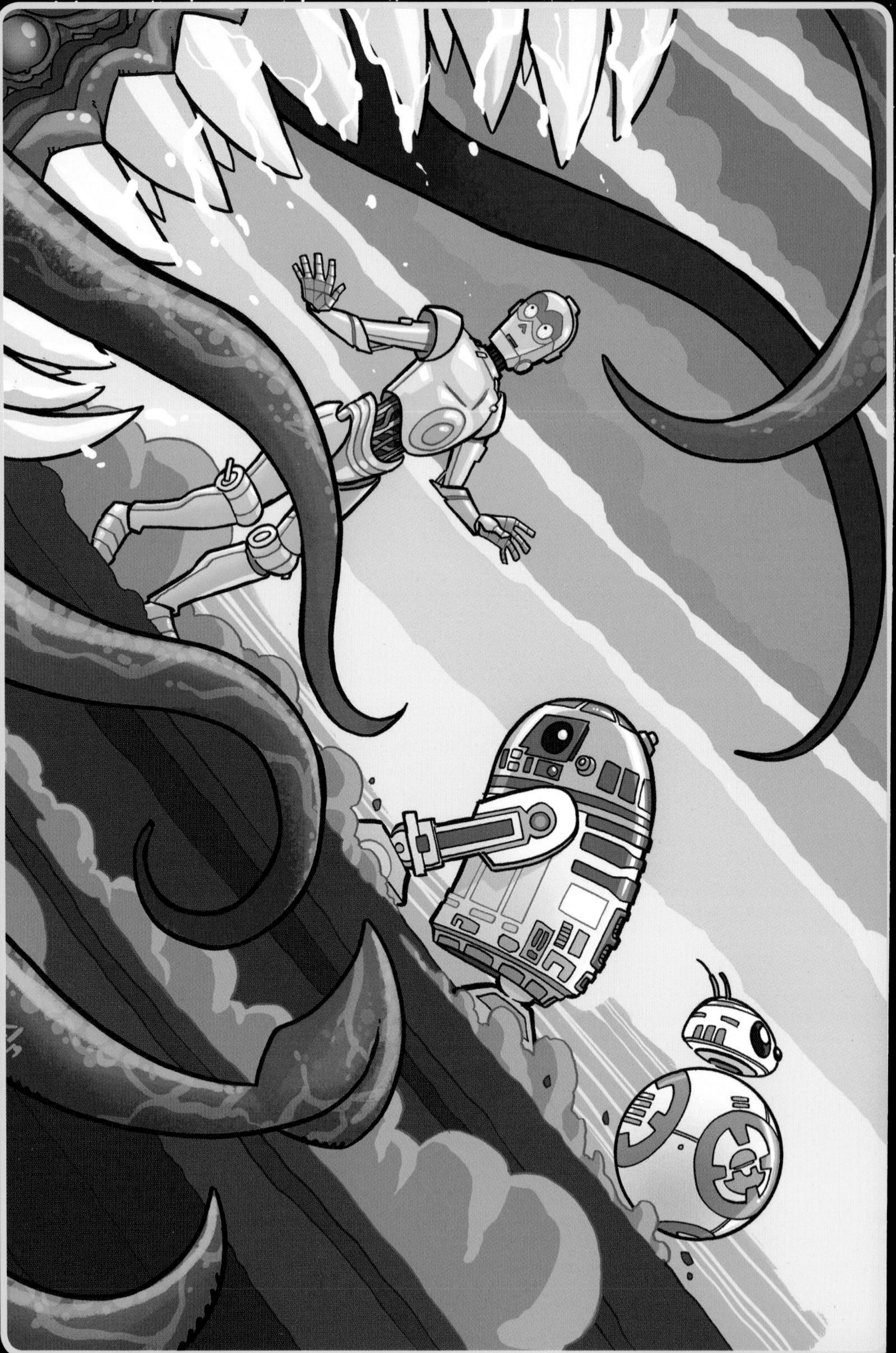

Art by Tony Fleecs

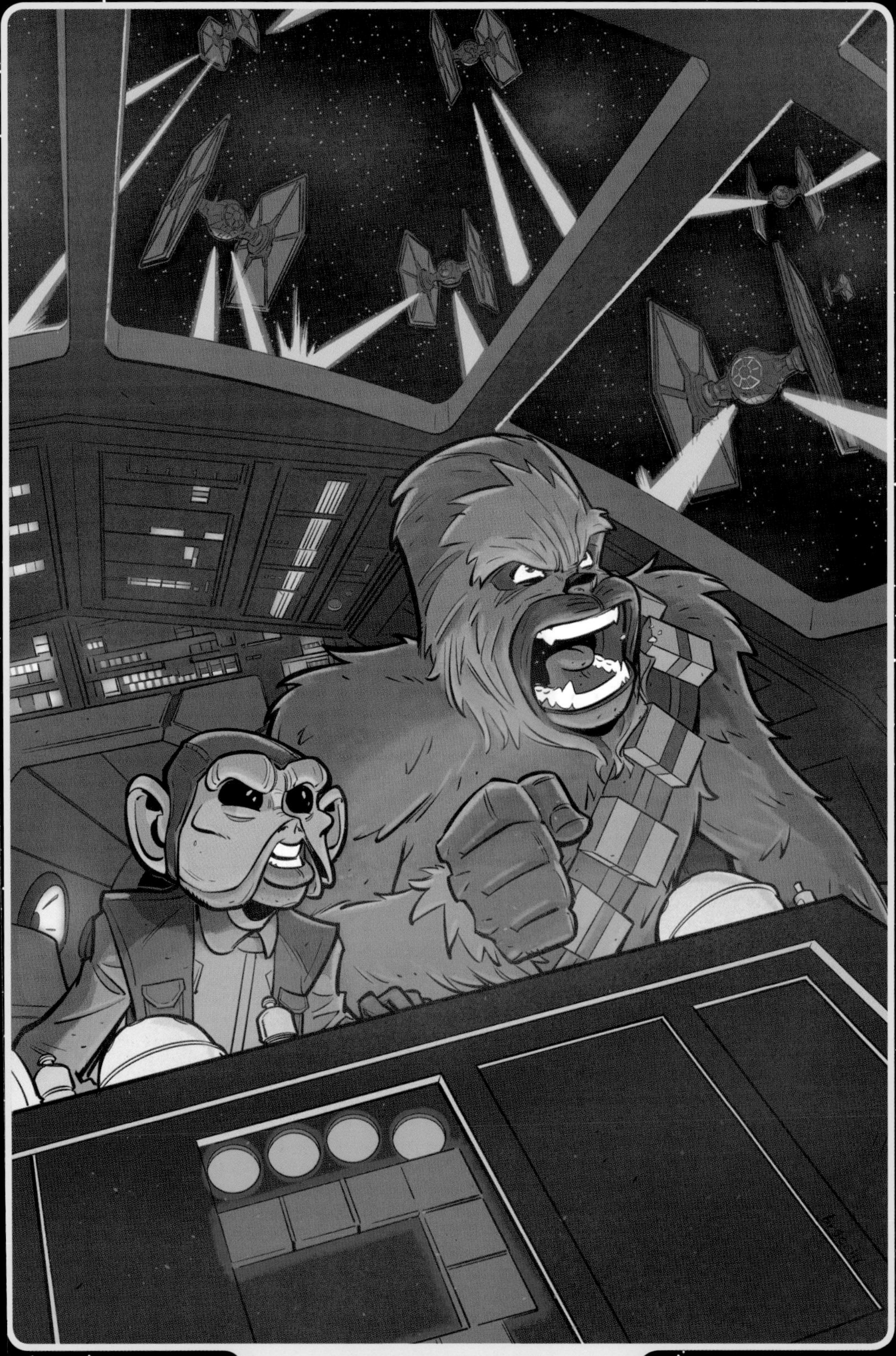

Art by Manuel Bracchi

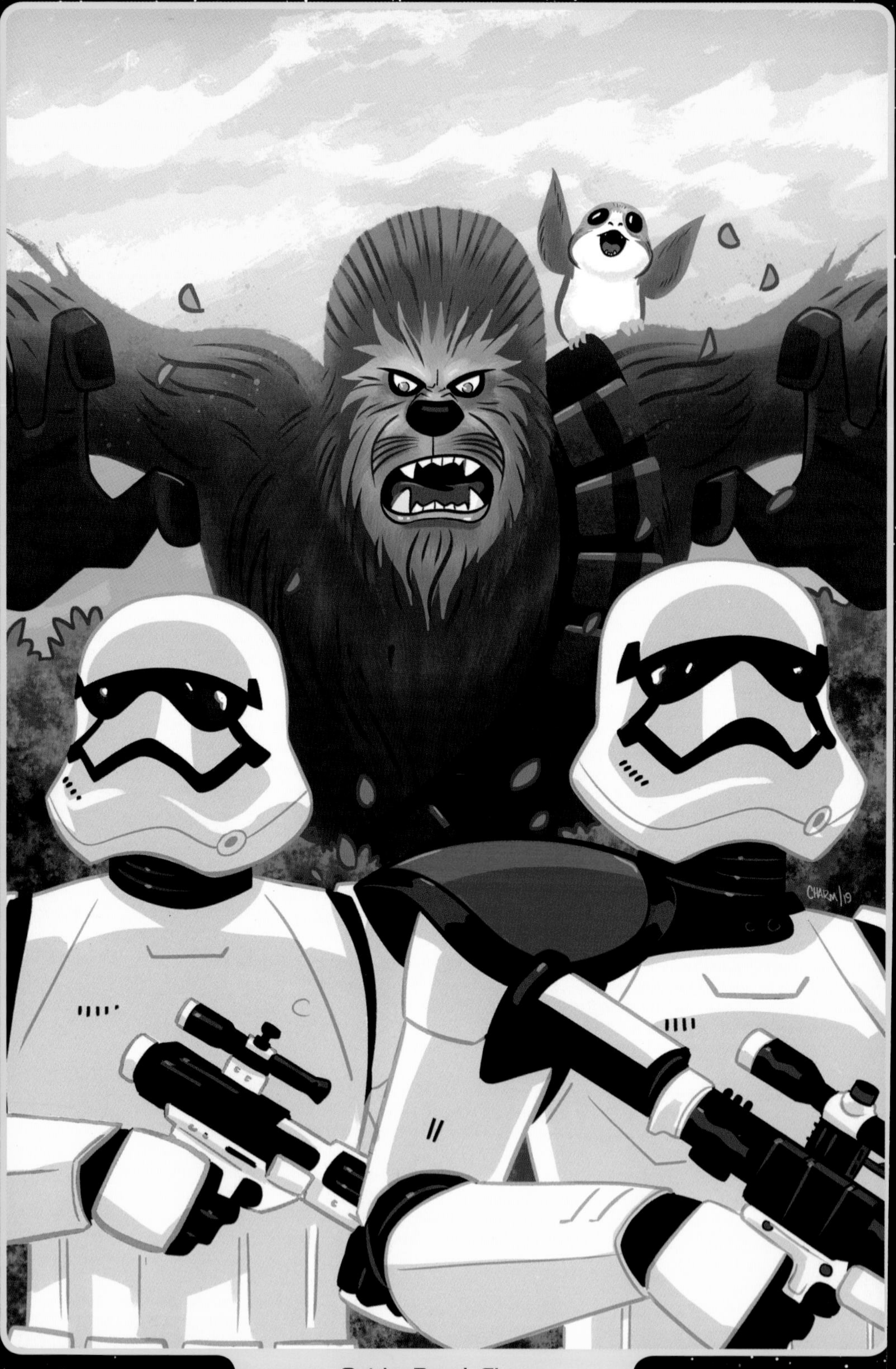
CHARM/19

Art by Derek Charm

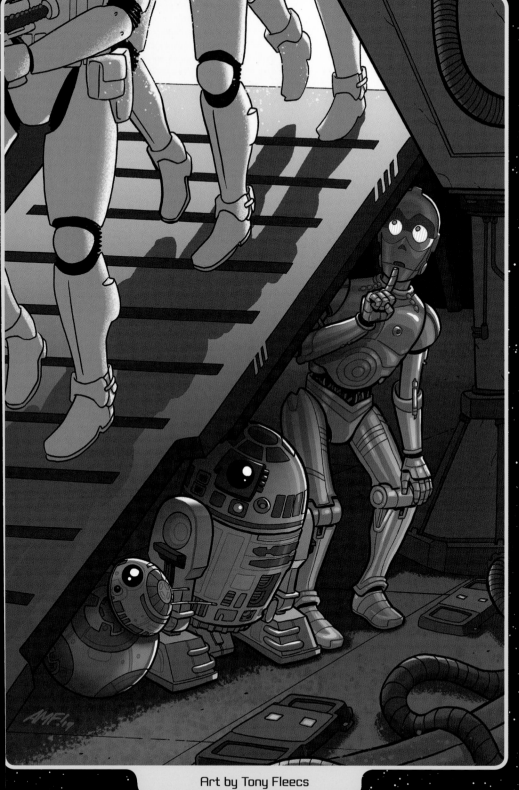

Art by Tony Fleecs

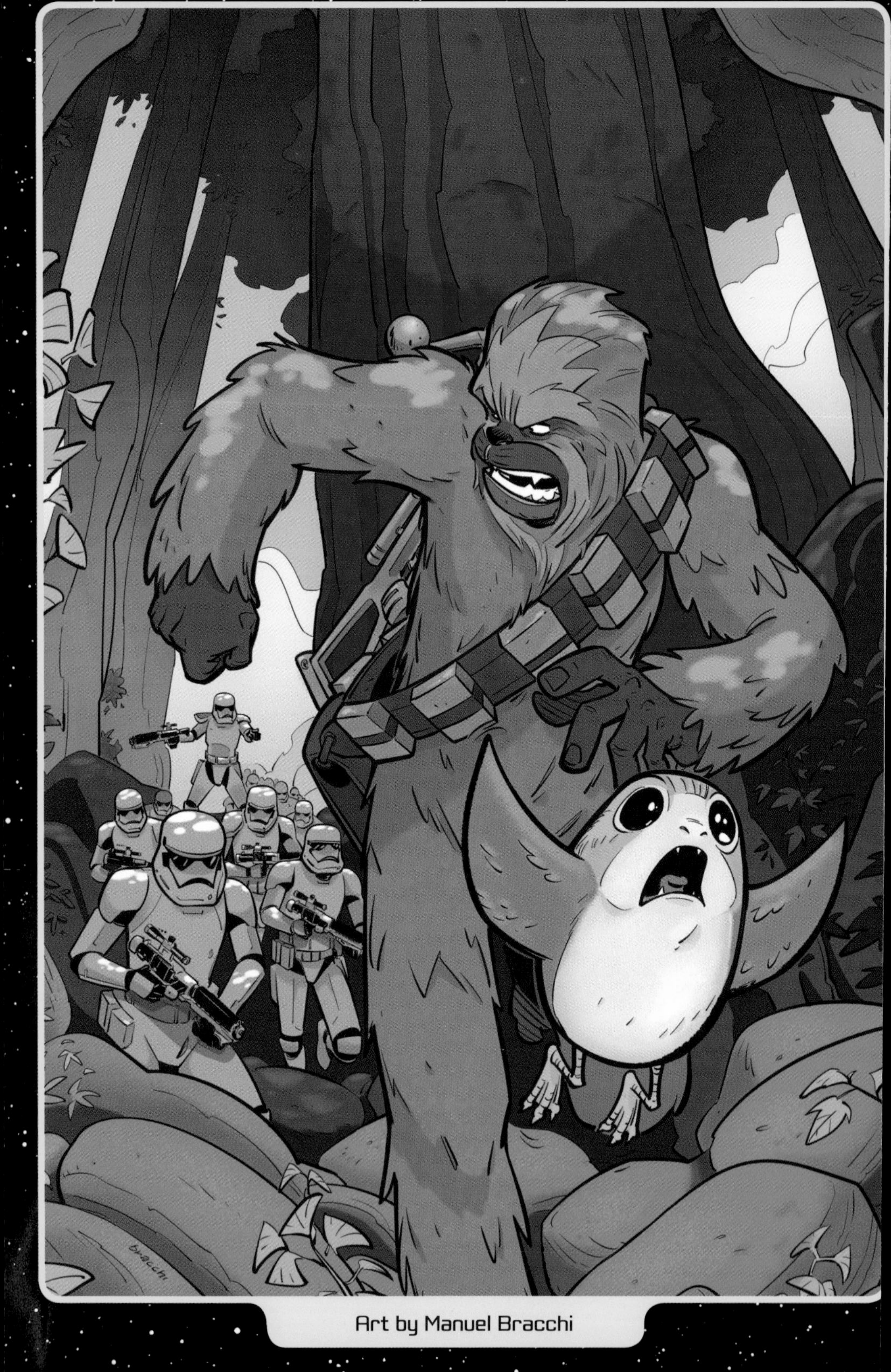

Art by Manuel Bracchi

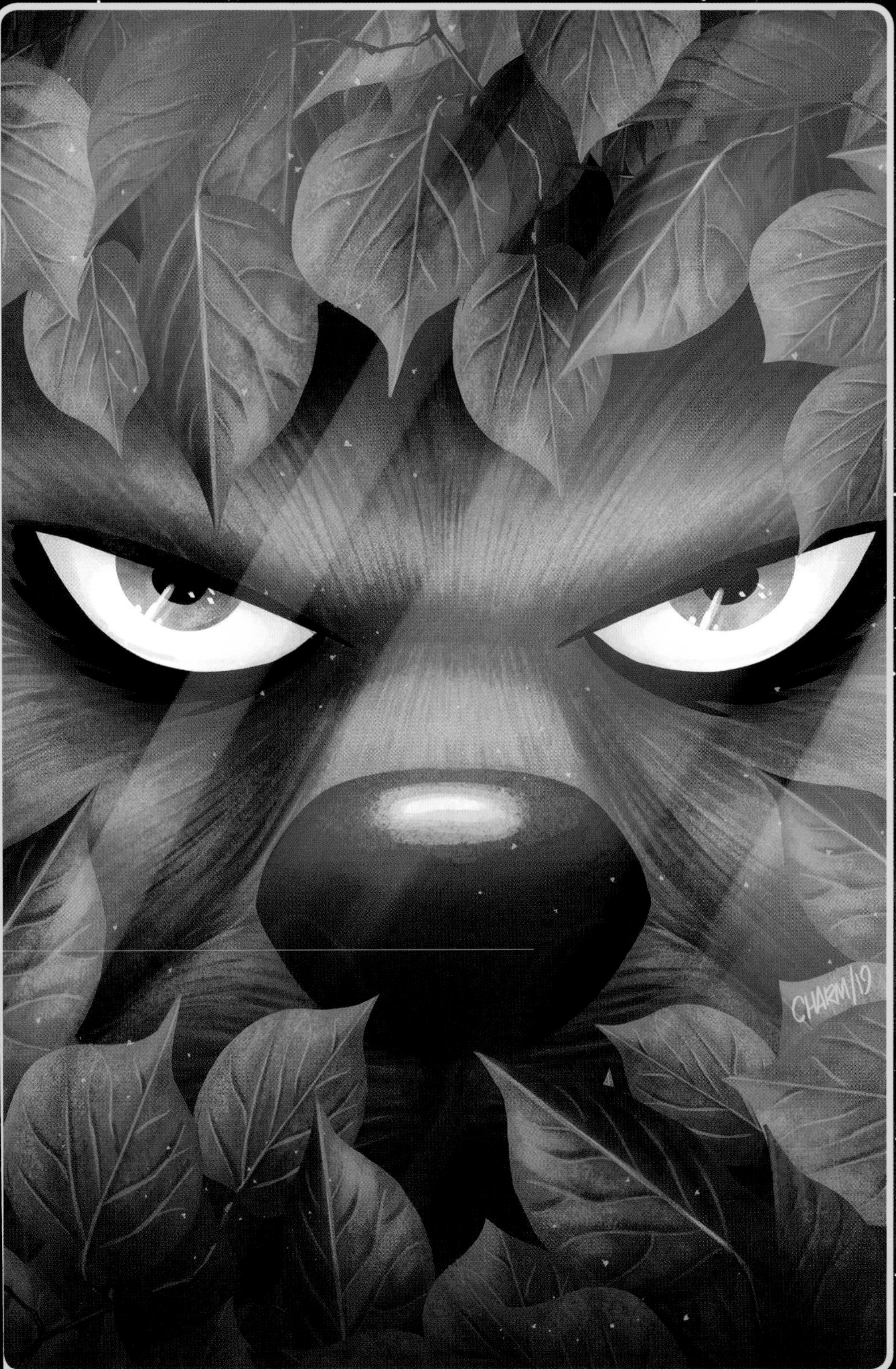
CHARM/19

Art by Derek Charm

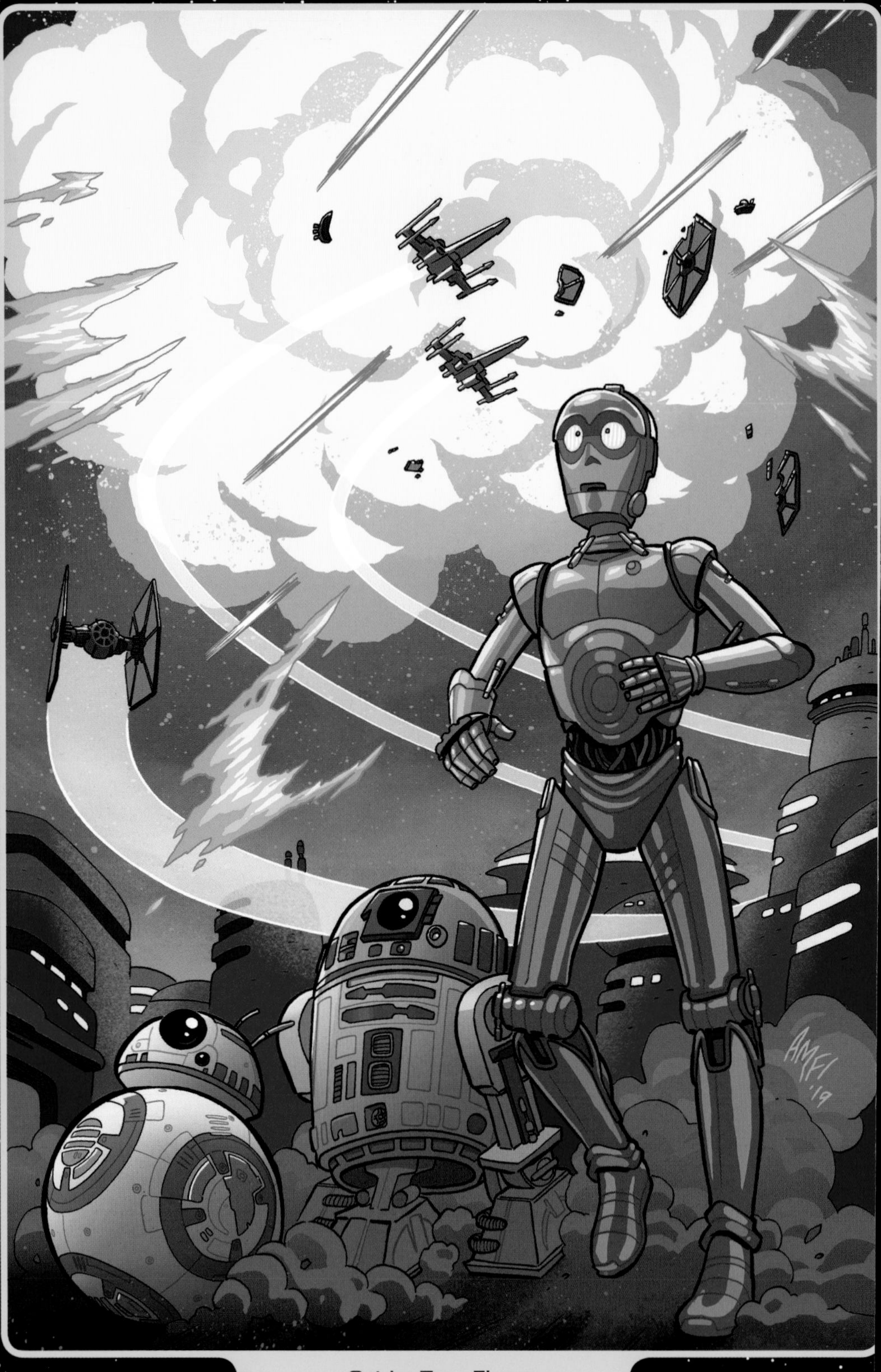

Art by Tony Fleecs

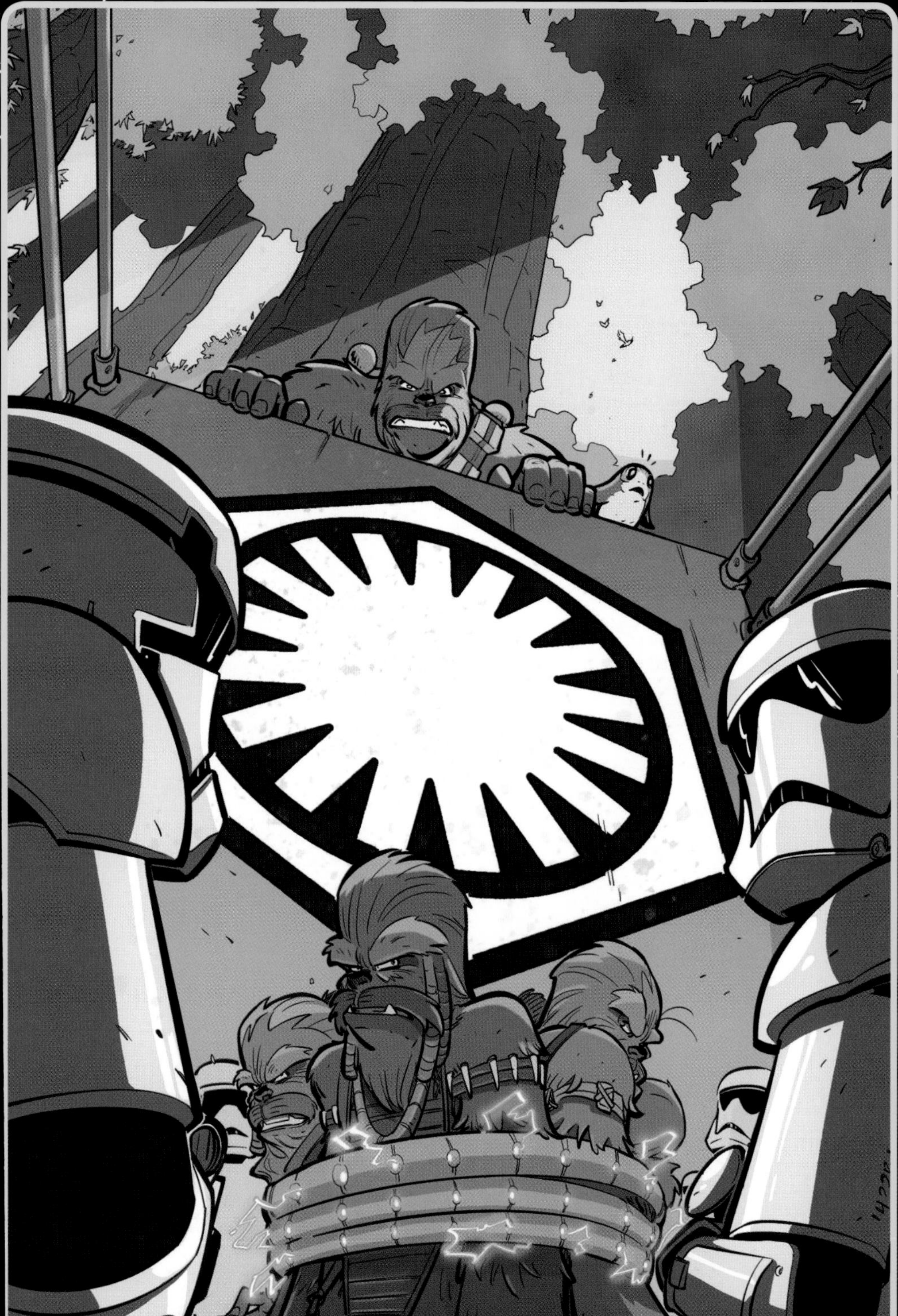

Art by Manuel Bracchi

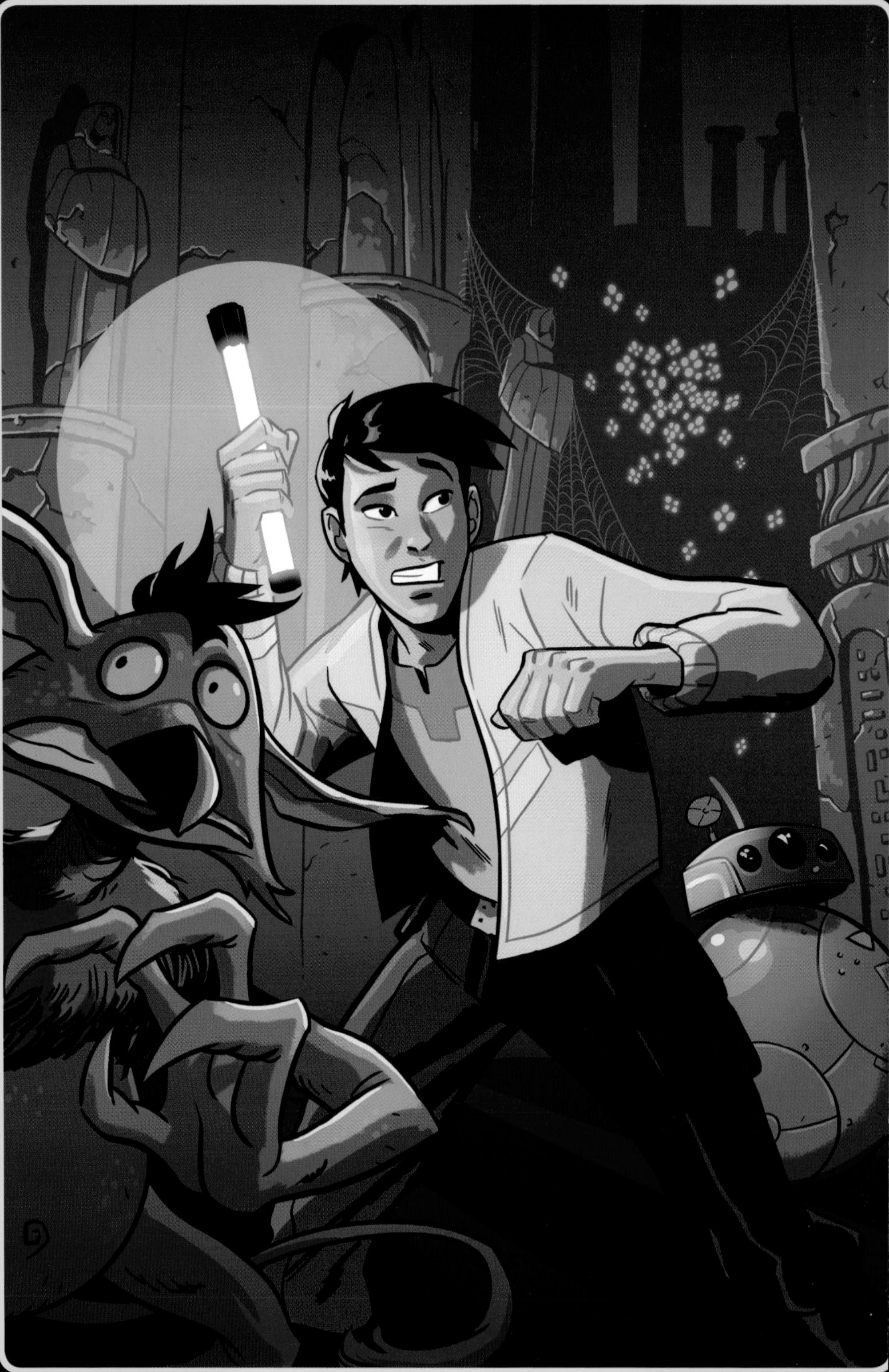

Art by David M. Buisan

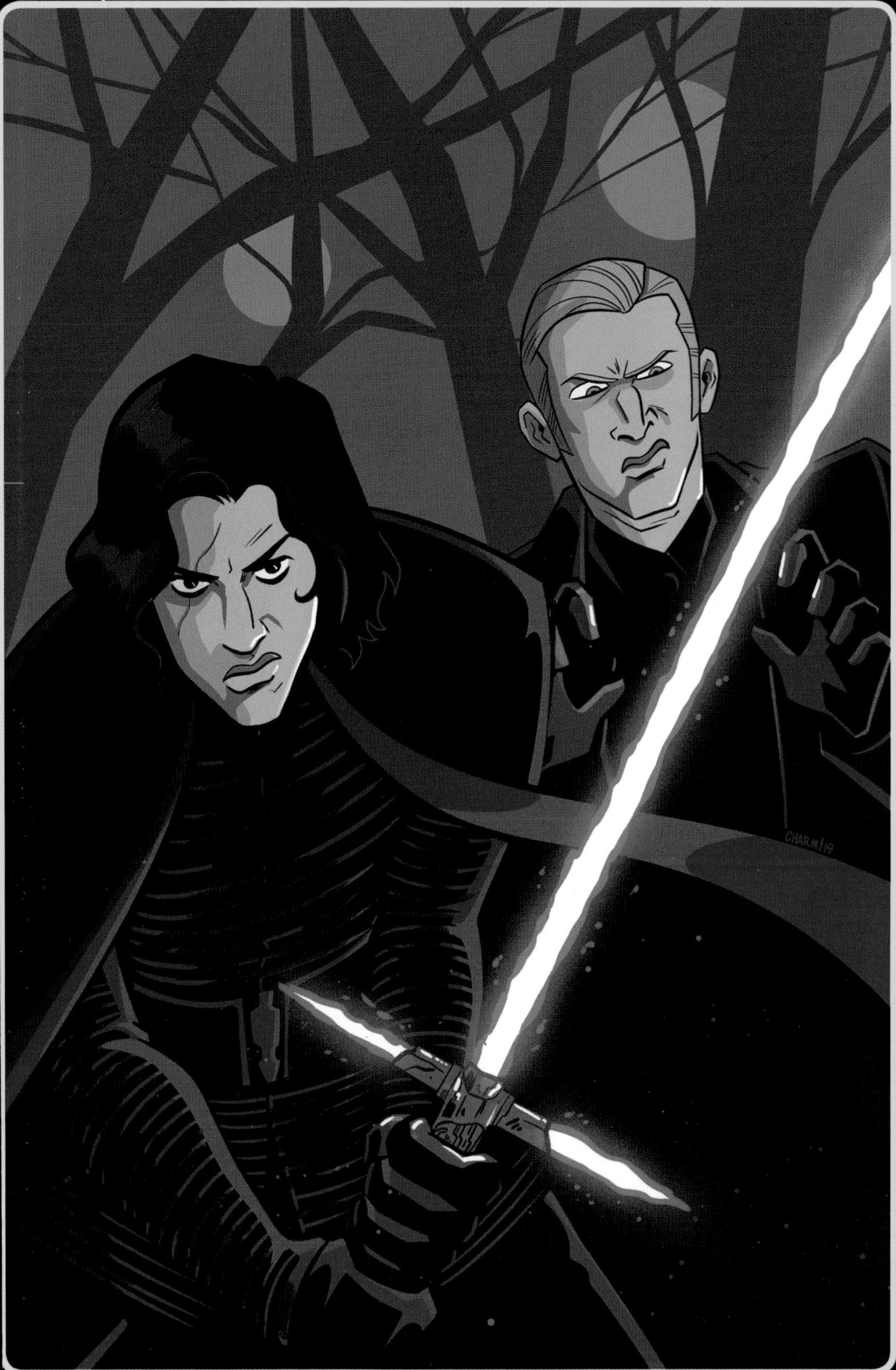
CHARM/19
Art by Derek Charm

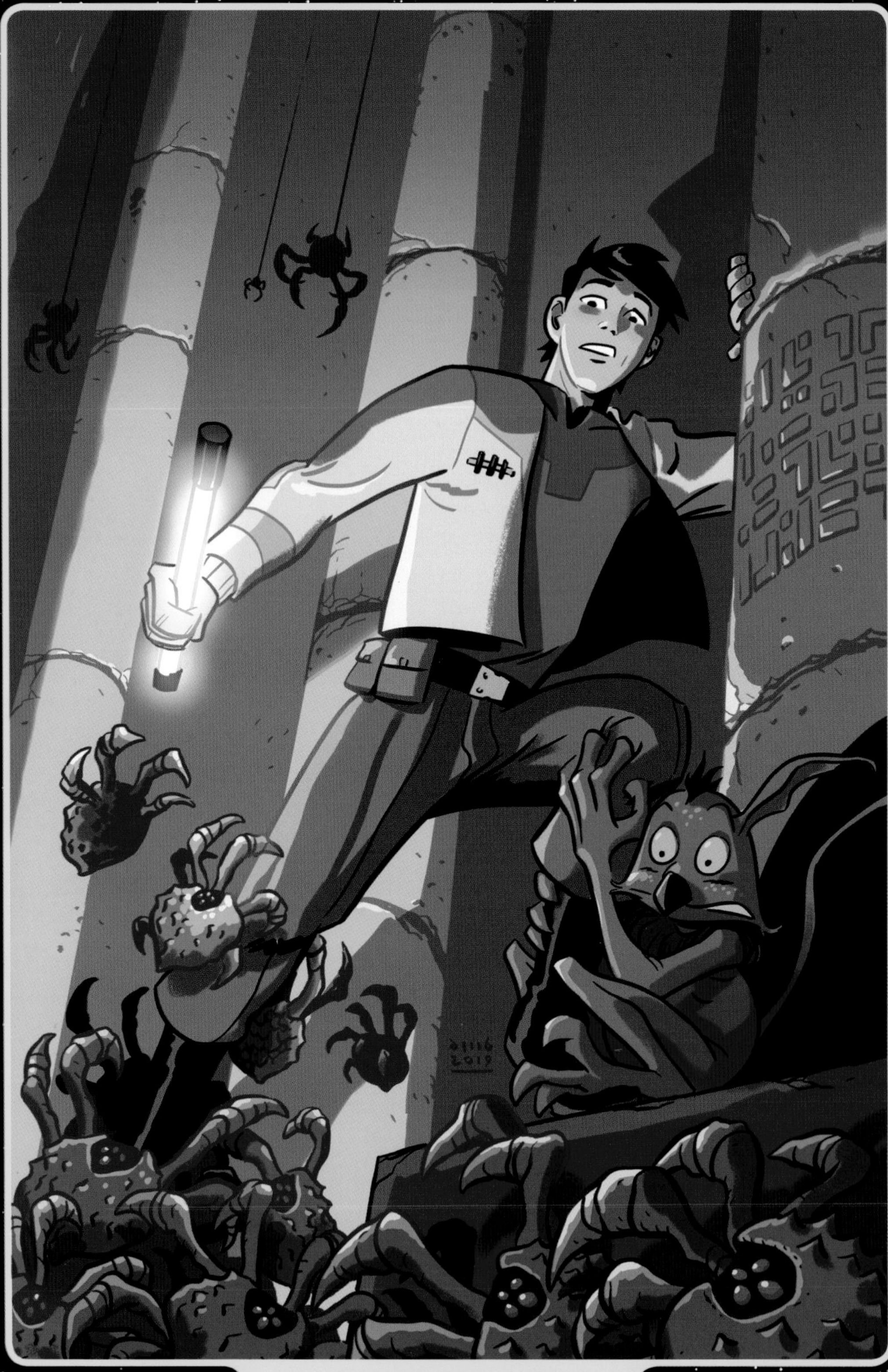

Art by David M. Buisan

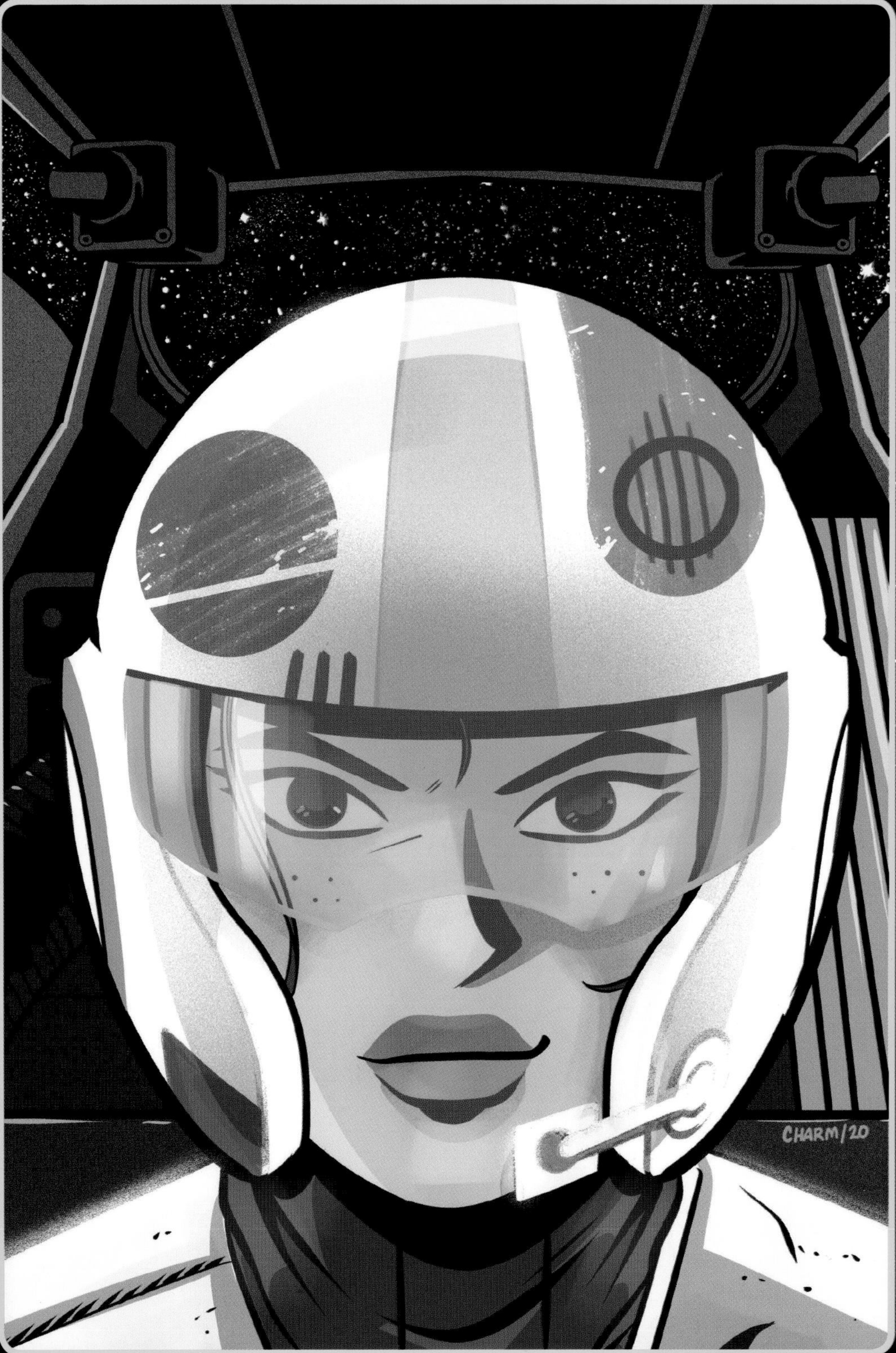
CHARM/20

Art by Derek Charm

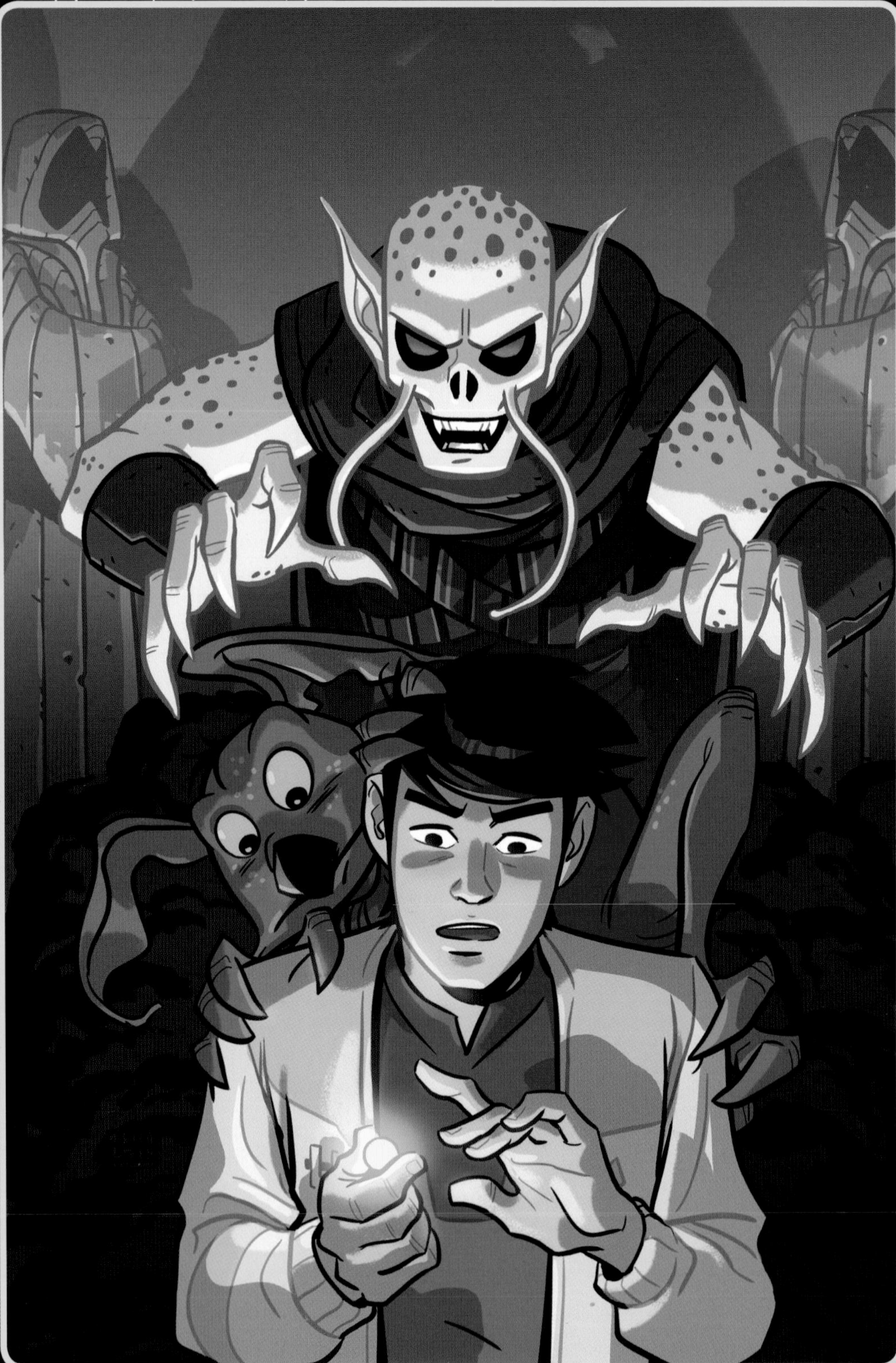

Art by David M. Buisan

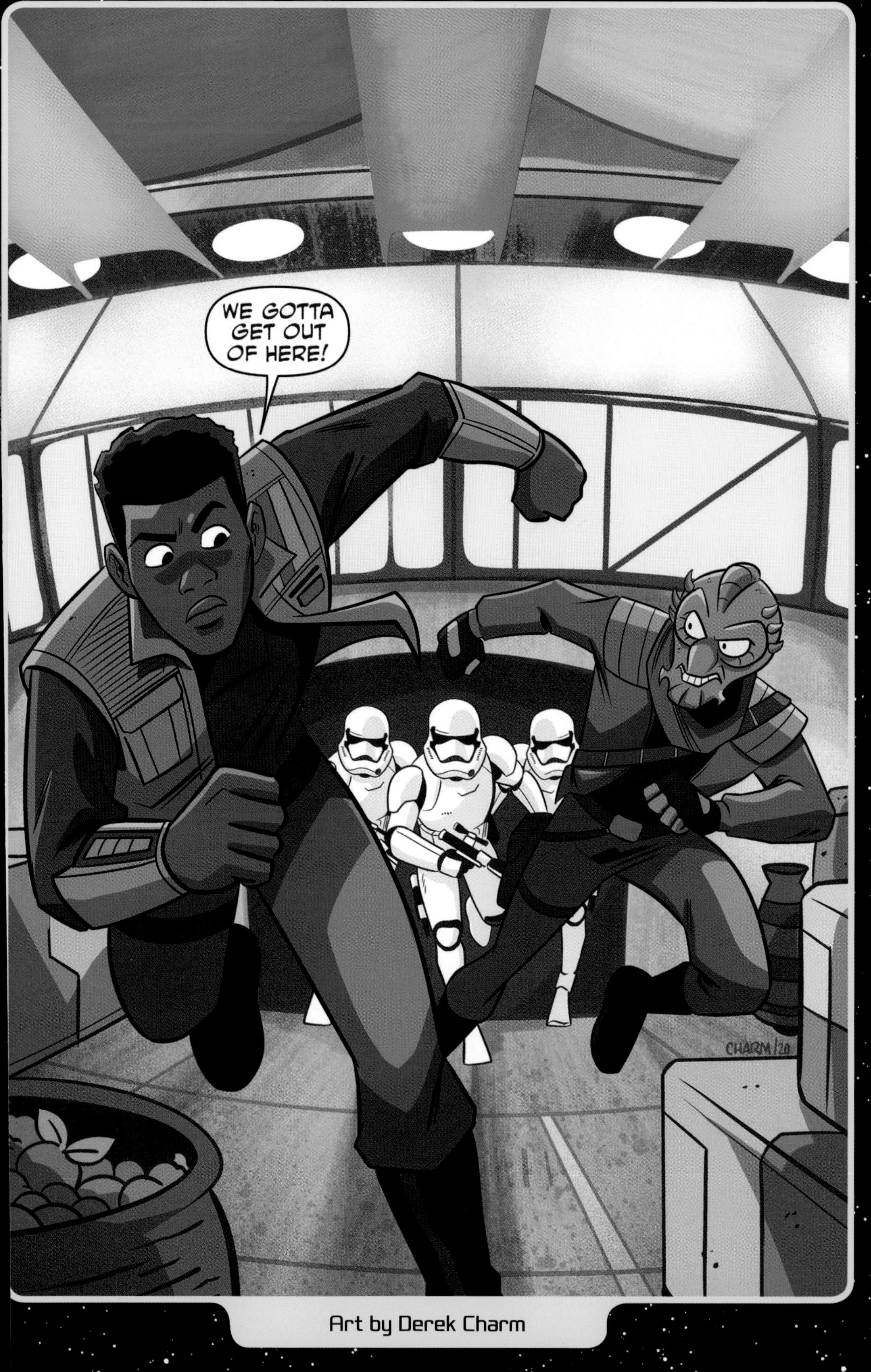
WE GOTTA GET OUT OF HERE!
CHARM/20
Art by Derek Charm

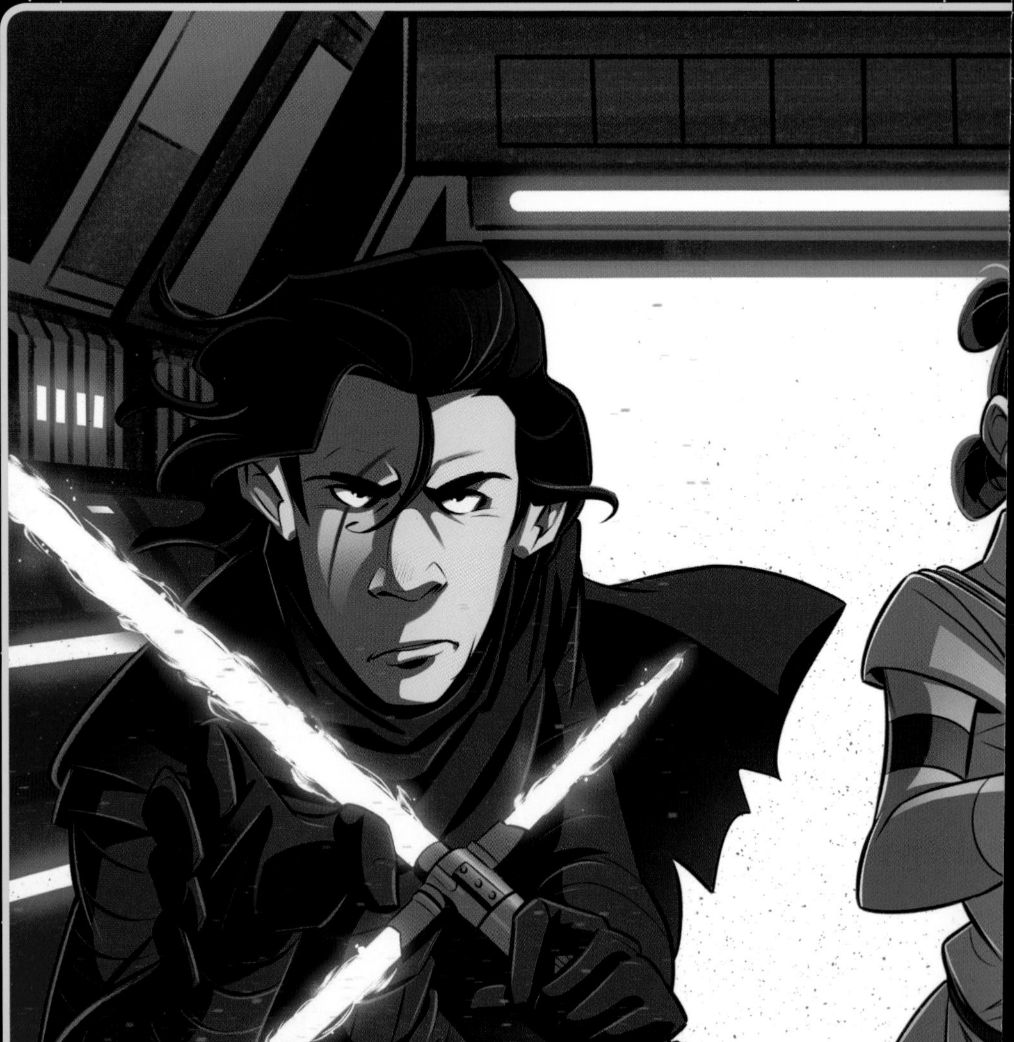
Art by Arianna Florean